About the Author

The Frobisher Trilogy is Jeremy Raylton's first published work. Being retired after spending forty-five years in various positions in a number of British and foreign airlines, in a number of countries, he and his wife have travelled widely to several far distant places. He enjoys gardening, walking and Rosé de Provence, in that ascending order.

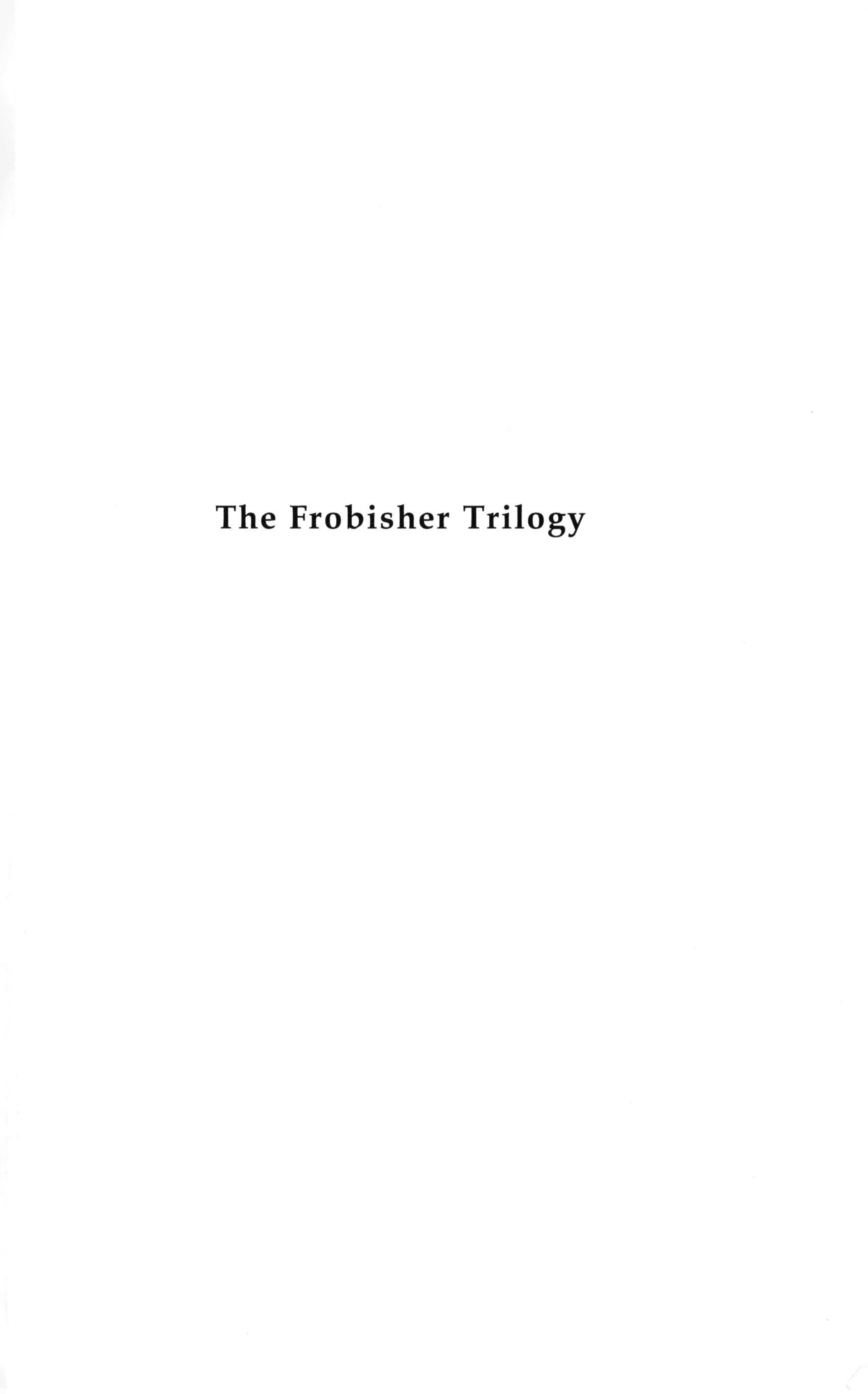

The Frobisher Trilogy

Jeremy Raylton

The Frobisher Trilogy

The Frobisher Letters

Frobisher's Diary

Frobisher's Other Diary

Olympia Publishers
London

www.olympiapublishers.com
OLYMPIA PAPERBACK EDITION

A CIP catalogue record for this title is
available from the British Library.

ISBN: 978-1-80074-178-2

This is a work of fiction.
Names, characters, places and incidents originate from the writer's imagination.
Any resemblance to actual persons, living or dead, is purely coincidental.

First Published in 2022

Olympia Publishers
Tallis House
2 Tallis Street
London
EC4Y 0AB

Printed in Great Britain

Acknowledgements

Frobisher was born on a whim, and he would not have survived infancy without the dedicated post-natal support of Ranald Noel-Paton. As he gained strength and needed grooming, my sister, Rosemary, spent many hours proofreading and improving his appearance, and throughout his childhood, my wife, Judy, consistently provided the encouragement to develop him into a worthwhile person whose exploits might one day interest people outside his family.

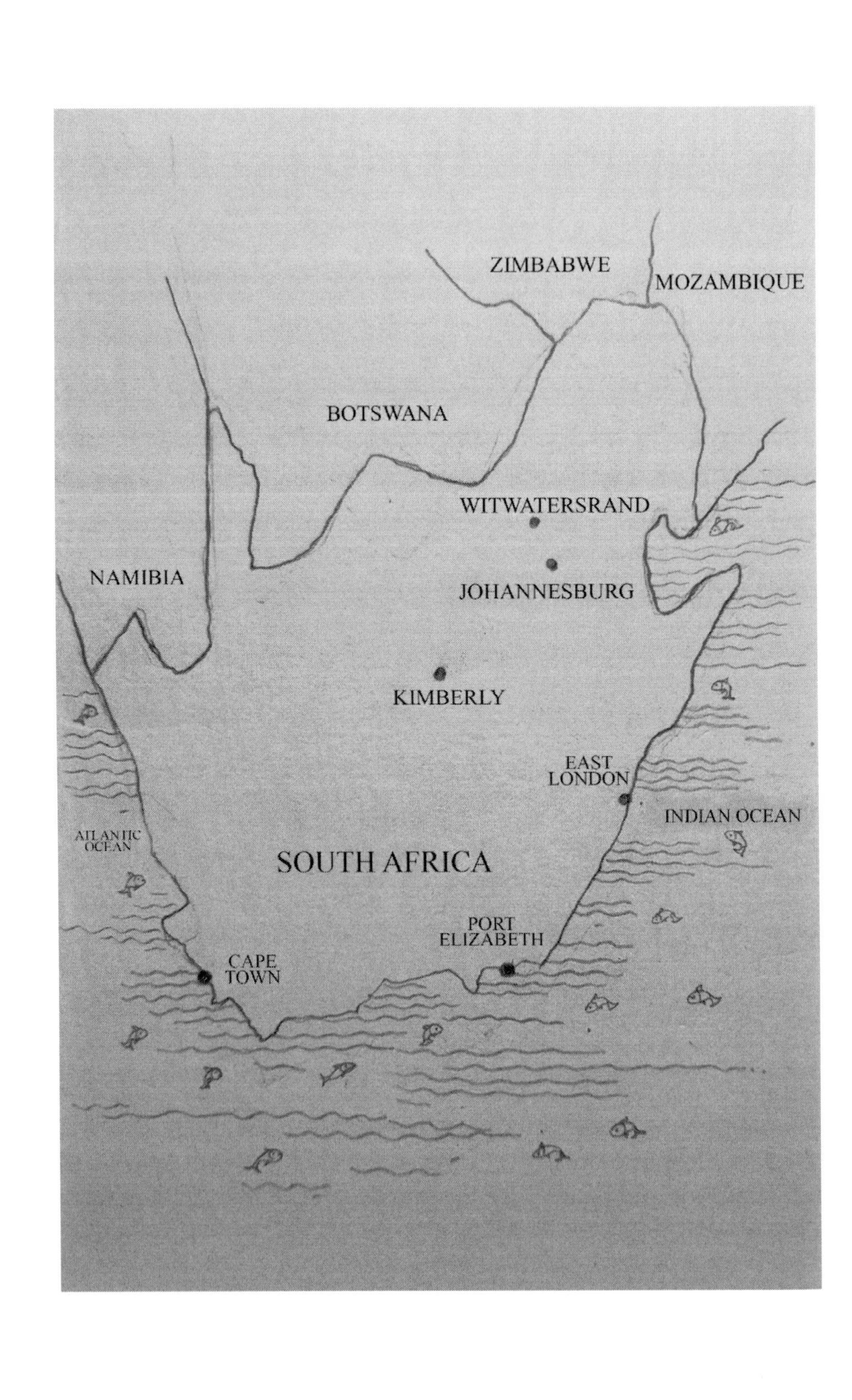
ZIMBABWE
MOZAMBIQUE
BOTSWANA
WITWATERSRAND
NAMIBIA
JOHANNESBURG
KIMBERLY
EAST LONDON
INDIAN OCEAN
ATLANTIC OCEAN
SOUTH AFRICA
PORT ELIZABETH
CAPE TOWN

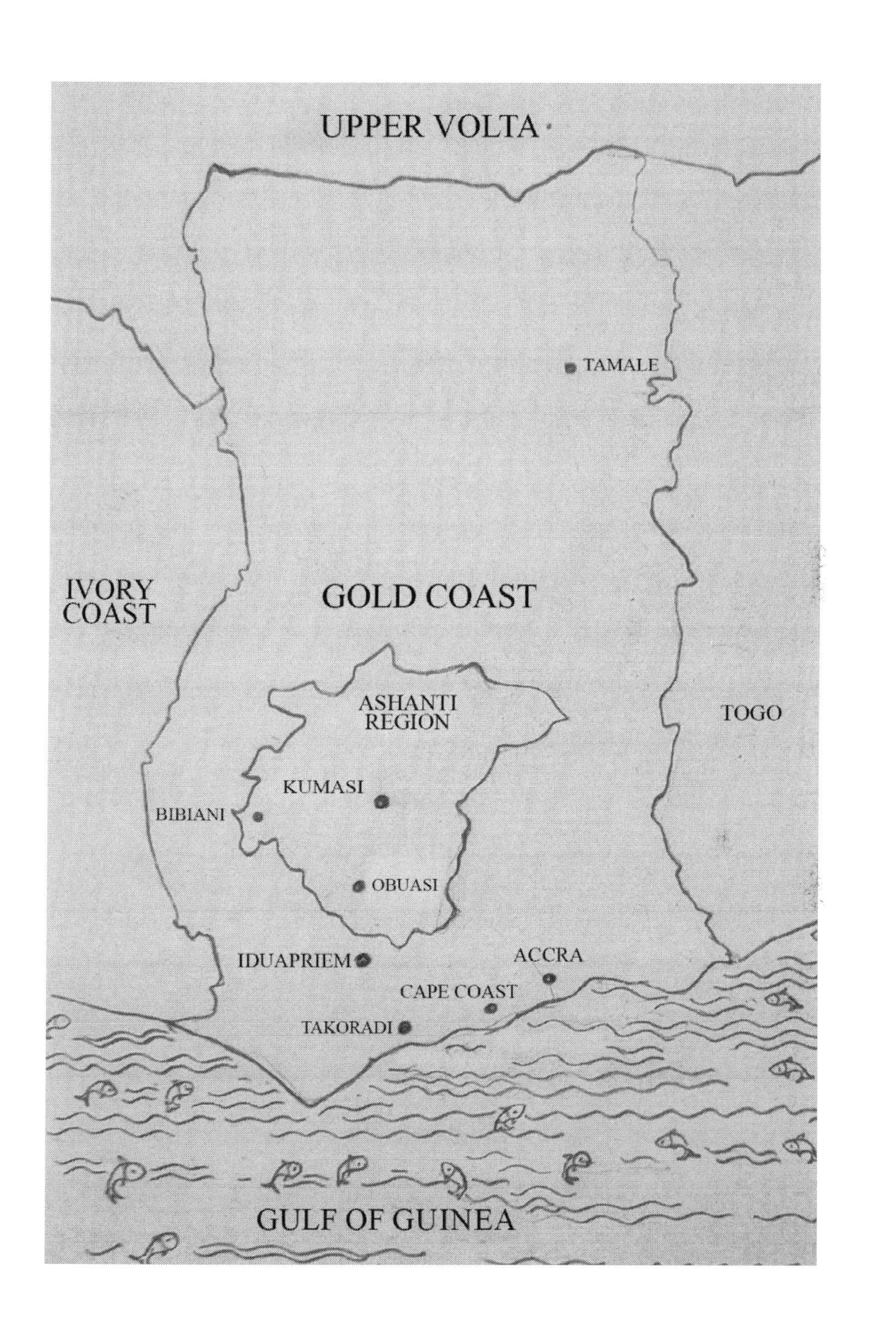

UPPER VOLTA
TAMALE
IVORY COAST
GOLD COAST
ASHANTI REGION
TOGO
KUMASI
BIBIANI
OBUASI
IDUAPRIEM
ACCRA
CAPE COAST
TAKORADI
GULF OF GUINEA

Editor's Foreword

When I bought Broadlands, a fine, country house in what was once a sizeable estate, little did I know that I would become privy to the life and adventures of a young man born almost one hundred and fifty years ago. An editor's job is to search for books that will interest and give pleasure to their readers, and here, almost literally on my doorstep, was the stuff of a story that I found absorbing; a story that portrayed Broadlands as the home of a loving family and a rather extraordinary young man.

In a deed box in the attic I found a bundle of letters written at the beginning of the twentieth century by Frobisher Broad, his father and his sister Hermione. There were also parts of a diary kept by Hermione. The letters covered a period of almost ten years while Frobisher was in Africa, and the diary some of the same time and a few years thereafter.

A chance meeting at the golf club enabled me to throw some light on one matter that was left without a satisfactory explanation in the letters, By trawling through numerous newspaper cuttings, corporate archives, military records, parish registers and notifications of births, deaths and marriages, I have been able to reconstruct a lot of detail relevant to the family and others mentioned in the letters.

When compiling *The Frobisher Letters* I found myself unable to resist imagining the circumstances that led him to leave Broadlands for South Africa, and by combining what we know from the letters and diary, with what I imagine the situation to have been, I feel that I have constructed a credible background to his departure.

Frobisher was the second son of a once well-to-do family, born and raised in the Shires. The family's wealth, once quite considerable, had been much reduced due to the inability of Frobisher's paternal grandfather to pick a winner in any of the many sports on which he wagered his inheritance. Much of what little remained when Frobisher's elder brother Quentin came of age, was spent on purchasing for him a commission in one of the less prestigious regiments of the line. He had been educated at Wellington College, and it had always been assumed that he would pursue a military career. Frobisher, on the other hand, had been sent to Eton, on the understanding that it would prepare him for any one of a wide choice of careers.

But his options were not overly attractive; the revenue from the estate was not sufficient to enable him to live at Broadlands without an income; he could 'go into the church' or seek his fortune abroad. He had never enjoyed the obligatory Sunday attendance at St. John's, and the thought of being involved in dispensing religious wisdom to unbelievers such as himself did not appeal to him. Accordingly, therefore, he took the one thousand guineas that his father raised from the sale of one of the few remaining family heirlooms and boarded a steamer bound for Cape Town.

Frobisher was just twenty when he left Broadlands; he had spent the two years since he left Eton helping his father run the estate and enjoying such of the obligatory social whirl as he could afford on the small allowance that his father gave to him. At Eton he had excelled at nothing but was always near enough to the top of the ladder, both academically and in sport, to be considered a well-rounded, young man, properly prepared to make his mark in life.

He was a good-looking lad, six feet tall, and had a head of fair hair that ensured that he was never short of a partner at the balls and dinner parties that were part of his life; but he had no airs or graces and was just as happy chatting to the gamekeeper about the pegs for the next shoot as to some debutante with a titled father in the House of Lords.

Frobisher and his siblings had been brought up in a close, loving family, one where respect for one's elders and betters was instilled in the children from an early age. Their father was always 'Pater' and their mother 'Mama', and they grew up conscious of their privileged place in society and their duty to maintain the family's status in the pecking order of the local gentry.

Never afraid of hard work, Frobisher did not relish the thought of some minor administrative post in one of the colonies that his father's connections could probably have secured for him, but rather he hoped to find a position in which hard work would be both satisfying and a means of supporting the home and estate in which he and previous generations of his family had grown up, and after much deliberation he had decided that South Africa offered the best chance of achieving his ambitions.

The eighteenth and nineteenth centuries had seen the European nations eagerly colonising any parts of the undeveloped world that held out the prospect of profitable exploitation, and Africa had attracted the attentions of a number of them. France had grabbed several colonies on the south coast of the Mediterranean and in West Africa; Belgium had taken a major slice of the centre of the continent; Germany and Portugal had both managed to gain rather less prestigious footholds; even Italy, no longer the maritime power that it had been a hundred years previously, had ventured across the Mediterranean and colonised a large area of sand between Egypt and Tunisia. Great Britain had raised the Union Jack on the West Coast and in East and Central Africa.

The Dutch had established several trading posts on the West Coast, but the jewel in their crown was South Africa; not only did it offer a harbour midway on the trade routes between Europe and India and beyond, but it offered enormous wealth to those who could successfully exploit its mineral riches. To one such as Frobisher, the country was clearly the first step on a journey that he hoped would not only make his fortune but also restore that of his impoverished family.

So it was with high hopes and the confidence of youth that Frobisher embarked on the ship that was to take him from the comfort and stability of his life at Broadlands to the less comfortable and stable way of life that he could expect in South Africa.

The voyage to Cape Town was certainly less comfortable than he had expected. His cabin, which he shared with five others, was several decks below the main deck, and his fellow travellers were, to say the least, a mixed bunch. A few were from backgrounds similar to his, but most were working-class men hoping to better themselves. Frobisher struck up a friendship with a young Scotsman, and with a young priest who felt that he had been called to spread God's word among the African savages that he felt sure were eagerly awaiting his arrival. Frobisher knew nothing about these savages, but thought it unlikely that they were eagerly awaiting the salvation that was on its way, but he admired the spirit of the cleric and they spent much time together during the voyage.

One morning, the ship's company awoke to their first sight of the land that was to change, so radically, the lives of those who were to disembark there. To Frobisher, eager to leave the constrictions of life aboard, it was hugely attractive; the top of Table Mountain, bathed in the morning sun, rose above a layer of mist, and although much of the town that he could see was nothing like the towns that he was used to, he was so eager to get ashore that he could forgive the narrow streets and humble dwellings.

He walked down the gangplank carrying his valise and made his way to the office of the shipping company, where he sought directions to a modest hostelry where he could stay until he found employment and permanent lodgings. Full of confidence and optimism, and undaunted by the fact that he was now thousands of miles from the protective cocoon of Broadlands, he was impatient to make a start on his new life.

It was some time after I had compiled *The Frobisher Letters* that I became aware that there was other material about Frobisher's life, both in Africa and after he returned to England. This material was in the form of two diaries and many sheets of paper, which only came to light in 2004 when the Ashanti Goldfields Corporation, for whom Frobisher worked when he returned to England, merged with Anglo Gold and vacated the offices in which they had been based for over one hundred years.

In a strongbox, found in the vaults covered with a century of dust, were two diaries, best described as exercise books, and various private and other papers of Frobisher's; some were very tattered and bore traces of ancient mud and damp and evidence of the attention of small rodents. The directors of the Ashanti Goldfields Corporation knew of my work in assembling *The Frobisher Letters* and since no descendants of Frobisher could be found, they sent the new material to me.

Frobisher's Diary, the contents of the first exercise book, was written when he was in Africa, and while it refers to many of the events mentioned in his letters, it goes into much greater detail, in some cases about matters about which he did not want his parents to know. It covers the time from when he left Southampton on11th December 1895 until he returned to England on 7th July 1904.

The second book, and a number of loose sheets of paper of varying sizes, covers the time from his arrival in England until 1922, and this material I have assembled as *Frobisher's Other Diary.*

And so, we have a trilogy. We cannot know whether all that Frobisher wrote was fact, but certainly much of it is verified in historical records of one sort or another, and what reason would he have to include inventions of his own, in documents that he must have assumed only he would see? He certainly did not do so to glorify his own achievements.

And what of the background that I have constructed to give credence to his reasons for leaving home and setting off to South Africa? Some details are confirmed in his letters and diary, and some seem to me to be entirely likely and are not at odds with anything that is known for sure. Whatever the case, I have had great pleasure in reading and recording Frobisher's writings and I hope that *The Frobisher Trilogy* will give pleasure to its readers.

The Frobisher Letters

Contents

New Personae

The Broad Family

Papa/Pater	Frobisher's father
Mama	Papa’s wife
Quentin	Their elder son
Frobisher	Their younger son
Hermione	Their daughter
Arthur	Hermione’s first child
Penelope	Hermione’s second child
Pamela	Quentin’s fianceé

The Retainers

Mary	Cook's assistant
Rob	Mary's son
Jackson	The gamekeeper
Old Jock	An ageing, much loved dog
Oscar	Old Jock’s successor
Betsy	A maid

Others

Fisher	Possibly Rob’s father
Roger Fellowes	The local solicitor
Caroline	Roger’s wife
Anthony/Tony	Roger’s son
Martin deVries	A Dutchman

Persons in South Africa

Sidney	One who lived by his wits
Tony Bellingham	An Old Etonian
Cecil Rhodes	A man of considerable influence
Rodney Shields	An Old Reptonian
Ocke, Helena & Ryneker	A Dutch family

Persons in the Gold Coast

Edwin Cade	Owner of a gold mine
Williams	Mine Superintendent
Cameron	Chief Engineer
Dr. Franz Werner	Chief Chemist
Dr. George Thomas	Chief Medical officer
Sgt. Miller	Chief of Security
Mensah	Frobisher's steward
Yeboah	Frobisher's Cook
Musa	Frobisher's night watchman
Ted Harris	

Chapter One

Dear Master Frobisher,

I 'ope as what you will not think me forwerd writing to you, but you as always been so nice to me, and I will be sorry to see you go to Africa, wherever that is.

I wish you a safe journey, and I ope as what you will soon come back.

Yors, Mary

Chapter Two

Cape Town 3rd January 1896

Dear Pater,

I arrived here two days ago after a very pleasant voyage. Happily, we were spared any rough seas en route. The accommodation was fairly basic, but very clean and not the hot cabin in the bowels of the ship that I had expected. Six of us shared a cabin, and my fellow travellers were a good bunch of chaps. One of them, a Scot, became a good friend. I know that you could not afford a first-class cabin for me, and I am forever grateful for your generosity, but I sincerely hope that when I return home I shall be able to find the money for a berth more suited to our family's status.

Very soon after my arrival, I discovered that there is actually no gold or diamonds here; both are found further north, and it seems that I shall have to travel there if I am to make my fortune and repay your kindness and generosity. I shall, however, stay here for at least a few weeks, for it is a most agreeable place with a climate to match.

Shipping is the lifeblood of Cape Town, and using the letter of recommendation that you so kindly gave to me, I have obtained a post in a Ships' Chandlers store. We provide everything that the ships need when they call in on their way to or from the ports of India and beyond. I have to say that some of the sailors are rather rough fellows, and they seem to think that I can provide them with female company as well as rope, drink and victuals. Believe me, Pater, even if I knew of any such wanton women I would not sully our family name by encouraging their sordid trade, and please do not embarrass Mama by referring to this.

Many of the people here are of Dutch descent; some can trace their ancestors back to the first Dutch colonists who arrived nearly two hundred and fifty years ago. I find them arrogant, and mostly resentful that we British have, as they put it, invaded their country, although more than seventy years ago many of them voluntarily 'trekked' north, as they call it, to find grazing for their cattle, and founded their own state, for they are basically of farming backgrounds.

Fifteen years ago, there was a minor war between the British and the

Boers, but it seems to have been an indecisive affair, and it has not defused the situation; I am glad that I am here in Cape Town, and not in Johannesburg or Pretoria.

I have found lodgings with an Indian family who have a house not far from the port. Apparently, a number of Indians were brought here by the British earlier in this century. I have a nice room, and am provided with breakfast and an evening meal, all at a very reasonable cost. I find some of the dishes rather spicy, for they eat only the food to which their race is accustomed, but I am adapting to it quite well. They are a very hospitable family, especially the daughter, who is forever asking me if there is anything that I want. Pater, if I am to make my fortune it will be in the areas presently controlled by the Boers. The major gold fields are around Witwatersrand, northeast of Johannesburg — or Jo'burg as they call it here — and the diamonds are to be found near Kimberley, which is southwest of Jo'burg. Increasingly deep mines are being used to extract these riches, but it is sometimes possible to find both in river beds, and a licence to prospect in this way is very much more affordable than a share in a mine. I will try to increase my capital by working hard, hoping that the political situation may soon enable me to travel north and try my luck.

Do give my love to Mama, and tell her that I am being very careful to drink only boiled water. When you write to Quentin, give him my best wishes, and tell him that there may be a war for him to fight down here before too long; and tell Hermione that I miss our games of tennis and croquet.

I hope to get a letter from you before too long, and I remain, dearest Papa, your loving son,

Frobisher

Broadlands, 10th March 1896

Dear Frobisher,

Your letter arrived yesterday and I was glad to hear that you arrived safely in Cape Town, and that you have found employment of a sort. Our family has never before been involved in 'trade', but needs must, as they say, and I hope that it may be short-lived.

I have passed on your news to your mother and Hermione, and they send all their love to you. I have not heard from Quentin for several months, and do not know where he is. I suspect that he may be in India, where there are always natives to be suppressed.

The pheasant season was very successful, but there were very few partridges or woodcock. I would like to put down more this year, but the cost is becoming exorbitant, and the present government is forever finding more ways to divest us of what little capital we have left. I do not know where we will find a suitable suitor for Hermione, for there is very little that I can offer in the way of a dowry, except a few acres of relatively unproductive arable land. Quentin will never get rich in the Army, and it is down to you to restore the family to its right and proper place in society.

It is not easy to run the house and the estate with so few servants, and only one gamekeeper cannot be expected to ensure that every drive is a good one. Poor old Jock got a thorn in one pad, and it turned septic, but he is back on four legs now, and is probably the only one of us without a care in the world.

But I must not burden you with our problems; you must live life to the fullest extent of your purse, and we all hope that it will not be long before you tell us that you are achieving your objective in travelling to South Africa, and that my investment in your venture is starting to pay off.

Your loving Father

Cape Town, 30th April 1896

Dear Pater,

Many thanks for your letter, which arrived on the mail boat yesterday. It is so good to get news from home, although I am sorry that the government is being so beastly; what rotten luck.

Try not to worry about Hermione, Pater; she is such a pretty and nice girl that I am sure that she will marry well, regardless of our fortunes.

I have changed my lodgings, but you can still write to me at the Ships' Chandlers until I travel north. I was well-suited with my Indian friends, and was even learning a few words of their language, but it became impossible for me to stay with them any longer.

One evening last week, after we had had our evening meal, I retired to my room and heard the father and mother go out. Shortly afterwards, their daughter knocked on my door, and when I opened it to let her in, she burst into tears. I asked her what the matter was, and she told me that her parents had just told her that she was to be married to a friend of theirs in India.

I said that I was sure that her parents knew what was best for her, but she said that she had never met the man, and that even if she had, she would only marry someone that she loved. I tried to reassure her that she would surely meet such a man, and she said that she already had, and that the man was me, and that she would do anything, anything, to make me love her.

As you can imagine, I was somewhat taken aback by this declaration, for although I had grown to like her, and been appreciative of the many little things that she did to make my stay more agreeable, I did not reciprocate her feelings, and even if I did, I was sure that neither you nor Mama would approve of any such liaison, and that it might be difficult for her to get membership of the club. I tried to comfort her as best I could, and I must admit to relief when I heard her parents return and she had to leave my room.

Pater, you must believe me when I say that I had given her no encouragement, and you will understand why I have had to change my lodgings.

I must end this letter now, as there is just time to catch the mail boat, which sails this evening; I will write again soon. Please do not mention any of this to Mama or Hermione, but tell them that I am well and in good spirits.

Your loving son,

Frobisher

P. S.

I have met a chap who has a good plan to make some money; I will tell you more in my next letter.

Cape Town, 2nd June 1896

Dear Pater,

It is a few weeks since I heard from you, but I know that you are very busy trying to save the estate, and you should not waste time writing to me. It would be a shame if you had to sell Broadlands; it has been in the family for so long.

Life here is not very different. We are in the middle of winter now, but it is still very pleasant, and the sun shines out of blue skies on many days. It can be very windy, but overall it is a very nice climate, and I am sure that it would be good for Mama's rheumatism. When I have the money, I would like to buy tickets for you, Mama and Hermione to come out for a couple of months, if you could spare the time.

How is Hermione? Has she got a beau yet? When she has he will be a jolly lucky fellow.

Do you remember that in my last letter I told you that I had met a chap who is sure that he can help me to make a lot of money? Well, his name is Sidney, and although he is not the sort that I would normally seek to mix with I have moved into a room in a house that he shares with another friend. I am not sure what it is that they do, something to do with finance, but they seem to be good at it, for they both always have a full purse.

Sidney is very good at a game called *Last Man Standing*; it consists of fifteen objects laid out in lines on a table, or a bar, or even the floor, and two people each alternately take one or more objects. The winner is the man who does not take the last. There are various rules that I do not yet fully understand, and the game can be played with stones, matches, corks, cheroots or any small object. Sidney usually loses the first game against a new opponent, but after that, he never loses, and last week he won more than three pounds in less than an hour.

He has promised to teach me how to win, but says that I must expect to lose a bit while I am learning. If I could get to know it well, I might be able to save up a bit of cash, and that would enable me to travel north to the goldfields.

It seems that it may be necessary to put the Boers in their place, and there is definitely something brewing; each ship from England or India brings in a few more troops. I think that I told you that there was a short war against the Boers a few years ago, but it solved nothing.

There is a mail ship due in the next couple of days, and I hope that there may be a letter for me. But whether there is or not, I will send this to you.

Give my dearest love to Mama and Hermione;

your loving son,

Frobisher

Broadlands, 24th May 1896

Dear Frobisher,

I was very concerned to read the postscript to your last letter. Surely you know that there is no lawful way to make easy money. Your grandfather once told me that if a man wagers you a guinea that his dog will sing our national anthem do not, under any circumstances, take the bet, for be sure that the dog will do just that.

I hope that you have come to your senses, and that you will no longer associate yourself with this man, for if you do not, you will lose what little money you have, and I cannot send any more to you.

Mama and Hermione send their love; Mama says to be sure to shake out your shoes or boots before you put them on in the morning, for scorpions and small snakes like to hide in them overnight.

Your concerned but loving Father

P. S.

We have had to dismiss Mary, Cook's assistant; it seems that she has been concealing the fact that she is with child for some months. She will not name the father, but seems convinced that he will come back and marry her, although she does not say from where. We shall be sorry to see her go, for she has been with us for several years, but we will not replace her, and the saving in her wages will be helpful.

Broadlands, 30th May 1895

Dearest Frobisher,

How are you? I miss you terribly; no games of tennis or croquet, and no one in whom to confide my girlish fantasies. I do hope that you are happy, and that you will soon be rich enough to come home.

I will ask Cook to post this letter for me when she goes into the village to get groceries, for as you know, Mama likes to read my letters before they are sent, in case, as she puts it, I have been *unladylike*. I am sure that I would never be that, but I am no less sure that she would not be happy with what I have to tell you.

Do you remember Anthony Fellowes? He came with his father to one of the shoots, shortly before you left. He is tall, with blonde hair, and has just come down from Cambridge and started working in his father's firm of solicitors. He is just four years older than me. His father is invited to shoots, but there is some past history of a dispute between our families, and I do not think that Papa and Mama consider Tony a suitable suitor.

Well, after the shoot we got talking, and before they left, he asked whether he could see me again. Without being too eager, and therefore, I am sure unladylike, I said that if he was in the area again, I was sure that Mama would like him to drop in for tea. Would you believe that he was in the area again only a few days later? After tea he and I went for a walk in the park. He is such a nice man, and so interesting, and I must say that I have quite lost my heart to him.

I know that you will say that I have not met many men with whom to compare him, but if the truth be told, I do not now want to meet any other men. His mother has asked Mama if I may attend a ball with them in London, and Papa and Mama say that it will be a good opportunity for me to meet some suitable young men; little do they know how fond I have become of Tony.

Do not, whatever you do, make any mention of this in your letters to Papa, and if you wrote to Cook, who would be thrilled to act as a go-between, the South African stamp would give the game away. No, you must keep this to yourself, and I know that you wish me every happiness; I will write to you again when I have more to tell you.

Look after yourself, dearest Frobisher, and wish me well.

Your loving sister,

Hermione

P. S.

Cook's assistant, Mary has been dismissed. Evidently she is several months pregnant and is not willing to name the father. I will miss her, for she was a friendly girl and very pretty.

Cape Town, 25th September 1896

Dear Pater,

You will wonder why I have not written to you lately; well, I have been out of Cape Town for three months. I will tell you about this, but first, I must thank you for the letters that I found waiting for me when I returned just a few days ago.

How splendid that you think that you may be able to keep Broadlands; I know how much it means to you, and I do so hope that you are successful.

You were, of course, quite right to warn me about Sidney, but he seemed to be a good friend, and I agreed to accompany him on a journey to some of the towns that have sprung up in an easterly direction along the coast. He said that there were good prospects there for his financial business, and that if I wanted to come along with him, he would let me in on the opportunities so that I too could make some money.

We went to Port Elizabeth first, and found lodgings in a rather seedy but cheap boarding house. Sidney spent most of the days out by himself; he said that he had private business to attend to, but every evening, we would go to a different bar, where he would play *the Last Man Standing* game with anyone who cared to take him on. He was invariably successful, and gradually amassed quite a lot of money.

From Port Elizabeth we moved on to East London, and each day, Sidney was again out and about, and each evening we frequented the bars. By now I had a good idea as to how it was that he was able to win so consistently, and he very kindly took it upon himself to give me the instruction necessary to make me as proficient as himself. As he had said would be the case, this involved me losing a bit to him, but I was certain that I could very soon recover that and make a great deal more.

I must emphasise, Pater, that there is nothing underhand about the game; there is, like chess, nothing hidden, and the players have free choice as to their moves; it is just a question of knowing which moves to make. I will teach you the game, if you like, when I return, although I know that you would never play for money.

One evening in our lodgings, Sidney was debating whether we should move on to Durban, quite a long way up the coast, when there was a loud banging on the door, and a couple of policemen burst into our room and arrested us both! Imagine my surprise, and my shame, that however innocent I might be, our family name should be tarnished in this way. We were bundled into separate trucks, and on the way to the police station, I demanded to know on what grounds I had been arrested. I was told that Sidney and I were accused of fraud and obtaining money by deception. I said that there was no fraud or deception involved in *Last Man Standing*, but was told that it was our daytime activities that had led to our arrest.

Pater, I will not trouble you with details of our incarceration; suffice it to say that it was unbecoming to a person of our class, and the food was neither sufficient nor tasty. Sidney and I were kept in separate cells, and only saw each other for an hour a day, when we were allowed to exercise in the prison yard. He was optimistic that he could buy his way out of trouble, but I doubted that the little money that I had would be enough to secure my liberty. After three weeks, we were brought before a magistrate, and during the hearing a number of witnesses gave evidence that Sidney had visited their homes and promised quick and substantial returns if they invested their savings with him. Needless to say, none of them had ever again seen a penny. Happily, none of them said that I had been with Sidney on these occasions, and nothing was said about our conducting the game of

Last Man Standing. I was dismissed with a caution about consorting with men of bad character, and required to pay most of my remaining money for costs, whatever they were. Sidney was sentenced to three years in prison, and all his money was taken and returned to his victims.

Pater, you must believe how sorry I am that this incident should reflect on our family, and I hope that it can be kept from our friends. Especially, I hope that it will not make it difficult to find a suitable husband for Hermione.

I have been taken back at the Ships' Chandlers, and am once again lodging with the Indian couple. Their daughter has gone to India and married a man of their choice, so I do not foresee any of the former complications.

I hope that my life can now return to the status quo, and that I can recoup what I have lost and start to build up a decent purse.

With all my love to Mama and Hermione, I remain,

Your chastened but loving son,

Frobisher

Chapter Three

Cape Town, 2nd November 1896

Dear Pater,

I hope that you, Mama and Hermione are all well. You will be preparing for the usual fireworks display on the front lawn, and I hope that you have decent weather for it. The estate staff do so much enjoy the evening, and although I know that the fireworks and refreshments cost a fair penny I am sure that it is worth it for the goodwill that results.

I had expected to be telling you now that I am back at the Ships' Chandlers my life had returned to normal, but that is far from the case. It seems that a considerable amount of our stock, mostly drink and tools, has gone missing. This was discovered when the quarterly stock-taking took place.

At first, the owner was reluctant to call in the police, for he has no insurance, and so could not hope to recoup his loss, but when he eventually did so, all the employees, including me, were subjected to some very aggressive questioning. Luckily, because I have not long been re-employed, and because it seems that the theft may have been going on for some time, I was not considered a prime suspect, and so I got off more lightly than the other two who work there. I am glad to say that the police confirmed that there would be no record of my involvement in the case; after the events in Durban I do not want to tarnish our family's name by seeming to be regularly involved with criminals.

The store supervisor, a Dutchman who I have always thought was rather a disreputable fellow, eventually confessed to the crime after what I suspect was some fairly brutal encouragement. It seems that he was known to the police with regard to an earlier case, and he will appear before the magistrate next week. He will probably be sentenced to several years' hard labour, and although I never liked him, I have to feel sorry for him.

However, his downfall has been to my advantage, for I have been promoted to the post of supervisor. I do not have many to supervise; until a replacement is found my command is just one young Dutch lad and half a dozen Africans who do the hard work, loading and unloading our goods, but my pay has been increased, and I hope that I will be able to return to Broadlands with a full purse that much earlier.

When I am not working at the store, there is not a lot to occupy my spare time, and I do not care to spend every evening, and most of the weekend, in the various bars, as a lot of chaps of my age seem to do. Some of those establishments make no secret of the fact that food and drink is not all that they can provide, and I am ashamed to say that on one of the infrequent occasions that I was in one, a very dark-skinned young woman made a most indecent proposition to me. You must believe, Pater, that I had in no way encouraged her, and I left the place without delay and will not go there again.

A couple of days ago, I met a fellow at the docks while I was supervising the loading of some of our goods onto a ship bound for Bombay. He is English, about my age, and although he did not go to one of the better schools, he is certainly a cut above some of the other English fellows out here. His name is Rodney Shields, and his family live in Norfolk, so I do not suppose that you know of them. He was on his way to Australia six months ago but was taken seriously ill when off the coast of West Africa and was put ashore here as he was unable to continue the journey. He recovered fairly quickly, and the shipping line took him on in a clerical position in their office here, and he so likes the place that he has decided to stay and try to find a better job.

He told me that he is a member of a sports club that has just been started here, and yesterday evening, he took me there as his guest. Most of the members are Dutch or English, and because the object of the club is to encourage sporting activities, they are nearly all in their twenties or early thirties. There is a small clubhouse with a billiards room with two tables, and a good-sized grass playing field.

Rodney asked if I would like to be a member, and I have agreed to. The membership fee is not expensive, and I hope that I will make friends with some of the members. As well as the sports teams, there is a trekking club. Trekking is a word in the local language, Afrikaans, derived from the Dutch, and it originally referred to transporting goods, usually by ox cart, across country. Now it also means travelling on foot, and as you might suspect this is a group who enjoy exploring the country outside Cape Town, and that would certainly interest me.

Before I left home, you told me about Table Mountain, and I see it every day as I go about my business out of the office. It is more than three thousand five hundred feet high, and there are a number of trails up and around the mountain; I would very much like to try some of them. I am told that there are many species of animals and birds there, and I will try to let you know what I see when I trek there.

Do give my fondest love to Mama and Hermione,

Your respectful son,

Frobisher.

Cape Town, 15th November 1896

Dearest Hermione,

I hope that you are well, and that your romance with Tony Fellowes is going well; he is a very lucky chap to be so well-liked by you, and I hope that he will soon be more than a friend. I have no female friends here, but there is lots to keep me busy, and I know that Papa has shown all my letters to you.

He will have told you that I have joined a club, and on last Saturday evening I was formally accepted as a member, having been proposed by Rodney Shields. What I did not know was that there was an initiation ceremony. This involved me standing on a table, dressed only in my undergarment, and reciting the club motto in Afrikaans five times, while balancing a glass of beer on my head. I am glad to say that I passed this test, but if I had known about it in advance I might well have decided not to join. I had thought that that kind of thing did not take place after leaving Eton, but looking back on it it was quite fun, and the other members said that I did it well. Do not, I beg you, say anything of that to Papa or Mama.

Next weekend I am going on a trek, a hike, with Rodney and a Dutch friend of his. We are going to try one of the trails up Table Mountain, and I am very much looking forward to seeing the birds and animals that live there. I need some proper climbing boots and other clothes, and happily I was able to buy them all from the store where I work at a discounted price. This is because I am now the supervisor.

Rodney is a nice fellow; he has told me that the reason that he was on his way to Australia when he fell ill was because he was expelled from school after he was found kissing one of the kitchen maids, and that because his father had political ambitions the family wanted Rodney where no breath of scandal could spoil his chances.

It seemed to me that to be expelled for such a minor reason was unfair; a chap at Eton who similarly broke the rules was only given a good flogging by the Head. I do wonder whether there was more than a kiss involved, but Rodney assures me that there was not. Anyhow, that would be no reason for me not to count him as a friend.

Last week was the busiest at the store since I have worked there. We had two ships in the port at the same time, one on its way to India, and the other on its way back from China. My African loaders kept muddling the stores, and I was fearful that the wrong stores would get loaded on the wrong ship; that would have been the end of my job there, but happily, I managed to sort it out before my boss found out.

I was sorry to hear that Mary had left; she was a nice girl and was always cheerful, but the saving will be a relief for Papa.

When I write again, I will let you know how the trek goes, and anything else of interest; meanwhile, all my best wishes.

Your loving brother,

Frobisher

Cape Town, 5th January 1897

Dear Pater,

I hope that you all enjoyed Christmas and New Year at Broadlands, and that the New Year shoot went well. I expect that the weather there was rather colder than it is here, for we are in the middle of summer, and although there is often a good breeze off the sea it can be quite uncomfortable indoors.

There was a party in the club on New Year's Eve, and we saw in 1897 with drinks and songs. Some chaps had rather too much to drink, but I can assure you, Papa, that I limited my own intake, and did nothing to be ashamed of.

Rodney Shields and I had decided that on New Year's Day we would explore some of the trails on Table Mountain, and we set off early, with some food and water in our packs. It was as well that we had not over-indulged on the previous evening, for the trails were rough and in some places quite steep, and one had to keep one's balance to avoid falling. But we made good progress, and after a couple of hours we could look down on Cape Town and pick out all the places that we knew.

There were many birds and animals that I had not seen before, and I made notes of their appearance in my pocketbook so that I could identify them when we returned to the town. I can now tell you that we saw a number of Rock Hyrax, a little furry animal, about the size of a large rabbit. They are called Dassies by the local people. There were several kinds of lizards and snakes, which we kept well away from, and many different sorts of birds, some of them brightly coloured. I am trying to identify these from the notes that I made. We saw a couple of small antelopes some way off, probably klipspringers, and had hoped to see elands, very large antelopes with long horns, but were probably still too close to town.

After eating our lunch, we climbed a bit higher up the trail, and it was then that I had a mishap. Leaping from one stone to another, I landed badly and twisted my ankle. I could feel that nothing was broken, but it was quite painful, and it put to an end our plan to climb higher up the mountain. It took us a long time to descend the trail, with Rodney taking some of my weight when the going was rough; there were no broken branches that I could have used as a support, and next time that we go trekking, for I shall certainly go again, I shall take a stout walking stick. We got back to town just before it got dark, and I put a towel soaked in cold water around my ankle. Five days later, it is still a bit swollen, but much less painful, and I can go about my business all right.

Papa, if you tell Mama and Hermione about my mishap, please be sure to emphasise that it was not a serious accident, and that I am now fully recovered; I do not want them to worry that I will do myself harm on future treks.

Your chastened and respectful son,
Frobisher

Cape Town, 28th February 1897

Dear Frobisher,

I was glad to get your letter and to learn that you had not seriously damaged your ankle on your trek on Table Mountain. I have assured Mama that it is nothing to be concerned about, and that it is a good thing that you are finding some interests outside your work.

The New Year shoot was one of the better ones in recent years; we were eight guns, and Jackson and Old Jock put on a splendid show, and all our guests said what a good day's sport they had. The bag was seventy-two pheasants, four woodcock, three hares, four magpies and a jay. I don't know if we will be able to afford to put down as many poults this year; Jackson is not as young as he was, and there are a lot of foxes about, especially in the Long Spinney, but Broadlands shoots have always been much enjoyed by our guests, and it would be a pity if they were no more.

I was very interested to hear of the birds and animals that you saw on Table Mountain, and I am sure that if you manage to get higher you will see even more. Kudu are considered good trophies by hunters in East Africa, and I seem to remember seeing the head of one mounted in the Great Hall at Nutbourne, along with all the other trophies that Edward came back with from Kenya. Let me know if you can identify the birds that you saw, and I will look them up in my encyclopaedia.

Your sister seems to be quite smitten by Anthony Fellowes, and I must say that he seems to be a nice chap. Mama is already talking about wedding dresses and bridesmaids, but I tell her that we must wait and see how the romance progresses. Anthony's father is a well-respected solicitor, and their land adjoins ours, although they cannot have more than five or six hundred acres.

Next time that you write I would like to know more about your job, what you do, and what prospects there are for you. You have been out there for more than a year now, and if you are to become a man of some substance, I think that you will have to make your mark in some other enterprise. That is not to say that I disapprove of your present employment, you did well to find a position so soon after your arrival there, but I am sure that you would like to think that in two or three years you could return to Broadlands with the means to live a full life and find a suitable wife.

We get reports in The Times of the problems that the Boers are causing, and even suggestions that it may come to war. I hope that that is not the case, and that if there is conflict, it will not be in the extreme south of the country. If it became impossible for ships to call in at Cape Town on their voyages to and from the east, it would seriously affect the value of our shares in shipping lines, and I would not wish to think that you might be in danger.

I must close now and take Old Jock for a walk; Jackson finds it difficult to exercise him enough, and I enjoy his company. Take care of yourself, my boy.

Your loving Father

Cape Town, 6th May 1897

Dear Pater,

I was so glad to hear that the New Year shoot was a success; I know how hard Jackson works to get the birds in the best coverts to give the guns a good day's sport. Old Jock must find it hard to put in a full day's work, but I know that he will never give up.

You asked for some details of my work at the Ships' Chandlers, so I will try to give you an idea of my duties. I told you in one of my letters that I am now the supervisor; I report to the manager, who is a Dutchman. The agents of the various shipping companies let us know when one of their ships will be calling at Cape Town, and what stores will be required; I then pass this information to the Dutch lad who is in charge of the African loaders, and he makes sure that everything that has been ordered, is ready and loaded on one or more of our carts in good time before the ship docks.

It may sound as though there is not much to my job, but believe me, Pater, that I have to check and re-check every detail of every load. The Dutch lad is not very reliable, and the loaders, all of whom are illiterate, often put the goods ready for the wrong ship. When I am satisfied that the order has been met, I then record the cost of each item and send an invoice to the shipping company. They are meant to settle each invoice before the ship docks, but there are often delays, and I have to use my best persuasive powers to get payment.

When the ship docks, usually early in the morning, I first check with the captain whether he has any additional requirements, over and above what we have been advised by his local agent; if so, he has to give me another docket, which I have to get approved by the agent before I can get the additional items taken from our warehouse to the docks.

Meanwhile, a gang of our loaders, usually four of them, are working with the ship's crew to load the stores on board. I am sorry to say that some of the loaders, and some of the seamen, are not entirely honest, and I have to urge the Dutch lad to make sure that all of our stores get on board and to get a receipt from the ship's purser. When that is done, that part of my job is finished, but the next part is about to start.

The stores ordered by the agents include everything from anchor chains to gunpowder, and from ship's biscuit or salted pork to marlin spikes. Often, a cask or two of rum is also ordered, and you can imagine that it is not easy to make sure that it reaches the ship's lock-up without being sampled by the loaders or crew. So far, I have been lucky in this respect, and more than one captain has commended my work.

Once the loading of stores, and other work necessary when a ship docks after a long sea voyage is completed, the crew are allowed ashore for a few hours before the ship sails; at all times there are half of the crew on board, but the other half are free to enjoy the various delights of the town. Some of them will come to our store and buy tobacco, knives, writing material or a host of other personal items. Some will go straight to the bars, and I am sorry to say, that some will seek the company of local girls.

When the ship is due to sail, the captain will tell the agent if any of the crew are missing, and the agent will then solicit our help in finding them. My labourers seem to know where to look for these men, and it is not often that a ship has to sail without a full crew.

I have introduced an arrangement whereby we charge the agents for any such additional services, and because they will be blamed, however unfairly, if the crew is not complete, they are willing to pay up. My manager is so pleased with this additional income, that he has said that I may keep half of it. It is not a great amount, but I am glad to have it, and I believe that he keeps the other half, for I have not seen it noted in the ledger.

After the ship has sailed, it is my responsibility to see what items need to be ordered to maintain our stocks at the correct level. Some are not available locally, and so I have to contact the agents of the shipping lines to arrange for them to be loaded on the next sailings from England, India or elsewhere. I must ensure that we are never unable to fulfil a ship's order, or we could lose that contract.

You will see from the above, Pater, that my job is a varied one. I have responsibilities to others, but I also have the opportunity to use my own initiative, and although some of the work is tedious, I enjoy meeting the ships' captains and pursers, and I get on well with the agents. But I do not think that I will stay here for more than another three months or so, and I may go north to see what prospects there are there.

I will, of course, let you know what I decide, and until then, I remain

Your respectful son,

Frobisher

Cape Town, 30th June 1897

Dear Pater,

I hope that you found the list of my duties here in my last letter to be interesting. In truth, they are not interesting, but it has been a position which has kept me in funds, and I now have a better idea of what I want to do while I am here in South Africa. I have several ideas, and when I decide which to pursue I will let you know, but you may be sure that it will be nothing that will reflect badly on me or the family.

Meanwhile, I have had something of an adventure. A week or so ago, I met a Dutchman in the club. He is one of the members, and has been in South Africa for several years. We got talking about what there was to do when we were not working, and he asked whether I had been up Table Mountain. I said that I had been some of the way up a few months ago, with Rodney Shields, but that I had sprained my ankle and had to come down without getting as far as we had hoped.

He said that some of the trails were quite dangerous, and that it was wise to take an African guide. One of the club servants, Msizi, evidently knows the mountain well, and will go with members when he is not required to be on duty in the club.

Well, one weekend when Msizi was not on duty, he agreed to guide Rodney and I, and we set off early on Sunday morning. We each took some food and a blanket and groundsheet. We had thought to take some water, for some parts of the trails are quite steep and it is hard work in the midday sun, although at this time of year the sun is not as powerful as it is at the end of the year, but Msizi said that there were many springs and small streams on the mountain where the water was very pure, clean and refreshing.

There are a number of different trails by which you can reach the top; some take as little as six or seven hours, but there are others, which are more interesting, and which can take ten hours or more. The trail that Msizi has suggested is not one of the longest or most difficult, but it will take us to the site of a large dam that is being built to supply Cape Town with water. Rainfall up the mountain is much greater than down on the coast, and it is intended to put an end to the frequent water shortages in town.

It is called the Woodhead Reservoir, and it is almost completed, and we thought that it would be interesting to see it. The route was not difficult, although there were places where it was necessary to go carefully over patches of boulders, large and small, and we reached the site of the reservoir in under three hours. It was a most amazing sight, and I fear that I cannot do it justice explaining it to you.

It is built across a gorge, and the dam wall is more than seven hundred feet from end to end; the height in the centre is more than one hundred and fifty feet. The material of the wall is stone, and this has mostly been cut from the local area, but everything else has had to be hand-carried by the workers up from the town. Although the top of the dam has yet to be completed, it is due to be officially opened later this year. It is now beginning to fill with water, and when it is full, it will be a most splendid sight. Rodney and I spread our groundsheets and blankets on a patch of scrub grass and much enjoyed the food that we had brought. We gave some to Msizi, for which he thanked us profusely, and went and got a goatskin bag full of the most refreshing water that I have ever drunk.

After we had eaten, we lay down on our blankets in the warm sun, and before very long, we were both asleep. I do not know for how long we slept, but we were woken by Msizi who said that the weather was going to be 'very bad'. And very bad it became, very quickly. A thick, damp mist was rolling up the hillside, and Msizi said that we should descend without delay. In the space of not more than five minutes it was not possible to see more than a few feet in front of you, and I can tell you, Pater, that I was very glad that we had him with us, for I doubt whether we would have found the trail by ourselves.

We came upon another pair of trekkers, also with a guide, and together, we carefully picked our way down the trail that only a few hours earlier had been bathed in warm sun. It was then that disaster struck us, for Rodney fell heavily and damaged his right leg so badly that he could not walk, even with a bit of wood as a crutch. I could not think how we could get him down to the hospital that he so obviously needed, but it was here that Msizi showed his true worth. Together with the other guide, using our blankets and groundsheets and two rough poles, they fashioned a crude stretcher, and, believe it or not, Pater, between them they got Rodney safely down to the town.

There was no mist on the lower reaches of the mountain, but the trail was far from smooth, and they managed to carry him without jolting his injured leg. I lost no time in putting Rodney in a carriage, and in quick order, we had him in the hospital. The doctor was able to confirm that no bones were broken, but he said that there was significant muscle damage, and if he had tried to come down on his feet, even with a crutch, he could well have caused permanent damage.

Rodney was strapped up, very firmly, and allowed to leave the hospital if he agreed not to leave his bed for the next three days. He was then to report back to the doctor, who would assess what, if any, further treatment was needed. I took him back to his lodgings, which are definitely more appealing than mine, and made sure that his African servant knew what was required of him. I felt that I should stay, but he insisted that he would be all right. He gave me two sovereigns and asked that I should give one to Msizi on the next occasion that I was in the club, and give the second to the other guide. I later found out that Msizi is Zulu for *Helper*, and he certainly lived up to his name.

The only animals that we saw were many dassies and several different species of birds, but you will understand that I did not pay much attention to them under the circumstances. I will provide a better record on my next trek.

Be sure to let Mama know that I am not taking part in any dangerous activities, and that I am in good health.

Your respectful son,

Frobisher

Broadlands, 30th August 1897

Dear Frobisher,

I have some very good news for you; your sister has become engaged to Anthony Fellowes. He is a most suitable young man, and I wholeheartedly support the marriage. Of course, his father is a solicitor, as is Anthony, but they are a well-respected firm, and I believe that Anthony has ambitions beyond his present work.

Mama is delighted by this development, and is discussing with Hermione details of the wedding dress, the bridesmaids' outfits, the flowers in the church and even the menu at the reception. The latter will of course, be held at Broadlands, and already some of the estate workers have asked whether there is anything that they can do to assist in the preparations.

I will end this now, as Hermione wishes to enclose a letter to you, and the post will be collected very shortly. I hope that this finds you in good shape, and I know that you will be as glad as I am about your sister's engagement.

Your loving Father

Broadlands, 30th August 1897

Dearest Frobisher,

What a lucky girl I am; I am going to marry Anthony! Last weekend he and his parents came to dinner, and afterwards, he and I went for a stroll around the rose garden. You can imagine my surprise when he went down on one knee and asked me to marry him. Of course I said 'yes'. Mama says I should have made him wait for an answer, but I was so happy that I could not possibly have waited for a moment.

We have not yet set a date, but it will probably be in October, and the reception will be here at Broadlands. Papa wants it to be a grand affair, with all the county invited, but I know that we are not as well off as we used to be, and I will try to convince him not to overdo it.

Mama is already making all sorts of plans, and I am sure that I will be kept very busy for the next two months, deciding on my dress, who are the bridesmaids to be, and a lot of other details.

I know that you will get on awfully well with Anthony; he is such a sweet man, and we will be so happy together.

I have to finish this now, before the post is collected; do write and tell me that you approve of my choice of a husband.

Your loving sister,
Hermione

Cape Town, 3rd September 1897

Dear Pater,

It is now three months since my trek up Table Mountain with Rodney Shields, and I have to admit that I have not been there again since then. That is partly because I have been very busy at work, with more ships than ever coming and going. And I have been giving a lot of thought as to whether I should stay here in Cape Town and try to find a more rewarding position, both financially and intellectually, or go north to where there seem to be real prospects in the goldfields for someone who is prepared to work hard.

I have decided, Pater, to move to Witwatersrand, where it is possible to stake a claim for very little outlay, and where, if you are lucky, you can get your money back and turn a profit in as little as three or four months. It all depends upon whether your claim is in the right place, and here, I have to admit that I do not have any knowledge of such matters, and I will have to rely upon getting advice from someone who knows the ropes.

You will say that if I am not careful I will be cheated out of my money, but I assure you that I will be careful not to put my trust in anybody that does not have a really good reputation. I expect to leave in two weeks' time, and I have told my Dutch boss of my plan. I think that he is genuinely sorry that I am leaving, but I have been able to find my replacement so he will not be left in the lurch.

Rodney Shields is going to take my job. He is completely recovered from his fall on the mountain, and does not much like his job in the shipping company. He went to Repton, so he has a fair education, and certainly knows more about the job than I did when I first arrived. He is very grateful to me for finding this position, and I shall be sorry to miss his company in Witwatersrand, but I am sure that I will make other friends there, and that I am doing the right thing. I do hope, Pater, that you approve of this change, and you may be sure that I will keep you up to date with my efforts to find gold.

I will let you have my new address when I get to Witwatersrand; until then, please give my love to Mama and Hermione, and tell them of my plans.

Your respectful son,
Frobisher

Chapter Four

Broadlands, 3rd November 1897

Dear Frobisher,

I was very surprised to learn from your letter of 3rd September that you are leaving Cape Town; I expect that you are already in Witwatersrand by now, and I hope that this letter reaches you in due course.

You know, my boy, that I will support you in whatever enterprise you choose, and I hear that there are fortunes to be made in the gold mines; my only concern is whether your lack of any experience of mining will prevent you from succeeding, but I know that you will give it your best shot, and I wish you every success.

I will close this now, as your Mama and I, together with Hermione and Anthony Fellowes, are going to a Hunt Ball in Oakham. Your mother and I are getting to the age when such events are less entertaining than they used to be, but it will be nice to see some of our old friends.

Your loving Father

Witwatersrand, 4th October 1897

Dear Pater,

I got your letter of 30th August just before I left Cape Town, and I was so glad to hear that Hermione is engaged to marry Anthony Fellowes. I do not know him well, having only met him when he and his father shot at Broadlands, but he seemed to be a decent chap. I know that there is some past history between our two families, but I am sure that the wedding will make that truly a thing of the past. I am so happy for Hermione, and I will write to her tomorrow.

My arrival here in Witwatersrand has been timely, for the discovery of major deposits of gold last year, far greater than the few previous findings, has transformed the place into a hive of frenzied activity. All sorts and conditions of men are here, all, like me, seeking their fortune.

I have learned that gold can be found in three ways; the one requiring the least capital investment is panning for what is called alluvial gold in river beds. It is unusual to find more than small specks of the metal in this way, but over a period of time it can be profitable, and all that is needed is a metal basin, called a pan, and some means of conducting water to the site if the river is dry. One has to stake a claim to a specific area of ground, but this is not expensive, and there is so much land available that you can move on when you want to.

Gold nuggets can occasionally be found in the same way, but more often it is necessary to dig for them, again usually in river beds. The pits can be quite deep, and ladders and ropes are needed, as well as equipment for the provision of water.

The third source of gold, and by far the most profitable, is by deep mining, following a seam of quartz rock. When brought to the surface, this has to be crushed and the gold extracted. This method is, you will understand, far beyond my financial means, unless I can find a partner with whom to invest my savings.

I will first of all try the inexpensive panning method, and I will let you know when I have staked a claim and started working it.

I was sorry to hear that you may sell the picture of Broadlands, painted by Thomas Gainsborough, for great-grandfather. I know that his work is becoming increasingly sought after, and I realise that Hermione's wedding will involve a considerable expense, but it will be a shame if it passes out of the family; I wish that I could do something to help you. I did manage to save quite a bit before I left Cape Town, but I will need this if I am to try my luck panning for gold, for there will be a lot of things to buy.

Do give my love to Mama and Hermione, and be sure to let me know when the date of the wedding is chosen.

Your loving and respectful son,
Frobisher

Witwatersrand, 5th October 1897

Dearest Hermione,

I was so pleased to hear from Pater that you are to marry Tony Fellowes. I am sure that you will make a wonderful, loving wife, and I hope that he will be everything that you want; let me know if he is not, and I will set him straight.

I am sure that you will be married before I get home, but you will be in my thoughts every day, and I will ask Mama to get something really nice for you as a wedding present. It is more than two years since I last saw you all, and it is strange to think that my little sister is soon to become a married woman. I hope that you will not think me presumptuous to look forward to being an uncle to your children, but I hope that I will be home long before then.

Life here is very different from that in Cape Town. There was a degree of sophistication there, albeit not much, but here it is a rather rough place; everyone is driven by the desire to strike it rich, and there are few of the niceties of life that we are used to. I am going to stake a claim in the goldfields and I am hopeful that a big find is just around the corner.

Papa says that he may sell the Gainsborough picture; it will be shame if he has to, but you must not reproach yourself that it is the cost of your wedding that makes it necessary, it is far more important than a picture, and when I am rich, we will buy it back again.

I send to you all my love, my dearest sister, and I wish you every happiness; it must be fun planning your wedding, and you must let me know as soon as a date is fixed.

Your loving brother,

Frobisher

Witwatersrand, 20th November 1897

Dear Pater,

Please excuse the lengthy gap since my last letter, but I have been working ten or twelve hours a day on my claim, and in the evenings, all I want to do is have a meal and get some sleep to prepare me for the next day.

You will be pleased to hear that I seem to have been lucky with the site of my claim, for I am regularly finding gold in my pan; not in large quantities, but I have several small nuggets and quite a lot of flakes. Every week, you take whatever you have found to the office and they weigh it; you are then credited with the value. I am happy to tell you that my credit stands at nearly fourteen guineas, and if my luck holds, I should have quite a sizeable purse in a couple of years.

I hope that you will soon tell me when Hermione is to be married. I am having my biggest nugget put on a chain, and I will send it to her as a wedding present. It is not very big, but it will be something to remind her of me on her wedding day and hopefully long after.

The political situation here is not getting any better, and it is hard to see how the dispute between the English and the Boers can be resolved peacefully. Several militias are being formed; groups of Englishmen who are prepared to fight alongside the army if necessary. I thought it my duty to join one and was surprised to meet a chap who was at Eton a couple of years ahead of me. I never knew him well, and he was known to be a bit of a chancer, but he has an interest in one of the deep mines and seems to be doing well. It is nice to have someone with the same background to share an occasional drink with, although I can assure you that I am not spending too much time and money in the bars with him or anyone else.

I will end this now, Pater, but I will write again soon; meanwhile, please give my love to Mama and Hermione.

Your loving and respectful son,

Frobisher

Witwatersrand, 2nd March 1898

Dear Pater,

I was so glad to get your letter telling me that Hermione is to be married on 14th July. I only wish that I could be there, for I am sure that you will do her proud, and that Broadlands will be a splendid place for the reception. I hope that she has got the nugget and chain that I sent to her as a wedding present. I am sorry that you have had to sell the Gainsborough, but as I told Hermione, I will try to buy it back when I have made my fortune.

You will be pleased to know that my claim is proving to be more productive than everyone thought that it would be. I have now obtained the titles to the land above and below it on the river bed, and I have a chap working for me. I have yet to find a really big nugget, but the ones that I have found, together with the small flakes of gold, have increased my credit to over one hundred guineas. I am considering digging some pits, to see if there is more gold beneath the surface, but that will be quite an expense, as I would have to hire a labourer or two.

You may remember that I told you that I had met an Old Etonian; his name is Toby Bellingham, and his family have an estate in Gloucestershire. It seems that they are well-off, and have funded his investment in one of the mines, and it is proving very profitable. I see him once or twice a week for a drink, and I have taken a few guineas off him at *Last Man Standing.*

I must end this short letter, for I have to go for Militia training; it seems increasingly likely that we will be needed before very long, and I want to be able to defend my claim if necessary.

Please give my love to Mama and Hermione, and my best wishes to Quentin when you write to him.

Your loving and respectful son,

Frobisher

Witwatersrand, 3rd March 1898

Dearest Hermione,

I was so glad to hear from Papa that you have fixed a date for your wedding; I do so wish that I could be there, but I am sure that it will be a splendid occasion and that you will look truly beautiful.

I hope that you got the little present that I sent to you a few weeks ago; it is not much, I know, but it is something that I myself have found, and it comes with all my love and best wishes for a happy married life.

Where will you live? I know that Tony works in his father's firm, and I hope that you will not be too far from Broadlands, so that I can see a lot of you when I return; although I don't suppose that you will want to see your boring, old brother when you have a fine husband to care for.

My prospecting is going quite well and I may try digging a few pits to see whether there is more gold beneath the surface. It seems that this is a very old river bed, and that thousands of years ago it was a really big river, so there may be more deposits a few feet down. I hope so, and I will let you know as soon as I have made my first million. Ha, ha!

I am sure that you and Mama are very busy with all the arrangements for your wedding; how splendid that the reception will be at Broadlands; I am sure that it will look its best and that the sale of the Gainsborough will be more than worth it.

Give my best wishes to Tony; he is a very lucky man.

And all my love to you, my dearest sister,

Your loving brother,

Frobisher

Broadlands, 17th June 1898

Dear Frobisher,

Your sister was married to Anthony Fellowes last Saturday, and what a day it was. The weather was perfect, and Broadlands looked its best, thanks in great part to the hard work put in by the estate workers. The lawns were perfectly mowed, the flower beds full of colour, and the bushes neatly trimmed.

There were only about seventy guests, as Hermione had said that she did not want more, but there were most of our friends and surviving relations, and a good turnout from Anthony's side. Several of Quentin's brother officers were also invited.

The reception was in a grand marquee on the front lawn, and we all sat down to an excellent meal. I had brought some of my best wine up from the cellar, and I think that I can safely say, that no one went home hungry or thirsty.

Hermione looked really lovely in her white wedding dress, and the four bridesmaids were beautifully turned out in pink and blue dresses. Quentin gave his sister away, looking very smart in his regimentals, and Anthony cut a fine figure in his morning-dress.

Altogether it was a splendid occasion, with much of the success being down to your mother, who had ensured that every detail was perfect. She is very tired now, and I hope that she did not overdo it, but she insisted on being fully involved and we were both very proud of our daughter.

The happy couple have gone to France on their honeymoon, and when they return will move into Chestnut Cottage, so they will not be far away and I am sure that we will see a lot of them.

It is a shame that you could not be here for your sister's big day, but I know that you will return home as soon as you have made your mark. Until then, look after yourself my boy,

Your loving Father

Witwatersrand, 10th August 1898

Dear Pater,

I was so glad to get your letter, and to learn that Hermione's wedding went off so well. I only wish that I could have been there to enjoy the occasion and see her married to Anthony, but it is good that Quentin was able to get leave from his regiment. In her last letter to me, Hermione described her wedding dress, and I am sure that she looked really lovely. How lucky that the weather was so good, and that you could hold the reception on the front lawn.

Here I can tell you that I have been really lucky with my claims; I have now got three pits dug in the old river bed, and we are finding nuggets fairly often. Still no really big ones, but together with the smaller specks I have been able to increase my credit to almost eight hundred guineas. It would be more, but I have had to hire a couple of labourers to work the pits, and a man to guard the site at night.

You will remember that I told you that I had met Toby Bellingham, who was a couple of years ahead of me at Eton. He has said that if I could find one thousand guineas, I could invest it in his mine. Pater, you may be sure that I have checked out his mine, and it is certainly producing gold at a good rate. I have not committed myself, and I will wait until I have the funds before I make a decision, but it might be a way of increasing my credit, faster than I can by working my claim.

I do not know how much news of South Africa you get to hear in England, but here there is no good news of the political situation. Sporadic fighting occurs in the Transvaal area, and the Boers seem to be preparing for all-out war to defend there and their so-called Orange Free State. Most of the diamonds are being found near Kimberley, on the western border of the Transvaal, so there is every reason for the British to bring it under their control.

Here the winter is coming to an end, and the weather will soon be very hot. I will be glad when the rains end, for much time is taken up in baling the water out of the pits. Some people have bought pumps to do this, but they are unreliable and expensive, and I prefer to leave it to my labourers and their buckets.

By the time that you get this letter you will be shooting the partridges; I hope that it is a good season, and also that when you get at the pheasants in October, the expense of the poults will have been worthwhile. Old Jackson must be getting on now, and without an under-keeper he will be kept very busy, but I know that he loves working at Broadlands and he will make sure that your guests are not disappointed.

I will write again before very long; meanwhile, Pater, be assured that I am working hard, to some effect, and will continue to so until I fulfil my ambition to help you to restore the family fortune and secure our position at Broadlands.

Your respectful son,
Frobisher

Witwatersrand, 14th August 1898

Dear Mama,

It was very good of you to remember my birthday; the card was much appreciated and it has pride of place in my little room.

I am so glad that Mr Gainsborough's painting sold so well, and that besides Hermione's wedding, Papa has been able to put Broadlands in tip top condition once again. I cannot imagine living anywhere else, and I so look forward to returning home and being with you all once again.

Papa will have told you that I have been lucky with my claim, and I hope that before long I will strike it really rich, as the saying here goes.

I am taking your advice about knocking out my shoes before I put them on every morning, and I am very careful about what water I drink. There is a woman who does laundry for us prospectors, so I am always dressed in clean clothes every morning, although by the end of a day's hard work they are ready to be washed again.

Do give my love to Hermione. Tell her that I will write to her very soon. I don't have her married address, so I will send the letter to you.

Your loving son,

Frobisher

Witwatersrand, 4th January 1899

Dear Pater,

Thank you for your letter; I am glad that you are having some good days at the pheasants, and that Jackson and Jock are still giving your guests what they expect at Broadlands.

Christmas and the New Year were not much celebrated here; everyone is too busy working their claims, but I did get together with Toby Bellingham for a couple of drinks on New Year's Eve. The mine in which he has an interest is not doing so well now, and I am glad that I did not take him up on his offer of a share in it.

My pits, I now have five, are proving very productive, although I did have what could have been a serious setback a couple of months ago. While one of my labourers was working at the bottom of my latest pit, about twelve feet down, one of the walls fell in and buried him. Luckily we were able to get him out very quickly, and he suffered no more than a good fright. While we were clearing the rubble out of the pit, we found that there were several good-sized nuggets in it, and since then we have had more success in the same place.

I am thinking that when my credit reaches five thousand guineas, probably in about a year's time, I might put the money into something else. I could go home and help you with the estate, but I would like to spend a few more years here and make a real success of my efforts.

You may be sure, Pater, that I will not risk what I have accumulated, and I would be glad of any advice that you may be able to give me; there are all sorts of opportunities here, from gold and diamonds to supplying the food and goods that everyone needs. You will say that the latter businesses are trades, and that gentlemen do not pursue such, but they are very profitable, and there is very little distinction here as to who is or is not a gentleman; a man is judged by the success of his efforts, and not by the family into which he was born.

It seems increasingly likely that there will be a full-scale war against the Boers before very long, they are forever harrying our people and need to be put in their place.

Give my love to Mama, and to Hermione when you see her next; and my best wishes to Quentin, if you are in touch with him.

Your loving son,

Frobisher

Chestnut Cottage, 10th April 1899

Dearest Frobisher,

You will think me a very bad sister for writing to you so seldom, but I have found that married life is very much busier than I had imagined it.

Apart from the social events, coffee mornings, dinners and balls, there are any number of estate duties that I have to attend to. If someone in the family of one of our people is ill I go and visit them and take a few things that they may need. I am also a member of the Ladies Circle, which consists of the wives of all the local landowners. We arrange flower shows and fêtes, petition the railway for better first lass carriages and a more convenient timetable, and keep the bishop advised as to the shortcomings of the vicar.

You may think that these are matters of little importance, and I must say that I am much of the same mind, but they are nonetheless an inescapable part of my life, and they do fill up some of the time that would otherwise have to be filled with needlework and piano lessons.

But I have some very good news for you, my dearest brother; I am with child, and expect to provide you with a nephew or niece in the middle of October. Papa and Mama are thrilled, and so are Tony and his parents. Tony is such a good husband, and I am sure that he will be a very loving father. Our house on the Fellowes' estate, Chestnut Cottage, is very comfortable, and despite the name, is quite big enough to accommodate a baby and a nursemaid.

You may remember that Cook's assistant, Mary, had to be discharged when she fell pregnant; well, she had a baby boy and she is coming to work for me when I have my child. It seems that the father of her child was a man called Fisher, although no one has ever seen hide nor hair of him, and she has called the boy Robert, Rob for short; he is a lovely looking little boy. They will live in, and when my child gets a little older it will be nice for him or her to have someone to play with.

We have not seen or heard from Quentin for ages; he is not a good correspondent, and his regiment does not give him much leave. But he has been promoted to Captain, so they must think well of him.

I am so glad that your claim is doing so well; I always knew that you would make a go of it, and that you would help to ensure the future of Broadlands. Do take care, and be sure not to get involved with the war that Tony says is sure to break out before very long.

I send all my love to you, my dearest brother,

Hermione

Chapter Five

Kimberley, 14th May 1899

Dear Pater,

You will be surprised to hear that I have left Witwatersrand and travelled to Kimberley. I told you in one of my letters that I was thinking of trying something else with the money that I had made with my gold claim; well, it continued to be very profitable, and a chap who had the claim next to mine, also a profitable one, offered me five thousand guineas for my claim. He felt that the two together would be an even more profitable operation, and he was probably right.

This stroke of luck meant that my purse was now more than twelve thousand guineas, and I felt sure that I could increase it in the diamond fields, where you can literally kick a diamond out of the ground if you are lucky. I have been here for a week now, and I am looking to see where I should invest a part of my money.

War seems to be imminent, and there is a sizeable contingent of the British Army in the town, which is just outside the border of the Boer's so-called Orange Free State. I will not part with any of my money until we see what will happen, but I think that there are good investments to be made, and I would rather not be involved in the actual search for diamonds.

I must finish this letter now, as the mail is due to be sent to Cape Town tomorrow to catch the mail boat to England. Please tell Mama that I am well and safe, and give my love to her and Hermione.

Your loving son,

Frobisher.

Kimberley, 10th September 1890

Dear Pater,

I fear that this may be the last letter that you get from me for some time. War with the Boers is inevitable, and preparations are being made here in case we are attacked by them.

All English men have been recruited into militia and issued with rifles; this is to supplement the quite small number of our soldiers in the town. I also have my pair of Purdeys, and a pistol that I bought in Witwatersrand, to defend my claim if need be. So I am well armed to do my bit if necessary.

A man called Cecil Rhodes, who has been the biggest player in the diamond mining business here, is organising our defences, and I am sure that we will give the Boers a good thrashing if they try anything.

Pater, please do not let Mama or Hermione have any concern on my behalf, and do not worry if you do not hear from me for a while, as it may not be possible to get letters down to Cape Town.

I must close this now and go for a training parade; there will soon be two soldiers in the family. Ha, ha.

Your loving son,

Frobisher

Kimberley, 12th October 1899

Dear Pater,

We are at war with the Boers. It was declared yesterday, and since then, there has been much activity to prepare the town for a possible attack; Kimberley is very close to the border with the Orange Free State, and the Boers will certainly have their eyes on the diamonds that have transformed the town into a prosperous community.

There will be no mail out of here until the situation is resolved, so I will try to record important events in this letter and then send it to you when communications are restored.

20th October 1899

We have been besieged by the Boers for almost a week. They completely surrounded the town on 14th October and since then, have tried continuously to break through our defences. They have a very large gun, with which they bombard us daily, but so far we have repulsed them and there have been very few casualties, although many of the buildings have been destroyed or damaged.

Luckily there are wells within the town, so we will not want for water, but food is already being strictly rationed, and we have been told that it may be necessary to kill and eat some of the older horses and mules.

I have not yet been engaged in any fighting, for the part of our perimeter that my group is responsible for has not yet come under attack. I have been put in charge of a dozen men who were working in the mines, and although they are rough sorts, I am sure that they will give a good account of themselves when asked to.

I often think of my former life at Broadlands, but you must not misunderstand me, Pater, when I say that I am quite enjoying the situation in which I find myself. Luckily, the greater part of my purse is held in a bank in Cape Town, so if I should be captured, I will not lose everything that I have worked for during the past four years.

10th January 1900

It is now three months since we were besieged, and conditions in the town are not good. All sorts of diseases have spread through the population, due to malnutrition and poor sanitation, but morale remains good and the Boers have not been able to break through our lines.

I have been engaged a number of times, and I am proud to say that my men have given the enemy a bloody nose every time that they have attacked us, and so far, none of us has suffered even a scratch.

The Boer artillery continues to be the greatest danger, and we have only some small field guns, which are of little real use against men with rifles on horses. My Purdeys have had hot barrels on several occasions, and I find it much easier to hit Boers, while trying to avoid hurting their horses, than high-flying pheasants coming out of the beech wood at home.

17th February 1900

The siege has been lifted! The relieving force broke through the Boer lines a couple of days ago, and the survivors made themselves scarce. It will be some time before things return to normal, but at least we are spared the daily efforts of the Boer artillery.

There is to be a military parade through the town tomorrow, and it is hoped that the railway line to Cape Town can soon be repaired, and we will be able to obtain all the many things that have been unobtainable for the past four months.

When things return to normal, I shall start to consider how I should seek to increase my purse.

I assure you, Pater, that I will not invest in any dubious venture, or any high risk business, but only in something that is safe and will give a fair return on my money. There is no opportunity to become involved in the diamond mining; the costs are very high and Mr Rhodes controls every aspect of it. I will see what other opportunities there may be.

18th February 1900

Pater, you will never believe this. I was watching the parade yesterday when who should I see but Quentin, leading a troop of very smart soldiers. I shouted out, but he could not hear me, so I followed the parade to their barracks, where I met Quentin. He took me to their mess, and over a few glasses of a very good port, he filled me in on his life during the last few months.

He spent some time in Cape Town after his arrival, and then his regiment was embarked on the train with a view to strengthening the defences of Kimberley. Before they got there, the Boers had besieged the town, and it was then a case of preparing for an attack that would break the siege. There were several unsuccessful attempts made over a period of two or three weeks, before they broke the Boers on 16th February.

He told me all about Hermione's wedding, and said that he felt that Tony Fellowes was a good chap; I am so glad.

It seems that the Boers have also laid siege to Ladysmith, a town several hundred miles to the east of Kimberley; there are evidently a large number of British troops there, as well as civilians, and they have been surrounded since November last year. Quentin's regiment may be sent there, but it will take a long time to get there.

I have just heard that the post will be leaving for Cape Town tomorrow, so I will end this now. Quentin and I both send all our love to you and Mama. Be assured that we are both safe and well.

Your respectful son,
Frobisher

Kimberley, 10th June 1900

Dear Pater,

So much has happened since I last wrote that I hardly know where to begin. But first I must thank you for all the letters that I received when the railway was re-opened. I hope that you have received the letter that I wrote during the siege; it now seems a long time ago, and life here has almost returned to normal, with diamonds once again being what involves everyone in one way or another.

Pater, I have made an investment which I am sure will be even more profitable than my gold pits were. I have bought a general store.

The previous owner and his entire family were killed by one of the Boer shells while walking in the town, and no one came forward with a claim to it. It cost me less than nine thousand guineas, and I have looked up the accounts and it was making a profit of more than a thousand guineas per month. In some ways, it is very similar to the Chandlers business that I worked in in Cape Town, except of course that we do not sell any nautical goods.

I know that you will be disappointed that I am involved in trade, but in fact, I take no part in the day-to-day selling of goods; rather I order what is necessary to maintain our stock, keep the accounts and supervise the three men that I have employed. We sell nothing perishable, but otherwise almost everything that the people here need. In our first month of trading we broke even, and I have no doubt that we will soon be in profit.

Quentin's regiment moved on shortly after they lifted the siege, and I have heard nothing from him since then. I know that Ladysmith was relieved shortly after Kimberley, so I do not think that he could have been there. He has my address here so I hope to hear from him before too long.

I was so glad to learn in your last letter that you have been able to bring the estate up to scratch again, and particularly that the roof at Broadlands has been repaired. I know how much you care for our family home. I was so sorry to hear that old Jock had died; he has been such a faithful friend for so long; I hope that Jackson will be able to train up another dog before too long.

I got a letter from Hermione with the bunch from you; what good news about her son; I will write to her very soon.

I must go now and do the day's accounts for the store and see what needs to be ordered to maintain our stock.

With my respectful love to you and Mama,

Frobisher

Kimberley, 12th June 1900

Dearest Hermione,

I was so glad to get your letter when the post came up from Cape Town after the siege was lifted, and I am delighted that you have made me an uncle to your baby boy. You and Tony must be so happy to be parents, and I know that he will lack for nothing now and as he grows older. Well done!

What a good idea to call him Arthur after our grandfather, and William after Tony's father; they are both good names and I am sure that he will bear them with distinction.

It seems as though employing Mary has been a very good move; you say that she is devoted to Arthur, and her son, Rob, will be a good playmate for him when he gets a bit older. I do so look forward to seeing you again, and to meeting my nephew, but I think it likely that I will be here for some time yet.

I have bought a general store here in Kimberley. I fear that Pater will not be too pleased, as he has always thought that the family should not be involved in trade, but it does represent a real opportunity for me to accumulate some money, and so make it possible for me to return home that much sooner. I do not become involved in actually selling goods to our customers, some of whom are rather rough types, but rather I manage the business and the accounts. I must admit that I find it rather fun, and much less risky than my gold pits.

You will have heard from Pater that I met Quentin here in Kimberley when the siege was lifted; his regiment was part of the force that drove the Boers off and relieved the town. He was in very good shape and is clearly cut out to be a soldier. He looked very smart leading his men through the town in the victory parade, and we met several times before he left to win the war somewhere else. We are indeed, defeating the Boers, but they are very hard to pin down, and those that escape from any engagement form up new 'commandos', as they call them, and harass our people somewhere else.

I must end this letter now, and go and get some sleep. Do give my best regards to Tony, and congratulate him on becoming a father; also give Arthur a big hug from his uncle in South Africa. And of course, I send all my love to you,

Your loving brother,
Frobisher

Broadlands, 3rd August 1900

Dear Frobisher,

I was indeed surprised to get your letter and learn that you now own a general store. As you said, I have never wanted the family to be involved in trade, but it does seem to be a sound investment, and it certainly is less of a risk than looking for gold; although you were very fortunate in that enterprise.

What a stroke of luck Quentin turning up in Kimberley, and how you both must have enjoyed telling each other of your varied adventures. I am glad that he is making a go of soldiering, and if he keeps it up he may in time become a colonel, or even a brigadier. Your great uncle George served under Lord Raglan in the Crimea, and distinguished himself by saving the lives of two wounded brother officers during the siege of Sevastopol.

Hermione will have told you that she is the mother of a fine boy, Arthur by name. She and Tony seem to be very well suited, and as they live on his family's estate we see quite a lot of them. Did she tell you that Mary, the maid that we had to dismiss, is Arthur's nanny? She has a boy called Rob, who is almost four years old now; he is a good looking lad, and he sometimes reminds me of you at that age.

I have a new dog, a cocker spaniel called Oscar, after another of your great-uncles who was very fond of shooting. He is only a year old, but quick to learn, and he may be able to retrieve a few pheasants when the season begins. I am going up to Scotland next week to have a go at the grouse with the Forsythes; it is some years since I have been there and I hope that I can do myself justice. Mama will go and stay with the Fellowes; she is very much looking forward to spending some time with her grandson.

We have had some trouble with gypsies setting up camp by the West Wood; they may not be as bad as their reputation but Jackson is sure that they are taking some of our pheasants, and by himself, he is not able to patrol as well as he did when we had Smith as under-keeper. I wish that you or Quentin were here to put them in their place, which is not on our land.

I hope that the war is over soon, and that you will have saved enough to come home. I am not getting any younger, and Broadlands needs someone who is able to keep an eye on the house and the estate and nip any problems in the bud.

Look after yourself, my boy,

Your loving Father

Kimberley, 4th January 1901

Dear Pater,

Thank you for your last letter. I fear that I have been somewhat dilatory over my correspondence lately, and my only excuse is the success of the store, which has kept me occupied for many hours every day.

I am glad to say that it has exceeded my expectations as to its profitability, and is even doing better than it was before I acquired it; although to be fair, trading was not easy in the months before and during the siege. I should be able to return home in a couple of years' time if things continue as at present, although I am tempted to see whether there may not be further opportunities here or in Johannesburg.

Now that that town has been taken by the British Army, it will not be long before business there flourishes once again. There is a stock exchange, and I might be able to increase my purse in that way; certainly most of the stocks will be rising in value now that the Boers have been driven out. But do not worry Pater, I will not speculate unwisely.

I hope that your visit to the Forsythes' grouse moor was a success, that you are having a good season at the pheasants, and that Oscar is learning his trade under Jackson's training; you will be glad to have a dog again.

Do give my love to Mama, and tell Hermione that I will write to her again soon.

Your loving and respectful son,
Frobisher

Kimberley, 3rd May 2001

Dear Pater

In an earlier letter I said that I was looking out for other possible investments; well, I have made one. I have bought the small hotel which is next door to the store.

It is not the sort of place that you and Mama would stay at in London, but it is a cut above the boarding houses that accommodate the riff-raff. It has only twelve rooms, a small dining room and a bar, and because it has a good reputation it is fully occupied most of the time. There is a housekeeper, two maids, a cook — I cannot call him a chef — and a barman. We keep our prices for food and drink a little higher than most of our competitors, and in that way, ensure that our customers are for the most part respectable.

Because I also own the store it is possible for the hotel to get many of the things that are needed at a discount, and I think that the two businesses will work together really well; but the proof of that pudding will be in the eating.

Pater, I fear that you will be displeased at this further venture into trade, but there are very few social distinctions here between one class and another; we all live and work in the same conditions, and an education at Eton is less important than an ability to survive and prosper in a very mixed environment.

Buying the hotel did take most of my purse, but so that I did not put all of my eggs in that basket I also bought two . . .

Editor's Note. The rest of this letter is missing.

Broadlands, 20th June 1901

Dear Frobisher,

Be assured, Frobisher, that you have my full support in whatever you do, and I hope that your efforts will be well rewarded.

I was indeed surprised to learn that you had bought a small hotel. You will think that I deplore your further venture into the world of commerce, but you seem to have a good head for business, and if the store and the hotel can between them make your fortune, then I wish you every success. I realise that times are changing, and we must adapt and change with them. I notice here at home that there is a feeling that our class has had its day, but I am happy to say that all our tenants continue to show the right respect for the family.

I fear that Mama is not in the best of health. She misses you and Quentin, but she drives great pleasure from her frequent visits to Hermione, and she has a great affection for Arthur. Doctor Tayler has prescribed a potion to ease her breathing, and she remains very cheerful, even when she is feeling low.

My leg is causing some discomfort, especially during the cold weather, but I can still get around the estate with the help of a stick, and I am more fortunate than some of my friends. Oscar is a great companion to me on these walks; Jackson has trained him to be a very good gun dog, and he is also very much at home in Broadlands.

The good news is that I had a letter from Quentin last week, and he has been promoted to Captain. His regiment has been involved in some heavy fighting, and has lost quite a number of officers and men. Nevertheless, he is in good spirits, and says that he is sure that the war will be over before very long.

Your loving Father

Chestnut Cottage, 28th June 1901

Dearest Frobisher,

I was so glad to hear about your hotel; now you are truly a man of property, and I am sure that you will get very rich, very soon. Papa may not sound very enthusiastic about the store and the hotel, but he is secretly very proud of you, and the fact that you are making your mark in South Africa.

I have some very good news; I am once more in what Mama would call 'an interesting condition'. I will have a baby brother or sister to Arthur in February next year. I hope that it is a girl, but I will be no less happy with another boy.

Papa and Mama are thrilled, and so of course is Tony. Mama seems to be a bit better than she was. She finds her breathing rather difficult, but still manages to walk round the gardens with me when she comes to visit. Papa complains about getting old, and I think that he finds it harder to manage the estate than he used to but he is very fond of Oscar, who never leaves his side during the day unless it is to be further trained by Jackson.

Mary is also very excited at the thought of another baby to look after. Her Rob is now five years old and is a lovely child. It seems that while she was pregnant before she had him, she spent some time with a retired schoolteacher who expanded her vocabulary, and improved her grammar and her speech. She is now very self-confident and can hold her own when talking to my visitors.

Tony is now a full partner in his father's firm; this means that I see less of him than I would wish, but he is such a good husband and father that I cannot complain. He says that we may move into his parents' house in a year or two, when it becomes too big for them as they get older. That would be nice, but I do not want to have to share him and Arthur with a lot of servants. Am I being silly?

It is great news that Quentin has been promoted. Father is very proud of him too, but Mama is always worried that he will be killed or wounded heroically leading his men into battle, although she tries to hide it. If the war is over soon, I hope that his regiment may come back to England, and it would be lovely if they were not far from here.

Do let me know how your hotel and store get on; I am sure that they will be very successful.

Your loving sister,

Hermione.

Kimberley, 7th November 1901

Dear Pater,

Thank you for your recent letters, and for your support for my commercial ventures, as you call them.

Alas, I have the worst possible news; my store and hotel were both burned to the ground last week. It seems that the fire started in the hotel kitchen, possibly as a result of an oil stove being overturned, and the fire engine that was summoned was unable to do anything but prevent the fire from spreading to the adjoining properties.

Happily it happened during the day, and no one was hurt, but all my possessions have gone up in smoke. Luckily, I kept my passport, the two diamonds, a small amount of cash, the deeds to my properties and your letters in a safe deposit box at the bank, so I am not quite back to where I started almost seven years ago.

The buildings were insured, but only for the structures, and that represented only a small part of what I paid for the goodwill and for all the goods in the store. By the time that I have paid off the suppliers' invoices and the staff in the hotel and store, I shall have precious little in my purse, and in any case I do not feel able to try to rebuild my little empire here.

But all is not lost. My diamonds are good stones, and if I can sell them well, it should be possible for me to make a fresh start somewhere else and build up my purse again. I will, of course, keep you informed.

I have much to do now, so I will close this letter with my fondest love to Mama and to you, Pater.

Your respectful son,
Frobisher

Chapter Six

Johannesburg, 14th January 1902

Dear Pater,

I have moved to Johannesburg. It took me some time to settle my affairs in Kimberley, but I did not feel inclined to become involved in another venture there, and there are certainly more opportunities here.

I managed to sell the land on which the store and hotel had stood for a reasonable sum, and I was left with something in my purse after I had paid the staff and my outstanding liabilities, so I was able to take a little time to see what I might do here in Johannesburg. Only three weeks after I arrived here, I learnt that one of the major hotels was looking for a Night Manager, and because of my hotel experience in Kimberley, I was offered the position.

It is not very well paid, but I do get a room in the top floor of the hotel and all my meals free of charge, so it will not be necessary for me to spend very much, and I think that within a year or so I will be once again quite well placed financially.

The work is not very onerous; apart from supervising the staff on duty overnight, I am responsible for meeting any guests arriving during the hours of darkness. Some of these are important persons, and it is up to me to ensure that their first impressions of the hotel are favourable, and that their varied requirements are satisfied. I am sorry to say that I have already had to tell one man that I was not able to supply him with a female companion; we are not that sort of establishment.

The sale of diamonds in Kimberley is controlled by Rhodes, so I was not made a good offer for mine there, as they want to sell them on at a profit. However, I have heard that there are people here who do not approve of the Rhodes' monopoly, and if I need to, I may be able to sell them here at a small profit. You may be sure, Pater, that I have put them, together with my other important items, into a safe deposit in the bank.

Hermione must be very close to having her baby; I hope that it's a girl, it would be nice for them to have a pigeon pair. Two young children to look after must be hard work; I am so glad that she has Mary to help her.

I must close this, for it is almost time for me to go on duty; I work from nine o'clock at night until seven o'clock in the morning. This means that I have most of the day, when I am not sleeping, to explore this town.

With fondest love to Mama and yourself, I remain

Your respectful son,

Frobisher

Broadlands, 20th January 1902

Dear Frobisher,

I was very concerned to hear about your misfortune regarding the fire. I am relieved that no one was injured, since you might have been held responsible, but it is a great pity that all your efforts to establish yourself have come to nothing, although I understand that it is no fault of yours.

What will you do now? With or without substantial means you will always be most welcome back here at Broadlands, and I must admit, that it would be nice to have a younger man around, to take over some of the estate duties, but I realise that you will want to make good your loss, and that is the determination that I admire in a man.

Do let me know what you intend, so that I can reassure your Mama that you are not depressed by your ill-luck.

I must admit that I was intrigued to learn that you had purchased two diamonds; that has turned out to be a very shrewd move. I hope that the sale of one or both will enable you to get back on your feet, although it would be splendid if you could bring them home with you when you return.

Hermione's second child is due very soon now; she has had an easy pregnancy, in no small part due to Mary's assistance, and is so looking forward to having another baby in the house.

It is time for me to take Oscar for his afternoon walk. He has turned out to be both a good gundog and also a devoted companion; he is very happy about the house, unlike poor old Jock, who was never happy unless he was out on the estate, seeking to put up a hare or pick up a shot pheasant.

Your mother has asked me to say that you must take care of yourself, and beware of anyone who expresses an interest in your diamonds. I am sure that you have told no one about them, but you know how she fusses.

Your loving Father

Johannesburg, 20th May 1902

Dear Pater,

This will only be a short letter, as I am in a hospital, and they want me to rest as much as possible. Do not worry; I am not in any danger, and I should be able to leave in a couple of days.

I have been gradually replacing my wardrobe, which you will remember was all lost in the fire. I needed a buckskin jacket, and was directed to a store on the outskirts of town. It was not a pretentious establishment, but it did sell good quality clothing at very reasonable prices.

There was a pile of jackets on the floor, and I bent down to pick one up; as I did so I felt a very severe pain in my right hand, and when I dropped the jacket I saw a krait that had been lying curled up under it. As I am sure that you know, the krait is a very small snake, but it has a very poisonous bite, and I made my way to the nearest hospital with all speed. I am told that I passed out soon after I arrived, and I woke up some time later in bed.

I evidently told them that it was a krait that had bitten me before I passed out, and luckily they had the right serum, so it was not long before I was on the road to recovery. Do not let Mama or Hermione worry on my behalf; I really am in no further danger.

One piece of good news is that the day before my accident, I was told by one of the hotel guests that I have got to know, that he might have a proposal of interest to me. I have no idea what it may be, but I will certainly contact him as soon as I can get out of here and listen to what he has to say.

The war really does seem to be near the end, and I hope that in my next letter I can confirm that it is over.

Your respectful son,
Frobisher

Johannesburg, 4th June 1902

Dear Pater,

Peace at last! There have been many celebrations here in Johannesburg and throughout the country, and everyone is hopeful that business of every sort will soon be even better than it was two years ago. Certainly the hotel in which I work has seen a considerable increase in the number of guests from overseas, many of them from England, who are looking for new opportunities in which to invest.

I was discharged from hospital a week ago, and apart from a swelling on my rather sore right hand, I am now fully recovered and back at work. You will remember that in my last letter I told you that one of our guests had said that he might have a proposition that would interest me; well, I saw him last evening and he told me what he had in mind.

His name is Mr Edwin Cade, and he has set up a gold mining company in the Gold Coast, a British colony in West Africa. Gold mining there has evidently only recently become properly organised, having previously been what Mr Cade described as a very ineffective, amateur effort, by a number of indigenous and foreign companies. His company, the Ashanti Goldfields Corporation, has the rights to mine in a region of the country some one hundred and twenty miles north of the capital town, Accra, which is on the coast. The conditions there are rather primitive compared with those here in Johannesburg, but the position which he offered to me, on the basis of my experience in Witwatersrand, is that of Mine Manager, and is well paid.

Pater, you will wonder whether this is a good move, and I have myself given much thought to it. My position here does not require any great effort, and apart from meeting some interesting and influential people, is not a very satisfying one, and will never make me rich. I enjoyed my time in both Witwatersrand and Kimberley, and I think that I am better suited to such work than bowing and scraping to my financial betters.

I have a week to make a decision, and if I decide to accept Mr Cade's offer I will leave with him by ship from Cape Town in the middle of next month. I will, in any case, write again before I leave.

Your respectful son,

Frobisher

Johannesburg, 21st June 1902

Dear Pater,

I have decided to accept Mr Cade's offer, and we leave for Cape Town tomorrow, with a stop en route at Witwatersrand. It will be good to see how the place has changed since I was there, and whether my claim is still being worked. I have heard that the production of gold has increased considerably in the last year or two, but I do not regret having moved on from there.

I have given in my notice to the hotel, and have a few days to settle my affairs here. I am already on the payroll of the Ashanti Goldfields Corporation, rather a fine-sounding name, so my purse will not be reduced and I have not had to sell the diamonds.

I must say that I am looking forward to this new challenge, and I can assure you, Pater, that I will give it my best shot and try to justify Mr Cade's confidence in my abilities.

There is no port in the Gold Coast that our ship can tie up alongside, so it will stand off shore and the disembarking passengers and their luggage will be taken ashore by ship's boat. I hope that we are blessed with calm water then, as I do not much like being in a small boat at the best of times; but I will not, of course, give Mr Cade any reason to doubt my fibre.

A new shipping line, Union Castle, has started sailings between England and South Africa, and we will travel in one of their ships, the *Alnwick Castle*. I am happy to say that Mr Cade has kindly booked me rather more suitable accommodation than that in which I travelled to Cape Town, nearly eight years ago.

So much has happened in those eight years, and I fully expected to be back at Broadlands long before now, but this latest opportunity should enable me to get home in three years at the most, and by then I will be able to help you with maintaining Broadlands and running the estate until Quentin leaves the army.

I have received no letters for the past two months, although I am sure that you will have written with news of Hermione's second child. I did tell the hotel that I was going to the Ashanti Goldfields in the Gold Coast, but I fear that there is little chance of them forwarding any mail for me. I will let you have a proper address when I get there.

Please give my fondest love to Mama and Hermione,

Your respectful son,

Frobisher

Cape Town, 11th July 1902

Dear Pater,

I am now back in Cape Town with Mr Cade, and we sail on Thursday at four o'clock in the afternoon. I am so much looking forward to this new venture and I am determined to make a success of it.

Our stay in Witwatersrand was very interesting. My old claim has turned out to be very productive, and the man who bought it from me has started to sink a proper mine where I dug my little pits. I was very pleased when he told Mr Cade that I had a real nose for gold, and that he was a lucky man to have secured my services.

Last evening Mr Cade kindly took me out for a drink to a bar that I visited once or twice when I lived here and who should I see at a table in the corner but Sidney, the man who caused me to be thrown into jail in Durban. He must have completed his sentence three or four years ago. He was talking to two men who I thought looked rather rough, and I made sure that he did not see me, for I would not want Mr Cade to think that I associated with jailbirds and riff-raff.

I understand from Mr Cade that the climate in the Gold Coast is very different from that here; it seems that there is thick forest over much of the country, and that at certain times of the year, there is very heavy rainfall for days on end. There is evidently a lot of fighting between the various tribes, but the Ashantis, the tribe who live in the region of the Ashanti Goldfields mine, are the strongest and most warlike and only recently were subdued by the British Army.

I will finish this letter now, it will travel with me on the ship, and I will add to it during the voyage, and then seal it and send it on to you with the ship, so you should get it before the middle of July. The whole trip from Cape Town to Portsmouth normally takes twenty days, so I expect that we will reach the Gold Coast in about a week or ten days, and I will write again when we arrive.

At sea 15th July 1902

We sailed yesterday, right on time at four o'clock. My cabin is small but very comfortable, and the whole ship has a very favourable appearance. The first class dining saloon is a good size, and the food is excellent. I had not expected to be booked in first class, but Mr Cade said that as a senior member of his company, it would not be appropriate for me to have a lesser status on board.

I have been able to spend some time on the bridge, and I found this most interesting. It seems that a Union Castle ship sails every Thursday at four in the afternoon from both Cape Town and Southampton, and they pass each other somewhere off the West African coast. The voyage takes about twenty days in each direction, so there must be quite a number of ships in the Union Castle fleet.

Tomorrow night we will be opposite, or abeam, as I have learned to say, Walvis Bay, the Bay of Whales. The port there was of interest to the Royal Navy, and was annexed by the British more than twenty years ago, to protect the sea route round the Cape of Good Hope. We have not seen any whales yet, but I hope that we may do so tomorrow.

The weather has been good and the sea calm so far, and I hope that I get my sea legs before we encounter any rough seas; I would be most embarrassed if Mr Cade found me with mal de mer.

At sea, 17th July 1902

Yesterday afternoon, we saw several large whales, and we have several times been accompanied by schools of porpoises; otherwise, the only living thing to be seen is the occasional albatross. They are able to keep up with the ship without seeming to make any effort, only moving their wings very occasionally, and otherwise gliding, sometimes very close to the surface of the water. They are beautiful birds, with a considerable wingspan, and I am not surprised that Coleridge reviled the Ancient Mariner for killing one.

Last evening I had a great surprise while I was walking round the deck to get some exercise. Do you remember that I told you that I met Toby Bellingham, another Old Etonian, when I was in Kimberley? He was the fellow who said that if I could raise one thousand guineas I could have a share in his diamond mine. It seems that on Toby's recommendation his father had made a very considerable investment in the mine, but it had proved unproductive, and had closed down, losing all their money.

Toby has been told to come home and face his father's anger; he is travelling in the cheapest type of cabin, as Toby put it, very close to the engine room. I bought him a drink in the first class bar, and felt sorry for him when he left me to descend to the depths of the ship. How fortunate that I did not lighten my purse in that direction.

At sea, 21st July 1902

Tomorrow we should reach our destination and leave the good ship Alnwick Castle. I have very much enjoyed the voyage, but I will be glad to get some good, solid earth beneath my feet. We will be put ashore at a fishing village called Takoradi, some way to the west of the capital, Accra. From there, we will travel up-country to Obuasi.

Yesterday afternoon I had a long talk with Mr Cade; he wants me to call him Edwin when there are just the two of us together, but I do not feel happy to show such familiarity with my employer, although I try to do so, so as not to offend him.

As the mine manager I will be responsible for all aspects of the operation when he is not there, which will be for most of the time. He has a foreman there, a chap called Williams; he is a Cornishman, and has experience working the tin miles there. I will have my own accommodation, a cook and another servant, all free of charge. And every other year I will have four weeks leave of absence. I am afraid that this will not enable me to get back home to see you all, for the voyage to England and back again, together with the time taken to get from the mine to the coast and back will take all of four weeks. I will pin my hopes on being in a position to leave the company after two years, but I have not so much as hinted this to Mr Cade.

You will understand, Pater, how much I am looking forward to this new chapter in my life, and how much I hope that I will make a success of it and that it will enable me to help you with the upkeep of Broadlands.

I will add a few lines to this letter when we sight the Gold Coast, and then give it to the purser to be posted when the ship arrives at Southampton.

Takoradi, 22nd July 1902

I was up early this morning, and when I went on deck I found that we were anchored off the town of Takoradi. There was a sandy beach with palm trees almost down to the water, for as far as I could see.

A number of small boats were milling around the ship; some were offering for sale their freshly-caught fish, and others, pineapples and other fruits, chickens and coconuts. The ship's chef was bargaining for some produce to add variety to the menu in the first class dining saloon.

We are to disembark within the hour, so I must end this letter now. I will write again as soon as we reach Obuasi; until then I send my love to you all.

Your respectful son,
Frobisher

Chapter Seven

Obuasi, 31st July 1902

Dear Pater,

I reached Obuasi yesterday with Mr Cade, and I have so much to tell you, but first I must tell you about our arrival in Takoradi and the journey up to the mine.

We were transferred to the little fishing port in a boat from the Alnwick Castle, and I must admit that as I looked back to the ship I wondered whether I was doing the right thing, but then I remembered you saying that whatever I do I must give it my best shot, and I resolved to put my Witwatersrand experience to good use in Obuasi.

The first night ashore we spent in a small hotel, or rest house, in Takoradi; it was not by any means luxurious, but it was good to have terra firma beneath me. The next morning we boarded a train, yes, a train, for the journey to Obuasi. The line was extended from Tarkwa to Obuasi earlier this year, and it will next be extended to Kumasi, the capital of the Ashanti region.

The train was a fairly basic affair, although those of us travelling in first class were at least enclosed in comfortable compartments, while the less fortunate passengers were crowded into open wagons. The train moved slowly, and seemed to stop for no good reason a great many times; sometimes it was because there was a tree across the line, in which case all the passengers got off and assisted in its removal.

Much of the journey was through dense rain forest; it was very hot and humid, and any number of insects found their way into our compartment. I had been warned about the mosquitoes that carry malaria, and you can tell Mama that I have a good supply of quinine.

Each time that the train stopped, often at a clearing in the forest, people would appear with fruit, eggs and other things to sell to the passengers. The pineapples and mangos did look very inviting, but I was not inclined to purchase the large rodents, evidently called Cutting Grass, which were held aloft by their tails and offered for sale. It seems that they are much prized for their meat, but I hope that there will be more familiar meals at our destination.

Our arrival at Obuasi was welcomed by a large crowd of men and women, most of the latter being clothed in bright, multi-coloured garments. As a major employer, Mr Cade is much liked and respected, and for a short time, I basked in his reflected glory. But I did not let this show, Pater, and I made sure that I was suitably deferential when he spoke to me.

Mr Williams, the mine supervisor, was there to greet us, and Mr Cade introduced me to him as the new mine manager. I got the distinct feeling that this was not good news to Mr Williams, but he shook my hand and said that I was welcome. We got into two lorries, Mr Cade in one and Mr Williams and I in another, and moved off through the crowd, who were now chanting songs of welcome.

Our accommodation, which consisted of a number of bungalows in a fenced compound, was not far from the station, and Williams, as he asked me to call him, showed me to my new home. There were three main rooms, a sitting room, which had a small table, a bedroom and a kitchen.

There was also a small room with a basin and a shower, and a rather primitive toilet. Outside the front of the building there was a large verandah, and I could imagine myself sitting there at the end of the day with a cold beer in my hand.

Lighting was by oil lamps. A small refrigerator, of a size to accommodate about five bottles of beer, was powered by kerosene. The furniture was basic and appeared well-used, and I wondered if perhaps Williams had been evicted from here to make room for me. His demeanour was certainly rather surly, but I gave him the benefit of the doubt and put that down to his Cornish background.

My household staff were lined up on the verandah to be introduced. The steward, responsible for cleaning, serving at the table and most other tasks was called Mensah; he told me that he came from the south of the country and seemed to be a pleasant chap; he assured me that he would look after me well. The cook, a small man from this area, introduced himself as Yeboah, and said that he was known to be an international cook. This sounded too good to be true, and I looked forward to the proof of that pudding being in the eating.

There was also a night-watchman, Musa, from the far north of the country; he was not fluent in English, but he assured me by miming deadly assault with his bow and arrow, that he would protect me from any intruders.

Williams left me to settle in and said that I should meet the other senior staff in the managers' lounge in an hour's time. Mensah served me a cold beer and unpacked my few belongings. I was much concerned as to where I should conceal my diamonds, for Mensah's duties clearly allowed him full access to all my possessions, and although he seemed a decent chap, I did not feel inclined to accord him my entire trust until I knew him better. After I took them from the bank vault in Johannesburg, I had kept them in a small pouch that I had had sewn into my belt, and it seemed wise to continue to keep them in this way. They are not very large, and do not change the appearance of the belt.

The managers' lounge was in another bungalow; there was a large room with a table and six chairs around it, and three smaller rooms, used as offices. On the doors of these were wooden plaques bearing the titles of the occupants. There was one for the chairman, one for the chief engineer, and one for the mine manager — my office.

Mr Cade and I, together with Mr Williams, the chief medical officer and the chief chemist took seats around the table, and I was introduced by Mr Cade. He said that I would meet the chief engineer later. His remarks about my experience in Witwatersrand were very complimentary, and he said that the company was lucky to have obtained my services. I said how glad I was to be here, and that I looked forward to working with my new colleagues.

We had a meal together of roast guinea fowl and fresh fruit, and then retired to our individual lodgings. Mensah had prepared my bedroom very tidily, and I was asleep within minutes of laying my head on my pillow.

All that happened yesterday, and I have written this letter early this morning before starting my duties. I will let you know all about them very soon but will close this now so that it can return to the coast on the train. You should address your letters to me c/o the Union Castle office in Takoradi; they will forward them to me here.

I do hope, Pater, that this will be the means by which I can return to you with a full purse before too long; meanwhile I remain,

Your respectful son,
Frobisher

Obuasi, 2ndAugust 1902

Dear Pater,

In my last letter, written just after my arrival here, I told you about my lodgings and the other managers. Since then, I have been fully instructed in my duties by Mr Cade, and have started to consider how the operation could be improved. Mr Cade says that that is the reason that he hired me, so you will believe that I am on my mettle.

For many years, large numbers of individuals, both indigenous and foreigners, have worked concessions to extract gold in this region. Some have had considerable success, but most have moved on after taking whatever pickings they found. The Ashanti Goldfields Corporation has acquired a large number of these concessions, and has installed the most modern equipment to extract gold from its ore.

The original workings were mostly fairly shallow pits, but mine shafts are now being sunk in increasing numbers, and the volume of rock brought to the surface each day is impressive.

Mr Williams, the mine superintendent, is responsible for the day to day organisation of the workers, the provision of food and water, transport and the general running of the mine. Mr Cade has made it clear that my responsibilities are to ensure that the pits and shafts are worked to the most profitable extent, and to suggest in which places further exploration should take place.

The chief engineer, Mr Cameron, is a Scot, and has spent some time at other gold mines in Africa, including, briefly, Witwatersrand, although at a different time from me. I get on very well with him, and he has given me a good understanding of the working of the machinery that moves, crushes and washes the ore. Huge crushing machines have been brought in and installed. The chemical leaching process, which extracts the gold from the ore, uses a cyanide solution. It is these two operations which require the services of the chief engineer and the chief chemist.

The chief chemist is a German, and he is not a very sociable fellow. His name is Dr Franz Werner, and he spends most of his time with a mask over his face, ensuring the safety of the leaching operation.

The chief medical officer is English, and his name is Dr Thomas. He is not much older than I am, and this is his first job, since completing his training at a leading London hospital. His hospital building here is rather less prestigious, but he is very conscientious, and works hard to treat the workers, all too many, who have accidents of greater or lesser severity. He also runs a clinic for the workers' families, and is never too busy to attend a difficult birth or a debilitating illness in their huts.

I have to say that Mr Williams is the least friendly of my new colleagues. I am sure that he resents my appointment, on which he probably had his eye, and when not in Mr Cade's presence he either ignores me or gives only the barest response to any question that I put to him. It is well that I have no responsibility for his work, for I am sure that he would conceal from me as much as he could, and only involve me if something went wrong.

Mr Cade is leaving for England next week, and has kindly said that he will take any letters that I have and post them on arrival at Southampton. I am making every effort to learn as much as I can while he is here, for I cannot rely upon Mr Williams for much help. He seems very keen that I should not know any details of his work, especially as regards the mine's transport. That is not in my remit, but as mine manager, I feel that I should know at least something of all aspects of the operation.

I must finish this now, Papa, for Yeboah has prepared my evening meal. I hope that you feel that I have done the right thing coming here, and I hope that some letters will be forwarded from Takoradi before very long.

I remain, your respectful son,

Frobisher

Chestnut Cottage, 3rd August 1902

Dearest Frobisher,

You have a niece. She is called Penelope, and she is such a lovely baby. Papa and Mama are thrilled to have a granddaughter, and Tony and I are very pleased to have a pigeon pair. I do so look forward to you being able to meet your new relations, although I understand that it will be some time before you can return to Broadlands.

Mary is such a help to me; I cannot understand how mothers can raise two young children on their own without help, although I know that most do; we are very lucky to have Mary.

Papa is very pleased that you have got this position in the Gold Coast. He reads and re-reads your letters, and when talking to their friends, he and Mama show how proud they are of you.

Mama is still not in very good health and I know that this worries Papa, but she is determined not to become an invalid, and comes over to see me and the children in the carriage at least once a week.

You will remember that Mary's son Rob...

Editor's Note. The remainder of this letter appears to have been damaged by rats or mice, and cannot be read.

Broadlands, 10th September 1902

Dear Frobisher,

I was very glad to get your letter of 2nd August, and to hear about your colleagues at the mine. They seem to be an assortment of nationalities, but I am sure that they are all competent in their various jobs. It is good that there is another Englishman there, and particularly that he is the doctor; I hope that you strike up a friendship with him.

It seems that Mr Cade is well-disposed towards you, and I hope that you justify the trust that he has placed in you; it is a responsible position that you hold, and you must remember that the well-being of your colleagues, and the workers at the mine, is to no small degree dependent upon the way in which you discharge your duties. You are still a young man, but your experience in South Africa should stand you in good stead, and I have no doubt that you will make a success of this enterprise.

There is not much for me to report from here; all is much as usual and we are getting ready for the first shoot on the estate. It is later than usual this year, but the poor weather during the recent summer has meant that the birds have not developed as well; but we have not lost many to foxes, so I think that we will put on a good show.

I am concerned about your Mama's health; she assures us that she is well, but I know that she is often in pain; the doctor says that there is no malignancy, and that there is no reason why she should not live for several more years. I am so glad that she saw Hermione married and become the mother of two fine children.

I look forward to hearing more about your life in Obuasi, and until then I am your loving Father

Obuasi, 30th September 1902

Dear Pater,

It is now two months since I arrived here, and I believe that I am now making a real contribution to the efficient running of the mine. But first I must thank you for the two letters that I got yesterday. One of them, written at the end of June and addressed to the hotel in Johannesburg, has somehow found its way here, and the other was forwarded from the Union Castle office in Takoradi. I also got a letter from Hermione.

I am so pleased that you approve of my decision to come here, and you may be sure that I am doing my best to justify Mr Cade's confidence in me. I was very glad to hear that Hermione had a girl; she must be three or four months old now, and I am sure that you and Mama are very pleased to have a pair of grandchildren. It is not good news that Mama's health is giving you cause for concern; do give her my best love, and tell her that I hope to be back home before very long.

The rainy period is coming to an end here, and that makes working the pits much easier since there is less water to pump out every day before digging can start. We are also sinking several mine shafts, and one of my jobs, in fact my first responsibility, is to decide in which direction to drive the horizontal tunnels from the vertical shaft. Sometimes this is made obvious by the nature of the rock; gold-bearing rock has a particular appearance, and veins of it can be either very short or very long. If we are lucky we find a long, rich vein and can follow it for several yards before it runs out.

I get on very well with all of the other managers, but I cannot say the same about Mr Williams. The other morning I was sitting on my verandah having my breakfast before going to work when I noticed a black girl of about twenty years leaving his bungalow. I thought that she was perhaps the sister of one of his servants, and when I mentioned it to him he said, with a wink, that she was a very good friend of his, and that if I wished, he was sure that she could become a good friend of mine. Of course, Pater, I assured him that I had no wish for such a friendship, and made that quite clear.

I sometimes go with George Thomas, our doctor, on short expeditions in the nearby forest. You may be sure that we never leave the tracks, but we do see a variety of animals and birds. There are any number of monkeys, and we have heard, but not seen, elephants; there are also some very unpleasant snakes, scorpions and giant centipedes, and George always carries a basic medical kit in case we get bitten or stung.

The mosquitoes are a permanent problem, and they are especially numerous now that the rains have provided them with breeding places; we all sleep under nets at night, but they seem to find their way through our defences; so far my quinine has protected me from the malaria.

Pater, I really am enjoying my time here, but I do increasingly look forward to returning to Broadlands; perhaps this will be possible this time next year.

I remain your respectful son,

Frobisher

Obuasi, 8th October 1902

Dearest Hermione,

I was so glad to get your letter telling me that you had a baby girl; many congratulations to you both. I imagine that she is now three or four months old. Penelope is a lovely name and I look forward to hearing all about my new niece.

Papa will have told you about my life here in the Gold Coast. Obuasi is not as nice a place as Witwatersrand, but I do enjoy the job very much, and I am proud of the responsibility that Mr Cade has placed in me. I have been able to make several changes to the way that the mining is done, and so far these have all resulted in a greater production of gold.

My colleagues here are a good lot, and I get on particularly well with George Thomas, the doctor, or chief medical officer, to give him his full title. We often go together into the forest and look at the birds and animals. George is not much older than me, and this is his first position since qualifying.

The only fly in the ointment is Mr Williams, the mine superintendent; he is a coarse fellow, who resents the fact that I have the position that he wanted. He does his job well enough, but there is something about him that makes me wonder whether he is not up to some mischief, and I keep a watchful eye on him without him knowing.

Your Arthur must be quite a big lad now, and I am sure that he enjoys playing with Mary's little boy; I am glad that she is looking after your children so well.

You would not believe it, but as I was writing that a large rat poked its head out of a hole in the wall and looked at me for a minute or so, before retreating into its home. There are a lot of them here; they come out of the forest because there is plenty of food to be had in the kitchens. There are also any number of cockroaches, a type of beetle, and when you go into a dark room at night you often crush them under your feet. We try to control these vermin, and our chief chemist, Dr Werner, is forever trying out new chemicals to poison them, without much success so far.

I hope that Mama's health has improved; and that Papa can be less worried about her, and I wish that I was not so far away, but I know that you will be a comfort to her, and she will be so pleased to have a granddaughter.

My lamp is getting dim, so it must need more oil, and I must finish this letter. I send all my love to you and your children, and my best wishes to Tony.

Your loving brother,

Frobisher

Obuasi, 19th April 1903

Dear Pater,

Please forgive me for not writing more often, but I have become very much involved in my work here. There are no full days off at the weekends, for the mine must be kept in production at all times, and in the evenings I am glad to have my meal and get into my bed. You must not think that the work is too much for me; it is just that having been given this responsibility by Mr Cade I must do everything that I can to justify his confidence in me.

You will see that I am doing that when I tell you what happened here recently. The gold that we produce is cast into ingots and stamped with a serial number and the mine's identification; it is then sent to London to be assayed and its purity confirmed, before it can be sold. Roughly once a month, the gold leaves here for the coast, to be carried to Southampton on the next ship.

The ingots are packed individually in wooden boxes, which are sealed with wax impressed with the company's seal. The boxes travel on the train to Takoradi under armed guard, and are signed for by the ship's purser, who checks that the seals are intact, and are then placed in the strongroom on the ship. The only weak link is the short journey through the forest from the mine to the station at Obuasi; this is in one of the company's trucks, but the guard is doubled for this and there have been no attempts to steal the gold.

Six weeks ago, when one of the six boxes in that consignment was opened in London, it was found to contain a piece of iron, and no gold. The wax seal was intact when the box was opened, but when examined afterwards it was found to have been impressed not with the company's seal, but with a coin of the same size. It seems that the purser saw an intact seal, but did not check that it was the same as the others.

You can imagine, Pater, that Mr Cade was much angered by this affair, and he has instructed me to investigate how this could have been done, taking priority over all my other duties.

I have interviewed the guards, the truck driver who took the gold to the station, and the guards on the train to Takoradi; they all assure me that the six boxes never left their sight for a moment, and I am disposed to believe them. If they had been involved, I am sure that by now they would have been far away with their shares of the theft. That being the case, the substitution must have taken place either on the ship or before the gold left the mine. The fact that a local coin was used for the false seal implies that the theft originated on the mine, for it is unlikely that anyone on board the ship would have had one.

There are only two keys to the strongroom on the mine; they are different, and both have to be used at the same time in order to open the door. I have one of them and Williams has the other. Mr Cade has copies of both, but they are kept in London. It followed, therefore, that the keys held on the mine must have been used.

When gold is put into the strongroom, or removed from it for transport to London, both Williams and I use our keys together; mine hangs from a ring on my belt, which I always wear in order to safeguard the diamonds.

Naturally, I asked Williams if he could explain the replacement of the gold by a piece of iron, and he said that he was as at a loss as to how it could have been done. I must admit that I feared that I could not solve the mystery, and as a last resort asked Mensah if he had at any time handled my key. He said that the only time was when Mr Williams had asked him to get it so that he could check that it had not been copied. I asked him how that could be, since I always wear my belt, and he said that it had been while I was in the shower, and since Mr Williams had said that it would only take a minute to check, he had not wanted to disturb me.

You will believe, Pater, that I lost no time in summoning the mine head of security, Sergeant Wilson, formerly of the Metropolitan Police in London, and together we went to Williams' bungalow and confronted him. He swore that he had never had my key, and that Mensah was lying, but a search of his clothes chest revealed a short stick of red sealing wax that had been partially used, a crude but effective copy of my key, and a coin, that when examined by Dr Werner, showed traces of sealing wax; all were concealed in a pair of socks.

He was forthwith dragged to the mine gaol by a pair of Sgt. Wilson's men, and I told him that he would remain there until Mr Cade's next visit, when he would be tried under local law. This could invoke the death sentence. Since it was due to be another two or three months before Mr

Cade came to the mine, and conditions in the gaol were not such as to make it likely that a prisoner would remain in spirits or good health, or indeed survive for more than a week or two. It was not long before Williams asked that if he could help us recover the gold he could be kept secured in better conditions.

This I agreed to, and the missing gold ingot was retrieved from beneath a floorboard in his bungalow. An effort had been made to obliterate the company's mark, but nothing had been cut off it, so I was glad to know that Mensah had not been a party to the theft.

I lost no time in reporting to Mr Cade that the gold had been recovered, and asked what he wanted me to do with Williams. His reply, which naturally took some time to reach me, was that he should be returned to England in irons to stand trial. I was not entirely sure what was involved in such restraint, but there were several sets of old slave leg irons on the mine, and they seemed to fit the bill. Williams and his guards leave here on the train tomorrow and he will be on the same boat as this letter.

I have to admit that it was to some extent by chance that my enquiry to Mensah led to the theft being solved, but Mr Cade says that I have more than justified his faith in me, and that my salary is to be generously increased. My colleagues hold me in greater respect, and the workmen evidently think that I have what they call a powerful juju when it comes to finding a guilty party.

I must close this now and go and have a last word with Williams; he has been no trouble since his arrest, and I have told him that since he had not disposed of the gold I will send a letter to the telling of his cooperation, and that this might reduce his sentence. For this he is grateful.

I now look forward to getting on with my job, and I hope to continue to serve Mr Cade well.

Your respectful son,
Frobisher

Broadlands, 2nd June 1903

My dear boy,

It is with a heavy heart that I have to tell you that your mother passed away yesterday. Her end was peaceful, and although she had lately shown some signs of a partial recovery, I have to feel some relief that the suffering that she bore so bravely has come to an end. The funeral will be held next week.

Quentin's regiment is now back in England, and he has been given leave in order to attend the funeral, and the estate workers have all asked whether they may attend, so I am sure that there will be a good turnout.

Your letter of 19th April arrived before she died, and she was so glad to know that you were making your mark so well in your new position. I congratulate you on bringing Williams to justice. I expect that the trial will be mentioned in the papers here, and if so, I will keep a cutting for you.

You will understand that I have much to do, so I will end this letter now. I will be very glad of Quentin's help over the coming days, and I hope that he will not have to return to his regiment too soon after the funeral.

Hermione is very much distressed by her mother's death, and has asked that I enclose a note from her before I seal it.

Your loving Father

Chestnut Cottage, 2nd June 1903

My dearest Frobisher,

I am so distressed by Mama's death that I hardly know what to write to you. She has been such a regular visitor to our home since I had Arthur, and she was delighted when I had a girl and that we called her Penelope, after her own mother.

The funeral will be a sad affair, of course, but I think that there will be many there who knew and loved our mother, and Papa will take some comfort from that. I am very glad that Quentin will be able to assist Papa with the arrangements, and I hope that his stay can be long enough to be of help in settling Mama's affairs.

Mary is being a great help to me at this difficult time; she is almost one of the family now, and Arthur adores her. I think that I told you that she had taken steps to improve herself, as she puts it, when she was carrying Rob, and she is now not only pretty but also very socially adept. There has been no sign of Fisher, Rob's father, and I have not raised the subject with her; she seems very happy to live with us and to have my two little ones and her own boy to look after.

Papa has told me of your success in finding the thief who stole the gold from the mine; what a clever brother I have, and how lucky Mr Cade is to have you working for him. I know that you enjoy your work there, but I cannot help hoping that you will come home before too long.

I must end this now, and take it to Papa to enclose with his letter to you. Think of me, my dearest brother, and do not grieve for too long over poor Mama's death; I know that she would not want that.

Your loving sister,

Hermione

Obuasi, 11th July 1903

Dear Pater,

I was so sorry to get your last letter and learn that Mama had passed away, and I wish that I could have been there to support you at her funeral. I am sure that Quentin has been a great help to you, and I hope that he has been able to stay on at Broadlands for a few weeks.

I know that Mama's health has not been good for the last year or two, and that she suffered from lack of breath, but I did not realise that it was likely to shorten her life, and I know how much you and Hermione will miss her. For my part, when I return to Broadlands it will not be with as much pleasure as I have anticipated, and the house will seem empty without her.

I continue to enjoy my life here; I spend quite a lot of my time assessing where it may be profitable to dig a new pit or sink a new shaft. The latter especially is a costly business, and if not successful can reduce the profitability of the mine quite considerably, so you will understand that I do not lightly commit to such work.

I will, of course, write again before very long, but meanwhile I feel for your loss and send all my condolences.

Your respectful son,

Frobisher

P. S.

Please give the enclosed letter to Hermione when you next see her

Obuasi, 11th July 1903

My dearest Hermione,

You will know how sorry I was to learn of Mama's death, and I know how sad you will be not to have her living nearby and visiting you and the children so often. She must have been suffering more than I realised, but she was never one to let her problems affect anyone else.

Do be brave in your loss; I am sure that Mama would not want any of us to grieve for too long.

I am so glad that Mary is being so supportive; it must be a blessing for you to be able to leave your children in her care while you attend to other matters and take care of Tony. I hope that he is doing well in his father's firm, and that he enjoys his work as much as I enjoy mine.

I must end this now and enclose it with my letter to Papa. I know that it will be a comfort for him to have you living close to Broadlands, and he will so look forward to your visits to him with his grandchildren.

Your loving brother,

Frobisher

Chapter Eight

Obuasi, 20th November 1903

Dear Pater,

I hope that you are well and that you are not missing Mama too much. I suppose that Quentin has had to return to his regiment some time ago, but now that it is based in England he should be able to get to Broadlands quite often.

I have some very good news. Two weeks ago I was in one of the old mines, checking that it was not flooding as that could be a threat to other nearby workings that are still in use. At the end of one of the tunnels, where the gold-bearing vein had run out, there was a recent fall of rock from the roof, and by the dim light of my lamp I saw a glitter. I thought that it was probably what they call Fools' Gold, an iron ore, but I put a bit in my pocket and when I returned to the surface I gave it to Franz Werner.

It took Franz a week to complete his analysis, but you will never believe what he found. It is not Fools' Gold, but the real thing and, this is the interesting part, it has a gold content almost twenty-five percent higher than that in the rest of our workings. That may not sound much, but it will have a huge effect on the profitability of the mine if there is a sizeable vein of ore of that quality.

This week, work has re-started in what has become known as 'Frobisher's Find', and the indications are that it is a thick vein which runs in the direction which would put it close to one of our other shafts. If that is the case, and if the vein continues at its present quality, we should be able to tunnel into it from the other shaft, and thus double the amount of ore extracted by working at it from both ends.

I am sorry if I am using mining terms with which you are not familiar, but you will understand, Pater, that I have had to learn everything about the business, far more than I had to know when I was working at Witwatersrand.

We have, of course, advised Mr Cade of this development; he is due to be here on one of his visits at the end of the year, and I hope that by then we will have extracted a good deal of gold from this vein. I am now examining all of the other disused workings, but I cannot hope to strike lucky a second time.

Please give my love to Hermione, and next time that you write to Quentin, or that he visits you at Broadlands, tell him that his baby brother is not only alive and well, but making a name for himself in the Gold Coast.

Your respectful son,

Frobisher

Broadlands, 15th December 1903

Dear Frobisher,

What very good news you told me in your last letter. You put the find down to good luck, but it was because you were carrying out your duties responsibly in the dangerous tunnel off the old shaft that you came upon the recent rock-fall. Well done my boy; I hope that Mr Cade is suitably impressed.

Since you moved to the Gold Coast I find that your letters are taking rather less time to reach me. I suppose that you time them to catch a sailing from Takoradi, and the sea voyage is obviously shorter than that from Cape Town. It makes me feel that you are nearer to us than before, and for that I am glad.

I have settled down into a routine since your mother passed away, and apart from my usual visits to various parts of the estate I try to call on Hermione at least two or three times every week. She is a good mother, and I very much like seeing my grandchildren. Arthur is now more than four years old, and is becoming a proper little man. Penelope is a dear, and I am trying to teach her to say 'Grandpa', but so far she cannot manage that.

Hermione says that she could not run the house, be a dutiful wife to Tony, and look after her children if it was not for Mary, who has almost become a housekeeper/companion rather than a nanny; what a change from her days as Cook's assistant.

I have to go and visit old Jackson, who I fear is not too well; I think that he caught a bad chill one day when the shoot took place in very heavy rain. The birds would not fly, and he spent a lot of time trying to get them out of the new fir plantation.

Keep up the good work, my boy,

Your proud Father

Obuasi, 5th January 1904

Dear Pater,

I hope that you are well, and that the cold weather that I imagine you now have is not proving too troublesome. As you can imagine, we have rather different temperatures here; not as hot as in South Africa, but the humidity is very high, and that is very tiresome.

I have so much to tell you that I hardly know where to start.

Mr Cade's visit coincided with the usual New Year celebrations, and this year we had much to celebrate. A week before Mr Cade's arrival, I had another bit of luck. I had for some time, been studying a map of the shafts and pits here, and it seemed to me that it was possible that what I had found was not an extension of the previously worked seam, but that we had hit a new one. If that was the case, then it should be possible to access it by means of a new pit or shaft some distance from the place where I first found it.

There were several places which I considered, but we could not try all of them, and I had to choose one for a new shaft. Well, three days after excavation started we came across a seam, whether the one that I had thought of or another. This is a very broad seam, not very far from the surface, and Franz Werner says that the gold content is as high or higher than that in the one that they now call 'Frobisher's Find'. What luck that was!

You can imagine how pleased Mr Cade was, and he said that he remembered that when we were in Witwatersrand together, the chap that had bought my claim there had said that I have a nose for gold, and to cut a long story short he wants me to use that skill, as he calls it, on a wider scale than just at Obuasi. He has offered me a position on the Board of Directors of the Corporation, based in London, responsible for improving the production of all their existing mines and suggesting where new investments should be made.

You can imagine, Pater, how proud I am to have had this recognition of my efforts, and how glad I am to have this opportunity to return to England, and I have accepted his offer. I will stay on here until a new mine manager is appointed and gets his feet under the table, but I should be back with you by the middle of the year or soon after.

I have suggested to Mr Cade that I be replaced here by Ted Harris, the chap who bought my claim at Witwatersrand. I expect that it is about worked out by now, and he would probably be glad of the security of employment here, rather than the risk of starting on a new claim. It will be some time before he can be contacted, and then he has to get here, but I am hopeful that he will accept Mr Cade's offer and I look forward to getting him started. He knows just as much or more about the job as I do, and I hope that he will have the same good luck.

Mr Cade is taking this letter with him back to England in a couple of days, and I hope that you will be as pleased as I am with this turn of events. I can now say that I look forward to seeing you again before very long, and I remain,

Your respectful son,
Frobisher

Broadlands, 23rd February 1904

Dear Frobisher,

I was so glad to get the good news in your last letter. To be a director of a major mining company before your thirtieth birthday is a considerable achievement, and the fact that it brings you back to England is a source of great satisfaction to me. I am only sorry that your mother is not here to share in your success; she was so proud of your advancement in both South and West Africa.

Hermione is of course delighted that you will soon be able to meet your nephew and niece, and also to get to know Tony. I must say that he has turned out to be a very good husband and father, and any rancour that may have existed between our families is now a thing of the past.

I hope that your replacement at Obuasi will soon be in place, and we all look forward to hearing when you will be home.

Your loving and proud
Father

Chestnut Cottage, 23rd February 1904

Dearest Frobisher,

What a clever brother I have! We were all thrilled to get your letter about 'Frobisher's Find'. Papa is so proud of your success that he is telling all our friends of your discovery and promotion. How lucky you were that Mr Cade visited the mine when he did, and that he thinks so much of you.

Tony and I are so glad that you will soon be back here, and able to meet our children; I have tried to explain to them who you are, but they are a bit young to understand.

Mary also is very much looking forward to your return, and to showing Rob to you. She is such a good soul, and looks after our children as if they were her own.

Do let us know as soon as you know the date of your departure from the mine, and we will start to get the red carpet out and make arrangements for a big party.

All my love from your loving sister,

Hermione

Obuasi, 18th April 1904

Dearest Hermione,

I was so glad to get your letter, enclosed with one from Papa. I am really excited to be returning to England, and to have such a good position in the company. When I get a place in London, you must come and see me often.

And when you come you must bring Arthur and Penelope with you; I am so looking forward to getting to know them. We will all go out to tea at a smart place and have lots of fun.

I hope that Quentin will be able to get leave from his regiment when I am back; it is four years since we met in Kimberley and I am ashamed to say that we have not corresponded. He must soon be due to be promoted to Major; I wonder whether he will stay in the army until he retires. If he does he will be following in Great Uncle Arthur's footsteps.

It sounds as though Mary has really made something of her life, and it will be nice to see her again. Rob must be a fine lad now.

Ted Harris, the chap who is replacing me as mine manager here, is due to arrive at Takoradi on the next ship, and I shall be very busy teaching him the ropes. Hopefully, I will be able to leave here in June, and I will let you and Papa know when I have a firm date.

Until then, I close with much love from your excited brother,

Frobisher

Obuasi, 12th May 1904

Dear Pater,

I hope that you are well, I am sure that you are finding plenty to do keeping the estate up to scratch, but you must not do too much and tire yourself.

I know that you must miss Mama terribly, although it is nearly a year since she died. I wish that I could have been with you and able to lend a hand during the past twelve months, but at least it will not be long now before I am back in England.

Ted Harris, the chap who is replacing me here as mine manager, arrived last week, and he is already getting his legs under the table. He will do a splendid job for Mr Cade, and he is very grateful to me for recommending him.

You may remember that he bought my first claim at Kimberley from me; well, he gave me a good price and he got a good deal. He extended the workings and dug several more pits, and found more gold there than I did. He puts his success there down to my ability to smell gold beneath the surface, and he told that to Mr Cade when they met on our way back to Cape Town, so I have much to thank him for as well.

When his claim was worked out he bought a share in another, and that too, turned out to be very profitable, but he wanted to be more involved in mining than owning shares in the business, so he was very glad to get this opportunity.

I seem to have written nothing except about Ted Harris, but I also have good news. Unless there is anything here to delay my departure I will leave Obuasi in a month's time, and I should be back with you early in July. You would not believe, Pater, how much I am looking forward to seeing you and Hermione, and Tony of course, and to meeting my nephew and niece.

When I next write it will be my last letter; until then I remain

Your respectful son,

Frobisher

Obuasi, 1st June 1904

Dear Pater,

This will be my last letter to you; I hope that it will catch the ship due to sail in a couple of days.

My departure from Obuasi is now fixed for 20th June and I sail from Takoradi on the Arundel Castle four days later. The ship is due to dock at Southampton on 7th July.

Ted Harris is now running the mine and has already had several good ideas as to how it might operate still more efficiently. He gets on very well with the others, and has made a very good choice of a new mine superintendent; I left the job of choosing a replacement for Williams up to him, so that he would be confident in his ability to work with him.

I have packed up my few possessions; they are mostly reminders of my time here and in South Africa, but do not worry that I will be bringing human heads or stuffed snakes.

As you can imagine, my departure calls for several parties, and my colleagues have very kindly presented me with a little copy of a local wooden stool. The Asantehene, the paramount chief of the Ashanti region, is said to sit on such a stool made of gold; needless to say mine is not large enough to sit on, but it is made of gold that we mined here, and it will be a very happy reminder of my time in Obuasi.

My servants, Mensah, Yeboah and Musa have all expressed their sorrow at my departure, but I have assured them that Mr Harris will be just as good a master. I was very touched when they gave me a little ivory elephant, made from a local animal that was found dead in the forest not far from the mine.

Please pass on my good news to Hermione; I am sure that she will be as excited as I am.

Your respectful son,
Frobisher

Chapter Nine

Hermione's Diary: One

(Found with Frobisher's Letters Ed.)

6th July 1904

Only a day to go. I wonder what F looks like now; after so long in Africa he must be as brown as a berry, and he is ten years older; I hope that I recognise him.

8th July 1904

He's back. F arrived home at midday, and what a reception he got when he reached Broadlands. Not only were Papa, Tony and me and our children there to greet him, but the estate workers and their families turned out and cheered. Mary and Rob, Cook and Betsy, our one remaining maid, were there too, and F was quite overcome to see how glad everyone was to see him home again.

I was really pleased that F got on so well with T; they have only met briefly before, and I had hoped that the past differences between our families would not cause any difficulty.

Papa had brought a couple of his best bottles of champagne up from the cellar, and Cook had made some tasty hors d'oeuvres. F met Arthur and Penelope, and Mary introduced him to Rob. There was so much to talk about that we could have been there all night. Papa said that F's letters had been a great source of comfort to him and Mama, and that he had kept all of them. F said that the letters that he got from Papa and me had made it seem that he was not so far from home, and had encouraged him when he had a setback, and that he too had all the ones that we had sent to him. I, of course, have kept every one of those that F sent to me. It seems likely that some have gone astray on their way to or from SA, and that would explain the periods when none of us got any.

It was really exciting when F showed us his diamonds. I had thought that they would be real sparklers, but of course they do not look like that until they have been cut and polished. When they are mined, they look rather like lumps of thick ice that have been broken up and coated with mud. One of them is bigger than the other, and F is going to have them valued when he goes to London.

F was quite tired after his journey, so it was agreed that we would all lunch at Broadlands tomorrow, and bring all our letters, which Papa said should go in the family archive to record an important period in our lives. Q is due to arrive tomorrow and will be staying for a few days, so the whole family, including our children, will be together for the first time ever.

I am so happy that I don't think that I will sleep tonight. F looks so well; brown and slimmer than when he left more than ten years ago. He has had such an interesting time, and his hard work has earned him a good position with the company in London. I hope that he soon meets a nice girl, for he would be a good father.

5th August 1904

F returned from London yesterday. It was the first time that he had met the other directors of the AGC, and he said that they had all congratulated him on his success at Obuasi. Their offices are in a good part of the City, and he has a nice secretary of his own. I hope that she is not too nice, for I am sure that he can do better for himself.

While he worked for Mr Cade at Obuasi the greater part of his salary was paid into a London bank account, for there was very little on which to spend money locally. F went to the bank, a branch of Lloyds, and found to his surprise that his salary and bonus amounted to a much greater sum than he had thought; he says that even with a London address he will be able to help Papa with the expenses of Broadlands.

He has found a small mews house and will be able to move into it in about a month's time. He will have to furnish it, and he has asked me if I would help him to choose the furniture and all the other things that he will need. I will be thrilled to do so; I love London, and it will be a good excuse to visit there, and perhaps stay for a night or two when he has got some beds.

F took his diamonds to a jeweller in Hatton Garden. It seems that they are of a good quality, and he will be given a valuation when they have been examined for clarity and their weight as cut gems can be estimated. In any event it sounds as though he made a good purchase.

Tomorrow F is coming to stay with T and I for a few days; it will be nice for him having some time getting to know A and P, and also to see Mary in rather different circumstances to those when he left England. She is now very much one of the family, and a great favourite with T, who says that she is much too pretty to be a nanny. Papa seems to have put behind him that she was once a servant, and he always has a kind word for her and a bon bon for Rob.

12th August 1904

Great news. F heard from the jewellers in Hatton Garden. They are really high-class stones, and though not very big, can be cut into some very fine gems. The larger one is particularly clear and free from something called inclusions, and would evidently make a splendid pendant when cut into a pear shape. Clever old F; he will decide what to do and then go and see the jeweller again. He did not buy them from Rhodes' syndicate, but from a private dealer who probably got them from someone who smuggled them out of the mine.

F is much enjoying his stay with us, but he goes to Broadlands every day to talk to Papa. I fear that Papa is not too well; he was so thrilled when F returned, and went to such lengths to make him welcome that he rather overdid it. He says that there is no need to bother a doctor, and that now that F will be down from London at weekends, the estate duties can be shared.

I think that the real problem is probably that he has missed the Glorious Twelfth for the first time in many years, and that he sees it as evidence of approaching old age.

15th August 1904

F went to London yesterday and saw the jeweller in Hatton Garden. He agreed a price for both stones, and although he has not told me how much, it is evidently very much more than he paid for them. I wonder what he will do with his riches.

20th September 1904

We all had tea at Broadlands, including Q, who always comes home when he has leave from his regiment. F said that he had a surprise for us, left the room, and came back with a large package, which he asked Papa to open. It was the Gainsborough. F said that the sale of the smaller diamond had realised more than enough to buy it back. It looks so good hanging in the sitting room, in the same place that it occupied for so many years. He then told us that he had also sold the larger stone; the money was put into an account that gives a good return, and the interest would be paid monthly into the Estate account. Papa was so overcome that he could not speak; he just embraced F for several minutes.

15th December 1904

T's father is going to retire next year, probably in April. He and Caroline will move into the cottage that we are in, and we will move into the Hall. This makes sense regarding the numbers; we are now six, including Mary and Rob, and they are just two, but I am not sure that I want to leave here, where we have all been so happy.

When Roger retires, T will become the Senior Partner; it is only a small firm, but it has been established for many years and it handles a good deal of business for people who live in the area. It will mean that T has to spend more time in the office, and he is not keen on that. I do not think that he is really happy being a solicitor, but he felt bound to go into the family firm, and he has always done a good job for their clients.

Chapter Ten

Hermione's Diary: Two

2nd March 1905

F has gone down to Cornwall to see whether there is any prospect of profitably recovering the small amounts of gold that have been found in some of the tin and copper mines there. He will be away for about a week.

When he is down at Broadlands at the weekends, he has made a habit of always coming over to our cottage for tea on Sunday afternoon. In this way he has got to know A and P and Rob well, and they look forward to his visits.

Last week I found him and Mary laughing together, and when I asked what the joke was, they showed me the note that she wrote to him before he left for Cape Town. F has kept it with all the letters that he got from Papa and me, and I told him that it should be put with them in the archive that Papa has put together.

Today Mary came to see me and said that she wanted my advice over a personal matter.

It seems that she was smitten by F's good looks from the first day that she came into service at Broadlands, and although she realised that nothing could ever come of it, she had never let her dream fade. Rob's father is not the Mr Fisher that she has always maintained, but she did not say who was.

The retired English teacher from whom she took lessons during her pregnancy was very keen on crossword puzzles, and used them as a means of increasing her vocabulary. This also introduced her to anagrams, so when Rob was born she decided that as a permanent reminder of the love that could never be she would invent Mr Fisher and create an anagram using his name; Rob Fisher; Frobisher. What a clever girl.

I asked her whether F was still the love of her life, and she said that after ten years apart she loved him more than ever. When I asked whether he felt the same, she said that she was not sure, but that he did seem to enjoy being with her. She was very anxious that Papa should not know of her feelings for F, and I too felt sure that he would disapprove of his son being romantically involved with a one-time servant, although he was always very pleasant to her and likes it when I take the two of them to Broadlands.

Of course, when we move to Broadlands in the next few months, it will be difficult for Mary not to show her feelings for F when he is down there for weekends. She asked me if I thought that she should resign her job as nanny to my children and leave the area, but I said certainly not; she should wait and see how things worked out.

Poor Mary; what a problem her feelings have caused for her.

12th March 1905

F returned from Cornwall yesterday. He says that there is indeed gold to be found there, but the quantity is not sufficient to make an operation by AGC profitable.

When we were alone, I told him that I had spoken with Mary, and asked him what his feelings were for her. Also, I told him about the non-existent Mr Fisher, and why she called her son Rob. He said that that was very nice to know, and that he had always thought her very pretty, but because she was in service with the family it would not have been proper to show any feelings for her; that was not something that Papa would approve of.

He then said that she had changed so much, for the better, while he was away that he felt that he could talk to her as an equal, and that he very much enjoyed her company, but still felt that Papa would not be pleased if things progressed from there.

I told him that Papa now looked upon her as almost one of the family, and that Rob got the same attention and affection from him as Arthur and Penelope. F was very pleased to hear that, and said how glad he was to be able to talk to me about it. I think that he now feels less constrained, and we will see what happens next.

30th April 1905.

We are back in Broadlands. Papa has arranged that T and I and our children have three bedrooms, and our own sitting room. This gives us our privacy when we want it, but we are always only a few steps away from Papa and we see him for much of the time. Mary is now the children's governess, rather than their nanny, and she and Rob have moved into old Jackson's house, which has been empty since he died; it is only a stone's throw away, and they spend much of their time at Broadlands as Rob takes his lessons with A and P.

T has been asked by Papa to manage the estate, and has already put forward some ideas as to how the costs could be reduced and the income increased. His father gave him a part of the proceeds of the sale of their property, and he believes that when the Broadlands farm is once more productive we will be comfortably off. He is still involved part-time with the solicitor's practice, where he remains a partner, and this gives him an income.

16th July 1905

Q has been promoted to Major and posted to the War Office in London. He cannot tell us what he does, terribly secret, but it means that he will not have to go overseas with his regiment, and he can still get down to Broadlands most weekends.

10th November 1905

Arthur's fifth birthday. We had a lovely tea party; Papa gave him a rocking horse, he loves it, and we can hardly get him to dismount. F gave him a clockwork train set, and Q left two nice books for him when he was last here. Mary, always practical, gave him a very smart coat, which he insists on wearing most of the time. The birthday cake had five candles on it, which he managed to blow out with a single breath, and he told us that his secret wish was that he could be six very soon.

2nd June 1906

F is engaged to Mary, can you believe it? He told me last week that he had told Papa that he wanted to marry her, and had expected to meet with his disapproval. But surprisingly, Papa said that he was delighted, and wished them both every happiness.

This, of course, was an excuse for another of Papa's champagne parties. Mary is so happy, and you can tell just by looking at her that her ten-year wait for Frobisher was worthwhile. F seems almost to be in a trance, and I suspect that Mary may have given up waiting and proposed to him; but there is no doubt that they love each other very much, and I am so glad for both of them.

They plan to get married in November. I hope that Papa may be feeling better by then; some days he is very depressed and sits all day by the fire; the doctor says that there is nothing clinically wrong with him, and that he is still grieving for Mama. But he does enjoy having the three young around him, and T has taken over most of the estate duties.

F is doing very well with AGC, and this cheers Papa, and the wedding may be just the thing to give him a new lease of life.

15th November 1906

F and M were married yesterday, in the same church as Papa and Mama and T and I were married. I was M's Maid of Honour, and the three children were her attendants. She wore a really beautiful dress, made by Betsy's sister. The reception afterwards was here at Broadlands, and all the guests said how lovely she looked, and that it was hard to believe that she used to be Cook's assistant.

Papa and F looked very smart in their morning dress, and Q, who was best man, was in his full dress uniform. Papa is not very well, but on occasions like this he seems to be almost like his old self, and he says that we should not worry about him.

F and M are honeymooning in Paris, and catch the boat-train today. M was nervous about going abroad, and said she feared she might not like the food, but F said that she may have the opportunity to travel overseas with him when he goes on AGC business, so she should get used to it.

10th March 1907

Q is engaged to be married. His fiancée is the sister of one of the officers who work with him in the War Office. She is called Pamela (I will have to mind my Ps and Qs) and is the same age as me. They came down yesterday and had lunch; Papa was quite taken with her, and thought that he knew one of her uncles. Next weekend they are going to see her parents; Q said that he hoped that they would approve of him, and Pamela said that everyone would approve of him. She is a very homely person, well suited to Q, and I am sure that she will be a good wife for him. They have not yet fixed a date for their wedding but are talking of the end of the summer.

18th July 1907

F and Q came down from London a couple of days ago, and we all had dinner together this evening. I thought that Papa looked as well as he has done recently, but he said that he felt very tired.

After dinner, he said that he had something to tell us. He called Q, F, Rob and me to the side of his chair, put his hands on our heads, and said with a breaking voice, “I am so glad and proud to have four such fine children.” He then kissed each of us goodnight and retired to his room.

I cannot write any more tonight, but I am very happy, especially for F and M, and I am sure that tomorrow will be a wonderful day as we all digest Papa’s announcement.

19th July 1907

Papa died in his sleep last night. He has not been well for more than a year, and I don’t think that he ever really got over Mama’s death, but he always seemed to rally just when we were getting really worried. The doctor says that his heart gave out, and that we should not think that he suffered.

T is being wonderful, and has started making all the necessary arrangements regarding the estate. Mary is very tearful, but has been so good at putting on a brave face and consoling the children, telling them that Papa has gone for a long rest but will be thinking of them.

I cannot imagine Broadlands without Papa. Through good times and bad, he has held the place together, and he and Mama made sure that their children never lacked for anything that they really needed; they loved us completely, and we loved them no less.

In the silence that followed Papa’s final remark, I saw F wink at M, who blushed and looked down; then she told us that Papa was indeed Rob’s father; that there was no Mr Fisher; and that it was Papa who had paid for her to be educated. I think that she must have told all this to F when they got engaged.

T obviously also knew about this, having drawn up Papa’s last will, but of course he could not tell Q or me since it was a matter of professional confidentiality. He took us aside and confirmed that what Papa said was indeed the case, and then Q went and hugged M and said that she was truly one of the family.

I took A and P over to M’s cottage, and told her how glad I was to know the truth, and that Rob could not have had a better father.

T said to M that if she would like Rob’s surname changed to Broad, it was a simple matter, and he would be happy to help her with it.

The evening had ended with a very happy family, conscious of its good fortune in the past and confident in its future. But our happiness was short-lived, and each of us is dealing with Papa’s death in our own way; but we are a strong family, and when the grieving is over Broadlands will once again be the happy place that it has been for so many years.

Chapter Eleven

The Ryneker Letters

These three letters were found in an old diary kept by Hermione while Frobisher was in Africa. Ed.

2nd February 1897

Got a letter from F, which I will certainly keep with the others, but as he has requested I will not show it to Papa.

Cape Town, 20th December 1896

Dearest Hermione,

I hope that you are well and that your romance with Anthony Fellowes is still going strong. You will not believe it, but your brother has also found someone who is something special. I will tell you all about her, but you must promise not to mention it to Papa or Mama. If they ask, tell them that this letter is just about my work at the Ships' Chandlers.

I met her at a party. Her name is Ryneker; she is the daughter of a Dutch couple, Ocke and Helena Mulder, who own a business importing all manner of goods for the Dutch community here. She is two years younger than me, and has the most beautiful golden hair. I cannot believe that she is interested in me, for she could have her pick of the young men in Cape Town, but since we met she has seen no one else.

I cannot begin to tell you what she looks like, but after you she is the prettiest girl in the world, and although I do not have any previous experience, I think that I must be falling in love. At Eton, we only mixed with girls at the annual sixth form dance, and they were mostly spotty and giggled when you spoke to them. The girls who came to dinner or dances at Broadlands always came with their boyfriends, and so I really am a beginner when it comes to girls.

Ryneker is much more experienced, as you would expect from anyone so beautiful, but I am sure that she has always behaved entirely properly with her admirers.

Her parents seem to think that I am a suitable escort for their daughter, and they do not keep her on as tight a rein as would be the case in England for a beautiful heiress. I use that word because her parents are very rich and she has no brothers or sisters.

At the weekends, when I am not working, we go for long walks, holding hands, and we tell each other about our lives. Mine is very dull compared with hers, for before coming to Cape Town she has lived in Holland and the Dutch East Indies. I have several times been invited to their house, which is a very grand place, and after the meal we are allowed to go to the library by ourselves.

Dearest sister, do not laugh at my stumbling progress into the world of romance. I will, of course, let you know if Ryneker should tell me that she shares my feelings, although I cannot believe that this would be possible. Meanwhile I repeat my plea that you say nothing of this to our parents.

Your lovestruck brother,

Frobisher

10th June 1897

Another letter from F; I am so glad that he is happy, like me.

Cape Town, 2nd May 1897

Dearest Hermione,

I hope that you are well, and that you are as happy with Tony as I am with Ryneker. She really is the most wonderful girl, and though you will not believe it, she says that she thinks that I am the nicest man that she has ever met.

We spend every moment together when I am not working, and I can tell you that we have got further than holding hands.

I think that her parents must consider me as a potential son-in-law, for last month her father suggested that we should get away from Cape Town together for a few days and get to know each other better. Can you imagine Papa saying that you and Tony should do such a thing? It seems that the Dutch are much less straight-laced than the English in that regard.

I do not know for certain that I want to marry her, but she does rouse feelings in me that I have not felt before, and I would be wretched if I could not see her.

I hope that you will not think ill of me, but Ryneker and I went to Port Elizabeth for three days at the end of last month and stayed in adjacent rooms in a very nice hotel. A gentleman never reveals any details of his amorous adventures, but you may be sure that your brother is now truly a man.

A few days after our return to Cape Town, Ryneker's father suggested that there might be a position in his firm that I might find more fulfilling than mine in the Ships' Chandlers. He went into no details, but he asked me to think whether I could imagine myself working in a foreign company and possibly living in a foreign country.

That is something that I have never considered, but if it meant that I spent the rest of my life with Ryneker then it is certainly something that I must think about. What do you think?

Once again, I must implore you to say nothing to Papa or Mama; Papa might be understanding but I know that Mana would be horrified.

Your loving and grown up brother,

Frobisher

18th July 1897

Poor F; I was so sorry to get his latest letter. I hope that he soon gets over his loss and finds another girl to care about.

Cape Town, 4th June 1897

Dearest Hermione,

I have the worst possible news; Ryneker and her family are leaving South Africa and returning to Amsterdam, never to return here.

I did not take the job that her father eventually offered to me, for I thought it better to show that I could make my way on my own, without being dependent upon his kindness. He quite understood, and said that it increased his respect for me.

Ryneker and I have had a most wonderful year since our trip to Port Elizabeth; I was intending to propose marriage to her very shortly, and I have every reason to believe that she would have accepted my proposal. I told her that before doing so, I must tell my parents of our friendship and plans for the future, and she agreed that I should.

And then, last week, she told me that her father had sold his business, and that the family was leaving for Holland in a fortnight's time. You can imagine my despair at that news. Her father said that he thought highly of me, and that if I went with them and married Ryneker he would make me a partner in his business in Holland.

What a choice I had to make. The thought of marrying Ryneker, and having a secure position was almost impossible to dismiss; but if I went down that path I would have failed in my efforts to secure the family home at Broadlands.

When I told Ryneker that I could not go with them she was distraught; she said that she could not live without me, and that she would stay with me in Cape Town when the family left. This show of her love for me made me very proud, but quite understandably her father said that she must leave with them, and since I could not support her properly on the income from my job at the Ships' Chandlers, I was obliged to tell her that our dream could not come true.

In two weeks' time I shall once again be on my own, with only happy memories of the last eighteen months to keep me company. We will say our goodbyes at the ship's side, and we will promise to write to each other, although I wonder if that might not be a mistake. Then I shall once again put all my efforts into justifying Papa's confidence in me.

With much love from your heart-broken brother,

Frobisher

Chapter Twelve
Editor's Postscript

Formerly the Mulders

I wanted to see whether I could be sure that Ryneker was not invented by Frobisher to give Hermione a sisterly interest in a fictitious romance.

The records of the Kamer van Koophandel, the Dutch Chamber of Commerce, go back well before the time when Frobisher lived in Cape Town, but I did not know the name of the company which Ryneker's father was said to have owned. The records, such as they are, in Cape Town, were equally unproductive, and it seems entirely likely that Ocke's firm there was not registered.

That might have ended my interest in Ryneker, had I not by chance met a Dutchman called Martijn deVries at my golf club. He had lived and worked in England for a number of years, and from his business card I learnt that his middle name was Frobisher; this seemed so unlikely as a Dutch name that I asked him how he had been named thus.

He was a most amiable fellow. He said that it was a long story, and he invited me to his house where he had a large metal box full of family documents dating back for over one hundred years. He was happy for me to trawl through these, and that was how I was able to pick up Ryneker's trail and follow it through one family called Mulder, to another called de Jager all the way to present-day Martijn deVries.

When Ocke, Helena and Ryneker Mulder, for Mulder was the name which they had in Cape Town, arrived in Holland after their precipitate departure from South Africa, their first concern was to assume new identities. Their ship docked in Rotterdam, where they had lived before going to South Africa some twenty years previously, and after passing through the immigration formalities they disposed of their passports and other documents identifying them as Mulders, and became the de Jager family.

Their business in Cape Town had been exposed to have serious accounting irregularities, and some of their customers were known to the police there to be less than upright citizens. They had also left behind them in Rotterdam, when they sailed to South Africa, a number of creditors who would be glad to have the opportunity to recover their losses.

Despite the change in their names they feared that they might still encounter in Rotterdam some of these less than friendly folk, and so Ocke chose Groningen as their next home; it was as far as it was possible to be from Rotterdam and still be in the Netherlands, and as the capital of the region it offered all the facilities and amenities necessary for the family to start a new life.

Ocke was not afraid of hard work when it was necessary, and soon found a job in a hardware store; despite this being a business in which he had many years of experience, he did not mention this to his employers, and was content to start at the bottom of the ladder, confident that he could work his way into a more rewarding position. Helena also found work in a shop selling fabrics and furniture, and their two salaries enabled them to rent a small but comfortable house on the outskirts of the city.

Ryneker got a part-time job with a florist; the work was undemanding, both physically and mentally, and this suited her well, for she had been obliged to tell her family that she was three months pregnant, and she had much on her mind.

Ocke had taken the news well, and since it was evident that Frobisher was the father he once again entertained hopes that he might join his family. He proposed writing to Frobisher in Cape Town, but Ryneker said that she did not want him to feel pressurised into taking on his paternal responsibilities, and since Ocke was now unable to offer him a meaningful position, it was unlikely that he would leave South Africa for the Netherlands, and that, anyhow, he did not know of her condition.

The de Jager family soon settled into a comfortable life in Groningen, and started the many preparations for the coming baby. Ryneker continued to work in the florist, and it was not long before she became much attracted to Jan deVries, the son of the owner, who was the day-to-day manager of the business. He returned her feelings, and accepted her condition, in view of which they decided to get married before she gave birth.

Ocke and Helena approved of the match, and two months before her due date Ryneker and Jan were married in a quiet ceremony, attended only by members of the two families and a few close friends of the deVries.

Seven months after leaving South Africa Ryneker gave birth to a fine boy, Luuk, who instantly became the focus of attention of both families. Ryneker loved Jan dearly, but could not forget her first love, whose name up to this point Jan had not known. When she told Jan that Luuk's father was called Frobisher she asked that Luuk's second name should be Frobisher. Jan agreed; Frobisher was, after all, history, and several thousand miles away, and he saw no good reason to deny Luuk his parentage.

And so the name Frobisher entered the deVries family tree, and the first-born son in each generation thereafter was so christened and my new Dutch friend is Frobisher's great, great, great grandson.

Frobisher's Diary

Contents

New Personae

At Sea

Jimmy	A red-headed Scot
Donald Scott	A would be missionary

Cape Town

Satish, Diya & Klara Modi	An Indian family
Lunga	Their boatman
Carter	The Ships Chandlers manager
Van Buren	The Superintendent
Sanjay	The Head Labourer
Nwazi	A resourceful Labourer
Frans	A Dutchman
Rodney Shields	An Old Reptonia
Sidney	A man who lived by his wits
Msizi	A Club servant and guide
Ryneker	A Dutch girl

Witwatersrand

Tony Bellingham	The "Manager" of a mine
Ted Harris	A Prospector

Kimberley

Cecil Rhodes	A man of influence
Ntotozo	Donald Scott's fiancée

Johannesburg

Edwin Cade	Chairman of Ashanti Goldfields Corp'n

Takoradi

Trevor Roper	A perspiring Engineer

At Sea

James & Sue Forster	Passengers to England
Nick Burton	A Man of doubtful probity

Chapter One
At Sea

11th December 1895

I have never kept a diary, always excusing myself by saying that I never had the time, and that in any case my life was too ordinary to be worth recording. But now I do not have those excuses; while at sea, I have all the time in the world, and when I reach South Africa, I am sure that there will be much to put on paper.

I cannot promise to add something every day; in fact, I can be sure not to; but I will try to mention anything and everything of interest while I am away from home. While I was at Eton one of my friends kept a pencil and paper beside his bed, and on waking, recorded everything that he could recall of his dreams. He never shared this record with us, and I wonder whether he continued the practise after leaving school, and if so whether he ever sought to publish it later in his life. For my part I do not dream often, and when I do only very rarely can I recall anything that I dreamt. So this diary will be factual, rather than a record of events that only happened in my dreaming mind.

Home already seems a distant memory, although we have only been at sea for a few hours. My school days, at prep school and then at Eton, and the brief period thereafter, when I did my best to avoid the social life expected of a son of the Broad family, seem far longer away than they really are. Life at Broadlands was easy, the only ever-present distraction being the need to find an occupation that would not only keep me in comfortable circumstances but also contribute to maintaining the estate, and hopefully to recovering some of the family's inheritance frittered away by my grandfather.

We left Southampton promptly at four this afternoon on board the steamship, the *SS Doune Castle*. This ship, which I have learnt not to call a boat, is some twelve years old and carries passengers in two classes, first and second. Papa apologised for being unable to afford a first class fare for me, which I quite understand, and I assured him that I would be happy to make the acquaintance of some of the men that I would be likely to be meeting and working with in South Africa.

There are no single-berth cabins in second class, and I have been allocated to a cabin containing no less than six berths. My companions for the next three weeks are a rather rough lot, but one of them, a red-headed Scot, seems to be an amiable fellow, although not a great conversationalist. He is called Jimmy, and he is going to South Africa to find work in the gold mines. The berths are arranged in three pairs of two, one above the other, and when I found my way to the cabin, there was only one, a lower one, unclaimed. I am not sure why a top bunk should be better than a bottom one, but we shall see.

The communal washing and toilet facilities are fairly basic, but there is a pleasant second class saloon, which is where I am writing this. There is a dining area at the aft end where we were served a tolerable evening meal. I think that the voyage will pass quite agreeably.

13th December

I have already failed to make a diary entry every day, but yesterday I was quite unable to do so. The weather turned for the worse and the sea became rough. This is not a large ship, of only about four thousand tons, and the strength and direction of the waves meant that it rolled from one side to the other, as well as pitching up and down. This combination of movements was enough to cause me some seasickness, and I spent most of the day huddled in a blanket in the saloon. I was much less affected than many of my fellow passengers, and especially Jimmy, who only left our cabin to visit the heads, as I have learnt to call them.

Today the sea is much calmer and I have spent some time on the aft deck, which is where the second-class passengers are allowed to take the air. There was nothing to see, but it was good to get out of the saloon, and the wind on my face was very refreshing.

In the saloon there is a noticeboard on which is marked daily the expected sea state and temperature, the distance run on the previous day and the anticipated date of arrival at Cape Town. Today it shows that we can expect calmer seas, a temperature of fifty-five degrees, that we covered three hundred and twenty-seven miles yesterday and that we should dock on 1st January. What a start I shall have at the beginning of the new year; and how many years will it be before I return to England and Broadlands?

There is evidently a daily sweepstake on the distance run; it costs a shilling to enter, and the winner, the person whose guess is nearest to the actual distance, gets the kitty. Although Papa does not approve of gambling, due to his father having gambled away much of the family's money, I think that as there is no risk of my losing more than a pound during the voyage, I will take a chance; it will provide a daily interest in our progress.

16th December

The past three days have confirmed that I shall not be writing in this diary every day, although I suspect that there may be more to record when we reach South Africa. This morning we saw two whales, quite close to the ship, but I do not know what sort of whales they were. When they expel the air from their lungs, they create a fountain up to ten or fifteen feet high, accompanied by quite a loud sound; they are very impressive animals.

Yesterday, I had a long conversation with Jimmy, who has completely recovered from his bout of mal de mer. He is twenty-one years old and has had very little formal education, having been required to work on his family's small sheep farm since he left school at the age of fifteen. He has a good sense of humour, and over a couple of beers we swapped stories about our lives. He is in awe of what he considers to be my lofty station in life, but is in no way jealous, and the details of what I considered to be a very normal childhood and school days interest him greatly. For my part I wonder at what I would consider a very hard life, without many of the creature comforts that I have always taken for granted, and it is very satisfying that he has turned out to be such a good fellow. I would rely on him if I ever needed help.

The meal this evening consisted of a fish pie. Needless to say, there is no wine on offer in the second-class dining saloon, but several brands of beer are available and also a very strong and aromatic rum at a very reasonable price. Jimmy much enjoys the rum, and is forever pressing me to have another, but I am not going to over-indulge.

19th December

There has been nothing of note to record during the past three days. The sea has been calm and the weather pleasant; we must be approaching the halfway point in our voyage, and I estimate that we will soon be rounding the western edge of the African continent and setting a direct course for the Cape.

Last night, I was approached by a group of chaps after the evening meal and was asked whether I played poker. We sometimes used to play whist as a family at Broadlands, and I was once instructed in the basic rules of bridge, but although I have heard of poker, I have never played the game, and have no knowledge of the rules. I was assured that this was no problem, and that I would soon pick it up, and somewhat reluctantly I found myself sitting with four of them at a table in the saloon. It seemed that my fellow players knew one another and more importantly had played together before, and therefore knew each other's style of play.

They explained the rules to me, and although there was a lot to take in and remember, I felt fairly confident when the first hand was dealt. My cards showed little promise, so I changed several, and ended up with five cards of the same suit. I seemed to recall that this was a good hand, but being unsure I only bet very cautiously. None of us could afford to lose heavily, and we had agreed that we would play for penny stakes. One player raised my bet; so did another; the remaining two folded, which meant that they took no further part in that game. Against my better judgement I raised my stake, and when we all displayed our cards, I found that I held what is called a flush, and that I had won nearly a shilling. They said that I was a natural and we continued to play.

Some hands I won, but more I lost, in both cases never being entirely sure why. When we called it a day, I was down three shillings and sixpence, and I have decided to play no more as I cannot afford to deplete my funds, and Papa would certainly not approve of my wasting my money in the company of what he would call 'undesirable persons'.

20th December

After the evening meal, my four new friends of yesterday asked if I would join them for more poker, but I excused myself, without admitting that I could not afford to lose. They said that they were sure that my luck would turn, and I was unable to avoid sitting down with them once again. Happily it turned out that their prediction was correct, for I ended the evening nearly five shillings to the good, showing a small profit over the previous night's loss. I now have a much better understanding of the game, and I do enjoy the bluffing that is an integral part of it, and if I can at least break even I will be glad to pass the evenings at the poker table. After all there is nothing else to do.

21st December

Early this morning, the ship came to a stop and anchored a little way off the shore where there was a large village; I learnt that it was called Takoradi and the country is the Gold Coast, which has been a British protectorate for more than thirty years. Many large wooden boats were drawn up on the sandy beach, and numerous modest houses and huts jostled for space in a large clearing in the forest of palm trees and dense greenery.

The ship's boat, manned by an officer and two sailors, took two of the first class passengers ashore, and when I asked the purser, who daily carried out a tour of inspection of the whole ship, who the passengers were he said that they were managers at one of the forestry and mining companies that operated up-country. After a short time the boat returned to the ship with a load of fresh fruit and vegetables, fish and other supplies. The event was a very welcome distraction, and I spent more than two hours on the after-deck, watching.

22nd December

This morning I was taking the air on the after-deck and got into conversation with one of the sailors who was polishing the rails. He told me that he was one of the crew who took the ship's boat ashore yesterday, and that he had had a most unusual experience. He had strolled along the beach for a hundred yards or so, while the fresh stores were being loaded on the boat, when he was approached by a young bare-breasted African girl with a basket of fruit. Thinking to buy a pineapple, he asked her how much they cost. She replied, "You give me white baby; I give you pineapple," and gestured invitingly towards the thick bushes that bordered the beach. He was about to tell her that he had no white baby when he realised what she had in mind, and he hurried back to the boat.

Papa would be horrified to hear this, and Mama would surely think that this was true of all Africans, and that on landing in Cape Town her son would be surrounded by would-be seducers. I shall not report this story in my first letter home.

23rd December

Today, the noticeboard declared that we had reached the mid-point of the voyage; I was a bit over-optimistic two days earlier. Yesterday, we covered three hundred and forty-two miles; I had estimated three hundred and sixty.

It also said that we would today be crossing the equator, and that the traditional ceremony would be held on the forward deck at two o'clock this afternoon. There was much discussion as to what form the ceremony would take, since none of the second class passengers had previously crossed the line, but one of the crew explained that homage had to be paid to King Neptune, and that this involved humiliation of his new subjects. Rumours spread that initiates would be put overboard and dragged behind the ship, that they would have to run naked twice round the deck, and that all body hair would be shaved off with a cutthroat razor.

Happily, the affair was much more civilised, and the only indignity was to have one's face covered in soap suds and shaved with a wooden spoon. One of the crew was dressed as King Neptune and sat on a barrel wearing a crown and holding a fishing rod.

The passengers who had not previously crossed the line each bowed to him and were presented with a certificate and a tot of rum. It was a nice diversion, and passed the afternoon very pleasantly.

I have to say that I am starting to look forward very much to the evening poker games. I can increasingly work out the chances of my hand being a winner, and I am beginning to know the betting habits of my fellow players. Two of them are fairly cautious as a rule, and if they raise the bet it is likely that they do in fact hold good hands, and unless I really do have good cards it is unwise to compete with them. The other two are much more likely to take risks, and on several occasions have scared off the opposition and taken the kitty with cards that I would not have expected to win. So far, I have had some success overall, and I am eight shillings and sixpence to the good. Jimmy sometimes watches us play, and I have to retrain him from cheering when I win a hand, which does not go down well with the other players. My guess of three hundred and forty-eight miles run on the previous day was only twelve short of the correct figure and was second best; but second-best gets no prize.

24th December

It is Christmas Day tomorrow, and preparations are in hand to make it as festive an occasion as possible. The second class passengers are invited to the first class saloon at noon, and will be treated to a Christmas dinner, together with the first class passengers. It remains to be seen whether there is turkey and plum pudding, but in any event it will be a nice change to escape our rather confined quarters. Jimmy is very excited by the invitation, and asked me what he should wear. I said that as long as he was tidily dressed and had a shave and shower beforehand he would be fine.

Yesterday's run was three hundred and fifty-four miles; I had guessed twelve miles less, but somebody evidently got closer than I did. However, I had more luck at the poker table. After five or six hands when I held indifferent cards, losing only a few pence, I was dealt the two, three, five and six of hearts. The chances of my getting the four of hearts, and thus a straight flush, were very small, but I crossed my fingers and drew one card, and to my great surprise I got the four. Even more luckily, one of the other players also had confidence in his hand, and he and I raised the bet several times before I equalled his last bet. We both showed our hands and my straight flush beat his three tens and two sixes, called a full house. I won two shillings and sixpence, my best win to date; the other players will want to take it off me tonight.

25th December

A calm sea and a warm sun got the day off to a good start, and in second class everyone was busy preparing for the dinner. The showers were used as never before and shirts were being ironed. Jimmy proudly showed me his dark blue trousers and matching shirt, and asked if he could borrow a tie from me; I said that his get-up was already perfect for the occasion and he beamed his thanks.

At twelve o'clock sharp, all eleven of us second class passengers presented ourselves at the door to the first class saloon, where we were welcomed by the captain. A similar number of first class passengers were already there, drinking wine and eating canapes prepared by the chef. The captain told us to get drinks of our choice from the steward behind the bar, and soon we were mingling merrily with our more financially-endowed shipmates. One of the ship's officers played some seasonal tunes on an upright piano, accompanied by one of the crew on a violin; this set the party mood perfectly and everyone was very relaxed.

Before very long we were all summoned to the tables, where we sat down with the captain and purser. I sat next to a fellow of about my age, who told me that he was travelling with his mother to meet up with his father in Cape Town. His father is the general manager of a trading company, part of the British South Africa Company, in Kimberley. On my other side there sat a young priest; Donald Scott, he told me that he was going to spread God's word among the savages in Africa. I was not sure that the savages were eagerly awaiting his arrival, but he was very earnest and I wished him every success. Opposite me sat Jimmy, who had seldom left my side since the party started.

When we were all settled the captain made a short speech. He said that it was not possible to provide the meal that we would have enjoyed at home, but that he hoped that we would all enjoy what the chef had prepared. And enjoy it we did. In place of the traditional turkey there was guineafowl, a bird somewhat similar to a hen which is evidently found in large numbers in West Africa. The birds had been obtained alive when we stopped at Takoradi. This was accompanied by a variety of vegetables, similarly obtained, that I had never seen before. The purser, who sat across the table from me, told us that there was yam, okra, sweet potatoes and groundnuts, and I found them all delicious.

The second course was a fruit salad, consisting of mangos, oranges, grapefruit and bananas, again all sourced at Takoradi. This was followed by cheese and biscuits. During the meal there was no shortage of drink on offer, and I noticed that most of my fellow passengers drank beer rather than the wine. Jimmy, needless to say, stuck to rum with every course.

At the end of the meal the purser rose from his seat and thanked the captain for agreeing to the meal being held, and the chef for making such good use of the victuals available. We were all bidden to fill our glasses for the last time and drank the Queen's health.

I was relieved that none of my companions had in any way let the side down, and back in our saloon we all shook hands and wished one another a Happy Christmas. While we were at dinner, one of the crew had placed on each bunk a small memento of the occasion; there were tea spoons with the ship's name on an enamel base, and mugs, glasses and coasters, all bearing the name of the *SS Doune Castle*. It was a very nice thought on the purser's part and much appreciated.

Needless to say, there was no poker tonight, and I found myself thinking of how the day must have been celebrated at Broadlands. Turkey, of course, with all the trimmings, plum pudding with brandy butter, followed by stilton and port. Crackers on the table, and the staff coming in and each being given an envelope containing one or more bank notes, according to their status. Who knows how soon I will enjoy all that again?

27th December

Life aboard has returned to normal, and with Christmas behind us, we are all looking forward to New Year's Eve and hopefully docking at Cape Town on New Year's Day. This is still forecast in the daily bulletins on the noticeboard, and I have noticed that the distance run has increased slightly in the past few days; I have, however, still failed to have a winner.

We saw a number of whales today; I was told by one of the crew that they were humpbacked whales, but I do not know if he was correct. As we sail down the coast of Namibia, a German protectorate recently established, an increasing number of birds visit the ship. Most are seabirds, which wheel around us effortlessly as we follow our course. Some that are not at home on the ocean are possibly engaged in migrating to or from the African continent, and many of them alight on our rigging and take a rest.

Yesterday's poker game started in the afternoon, rather than after our evening meal. My luck has changed for the worse, and despite holding two or three very reasonable hands I ended the day six shillings the poorer. This has all but wiped out my earlier winnings, and I have only three more days to recoup the loss, for I doubt whether we will play on New Year's Eve.

30th December

There is now a definite air of anticipation on board; our arrival at Cape Town continues to be forecast for eight o'clock in the morning of New Year's Day, and we will be seeing the new year in just a few hours earlier with the usual celebration. This will evidently not be on the scale of the Christmas Day dinner, but a notice on the board says that the captain and some of the ship's officers will be coming to the second class saloon for an hour or so after supper, accompanied by the two musicians. I feel sure that they will also be accompanied by beer and rum and that our voyage will end on a high note in every sense.

For my part, it has been a very interesting and enjoyable experience, and in several ways has left me better prepared for my time in South Africa than I was when I left Southampton. The friendship with Jimmy, in particular, and to a lesser extent the realities of living in close quarters with my other second class shipmates, has given me a totally new outlook on what Papa would call the working-class, and I believe that I am a better man for it.

I have never won the prize for the daily run, but last night I had a run of good luck at the poker table, winning no less than twelve shillings, and this evening, our last game, I managed to break even, so that I have almost won a pound during the voyage. I believe that I am now a tolerable player, and will be prepared to join in a 'school', as it is called, elsewhere if invited, although I do not expect to win a fortune at the poker table.

1st January 1896

This will be a brief entry. We docked at eight o'clock, as forecast, and have been told that we will be able to disembark in a couple of hours' time, so I have time only to report on last night's party. It was very informal; the captain and the purser mingled with all eleven of us, and a steward made sure that we were never without a drink. Jimmy sank two or three rums, and then went up to the ship's officer playing the piano and surprised us all by singing several songs accompanied by the pianist, ending up with Auld Lang Syne. He has a surprisingly good voice, and we all joined hands and sang along with him to welcome the New Year in, albeit a couple of hours early, as the captain's party had to go and do the honours with the first class passengers at midnight. It was a good ending to both the voyage and the old year; who knows what the new one has in store for me?

Chapter Two

Cape Town

3rd January

Yesterday was a very successful start to my time in this country; not only did I find lodgings, but I also got a paid position. I hope that this is a foretaste of the success that I shall have here, but I will be realistic and simply be grateful for a good start to my new life.

My lodgings are with an Indian couple, Satish and Diya Modi. He has a small but very nice house, and I have a comfortable room with my own bathroom. As well as a bed I have a desk and an armchair and I think that I shall be well-established here as my rent, one pound a week, includes breakfast and an evening meal.

Satish has a small business which caters to the Indians who have come here to work and remit money to their families in India. His business provides clothing, tools and financial help, and it seems to be a profitable undertaking, to judge by his house.

He has a daughter aged about eighteen or twenty called Klara, and she evidently acts as his bookkeeper and secretary. She smiled politely at me when we met, and said that I should let her know if I needed anything.

The position that I have got is with a Ships' Chandlers in the dock area, and I am to start on Monday next week. I was interviewed by the manager, an Englishman called Carter, and he told me that I am to be the assistant to the superintendent of lading, who is in charge of the labourers, mostly Africans, who carry the supplies to the ships that we service. The superintendent is a Dutchman, a rather unpleasant type; he did not seem pleased to have me join the business, but very soon was keen to advise me of my duties, most of which seemed to be his, and I suspect that he will look to have an easier life with me as his dogsbody. I will find my way cautiously and be careful not to antagonise him, but I do not intend to do his work for my wage.

6th January

I have spent the past few days finding my way about Cape Town. It is not a large place, most of the businesses are clustered around the dock area, and the European inhabitants live in one area to the west of the harbour. There is a large area to the east of the town where the Africans live in what is called a shanty township, and the Indians mostly live together in little groups.

There is a very defined class structure. The Dutch and English who manage the commercial businesses, and a few other Europeans, are at the top of the tree; below them are the other Europeans who are employees. The Indians, most of whom are labourers, come next, and the local Africans are at the bottom. This seems to be rather unjust, since it is their country, but they are mostly completely uneducated and not able to hold positions of any responsibility. They do however in most cases benefit from being employed, and are therefore able to raise their families in better conditions than they would otherwise do.

My funds do not enable me to stay at one of the European boarding houses, and this may mean that I do not mix with my fellow Englishmen, but I expect to come across them in the course of my duties and when I can afford to do so I will seek to change my lodgings.

8th January

I started work today, and very soon found that I had been correct in my appraisal of my superior, the superintendent of lading. His name is van Buren; I am just Broad. He comes from Rotterdam and I have some difficulty in understanding his accented English. He has been here for five years, and although he is not forthcoming about his past I get the impression that it was expedient for him to leave Holland, possibly a step or two in advance of the law.

My duties are not in themselves difficult, and can best be described as ensuring that the right goods are delivered to the right ships on time. The company services the ships of several shipping lines, and we are advised in advance of the dates on which 'our' ships are due to dock, and whether they are bound to or from England. Their actual requirements are not known until they arrive, and they are evidently always keen to spend as little time here as possible. I was told that sometimes we have to service two ships at the same time, and it is then that it is particularly important that there are no mistakes made. Since the superintendent cannot be in two places at the same time it is necessary for him to have an assistant.

One of the ship's officers gives us a list of their requirements as soon as they are alongside the dock, and it is then my job to have the various items brought from our warehouse and carried on board. If we do not have something on the list, I have to try to obtain it from one of our competitors. In this case the price will be greater, but it is a case of mutual assistance, since there will be a time when we have something that they do not.

On ships bound for England there will often be passengers, mail and goods to be loaded, as well as the usual food and water; the passengers are sometimes Englishmen who have made their fortunes, and the goods are often how those fortunes were made. Gold and diamonds are sent back to British banks and Dutch diamond dealers. I wonder how I might become one such passenger and how I could make Papa proud of me.

I have eight men under me, and I was introduced to them by van Buren. They seemed to be decent fellows and I am sure that we will get along well together when I have learned the ropes. One of them, Sanjay, an Indian, is the foreman, and he assured me that he and his men, all of whom are Africans, were all hard workers and entirely honest. Van Buren's comment that there was no such thing as an honest African seemed to be unnecessarily offensive, and was not unnoticed by the men.

10th January

My second day at work, and I was immediately thrown in at the deep end. One of our ships, bound for Bombay, docked at nine o'clock, and van Buren and I were the first to board her. We went to the office of the ship's purser, where he offered us a tot of rum and handed a list of their requirements to van Buren. He handed it to me, and told me rather brusquely to 'get on with it'. He seemed in no hurry to leave the purser's rum bottle, and so I left the ship and went to where our labourers were waiting for their instructions.

The list contained about twenty items, ranging from fresh water and dried meat to ropes and coal. I had no idea whether we had everything on the list in our warehouse, and in fact, having seen it I was pretty certain that we had no coal there. Happily Sanjay, who speaks good English and seems keen to get on the right side of me, took the list and assured me that we could supply everything that was wanted.

He gave orders to the men, and six of them went to our warehouse to select the various items stored there. The foreman and I, together with the other labourer, went to the yard where the coal was kept in sacks. I told the storekeeper how much was wanted, and the foreman told me that it would be put on large wagons and taken to the ship's side, when it would be taken on board by the ship's crane. We left the labourer there and went on to where the water was stored in large, wooden barrels. Here, we said how much was needed, and I was told that the barrels would be taken on board in the same way as the coal.

We then returned to our office, where I found van Buren back from the ship. The purser's rum had not made him any more agreeable, and he had no words of approval for what I had arranged without any help from him. He then started to put the cost against every item on the ship's list, taking the costs from our price list. I asked him if he would show me how the various items were costed, but he said that that was not my job and that I should go to see if the loading was going satisfactorily.

The captain wanted to sail on the evening tide, and when I returned to the quayside the coal sacks were already being hoisted aboard. The wagon with the water barrels was waiting its turn with the ship's crane, and our labourers were hurrying up and down the gangplank, loading the other items.

By six o'clock the loading was completed. Van Buren took the bill of lading to the purser who signed it on behalf of the captain; he kept one copy and van Buren the other. He said that I could leave while he had a few words with the purser and I went back to our compound and thanked Sanjay and the labourers for their work. I got the impression that they had never before been thanked for doing anything.

The ship sailed shortly after seven o'clock, and van Buren told me that I could stand down. It was a very interesting day, and I feel certain that I could do van Buren's job with no difficulty. Possibly he feels the same, and sees me as a threat to his easy life. I will have to be certain not to give him any excuse to find fault.

20th January

I see that it is nearly two weeks since the last entry in this diary. This is because there has been nothing of great interest to report. My work at the docks has involved only one of our ships, and I have had the opportunity to find my way about in that area, discovering where the other Ships' Chandlers have their compounds and getting to know their men. This is important, as I need to be on good terms with them when we need to get from them an item which we do not have.

It seems that van Buren is well known to everybody in the docks, but I notice that there is some reserve when people speak of him, and they seem to be glad to be able to deal with me when they need something from our store. One of the other companies is a Dutch one, and it seems that they service as many ships as we do, perhaps even more. One of their men is a Dutch fellow called Frans, not much older than me, and he told me that one evening he would show me the best places in Cape Town.

We met yesterday after work and he took me to a bar in one of the side streets on the edge of town; it was a busy place, and I recognised several of the men that I had met at the docks. We had a couple of beers, and I made several friends. And then Frans said that we should go to a club that he knew which he was sure that I would find interesting. I did not really want to go but agreed to rather than seem ungrateful.

When we reached the club I immediately recognised the name, for it was a place where some of the sailors from our ships used to spend their money when they were in port overnight. It was in a very seedy area, and when we were inside I was not surprised to find that there were a number of very scantily-clothed young women offering drinks to the clientele. It was not only drinks that they were offering, and it was with some difficulty that I persuaded one of them that I needed a beer before I could contemplate anything else. We sat down in a corner of the very dark saloon, and I determined that as soon as I had finished my beer I would make my excuses and leave. However, as it turned out, before very long Frans had agreed to sample the charms of one of the girls, and I was able to finish my beer, and go. As I got up I saw that van Buren was sitting at a table on the far side of the room with one of the girls; I hoped that he had not seen me, and hurried back to my lodgings with the Indian family.

I feel very ashamed at having been led into such an establishment, and I decided that I will restrict my contact with Frans to matters involving our respective businesses. Above all I hope that van Buren did not see me in the club, for I do not wish it to be thought that it is the sort of place that I like to visit, or that I would take advantage of the other services on offer.

28th January

It is now nearly a month since I landed in Cape Town, and I already feel established in my job; I also know my way around the town, especially which areas to avoid after dark. There is not a lot to do in my spare time, for I cannot afford to join the European club and there is not much in the way of entertainment for the public. I have, however, found that I very much enjoy fishing, and many evenings after work I take my rod down to the harbour.

Satish Modi owns a small boat, and one of his African employees acts as boatman when he or any of his guests want to spend an hour or two relaxing on the water. Satish has very kindly said that I may use the boat whenever I want, and I have struck up a good relationship with Lunga, the boatman; he tells me that his name means 'be kind'. He took me to a shop near the docks where I bought a second-hand rod for a very reasonable price, and he is teaching me how to use it to good effect. We do not go out very far from land, but Lunga knows where there are always fish, and I always catch a few. Some I give to him, and some I take back to my lodgings, where Diya cooks them and serves them for our evening meal.

We never fish too close to the harbour entrance, for there are always many seals there, and if they take a fish which is on the end of your line you will certainly lose the line and possibly the rod too, and the hook may prove fatal for the seal. The fish that I catch are not very big, but I have seen boats come in to the harbour with marlin and sharks that are nearly as big as our boat. I would very much like to catch a fish that size, but the hire of a boat for a day, and the cost of a suitable rod and other equipment is far beyond my financial state at present; when I have made my fortune here that is one of the things that I will do.

12th February

One of our ships docked yesterday, on its way back to Southampton from Calcutta. Apart from the usual revictualling and replenishment of coal and water, there were a few minor repairs necessary, and the captain said that he needed them done in thirty-six hours. I was in the office, checking the ship's requirements against our stock, when a couple of the crew came in; they were allowed to come ashore until midnight, and asked if I could recommend somewhere that they could get a drink and a woman. I was shocked at this blatant request, and told them that having fairly recently come to Cape Town, I could not help them, but I told them that my superior would be able to do so, and directed them to van Buren, who was berating one of the labourers for dropping a box of fruit. A couple of minutes later, the seamen left with broad grins on their faces. I asked van Buren where he had directed them, and he said that it was to a club that he had heard of; evidently he had not seen me there a couple of weeks ago, and was not going to admit that he patronised it; I wonder if Mr Carter would be pleased to know of his superintendent's out-of-hours pursuits, as he struck me as a very proper gentleman when he hired me.

4th March

The time passes very quickly here, and I can hardly believe that I have been here for two months; when I arrived, I knew nothing of South Africa, and although Cape Town is only a very small part of this huge country, it is a very important part. Everything that is not available locally passes through the port, and I like to think that if I am doing my job properly I am in a small way contributing to the prosperity of the country. I often find myself dreaming of my being successful in the goldfields, but it will be some time before I can think of leaving Cape Town.

I hope to have a letter from Papa before very long, and it will be good to have news of my family and Broadlands. The voyage to England takes three weeks or more, depending upon the speed of the ship and whether it makes any intermediate stops, but the outgoing mail sometimes waits here in Cape Town for up to a fortnight before there is a sailing, and so it may have been six weeks before the letter that I wrote when I first arrived was delivered. I will aim to write once every two months and hope to receive a similar number of letters, but I will, of course, report anything of special interest.

I know that Papa is very worried about his finances, and how he can keep Broadlands in a proper condition, and I very much hope that I can be of some help to him before too long, but there are no well-paid jobs here in Cape Town that I could hope to land, and I must try to save enough to enable me to head north.

6th April

Last night I had a most unsettling experience. As soon as I got home from work, Klara knocked on my door, and when I opened it, she burst into tears. I asked her what the trouble was, and she said that her parents had told her that she was to be married to a friend of theirs in India, who she has never met. She said that she loved only me, had done so from the first time that we met and that she would do anything, anything, if I could help her avoid this marriage. I said that I was very sorry but that there was nothing that I could do. I have every sympathy for the girl, but I cannot become involved in a family matter, and I do not share her feelings; I fear that I must find alternative lodgings before the situation becomes embarrassing to all concerned, and I would not wish to abuse the hospitality of the Modi family, who were kind enough to take me in when I first arrived here three months ago.

10th April

Yesterday I got a letter from Papa. Although it was mostly about how difficult he was finding it to keep Broadlands in a proper state, it was very good just to have this contact with home, and to hear about my family. I shall keep all their letters and be able to read them again whenever I want.

Yesterday, I had a chat with Satish, and I told him that Klara had come to me and told me about the proposed marriage. I was not going to say anything about her protestations of love for me, but Satish very tactfully said that he thought that she had other ambitions, and he thanked me for being a proper, English gentleman. He agreed that it would be for the best if I found new lodgings, and he recommended a small hotel in which he has an interest. He said that he would arrange that I could stay there on the same terms as I had in his house, and that I could continue to use his boat. What a nice man he is; a real Indian gentleman.

22nd April

I have moved into the hotel recommended by Satish. It seems to be a well-run establishment, very clean, and my room is well-appointed, with a small balcony from which I can just see some of the port. There are two other English guests, and I will be glad to expand my circle of acquaintances, as at present, I tend mostly to meet people involved in the port.

When I get settled here, I will write to Papa and let him have all my news, although I will be careful not to give him cause for concern about Klara.

Last evening, I met a chap called Sidney in a bar not far from my hotel. He was playing a game I do not know with a number of matches and was challenging anyone to beat him. The stakes were only a shilling to start with, and I noticed that he often lost the first game or two, but after that Sidney never failed to win, and in the course of the evening he must have won several pounds. When there were no more men wanting to play with him, he and I sat down together with a couple of beers.

Sidney has been here for nearly three years, but was evasive about his employment, saying that he was 'in finance' and that he did 'this and that' for a number of people. He was well dressed, passably well spoken, and said that his father had a grocery business in Huddersfield. When I asked him why he had come to Cape Town he said that Huddersfield had got too small for him, and that he had always wanted to see more of the world.

I asked how it was that he always seemed to win, especially if the loser had doubled up his stake, and he said that it was just a case of knowing how to outplay your opponent and would not give me any details. When we parted, we agreed to meet again, in a different bar, in a few days' time, when he might let me into the secret of the game.

I wrote to Papa yesterday and told him that I had moved out of my lodgings with the Indian family, but not why, I also told him, without going into any details, that I may have found a way to make some money.

2nd June

I wrote to Papa yesterday and told him about Sidney, and the game that he plays. It is called *Last Man Standing*, and although it is a very simple game, with one's opponent able to see all the possibilities, just like chess, it is not often that they make the right choice of move.

Eighteen small objects, matches, bottle tops, counters or even pebbles, are laid out in three lines of six on any flat surface, and the two players alternately take one or more of the objects from any one of the three lines. The winner is the man who does not take the last object. It is as simple a game as it sounds, and can be played anywhere with any suitable objects to hand. But there is, of course, a sequence of moves which makes it very difficult for anyone not in the know to win.

A couple of days ago, Sidney asked me to go with him on a trip to Durban and Port Elizabeth, both situated on the coast to the east of Cape Town. He says that there are good prospects there for his financial interests, and that he will let me in on the secret of winning *Last Man Standing* so that I could make some money. I told him that I could not take so much time off from my job with the Ships' Chandlers, and that I would probably lose my position, but he said that if I did, he would make good what I would have been paid.

I am not entirely sure that a journey of five hundred miles or more to Port Elizabeth, and much more than that on to Durban, is a good idea, and I do not know how we would travel, but it would be a good opportunity to see more of this country, and if I could make some money as well it would certainly be time well spent, so, rather reluctantly, I have agreed to go with him.

Mr Carter was very decent when I asked for unpaid leave; he said that they had managed before I was hired and he was sure that they could survive without me for a while, and that my job was waiting for me when I returned. I told Sidney of this today and he said that we would leave next week; I must say that I am quite excited at the prospect.

7th June

Yesterday, we left Cape Town for Port Elizabeth on the recently constructed railway. The train was very crowded, and it moved very slowly compared with the trains in England. We stopped overnight at a place called George Town, which I understand was the site of one of the first British settlements in South Africa. There was no accommodation provided, or available, so we had to sleep on the train. This was not an enjoyable experience, and I was very glad when we arrived at Port Elizabeth this afternoon and I could say goodbye to my fellow travellers.

Sidney has found rooms for us in a cheap boarding house; they are not as well appointed as my room in Cape Town, but since Sidney is paying, I cannot complain, and all I want to do now is have a good night's sleep in a bed. Sidney says that tomorrow he will be busy setting up contacts for his business, and so I will have an opportunity to see something of the town.

9th June

As the name suggests, Port Elizabeth is very much dependent on the port for its prosperity, and it is indeed prosperous. It is more British than Cape Town, with a German history as well; it values its administrative autonomy, and has a thriving export business, as well as being the destination for a lot of British goods. It is now the middle of winter here, but the temperature is very pleasant and only the wind makes the days less enjoyable. There are a number of bars and restaurants where one can get a good meal at a fair price, and when I get to learn the secret of '*Last Man Standing*' I am sure that I will be able to put a few pounds in my purse. Sidney has said that he will show me how it's done this evening, and I am quite excited at the thought.

10th June

I now know how to win the *Last Man Standing* game. Sidney and I played for a couple of hours last evening and as he had warned me, I lost every game, and almost a pound. He then told me how it was that he could always win, and it really is very simple. Of course, if you come up against someone who also knows the secret then you will lose as often as you win, but it seems that the game is new to South Africa and that the chance is small.

This evening I went for a drink in one of the bars near our lodgings and was able to interest one of the drinkers in the eighteen bottle tops that I had arranged on my table. He asked what I was doing and I explained that it was a game that I had recently come across and would be happy to play with him. We agreed that the stake would be for a beer paid for by the loser. I was able to spin the game out for a while before I lost, and my opponent was delighted with how easy it had been to get a free beer.

I asked for a return match, and said that as I still had an almost full glass could we play for a shilling. Emboldened by his success he readily agreed, and I soon had his shilling. Eager to retrieve it, he suggested that we played double or quits, and before very long I had eight of his shillings; he shook his head and said that he thought that he knew how to repeat his first success but that he was not able to remember exactly how he played. I said that I would be glad to play with him tomorrow if he was in the bar at the same time. He said that he would work out a winning system before then and I should be sure to have enough money with me.

11th June

My opponent of yesterday duly turned up at the bar this evening, and after I had allowed him to win a couple of games, which he said was because he had worked out a sure winning system, I was able to relieve him of more than three pounds. This was because he insisted on playing 'double or quits', several times after his initial loss. There seemed to be some feeling among the patrons of the bar that I was in some way playing unfairly, but there is no way that one can cheat; you either know how to win or you lose.

30th June

Sidney said today that his business in Port Elizabeth is nearly finished, and that he wants to go to East London, which is a little to the east of here, on the way to Durban. I am happy to go along with him; I have won quite a lot of money in the bars of Port Elizabeth, and I am sure that I can do the same anywhere that we go. Sidney says that we should go next week.

10th July

We arrived here in East London yesterday, and I find that it is a pleasant little town on the Buffalo River; it is not as large a place as Port Elizabeth. Sidney says that there are nevertheless plenty of opportunities for his business, and that I should be able to find people to play *Last Man Standing* with me while he is at work.

20th September

It is more than two months since I wrote in my diary, and they are two months that I would rather forget. One evening, Sidney and I were debating whether we should move on to Durban when two policemen burst into our room; we were arrested, taken to the police station, and put in separate cells, without any explanation. On the next day, we were taken to the local prison where I was eventually able to learn that we were suspected of obtaining money by false pretences. I tried to explain that there were no false pretences involved in *Last Man Standing*, and offered to show the police sergeant how it was played. He said that it was of no interest to him, and that our crime was taking money from people and promising high returns that never materialised. I said that I knew nothing of that, and he said to tell that to the magistrate.

Sidney and I only saw each other for an hour every day, when we were allowed to take exercise in the prison yard. He said that he was sure that he could buy our way out of this situation, but he was wrong. After three weeks in prison we were taken before a magistrate, where a number of people testified that Sidney had taken money from them but they had never seen a penny of the profit that he promised.

Luckily, I had never accompanied Sidney on any of his visits, and nobody had seen me with him, so I was discharged with a warning not to associate with criminals, and had to pay most of my money for 'costs', whatever they were. Sidney was sentenced to three years in prison and all his money was taken, to be returned to those that he had swindled. I have certainly learnt a lesson from my friendship with him.

27th September

I returned to Cape Town yesterday and went straight to see Satish Modi; he was glad to see me, and was able to offer me the same room in his hotel that I had occupied before I went to Port Elizabeth. His daughter has left for India, to stay with Satish's brother's family, and Satish and Diya are leaving for Bombay next month to make arrangements for the wedding. Today, I went to see Mr Carter at the Ships' Chandlers, and he was as good as his word, and said that I could start work again as soon as possible. I am really very lucky to be able to pick up where I left off three months ago.

At the shipping office there was a letter for me from Hermione; it was written four months ago, and it was fortunate that I ever got it. I am so glad that she has met Tony Fellowes and that she likes him. I do not know him well, but his father's firm of solicitors is well thought of. She told me that Mary, the kitchen maid, has become pregnant and had to be dismissed. I am sorry for her; she was a nice girl, very pretty, and wrote a very sweet letter to me when I left Broadlands.

15th October

For the past few days there has been turmoil at our compound. The quarterly audit of our inventory took place last month, and a lot of items were missing. They were mostly tools, but also quite a quantity of drink and biltong. The police have questioned all the employees, including me, and were making no headway until one of the African labourers, Nwazi, said under interrogation that van Buren had made him take the goods from the store without a signature and bring them to his house at night. He said that if he had not done this, van Buren would have sacked him, and he would have not been able to support his family. With this evidence the police raided van Buren's house and found many of the missing goods; the remainder he had already sold on. Van Buren was arrested and will be tried in the magistrate's court next month; there is little chance of him escaping a prison sentence. He was, however, decent enough to tell the police that he had made his accomplice take the goods against his wish, and Nwazi was let off with a caution. Mr Carter did not dismiss him, and I am sure that he will be a very trustworthy worker from now on. The outcome of this is that I have been promoted to the position of superintendent of lading, with an increase in my salary and have been asked to find an assistant. The extra money will make good what I lost over my involvement with Sidney, and hopefully I will begin to accumulate a decent purse.

29th October

Two days ago I met an English chap called Rodney Shields. Six months ago he was on his way to Perth in Australia when he was taken seriously ill and put ashore here and transferred to the hospital. He is now recovered and he likes it here and has got a job in the shipping office. He went to Repton, and does not seem to be without funds, for he has joined the club, which has mostly English and Dutch members. It evidently has good sporting facilities and he invited me to go as his guest one day soon. It would certainly be a good way to get to know people who might be useful contacts.

1st November

Yesterday I went to the club with Rodney; it has a small but substantial clubhouse and grounds which include a decent cricket pitch. Over a drink in the bar the club secretary asked me if I would like to join, and I was surprised to discover that the membership fee was within what I have been able to put aside since I was promoted. Rodney sponsored me, and tomorrow I have to undergo the initiation ceremony in front of the other members. I am not looking forward to this, but Rodney assures me that although he cannot divulge the details it is just a bit of fun, and not as humiliating as he experienced when he first went to his school. I hope that he is being straight with me.

3rd November

Yesterday I became a member of the club. The initiation ceremony consisted of me standing on a table in my underpants, reciting the club motto in Afrikaans five times, while balancing a full glass of beer on my head. I managed to get through it without forgetting the motto or spilling the beer, and got a round of applause for my efforts from the assembled members. I will not give the details to Papa, as I think that he might consider such behaviour as letting down the family name.

20th December

Today I met a girl who may have changed my life. Her name is Ryneker, she is Dutch, and her father has a business importing goods from Holland to sell to the Dutch population here. I could write pages about how beautiful she is, and how lucky I have been to meet her. She is a couple of years older than I am, and has seen much more of the world, having lived in Holland and the Dutch East Indies before coming to Cape Town.

I will tell Hermione about her; for I feel as though the whole world should know how lucky I have been, but not Papa or Mama, who might not approve of me being involved with a foreigner whose father is in trade. There will be something to record every time that I see her, but it will be locked away in my mind and not set down in these pages where anyone might see.

3rd January 1897

I can hardly believe that I have been here for a year; so much has happened in that time. Most recently, Rodney and I went trekking up Table Mountain on New Year's Day. There were places on the trail where there were really good views of Cape Town, and we saw many different birds and flowers. We also saw many rock hyrax, little brown animals about the size of a guineapig; they are called Dassies by the locals.

After a picnic lunch we were going to go a bit higher up the trail when I twisted my ankle quite badly. Luckily nothing was broken, but we had to come back down very slowly with Rodney taking some of my weight. Cold water bandages back at my lodgings reduced the swelling quite quickly, and I can now put most of my weight on it. Next time that I go trekking, and I will surely go again, for it was very interesting to see birds and plants that I have never seen before, I will take a stout walking stick.

Ryneker was very concerned and said that if I must go on dangerous walks then she should go with me. I am not sure that she would enjoy them much but it is nice that she worries about me.

20th April

Nothing out of the ordinary has happened during the last three months. I see Ryneker almost every day after I finish at the Ships' Chandlers, and we go for long walks, holding hands. It is surprising that we have so much in common, considering how different our backgrounds have been. We have not talked about what the future might hold for us, but she tells me that her father and mother like me and are very happy that I am her boyfriend.

To my surprise, when I last met her father he took me aside and suggested that it might be a good thing if Ryneker and I got away from Cape Town for a few days, to get to know each other better. I have always behaved very properly with her, and although I know that she has had a lot of boyfriends in the past, both here and in Holland, she has never suggested that they were serious relationships.

When I told Ryneker about this she said her father had already asked her if she would like to spend a few days with me and she had said that she would, and she hoped that I was not shocked. I said that I thought that it was a terrific idea, and that we should make the arrangements. She said that her father had already done that, and that he had paid for our travel and for a hotel in Port Elizabeth next week. I was very surprised that all this had been arranged without me knowing, but I am certainly not going to object. I expect that we will be better accommodated in Port Elizabeth than Sidney and I were, but I have not mentioned that trip to her and I hope that we do not meet anyone there who remembers me.

I will ask Mr Carter if I can have a few days leave, and I hope that he agrees. I now feel very confident in my work as superintendent of lading, and I am glad to say that so far, there have been no occasions when the goods have been put on the wrong ship. I get on very well with the Indian foreman and the African labourers, and they say that I am a much better boss than van Buren was. That is probably because I do not shout at them and criticise everything that they do, and I will try to find an assistant who behaves in the same way.

I remember that when I first started keeping this diary I intended to write something every day, but really every day is very much like all the others, and it is more a question of writing about unusual events. Papa has asked me to let him know just what my duties are so I will tell him how my working days are spent.

Rodney and I are talking about another trek up Table Mountain and hope to do better than last time. There are some trails where one can camp overnight and explore the top of the mountain, and I expect that there will be many birds and animals there that I have not seen. We will go well prepared, for we know from past experience that things can easily go wrong.

2nd May

I can hardly believe that the last few days really happened. Ryneker and I spent three wonderful days together in Port Elizabeth, and we both feel that we want to spend the rest of our lives together. A gentleman does not talk about some things, and I shall only say here that we now know all about each other.

When we got back, Ryneker's father asked if I would be interested in a job with his company. This would presumably be if Ryneker and I got married. He said it might mean moving to Holland and working there. I love her very much, but I must think about it very seriously and how such a move would affect my hopes to help restore Broadlands. I do not think that Papa would like to think of me working for a Dutch merchant.

4th June

Today has been the worst day of my life. Actually it was yesterday, for I am writing this at two o'clock in the morning.

Ryneker was waiting for me outside our compound when I finished work and I could see straight away that something was wrong. She was crying and she rushed into my arms and hugged me, and it was some time before I could get her to say anything; and when she did she had the worst possible news. Her father has sold his business here and the family are leaving for Holland before the end of the week.

I asked why her father had taken this sudden decision, and she said that she did not know the details but there had been some problem with his bank.

She said that she had told her father that she wanted to stay in Cape Town with me, but that he had said that the whole family must leave, and that if she wanted to marry me I must go with them to Holland. Of course I said that I would go and talk to her father and try to persuade him that we could stay here, but she said that would not do any good, and that if I really loved her, I would go with them.

I really do love her, but without any idea of what I might do in Holland I do not think that I can give up my plans to make my way in South Africa. I tried to tell her this, but it only made her cry more and there was no way that I could comfort her. We walked around the town for several hours, not saying anything, both hoping that the other could find a way out of the problem. Of course, there was no way out, and when I left her outside her parents' house at midnight our kisses had all of the passion but none of the hope of our previous partings.

Tomorrow, after work, I will go to their house and try to reason with her father, and hope that his wish to make Ryneker happy will make him change his mind, for I cannot be happy here without my Ryneker. I do not think that I can sleep tonight.

5th June

I went to Ryneker's house after work, to find the family packing their possessions for the voyage to Holland. Her father said that this was a last chance for me to accept his offer of a partnership, and to marry Ryneker, but I had to tell him that I could not. I begged him to agree that Ryneker could stay with me in Cape Town, but he said that that was not possible. I asked politely why he had made this decision to sell up, and he said, rather vaguely, that it had become impossible to work without the support of his bank.

Their ship sails in two days' time and I will try to spend every minute of that time with Ryneker, although she says that that will make our final parting even more difficult. I will, in any case, be at the dock when they board their ship.

7th June

Ryneker and her family sailed out of my life this afternoon. I said goodbye to her on the bustling quayside, but could not say any of the things that were in my mind. Her father said that he understood my position and was sorry that I could not become part of their family in Holland. Her mother, who has always been very kind to me, said that she hoped that I would soon find someone else. Ryneker just held me and sobbed without saying anything while I tried to comfort her, until her mother gently separated us and led her up the ship's gangplank.

I cannot imagine life without her; her laugh, her smile, and the soft warmth of her beautiful body. We have agreed not to write to each other, as that would only make us more unhappy, and delay both of us coming to terms with the reality of the situation, for there is no way that we can be together again in this life. There is nothing more that I can write here in my diary

14th June

It is a week since Ryneker left, and I have been working hard at the Ships' Chandlers to keep myself occupied, with less opportunity to think of her. I will see if Rodney would like to make another attempt to get to the summit of Table Mountain; it would take my mind off my loss and I enjoy Rodney's company.

29th June

Once again, our plans to reach the summit of Table Mountain and explore the country up there, have come to nothing. A Dutchman at the club suggested that it was wise to take a native guide, and that one of the club servants had taken several members up; we contacted him, he is called Msizi, and when I asked him, he agreed to take Rodney and I next week. We made sure that we made all the necessary preparations for at least a couple of nights on the trek and set off in perfect weather.

We had chosen a route that promised the best scenery, and although it was hard going in some places it was well worth it. We reached the site of the Woodhead reservoir, a dam being constructed to supply Cape Town with fresh water, and stretched out on our blankets in the sun for a short rest. Of course, we fell asleep, only to be woken by Msizi who said that very bad weather was coming. And he was not wrong; within fifteen minutes the sun was obscured in a thick damp mist, and it was hard to see the track. We met another couple, also with an African guide, and we set off down the mountain; where we had walked up in bright sunshine only a few hours before, it was now hard to see the way down.

We were making good progress when Rodney fell heavily, and when we got him back up he was unable to put any weight on that leg. We were only about half the way down, and I could not think what we could do, but the problem was solved in no time by Msizi and the other guide. With two stout poles cut from the bush and two of our blankets they fashioned a stretcher, laid Rodney on it, and carefully picked their way down the trail. As we got lower, we came out of the mist, and the going was easier and before too long we were back in the outskirts of the town.

I managed to find a horse-drawn cart, and we put Rodney on it and I went with him to the hospital. There we found the doctor who had cared for him when he was taken off the ship to Perth some nine months previously; after examining Rodney's leg he said that there were no bones broken but that there was considerable muscle damage, and that his ankle had been badly twisted, and that it was well that we had got him to the hospital before any permanent problem could develop.

I was prepared to stay with him at the hospital, but he assured me that it was not necessary; he gave me two sovereigns to give to Msizi and the other guide. When I gave his to Msizi, he told me that his name meant 'Helper' in the Zulu language, and he certainly lived up to it.

It is now twice that Table Mountain has frustrated our efforts to reach the top, and if I was superstitious I might think that there was some curse upon us; but I do not believe in such nonsense and I have not lost my ambition to explore its summit.

15th August

I have been remiss in neglecting this diary for the last six weeks, but truth to tell it was not until today that there was anything of interest to record; but today there certainly was. I was standing on the quayside while my labourers were loading coal onto a ship bound for Portsmouth, when one of them shouted that there was a fire in the coal bunker. I hurried on board, and saw that there was indeed smoke coming from the pile of coal already loaded. The coal is delivered to the ship's side in sacks, which are unloaded from the wagons and laid on a large net. The net is then hoisted by one of the ship's derricks and swung over the open hatch of the coal bunker. One of the labourers is hoisted with the net, and when it is in the right position he cuts the cords tying the sacks and the coal spills out.

To find out how there could possibly be a fire in the bunker was not the first priority, for if it was not quickly extinguished it could weaken and hole the steel hull of the ship, which would then sink to the bottom of the dock. I sent one of the labourers to the Harbourmaster's office so that the firefighting equipment could be brought alongside.

It was Nwazi, the labourer who had been involved with van Buren, who spotted the fire, and he now repaid in full the confidence shown to him by Mr Carter in not dismissing him. He shouted to his colleagues on the dock to load a net with some of the barrels of water that were waiting to be loaded. The ship's crew realised what he had in mind and when the net was loaded they lost no time in swinging it over the hatch of the coal bunker. Nwazi clambered onto the net and when it was over the smoking coal he knocked out the bungs in the barrels. The water found its way through the pile of coal, that had already been unloaded to the source of the smoke, and very soon, there was no smoke to be seen. It was then that the port's fire engine arrived, and although there was no sign of any fire, the firemen were sent into the coal bunker to ensure that it could not reignite.

The captain had been watching the drama, and I joined him when the firemen declared that there was no further danger of the fire reigniting. He asked to see the man who had spotted the smoke in the first place and I called Nwazi to the bridge where the captain thanked him for his quick thinking, without which the ship could have been lost. He left the ship with two sovereigns and, even more important to him, a letter on the ship's notepaper, signed by the captain, telling anyone 'to whom it may concern', that if Nwazi ever applied for a job he was strongly recommended by the captain.

Mr Carter had of course, been advised of the incident, and he personally thanked Nwazi for having advanced the reputation of the company, and told him that he was promoted to senior labourer with a small increase in his pay. Altogether it was a good day for Nwazi, and the company.

Then it was necessary to find what had caused the fire in the first place, for if it had happened once, it could happen again. The way in which the coal was loaded meant that there was always a cloud of coal dust in the bunker which for safety reasons was divided into several separate compartments with large, iron-hinged doors between them. As each was filled the door was slammed shut by one of the ship's crew, and it seemed possible that when one door was shut it caused a spark which ignited the coal dust in that area. Such a thing had never been known to happen before, and it was the bosun's view that one of the crew had been smoking and dropped a still-glowing butt end into the bunker. I don't suppose that we will ever know the truth of the matter, but we can be thankful that what might have been a serious loss was averted by Nwazi's quick thinking.

20th August

I have made up my mind that I will go to the goldfields in the north of the country, probably in October, by which time I should be able to find someone to replace me at the Ships' Chandlers for I would not want to leave Mr Carter in the lurch when he has been so good to me. I think that Rodney might be interested, and I will ask him. Also, by then, with two more months' pay, I will have enough saved to live on until I start to find gold.

3rd September

I have today written to Papa, telling him that I am going to Witwatersrand to try my luck in the goldfields. I know that he will think that this is something of a risk, for I have not had any relevant experience, but I have spoken to a number of people with first-hand knowledge and it seems that one only needs a small investment and a lot of luck. I have saved enough from my superintendent's pay for the travel and the basic equipment, and if I am ever to be able to do anything to support Papa and Broadlands I will have to earn a lot more than I do at the moment.

I expect to move next month, and I have told Mr Carter that I will be leaving the Ships' Chandlers. I have much to thank him for, and when he said that he would like me to stay until he found a replacement for me, I told him that I had already found one. Rodney Shields has been working at a very boring job in the Shipping Line's office, and he would be well able to take on my position. Sanjay and Nwazi would support him well until he learned the ropes and I am sure that he would enjoy the work as much as I have. Mr Carter said that he would like to meet him as soon as possible and I will arrange that.

2nd October

Yesterday I got letters from both Papa and Hermione; written on 30th August these are the quickest that I have ever received. The really good news in both is that Hermione is engaged to Tony Fellowes. I will write to both of them before I leave here tomorrow, but at the moment, I am busy packing up my few possessions, arranging for my mail to be forwarded when I have a new address, and telling Rodney everything that I can think of about his new job, for Mr Carter was pleased to offer the position to him.

I have enjoyed my time in Cape Town, and in many ways I am more of a man than I was when I arrived here almost two years ago. I have been arrested, fallen in love and faced danger on Table Mountain. I have worked hard and become good friends with people of several different races. I believe that I can achieve my ambition to help Papa to keep Broadlands, and I look forward to trying my luck in the goldfields.

Chapter Three
Witwatersrand

14th October

I never realised how large this country is, nor how far this place is from Cape Town. The first part of the journey was by train to Kimberley, which is where the line ends. The train was slow, crowded and the facilities were basic; it stopped frequently by day and completely for two nights en route. My fellow passengers were a mixed bunch of chaps, many of them, like me, going to the goldfields intent on making their fortunes. A few had already worked there and were returning to their claims after a few weeks in the Cape. From these I was able to learn much about the different ways in which gold could be found and I am more hopeful than ever that with a little luck I can make a success of this venture.

From Kimberley I travelled mostly in horse-drawn wagons or on horseback, and I was mightily glad to arrive here yesterday and find a room in one of the many lodgings housing the prospectors, for that is what I am now.

This morning I went to the Claims Office, where I was told that all the most promising sites were already being worked, and that I could only get title to a part of an almost dry river bed where gold had yet to be found. I went and had a look at the site, where several claims were already staked out, and decided that I would try my luck there. Back at the Claims Office I paid the fee and saw my name entered on the claims record, and on the map which showed the area of each claim. It was disappointing not to be able to get a stake in an area where gold has already been found, but that would have been more expensive than I can afford and my site is much cheaper.

I then went to the general store, where I bought a couple of pans, a sieve, some wooden planks and stakes, a pickaxe and spade, tools and nails, a bucket, a tarpaulin and a length of rope. I also bought a small wooden shed and a Colt revolver. I paid for the shed and the other purchases to be taken to my claim, where I was proud to see it take its place. The adjoining site on one side, downstream from mine, was already being worked, and I introduced myself to the chap there. He has only recently staked his claim, and has as yet found no gold, but he was happy to share with me what he knew about panning and I think that he will be a good neighbour.

It has been a very busy day and I am very pleased with what I have done; I cannot wait until I start actually to search for gold, and that will be tomorrow.

15th October

For the last two days I have been setting up my claim, in preparation for actually starting my search for gold. I have made a dam in the river, and diverted the flow, so that it created a small pool, so that the water tumbling into it is held briefly before it continues on its way; this means that anything washed into the pool falls to the bottom and can be examined to see whether it contains small flakes of gold. The river is very low at the moment, and when the flow increases I will have to modify my construction.

With the dam in place I spent the last two hours of daylight disturbing the riverbed upstream of the dam, so that all the silt at the bottom of the stream was washed into the pool. Tomorrow I will start to sieve and pan what is there, and hope to strike gold.

16th October

I was up early this morning and got to my claim as the sun was rising. I removed the planks which divert the water so that the pool drained out, leaving a lot of silt and small pebbles in the bottom. My neighbour had expressed surprised at my construction, saying that simply panning the silt at the bottom of the riverbed was the easiest way to find gold, but one of my companions on the train had told me that my way had a better chance of disturbing flakes and even nuggets, and had been very successful for him.

I pegged out the tarpaulin so that it formed a flat surface with a gentle slope down to the edge of the water and piled a spade-full of silt and pebbles onto my sieve. Anything of any size was caught, the water ran down the tarpaulin into the river and the silt was left on the tarpaulin.

I put a handful into a pan with some water and gently rotated it so that the water took the silt over the edge of the pan, leaving behind the small pebbles that had passed through the sieve. It was here that there would be any gold that had been swept into the pool.

Like any prospector, I have dreamed of finding a large nugget with my first panful, but that was not to be, and by the end of the day, after many sievings and pannings, I was still without my first golden flake, and my neighbour was saying that I was wasting my time. Since he has yet to have any success I had to restrain myself from criticising his efforts.

My arms and shoulders ache, but I am sure of success tomorrow.

18th October

I did not have success yesterday, but today, just before I knocked off for the day, I found my first gold. Only three small flakes, but enough to show that the claim may prove productive. I proudly showed my gold to my neighbour, and he said that I had been lucky; I said that I hoped that he would be lucky too. Tomorrow I shall disturb the riverbed deeper than before and gradually work upstream towards the edge of my claim.

1st November

The last two weeks have been the most exciting of my life; I have not found gold every day, but by yesterday, I had enough to take to the mine office and have it weighed. I was surprised to be told that it was worth eighteen pounds, and this was credited to my account in the ledger that records every declared finding. I have been told that some prospectors who find a rich seam prefer to keep it secret, and hold onto the gold rather than hand it in and be credited, but this must be risky, for this place is pretty lawless. It is for that reason that I bought a revolver, which I keep close to hand at all times.

12th November

My good luck continues. Yesterday I found a small nugget; I have not yet had it weighed, but I estimate that it weighs as much or more than twenty good flakes. I am gradually digging deeper into the riverbed, and not many pans do not have a flake or two in them. My neighbour has admitted that he was wrong about my method, and he has himself started to create a dam and a pool.

17th November

Yesterday, I took the gold that I have found during the last two weeks to the mine office to be weighed. There were several small nuggets and quite a lot of flakes and small specks, and the valued credited to me in the ledger was thirty-five pounds; at this rate, I will be able to return Broadlands with a full purse in a couple of years, but nothing is certain in this business, and a claim can run out of gold just as quickly as it first promises riches.

8th January 1898

How quickly the last two months have gone. I have continued to find gold fairly regularly, but not as much as I did in November. A flash flood washed away my dam and pool, and that took some time to rebuild; but it was a blessing in disguise, for the new silt contained some nice flakes, but no nuggets. I have now worked my way up to the upstream boundary of my claim and am considering how I may improve the rate at which I find gold.

One way would be to buy the title to the claim upstream of mine, and another would be to buy out my downstream neighbour, who has had limited success, although using my method, and increasingly says that this is not the easy way to make a fortune that he was led to believe. I have more than five hundred pounds to my credit and could afford both, but I have heard that digging pits beside the riverbed can be very rewarding. I must make up my mind what to do, for my claim is all but exhausted.

1st February

I have bought the claim upstream of mine, and am working it by the same method as before. It is proving to be moderately productive, but not as much as my first claim. So I have decided to see whether I can be lucky by digging a couple of pits, one each side of my original dam. I have also made an offer to my downstream neighbour; not a big one, for I must not reduce my credit by very much. We will see whether he accepts it.

I cannot by myself both dig the pits and continue to pan the silt, and I will need to divert some water past the pits so that the silt can be washed out of the pans; I need someone to work for me, but I cannot afford to pay very much and there are plenty of better paid jobs, especially in the deep mines which are being dug.

7th February

Last night, in one of the many bars that have sprung up, I got talking to a chap called Toby Bellingham. He was at Eton, a couple of years ahead of me, and his family, who are evidently very well off, have invested heavily in one of the mines here, and Toby has been sent out to keep an eye on it. He admits that he knows little about mining, but he is enjoying posing as a mine owner.

I told him of my claim, and he said that it sounded very hard work for very little return. He does not understand how satisfying it is to see a few flakes of gold at the bottom of your pan, and the ever-present hope of finding a really big nugget. He suggested that we meet again before too long, and I will be happy to do so for there are very few people here with the same background as I.

I was leaving the bar when I had a real surprise. Cleaning the tables and emptying the spittoons was none other than my erstwhile fellow passenger, Jimmy. When he saw me, he rushed over and shook my hand hard enough to break it off. I asked him to have a drink with me, but he said that as an employee it would not be proper, so we agreed to meet in another bar not far away in an hour's time when he finished work. We met and had a long talk. He told me that he had had a number of jobs in Cape Town and had come to the goldfields two months ago with what he had saved to see if he could buy a bit of land and have a little farm; if he did he would ask his Scottish girlfriend to come out to South Africa and marry him. I remember that he had worked on his father's farm before leaving England.

Land is cheap here away from where gold has been found, and he had been able to buy a plot of about fifteen acres, where there was good soil and a stream. He was willing and able to build his own house, but did not have enough money remaining after buying the land with which to buy the timber and other necessary material, and his job at the bar did not pay well enough for him to be able to save what he needed.

Jimmy seemed to be the answer to my need for someone to work with me, but I doubted whether I could afford to pay him enough. I explained my situation and he straight away said that he would very much like to work for me. We talked about the money, and I was reluctantly coming to the conclusion that this was not to be, when I had an idea. I told him that as well as his basic wage, I would give him ten percent of what I got for the gold that we found. This might be very little, but if we were lucky he might be able to build his house in a year or so.

Jimmy was very happy with this, and we shook hands on the deal. He said that he did not need to give any notice, and that he would be at my claim early tomorrow. I think that I have been very lucky to find Jimmy, and I have no doubt that he will be a very dependable worker. Quite apart from anything else it will be nice to have someone to talk to while I am working. I will sleep well tonight.

10th February

It is now three days since Jimmy started working with me, and what a worker he is. We have one pit down about four feet, and when Jimmy is digging at the bottom only his red hair can be seen. The sides of the pit have to be shored up with planks to prevent them from collapsing, and Jimmy does this very well; he says that back at home he had to do any number of odd jobs on their farm, and that he is enjoying his work with me.

So far, we have found only a few flakes of gold in the pit, but we have now reached the level of what I suspect was the old riverbed, many hundreds of years ago, and I am eager to see whether this gamble will pay off. While Jimmy was digging I created a sluice with wooden planks, and this brings water from the stream to the side of the pit. Tomorrow, we will start sieving and panning; perhaps by this time tomorrow I will be rich.

12th February

I wrote nothing yesterday, because when I got back from the bar, I was unable to put pen to paper. Our first day of panning the silt from the pit produced two small nuggets, bigger than anything that I have found so far, and a number of flakes of gold. This called for a celebration, and Jimmy and I had more drinks than I can remember. I do remember that I was unsteady on my feet when we left the bar, and that Jimmy, who seems unaffected by drink, supported me back to my lodging. I shall not repeat this, for it does not reflect well on me, and I shall certainly not tell Papa.

Today, we continued to sieve and pan the silt from the bottom of the pit, and it continues to reward our efforts. We found the biggest nugget so far, and the flakes of gold are noticeably heavier than the first ones that I got from the bed of the stream. I will take my gold to the mine office tomorrow and see how much I will be credited.

13th February

My gold was weighed at the mine office, and I was credited with ninety-seven pounds; most of this was down to the big nugget. I have started a ledger to record Jimmy's share, and the first entry was for ten pounds. Jimmy is thrilled by this, and I can see that he is already thinking of married life on his own farm.

27th February

The past two weeks have been the most exciting of my life. Every day we have found some gold; sometimes more than one nugget, and always some good-sized flakes. We have started a second pit, on the opposite side of the stream, and Jimmy is making good progress with it.

I will write and tell Papa of my success, and I hope that he will be proud of me and my efforts to be able to contribute to Broadlands when I return there. I do not know when that may be, or for how long my claim may continue to deliver gold, but I am greatly enjoying the hard work and the success and also the companionship that I share with Jimmy.

17th April

I see that it is more than six weeks since the last entry in this diary. That does not mean that there has been nothing of interest to record, for that has been the case almost every day, but the hard work at the claim makes me disinclined to sit down and write when I get back to my lodging.

Today, we found another big nugget. I estimate that it weighs about two ounces, and it will certainly contribute well to the credit on my ledger at the mine office. That now stands at over one thousand pounds, and Jimmy has nearly one hundred. He has asked me to give him only what he needs to live on so that the rest accumulates and advances the day when he can start to build his house

7th June

It is a year since I said goodbye to Ryneker. I try not to think of her, for that makes me sad, but I cannot help wondering what she is doing in Holland, and whether she has found someone to replace me in her heart. I know that no one will ever replace her in mine, and even if I wanted to there is no opportunity to do so here, where the only females are ladies of less than perfect morals, working in the bars.

When I am working at the claim I am too busy to let my thoughts stray, but the evenings are another matter, and I find that I can best forget her when I am in a bar with Jimmy or other prospectors. It would be all too easy to become dependent upon drink, but I will not go down that path.

The claim now has three working pits, and I have employed a labourer so as to reduce the hard work that Jimmy has been doing so well. It seems that I am getting quite a reputation among the prospectors for being lucky, and all the available claims around mine are being bought up as others elsewhere cease to be productive.

Some time ago I bought the claim of my downstream neighbour and worked the bed of the stream there; but it produced very little gold and I decided against digging pits and I proposed to sell it. Jimmy asked if he could buy it from me, for he thought that if pits were dug it might do well. It would be good for him to have a claim as well as his farm, and because he has become such a good friend I transferred the title of the claim into his name and told him that it was an advanced wedding present. He could not have been happier or more grateful.

4th August

I got a letter today from Papa telling me about Hermione's wedding. I am so glad that it went off well, and I wish her and Tony every happiness

Last evening, I was having a drink with Tony Bellingham when he said that he would like to make me an offer. I thought that he wanted to buy my claims, but it turned out that he wanted me to invest in his mine. He said that for one thousand pounds I could buy a share in it. I have some time ago looked up the published reports, and it seems to be very profitable, but I am not sure that I want a part of another business. I told Toby that I would think about it and he said not to think for too long as there were plenty of people keen to invest and he was doing me a personal favour.

20th August

I have told Tony Bellingham that I will not be taking up his offer, and I feel sure that that is the right thing to do. My claim continues to do well, and I now have more than four thousand pounds to my credit, and I see no reason to risk any of them, for there are a number of things which can seriously affect deep mines. Flooding is the most common, and collapse of the lining of the shaft sometimes occurs and can bury the men in the mine at the time. Quite apart from that, the cost of the necessary machinery is considerable.

12th December

I feel very guilty that I have written nothing here for almost four months, and I have no excuse to offer. My claim has continued to exceed my expectations, and apart from one occasion, when heavy rain caused flooding in one pit, there have been no problems. We have found several really good nuggets, and there is no sign that we are reaching the end of what seems to be the level at which the gold was laid down many years ago.

I have decided to extend the two original pits horizontally at the bottom, rather than dig deeper, for it must be unlikely that they are in the only places where there is gold. I have hired two labourers to do this work, and put Jimmy in charge of them. They seem to think that his red hair means that he is some god, or possibly devil, and take care not to give him cause to criticise their work.

1st January 1899

There is no holiday here today, nor was there at Christmas, for everyone is dedicated to mining, and a day without work, is a day without profit. It is the second anniversary of my landing at Cape Town, and I took the gold found during the last ten days to the mine office. My credit there now stands at over six thousand pounds, and Jimmy has nearly a thousand in my ledger. At this rate, I should have ten thousand by the middle of the year and I have been giving some thought as to what other enterprise I might turn my hand to. Here there is nothing but gold mining, but in Kimberley it is diamonds that have drawn hundreds if not thousands of prospectors. Like gold, diamonds can be found on or near the surface, where they have been brought down by rivers over many years, or in the deep underground seams, or pipes, where the real money can be made.

With my six thousand pounds I could buy a share in an existing mine, but I would wish to be actively involved in any venture in which I had invested, and I do not relish the prospect of being away from the real action. I could buy a surface claim, but I am sure that all the best claims are already staked and being worked, and if I did I would be lucky to find a good stone, and there must be other ways in which I could increase my purse without any great risk or expenditure.

2nd January

Today could have been the end of my mining career. There has been heavy rain lately, and it caused the boarding in one of my pits to collapse. One of the labourers was buried in the wet mud, and I must say that I feared for his life; but Jimmy, the other labourer and I worked with our hands and buckets, and managed to get the unfortunate man's head clear of the mud before he was suffocated.

People from neighbouring claims also rushed to help, and before long we had him out, washed down and recovering in my hut. This could have been so much more serious, and it has given impetus to my thoughts about doing something else.

10th March

It has taken some time to repair the flooded pit and resume mining it. The man who was buried when it collapsed recovered very quickly and said that he wanted to continue to work in the pit. He ascribed his survival to Jimmy, and said that he wished to work with him for the rest of his life. This I could not promise, but I said that his job was safe as long as I owned the mine.

I have let it be known that my claim may be up for sale, and I have already had a number of people declaring their interest. It seems that the pit collapse has not reduced its value, and indeed, with that pit back in production, we are now finding no less gold than before. The owner of a nearby claim has asked for first refusal; he is a nice chap who has turned his experience of mining tin in Cornwall, to extracting gold from the South African soil, and I would think the claim in good hands if he bought it.

12th April

Today I signed over my claim to my neighbour from Cornwall, Ted Harris, who outbid two other prospectors, and such is its reputation that he paid me an astonishing three thousand pounds for it. As part of the deal he agreed to continue to employ my labourers, and he was also keen for Jimmy to stay. I gave Jimmy three hundred of the three thousand, and when I closed his ledger and transferred the balance to the bank, he had almost two thousand pounds. This, he said, was enough for him to build his house, buy some farming equipment and seed, and pay for the passage to Cape Town of his intended, but he was happy to stay on with the new owner for the time being while he started on his house in his spare time. I understand that he also told the labourer rescued from the flooded pit that when he needed a farm hand, he would be happy to employ him. It seems that everyone will do well out of the sale of my claim, and I will now make arrangements for my move to Kimberley. Witwatersrand has been good to me, and I like to think that I leave it having done some good to others.

3rd May

All the arrangements have been made, and I leave for Kimberley tomorrow. The journey will be somewhat less onerous than when I travelled in the opposite direction a year and a half ago, although there is still no railway. Last evening Jimmy and I had a few drinks together, and he thanked me for making it possible for him to realise his dream of a little farm. He said that if ever I came back to Witwatersrand, I must stay with him on his farm, and I assured him that I would.

Chapter Four
Kimberley

10th May

How different this place is from Witwatersrand. A sizeable town has sprung up on the back of the wealth created by the success of the diamond mines, and there is a degree of sophistication that was entirely lacking in the last two years of my life. There are brick buildings and paved streets, stores selling every sort of goods and several decent hotels. The only fly in the ointment is the threat of war with the Boers that hangs over the town, and some men who had their wives here have sent them back to Cape Town.

In this situation I think that it would be unwise of me to invest in any undertaking, and I shall wait and see what happens; in the meantime, I will make it my business to understand all about diamond mining. A British regiment is stationed here, ready to protect the diamond fields from any Boer ambitions, and I am sure that we will be perfectly safe should they be unwise enough to try anything.

All the men here are required to join the militia, and there is training every evening after the day's work. A man called Cecil Rhodes is the most important man in the diamond business, and he is organising the defence of the town should there be an attack. I have my two Purdeys and the Colt that I bought when I first arrived in Witwatersrand, so I will be well-able to defend myself, should it be necessary.

6th June

How good to hear from Hermione that she is to have a child. I am so looking forward to being an uncle, and by the time that I get back to Broadlands he or she will be old enough to listen to my stories about South Africa.

I am glad that Mary, who used to be our kitchen maid, is to be employed by Hermione as her child's nanny, and that she and her son Rob will be well cared for. She was such a nice girl, and I always thought that she could do better for herself than work for Cook, who seldom had a good word to say for her.

14th September

It seems that war is inevitable, and Rhodes has had a barbed wire fence put up around the town, backed up by a number of watchtowers and trenches, from which our soldiers can fire on the Boers if they try to penetrate the wire.

11th October

War on the Boers was declared today. I do not know whether I will be able to keep my diary, that depends upon whether we actually see action against the Boers. There will be no mail out of here to Cape Town and England for the foreseeable future, but I hope that I can eventually let Papa and the family know how I fared. The militia have been summoned, so I must end this here and hope to be able to continue later.

14th October

Today a Boer column appeared at daybreak and they quickly encircled the town, cutting off the roads south to the Cape and north to Witwatersrand. They seem to have a number of guns, but they have kept these back, out of the range of our rifles. The Boer commander approached at midday, under a white flag, and met with Rhodes and the colonel in command of our regiment. We learned afterwards that he demanded that the town be surrendered, and said that our military would be properly treated as prisoners of war, and that all civilians would be interned in a camp that would be built.

Needless to say, the man was sent back to his men with the assurance that the next Boer who came within range would be shot. They are a rag-tag bunch, without proper uniforms and with a variety of rifles and other weapons, but there are a lot of them, and they are fighting for what they believe to be their land; I think that we can expect some action before very long.

20th October

We have been besieged by the Boers for almost a week. They completely surrounded the town on 14th October, and since then have tried continuously to break through our defences. They have a very large gun, with which they bombard us daily, but so far we have repulsed their attacks on the town and there have been very few casualties, military or civilian, although many of the buildings have been destroyed or damaged.

Luckily, there are wells within the town, so we will not want for water, but food is already being strictly rationed, and we have been told that it may be necessary to kill and eat some of the older horses and mules.

I have not yet been engaged in any fighting, for the part of our perimeter that my militia group is responsible for has not yet come under attack. I have been put in charge of a dozen men who were working in the mines, and although they are rough sorts I am sure that they will give a good account of themselves when asked to do so.

I often think of my former life at Broadlands, but I have to say that I am quite enjoying the situation in which I find myself. Luckily the greater part of my purse is held in a bank in Cape Town, so if I should be captured I will not lose everything that I have worked for during the past four years.

10th November

It is nearly a month since the town was besieged, and the daily bombardment by the Boer artillery, and the nightly skirmishes along our perimeter mean that we get very little sleep. Morale is still good however, and we are told that a military column is on its way to lift the siege. Cecil Rhodes asks everyone to use the minimum of water, and there is not a man amongst us without a beard, albeit one in sore need of the attention of a good barber.

25th December 1899

Last night, my sector of the perimeter came under attack by about thirty Boers. I have only a dozen men, but the groups on either side of us gave very effective support and the attackers were driven back, taking several dead or wounded colleagues with therm.

It was not a good start to Christmas, but a two-day truce has been agreed with the Boers, so hopefully we can at least get a bit of sleep. Christmas dinner will not be a festive affair; we are very short of food; what pigs and chickens that we had have long since gone into the pot, and we now have to kill and eat some of our mules. There is still a little grain left in the store, and a small loaf once a week is a real treat. Happily the wells are still providing clean drinking water, but if they run dry I can see it becoming a choice between surrender and dying of thirst.

10th January 1901

It has not been possible to celebrate the new century as we would save wished, but there has been no shortage of fireworks, thanks to the Boers.

It is now three months since we were besieged, and conditions in the town are not good. All sorts of diseases have spread through the population, due to malnutrition and poor sanitation, but morale remains good and the Boers have not been able to break through our perimeter.

I have been in action a number of times and I am proud to say that my men have given the enemy a bloody nose every time that they have attacked us, and so far, none of us has suffered even a scratch.

The Boer artillery continues to be the greatest danger, and we have only some small field guns which are of little real use against men with rifles on horses. My Purdeys have had hot barrels on several occasions, and I find it much easier to hit Boers, while trying to avoid hurting their horses, than high-flying pheasants coming out of the beech wood at home.

17th February 1900

The siege has been lifted! The relieving force broke through the Boer lines a couple of days ago and the survivors made themselves scarce. It will be some time before things return to normal, but at least we are spared the daily efforts of the Boer artillery. There is to be a military parade through the town tomorrow, and it is hoped that the railway line to Cape Town can soon be repaired and we will be able to get all the many things that have been unobtainable for the past four months.

When things return to normal I shall start to consider how I should seek to increase my purse, but there has been very little on which to spend my money and my balance has not much been reduced. I will not invest in any dubious venture, or any high risk business, but only in something that is safe and will give a fair return on my money. There is no opportunity for me to become involved in the diamond mining; the costs are very high and Mr Rhodes controls every aspect of it; I will see what other opportunities there are for me.

18th February

Quentin is here, in Kimberley! I was watching the parade yesterday when I saw him marching at the head of a section of troops. I could hardly believe my eyes. I shouted, but he did not hear me, so I followed the parade to the barracks and met him there. He took me to their mess where we had a few drinks and he told me that he had been in Cape Town for a short time before the war started, and that his regiment was now on its way to Ladysmith, which is also besieged by the Boers.

He left England in August last year and so he was able to bring me up to date with all the news of our family. He says that Papa is ageing, but is so glad that the sale of the Gainsborough meant that he could give Hermione a good wedding and also start to put the estate in better shape.

Quentin will only be here for a few days before leaving for Ladysmith, but it is so good to see him, and I must say that he looks very smart in his uniform; I will let Papa know that we met in my next letter.

3rd May

Today I became a shopkeeper; what would Papa think? I was in one of the general stores which has reopened, talking to the owner, and he told me that he was going to leave Kimberley and return to Cape Town. He said that before the siege the store had been very profitable but that he wanted to have a similar business in the more peaceful atmosphere of the Cape.

I asked him what he was asking for the store, and after a bit of bargaining we settled on five thousand pounds for the store and what little stock remains after the siege. This is about half of my purse, but he showed me his accounts for the year before the siege, and I have good reason to expect to recover the cost and start to show a profit before the year is out.

There are three men who work in the warehouse and deliver orders throughout Kimberley; they have worked at the store for several years and the owner said that they are hard workers and completely trustworthy. He will show me the ropes until he leaves, and help me to order the goods that are needed to fill our empty shelves. This venture is very exciting, and I feel sure that it will be a profitable one as long as the Boers do not win the war.

4th May

Today I made a record of all the goods that remain in the store, and placed orders for all the items that I need. Since the siege lifted there has been a demand for all the things that were unobtainable while we were cut off by the Boers, and there must now be a good opportunity to make a profit. Because he was not planning to stay here, the previous owner had not taken advantage of this situation and had placed no orders, and so many of our shelves are empty. It will be at least two and possibly three weeks before my goods arrive on the train from Cape Town. In the meantime, I will try to sell what we have, and to build a good reputation with my customers.

29th May

The goods that I ordered three weeks ago arrived on the train today, and I and my three men have been busy collecting them from the station and putting them on our almost empty shelves. My purse, which was almost halved when I bought the store, has been further reduced paying for this order, but if I am to make good profit I have to have a wide selection of goods to sell, and I think that I am now in a position to take advantage of the situation here. I shall have to work hard, and I will need a stroke of luck, but I am really hopeful that I will make a success of this.

1st August

It is three months since I bought the store, and I am glad to say that it has exceeded my expectations as to its profitability. This is partly because one of our three competitors went out of business and ceased trading, and many of their customers now come to my store. I have to place orders for more goods almost every week, and I am learning which items sell quickest and so need reordering on a regular basis. If the business continues at the present rate I will have recovered what I paid for the store, and the orders that I have placed, by the end of the year as I had hoped.

7th October

I have found that being a storekeeper is a very demanding occupation. My men are good workers and reliable, but I have to open up the store at seven o'clock, six days a week, and lock it up when it closes at six in the evening. I then have to record the day's sales and decide whether I need to place any orders, which I usually do once a week. On Sunday I bring the accounts up to date, and this is when I get to know how the business is faring. I am glad to say that so far there has not been a week when we have failed to turn a profit; not always a large one, but overall I am very pleased with how this venture is turning out, and I am sure that I will be able to return home by the end of next year with enough in my purse to help Papa.

1st November

Today I had a great surprise. I was in the store, attending to a customer, when another man, who looked to be English, came in and started to examine the shelf on which the note books, pens and ink and all such writing materials were displayed. I have to say that there is not usually a great demand for these goods, but I need to be able to respond to requests for them so as not to lose the customers to one of my competitors.

When I had finished dealing with the first customer, who had placed orders for a considerable number of tools, I went to introduce myself to the new arrival. I had the impression that his face was familiar, but could not place him. He, however, evidently had a better memory than I, for he extended his hand and said how surprised he was to find me here. It was then that I remembered; it was Donald Scott, the priest with whom I sat down to Christmas Dinner on the ship nearly five years ago.

Today, he was not wearing a white clerical collar, and was dressed no differently from any other person in the town. I invited him to my back office where over a couple of beers we told each other what we had been up to.

He had come to Kimberley three months ago, having spent his time in Cape Town and then Port Elizabeth, where he had tried to set up missions where he could convert the Africans to Christianity. He had had no success in either place, and had come to Kimberley to make a last effort to spread God's word; he had started a small school for children aged five to ten, hoping that they might be more receptive than their parents.

Several European families had enrolled their children, and also some of the more affluent Africans. He has appointed an African lady who had a degree in English from the University of Cape Town, which had recently admitted women, as the headmistress, a rôle which involved her in teaching all subjects to the dozen or so pupils, while he provided the religious instruction.

All was going well, with the prospect of there being more pupils joining for the next term, when he fell in love with the headmistress. She felt the same way about him, and they were now living together in his small house, the downstairs room of which was the schoolroom. They hoped to get married.

This situation had caused Donald great confusion and soul searching. His vows did not permit such an arrangement, but he did not want to give up either his love or his service to God. It was not unusual for Europeans to form attachments to local women, and there was not then any great social stigma involved, but Donald's concern was the opinion of the Almighty rather than that of Kimberley society.

One night, a week ago, Donald had a dream; he dreamt that God was speaking to him. He commended Donald for his attempts to spread His word, and He also said that Donald's love was pure. He said that Donald could best serve him by teaching, rather than preaching, and that he should renounce his vows and live as a teacher and a husband.

Donald asked me whether he thought that he was imaging these words from God simply to resolve his problem, but I said that from what he said, it was entirely likely that his sincere wish not to break his vows had been seen and applauded by the Almighty. I said that I thought that he should do as God had directed, and that it could only enhance his reputation as a teacher in the town. He thanked me, and said that he would bring his lady to meet me.

I must say that I was not happy having to act as God's interpreter, but Donald needed help in making a decision and I thought that his happiness would be best assured if he renounced his vows and taught his religion to children, European and African alike. I looked forward to meeting his lady, and I suggested that they come on a Sunday when I would not be distracted by work at the store.

10th November

Donald brought Ntotozo to meet me on Sunday; her name evidently means joy or happiness, and she is certainly bringing happiness to Donald. She is a striking woman, tall with a good figure, and an excellent command of English. I am sure that her education qualifies her well to teach children in all the basic subjects, and that there is every chance that their little school will flourish. The parents of the children pay a small fee, and Donald, when not teaching the scriptures, has been offered a position at St. Cyprians church, which pays him a small salary. I have to applaud their devotion to each other and their work, and I wish them success and every happiness.

20th December

Christmas this year will be celebrated with much more traditional festivity than was possible last year during the siege. My store and the other two are now able to offer a very wide range of goods, and meat and fowls are supplied to the butchers by the local farmers. Diamonds of a good quality are found regularly, and the town as a whole benefits from the prosperity of the prospectors.

My store continues to exceed my expectations as to its profitability, and I have a large number of regular customers. I should be able to return home by the end of next year with a heavy purse, and it would be so good to spend Christmas at Broadlands with the family.

10th January 1901

I spent Christmas Day with Donald and Ntotozo at their house. The school children had decorated their classroom with streamers and balloons, and only the absence of holly and mistletoe made it different from an English Christmas. We dined on roast guineafowl, as we had on board ship five years ago, and in place of plum pudding Ntotozo had made a very rich fruit cake, on which we poured brandy and set fire to it.

Their school has been a success and now has more than twenty children attending it. Another teacher has been employed, and they are looking for more suitable premises as there are now two different classes for the children and their house does not have a second classroom. Donald has taken up the offer of a position at St. Cyprians church; he does not act as a priest but rather as a verger and general factotum.

I have just finished drawing up the store's accounts, and I am glad to be able to record that it has proved to be a very good investment. My monthly profit is almost double what the previous owner achieved, and as the prosperity of the town increases, so does my business. My balance at the bank is now once again more than ten thousand pounds, and is increasing at the rate of almost a thousand pounds every month.

I am beginning to think whether there are other ways by which I might increase my purse, and now that the siege of Johannesburg has been lifted, there must be opportunities there; perhaps a second store if I could find a reliable person to manage it.

30th April

I have bought a small hotel. It stands next to my store, and has twelve rooms. The price was seven thousand pounds and I could not afford to buy it outright without spending almost my whole purse, but I have been able to borrow the money from the bank, where the success of the store means that my credit is good, and I will repay the cost price over twelve months.

The hotel is rather run down, and the guests are not from the top of the social scale, but I am going to make it rather smarter than it is at the moment, and raise the charges so that it only attracts a better class of guest. This will cost a bit, but there is always a demand for accommodation here, and there is no shortage of money in people's pockets.

There is a staff of five, a housekeeper, two maids, a cook and a barman. I will keep them all while I see who is able to provide the standard of service that I am looking for. The housekeeper is a sensible woman, and I may make her the manager if she impresses me.

I now have no time to myself; if I am not in the store, I am in the hotel, but I am very pleased with how my time here has developed, and the thought of returning to Broadlands makes my hard work worthwhile.

15th July

Both my ventures continue to prosper, and the hotel in particular is proving to be very profitable. The housekeeper has proved to be a very competent manager, and we have attracted a good class of guest, partially due to the really good food produced by the cook. Unfortunately, I have had to dismiss the barman, who was drinking almost as much as he served to the guests; I have hired a young woman to replace him, she seems to have a good rapport with the guests and the bar takings have increased considerably.

With the hotel in good hands I can concentrate on my store, and this also is doing well, and will show a sizeable profit at the end of the year, but I continue to wonder whether there is not some other way to increase my purse that would not take up so much of my time, for I have very little social life, apart from regular visits to Donald and Ntotozo.

15th August

Today I got a letter from Hermione, and I am so glad that she is to have another child. I am sure that she is an excellent mother, and it is good that she has Mary and her boy Rob with her. I hope that I can get home before too long, for I am missing my family more than I expected. Both Papa and Mama are evidently not in the best of health, and I know how much he worries about the future of Broadlands.

30th October

When I did the end-of-month accounts last night, I was surprised at how much I had made, and I think it would be prudent to invest some of my purse where it will be safe, and not pursue the thought of another store. I will take a look at the markets tomorrow.

2nd November

I have bought two…

Ed. The rest of this page is missing, possibly chewed by rodents.

4th November

Disaster! Both my store and the hotel were destroyed by a fire yesterday. It seems that it started in the hotel kitchen, possibly from a pan of hot oil, and it spread quickly to the store and the house on the other side. By the time that the fire cart arrived it was not possible to save any building, and all three have burned down to the ground. Happily, it happened during the day, so there were no guests in the hotel, and all the staff from my two buildings and the occupants of the other house were able to escape injury.

My buildings were insured, but this will not cover the value of the contents, and what I get will just about pay off the loan from the bank. What is more, I have ordered and paid for a quantity of stock for the store and food for the hotel, and when this arrives, I will have no option but to sell it to my competitors at a loss.

I have always kept my passport and the deeds to the properties, together with a small amount of cash in a safe deposit in the bank, and happily, I put my diamonds there yesterday, but all my other possessions, my clothes, my Purdeys and revolver are lost. It is fortunate that I had taken this diary with me when I went to the store.

Donald and Ntotozo have said that I can stay with them for as long as I like, but when all the necessary paperwork is completed I will definitely leave here and try my luck in Jo'burg, as it is locally known. Perhaps the fire was a sign from Donald's God that it was time for me to move on.

10th December

The insurance claim has been settled, and I have paid off all my staff at the store and the hotel. The goods that arrived after the fire were sold on, but, as I had expected, at a loss to me. The one bit of good news is that I have been able to sell the land on which my buildings stood; it is in an area which is being developed, and although I was not in a position to negotiate a high price it has given me enough to live on for a few months.

This year has been such an interesting one, and I am proud that I was able to make a success of both the store and the hotel; had it not been for the fire, I believe that by this time next year I would be on my way back to Broadlands. As it is, I shall have to turn my hand to something new, and I hope that there will be an opportunity in Jo'burg for me to replenish my purse. Donald tells me that he has said prayers for me, and I am very willing to believe that they will be answered; I need all the good luck that there is on offer.

Chapter Five
Johannesburg

3rd January 1902

I arrived here yesterday and I am surprised at how quickly the town has recovered since the siege was lifted a year ago. Gold is being found in many places in the Rand, and deep mines are being dug to follow the seams of quartz. If I am to stay here I must find a position, for everything here is expensive, and the money that I was able to bring from Kimberley will not last for ever.

I will not return to prospecting, for I have neither the money nor the inclination, and I do not want to spend my time bending over a pan or digging a pit. I will spend some time in the bars of the better hotels and try to learn from their patrons what opportunities there may be for me. Meanwhile, I have a good room in a small, well-appointed lodging, and will replace the clothes and other possessions that I lost in the fire.

25th January

I have a position. A couple of nights ago, I was chatting with the barman at one of the better hotels in town, and he said that they were looking for a night manager, as it was not unusual for guests to arrive late or need to leave very early. I said that I might be interested, and when I went there yesterday, he told me that I should go and see the manager. He is a young man who came out from England two years ago, after working in a hotel in Manchester as an apprentice; he felt that it would be a long time before he had a position of any standing in England and had come to South Africa where his experience would be valued.

We got on well together, and he thought that my experience with my small hotel in Kimberley made me well-suited to the job, and he offered to employ me with immediate effect. The pay is not comparable with what I have been earning from the store and the hotel, but I have free accommodation in the upper floor of the hotel, and all my meals are free, so I will not have any great expenses. I accepted his offer, and I will start in two days' time, when I will have bought some suitable clothes.

I have thought of selling my two diamonds but the buying and selling of them is very much controlled by Cecil Rhodes and I could not get a good price if I went through his business. I bought them from a chap who said that I should not ask where they came from, and he asked a lot less than I would have paid if I bought them on the official market. Naturally, he said that they were good stones. I know nothing about diamonds, and in their present state, they look more like small bits of rock rather than precious stones, but I thought that the seller seemed honest and I took a risk and bought them.

1st March

I am very much enjoying my job; it does not entail any very hard work, but I find it very relaxing after working in my store and hotel. I come on duty at nine o'clock in the evening, an hour before most of the staff finish work, and I am told whether to expect any late guests. During the night, there is always a cook on duty, in case a late guest wants a meal or one leaving early wants breakfast before he leaves. I am in charge of the bar, and am allowed one drink on the house. I often pass the time talking with the cook; he came from the Manchester hotel with the manager, and hopes one day to have his own restaurant here or in Cape Town. He has many amusing stories about some of the past guests, and the time passes very quickly, though I must admit that I sometimes drop off to sleep in the small hours when there is no activity.

A couple of nights ago, a guest asked me if I could tell him where he could find a woman for the night, and offered me two pounds if I looked the other way when he brought her back to his room. I told him in no uncertain way that neither I nor the hotel could countenance such behaviour, and he went out muttering about prudish standards and did not return before I went off duty.

I hand over to the day staff at eight o'clock, having paid in any cash taken at the bar, and tell the manager whether there has been anything to report overnight; I have my breakfast and retire to my room to sleep. I normally get up in the middle of the afternoon and go out to get a breath of fresh air. I do not know for how long I will keep this job, but at this time it suits me very well and I have got to meet some very interesting and influential people, some of whom tend to stay on in the bar for a drink or two when the day staff have left.

20th May

I am in hospital. Yesterday afternoon, I was choosing a leather jacket from a pile on the floor of one of the stores when I felt a sharp pain in my right hand. I dropped the jacket and found that I had been bitten by a krait, a very small and poisonous snake. I rushed to this hospital, where I passed out, but not before I told the doctor what had happened. They administered the appropriate antidote and brought me round fairly quickly, and before very long I was feeling very much better. They say that they will keep me here overnight in case of any complications.

3rd June

Today I had a long talk with one of the hotel guests, a Mr Edwin Cade, and we got on very well together. He has been involved with a gold mine here for some time and is now going to set up a mining company, the Ashanti Goldfields Corporation, in West Africa. He got my name from Ted Harris, the man who bought my claim in Witwatersrand. Ted evidently told him that as well as being a hard worker, I have several times made decisions which resulted in finding better yields of gold.

Mr Cade asked me whether I would be interested in the position of mine manager, at a place called Obuasi in the Gold Coast. I told him that I knew nothing about West Africa, and he said that the mine was a long way from Accra, the capital of the protectorate, surrounded by rain forest, that there were already some fairly inefficient operations there, run by both indigenous and foreign companies, and that he believed that there was a lot of gold waiting to be found. He thought that I might be the person to find it.

The position is well paid, and I have a week to think about his offer before he leaves for Cape Town. It seems that the war will soon be over, but I do not think that there are any opportunities for me here that will enable me to fill my purse, and I am minded to take up his offer.

19th June

I accepted Mr Cade's offer, and have given in my notice at the hotel. He has very generously already put me on the payroll of the Ashanti Goldfields Corporation, so I have no need to sell my diamonds. We leave for Cape Town in two days' time and are making a brief stop en route in Witwatersrand, where Mr Cade has some business to complete. It will be interesting to see how it has changed since I left there, and I hope that I get an opportunity to thank Ted Harris for putting in a good word for me.

I would very much like to see Jimmy again while we are there; by now he has probably got his house built, his little farm set up, and hopefully has been joined by his Scottish lady, but I do not know whether there will be time for that.

24th June

I have been back in Cape Town for a couple of days. We spent two days in Witwatersrand on the way, and we met Ted Harris at my old claim. He told Mr Cade how productive it had become, and said that he is going to sink a shaft near one of the pits. He said that I have a real nose for gold. I did not get to see Jimmy, so I sent a letter to him; he will not know my next address and I fear that our paths will not cross again.

Mr Cade has business to attend to during the days here, but in the evening we have a drink together and he tells me more about his plans for the Obuasi operation; he means to try to buy up some of the small mines and make them more efficient. It sounds as though there is a really good opportunity there; it seems that he has the necessary capital and if there really is as much gold as he believes then I think that this will be a chance for me to get a full purse before too long and be able to return to Broadlands.

I have told Papa that I have accepted Mr Cade's offer, and I wonder what he will think; I hope that he is not disappointed that I have not made more of my time in South Africa, but I think that he will be glad that I have this new opportunity, and that I am now considered to be capable of holding a relatively senior position in the gold-mining business. I look forward to his next letter.

27th June

Today I went to the Ships' Chandlers and saw Rodney; Mr Carter has been unwell for some time so Rodney has been in charge, and he seems to have taken to the job like a duck to water. He has negotiated a takeover of one of the other Ships' Chandlers, almost doubling the size of the business, and is obviously well-respected at the docks and at the club. I also saw Sanjay and Nwazi and the other labourers; they said what a good boss Rodney is and that they were sorry that I was leaving South Africa. Tomorrow, I will go and see Satish and his wife.

This evening, Rodney and I went to the club, where I met several old friends. Some members asked whether it was now too late to make a fortune in gold or diamonds, and I said that I thought that it would be a long time before they were exhausted. I also saw Msizi, who was our guide on our ill-fated trek up Table Mountain; he is now a senior steward at the club, but also acts as a guide for members.

2nd July

I called on Sanjay and Diya today and they kindly insisted that I lunch with them. Their daughter, Klara, was married nearly six years ago; she lives in Bombay with her husband, who is a government employee, and has already presented them with a grandson and granddaughter. Satish has sold his interest in the small hotel and says that as he gets older he likes to spend more time in his boat or in the pretty garden that Diya has made behind their house. They were good to me when I first landed here, and I am glad that they are well and happy.

10th July

Tomorrow we sail, and this evening Mr Cade took me out for a last meal in South Africa. It was a lovely evening, and as we sat outside on the verandah of the restaurant he said that I could expect a very different climate in the Gold Coast, where it is evidently very humid and not as hot as South Africa. There are two periods of heavy rain each year, the long and the short rains, and the land around the mines is mostly rainforest.

As we left the restaurant I saw Sidney, who got me arrested in Port Elizabeth, talking to two rather rough-looking fellows on the other side of the street. I made sure that he did not see me, for I would not wish Mr Cade to think that I knew such men, and even less, to know of my incarceration in East London. Sidney has obviously either completed his sentence, or possibly more likely bought his way out of gaol, but I expect that he will again be in trouble of one sort or another before very long.

Chapter Six
At Sea Again

11th July

We sailed today at four o'clock on board the *SS Alnwick Castle*. This ship was only built a year ago, and is therefore in very good condition. She replaces a ship of the same name that was wrecked in October 1894. Mr Cade has booked us in two of the few first class cabins, and I must say that I am travelling in much greater comfort that I did on my way out. There are also some second class cabins, but the majority of the accommodation is third class.

The ship was built to take advantage of the increased traffic to and from South Africa following the discovery of gold and diamonds and to carry the mail and cargo; it has a speed of fourteen knots. I expect that there will be betting on each day's run, and I hope that I am more successful this time; I calculate that we should cover about three hundred and thirty miles per day, and I will make my bets around that figure.

Dinner on board this evening was very different from the meals on the outward voyage to Cape Town; there are only six first class passengers, and we are expected to dress smartly for the meal. We were served by two stewards, one bringing the food and the other making sure that we did not go thirsty, and it was a real treat to have lamb chops, brought from England in the ship's refrigerated store, after so many years of beef and chicken. There was a choice of wines, and after the meal, when Mr Cade and the other gentleman smoked their cigars, coffee and liqueurs were served. I could get used to this sort of life, which is in stark contrast to what I can expect up at the mine.

14th July

There is very little of interest to record on a daily basis. Life on board is very comfortable and we have enjoyed good weather, but there is very seldom anything but blue water to see in every direction, and I miss the company of Jimmy and the others that I had on the outward voyage. Mr Cade tells me about the mine at Obuasi and what will be expected of me there, and I am cautiously confident that I will be able to justify his confidence in me.

Today we passed abeam, as I have learnt to say, Walvis Bay, the Bay of Whales, in Namibia, but no whales were to be seen. The area around the bay has been annexed by the British, as there is a port there and it is strategically important in protecting the trade route around the Cape. So far I have had no luck with the daily run; the ship seems to be steaming at less than fourteen knots.

15th July

Today I had a real surprise. I was sitting out on the deck in the sun, looking at the area where the second and third class passengers are allowed to exercise, when I saw Tony Bellingham. It was he who offered me a share in his family's gold mine at Witwatersrand for one thousand pounds. I invited him to the first class saloon and bought him a drink, while we told each other what we had been up to during the past five years. His story was a less successful one than mine.

Although he knew nothing of mining when he arrived at Witwatersrand, as he had admitted when we first met there, he had felt that as the representative of the family which owned a large share in the venture he should take an active part in the day-to-day management of the mine, and had made several bad decisions which resulted in heavy losses. He is now on his way home, in third class, to face the wrath of his father.

16th July

Whales at last! Not a lot of them, and I did not know what sort they were, but it was nice to know that we were not alone on the ocean.

18th July

I won yesterday's daily run sweepstake; because there are not many passengers on board I only got fourteen shillings, but I did guess the exact mileage, which had not been done before on this voyage.

This evening Mr Cade asked if I played bridge; Papa and Mama often play with guests at Broadlands but I have never learnt the game. I thought it best not to say that I can play poker and *Last Man Standing*.

20th July

Today I had a long talk with Mr Cade. He asks me to call him Edwin when we are alone, but I think that would be disrespectful. He has explained my duties and responsibilities and told me what servants I will have; I do not know quite what to expect in that respect, but I do not imagine that it will be anything like life at Broadlands, where some of our servants have been with the family for years.

I am entitled to four weeks' leave after a year in the job, but since it would take all of that time to sail to England and back, I will not have an opportunity to see my family next year, and the only holiday that I will have is possibly a few days on the coast. I hope that by the end of the second year, when I will be due for eight weeks' paid leave, I will be able to go home and stay there.

We will go ashore tomorrow at Takoradi, where the ship stopped on my outward voyage. There is evidently still no way for a vessel of this size to get close to the shore, and we will be taken off in the ship's boat. I am reminded of the sailor who was offered a pineapple in exchange for a white baby, but I will not tell Mr Cade about that.

Chapter Seven
Obuasi

22nd July

Here I am at Obuasi, the mine manager for the Ashanti Goldfields Corporation. I am so lucky to have been offered this job, and I will do it to the best of my ability and hopefully make Papa and Mr Cade proud of me.

When we came ashore at Takoradi yesterday, my first impression was how green everything was. There are palm trees on the edge of the beach, and around the town the bush, as it is called, was thick forest with every sort of tree and creeper; I would not wish to have to venture into it

The climate is quite different from South Africa; here it is very humid and not as hot as it was in Witwatersrand. There are many mosquitos, and Mr Cade has given me some pills to take so that I do not catch malaria from their bites. I am told that there are also a number of very poisonous snakes, and that it is wise to wear leather boots that protect your legs beneath the knees if you are working away from the buildings. I will hope not to be bitten by another snake; my experience in Jo'burg was not pleasant.

We spent the first night in the Rest House at Takoradi, a small, comfortable place which caters for senior staff arriving or leaving by sea. Apart from Mr Cade and me, there was a chap called Malcolm Forrest who had arrived from England a couple of days ago on his way to one of the forestry companies not far from our mine. I thought that he was joking when he told me his name, but he really is called Forrest.

This morning, we boarded the train at seven o'clock and were told that the journey to Obuasi would take about seven hours, but that if the line was blocked by fallen trees, which evidently is not uncommon, it would take a lot longer. Much of the journey was through dense rain forest, with only a few feet between the train and the vegetation. There were a number of villages in clearings on the way, and as we approached each one the train's whistle announced its arrival. This was the signal for a crowd of the villagers to appear, some selling fruit and vegetables, some hoping to hitch a ride up the line, and some just to look at the train. The line was only opened very recently, and the passage of every train is an exciting event.

The first class carriage was comfortable enough, and a steward served us with warm beer and fruit drinks. The other passengers rode in open carriages, and were totally exposed to the sun and for several months each year the rain. The peak of the rainy season was evidently last month; it is dry today and we can look forward to dry days before very long, although there will be occasional storms.

23rd July

When we arrived here yesterday evening, we were met by the mine superintendent, Mr Williams. He did not seem very pleased to see me, and Mr Cade told me later that he had hoped to be appointed to the position of mine manager. I will have to keep an eye on him.

There was also a crowd of the local people, some dressed in bright coloured garments, to welcome Mr Cade, as by far the largest employer in the region he is very popular.

Williams took me to my bungalow where my staff were lined up to greet me. The steward, who is responsible for the smooth running of my home, is called Mensah; he speaks good English and seems to be a nice fellow; he comes from the south of the country, near the capital, Accra, and has worked at the mine for some time as steward for the manager of one of the previous companies before it was bought by Mr Cade. He produced a letter of recommendation from his former master, which, if true, showed him to be a most reliable fellow.

Yeboah, the cook, introduced himself in less than perfect English; he comes from a village not far from the mine. He said that he was well known to be an international cook, and he too, had a letter from his previous master. This said, and I must record it verbatim, 'Yeboah has worked for me as a cook for three years, during which time he has produced my meals entirely to his own satisfaction'. He was very proud of this, and I have to hope that he is never disabused of his conviction that this is a recommendation of the highest order.

I was surprised to find that I also have a gardener, called Felix, although I cannot imagine why, and he is responsible for the area around my bungalow. There are several flowering shrubs, some fruit trees, mangos lemons and pawpaws, a flowerbed with some rather sad marigolds, and a small area of what could optimistically be called lawn. His testimonial letter bore evidence of it having been kept close to the body of a manual worker in a hot, humid climate for some time, and was all but illegible due to sweat stains. I could decipher, however, that Felix had great confidence in his god, and that he was always willing to explain the failure of a plant as something for which he was not responsible. He too, spoke little English, but he seems to be a cheerful fellow.

The fourth member of my staff is Musa, the night watchman; he comes from the north of the country and speaks only a few words of English. Mensah told me that he is on duty outside my bungalow from six in the evening until six in the morning. He carries a wicked-looking spear and is seemingly well-equipped to protect me and my property from any attempted burglary by the local villains. Yeboah did say, however, that there has been no trouble lately, as the mine gives well-paid employment to a large proportion of the male population in the area.

This evening we ate dinner in the conference room of the headquarters bungalow, and Mr Cade introduced me to the other senior staff of the mine. He was very complimentary about my experience in South Africa, and said that the company was lucky to have got my services; and that he was certain that I would soon increase its profitability. I said that I was glad to be here, and that I looked forward to working with my new colleagues.

The chief chemist is Dr Franz Werner, a German; he is responsible for the process of extracting the maximum amount of gold from the ore. He seems to be a congenial fellow, and he said that he looked forward to processing the ore that he hoped that I would find in new pits.

The chief medical officer is Dr George Thomas; he is not much older than I, and is here to gain experience in an environment without much of the basic equipment that he would have at home. Apart from dealing with injuries to the mine workers he has set up a clinic to which the local people can bring their cuts, sprains and other problems.

The chief engineer is Cameron, a Scot; he was introduced without a first name and I did not like to ask why. He has spent some time in South Africa before moving to the Gold Coast, including a few months in Witwatersrand, but that was before I was there, when most of the gold was found by panning, and before the discovery of major seams necessitated the use of pits and sophisticated equipment. He not only is responsible for keeping all the mining machinery in good working order, and there is a lot of it, but also deciding the best places to sink new shafts.

Williams was also there, and I gained the impression that the others had much the same opinion of him that I had formed on our brief meeting on my arrival. He is responsible for the day-to-day organisation of the workers, the provision of food and water and the transport. He reports to me as mine manager, and I am sure that if something goes wrong he will seek to lay the blame at my door.

The last member of the management team is the chief of security, Sgt. Miller; he used to work in London in the Metropolitan Police. He was not present at the meeting as he was evidently escorting a shipment of gold to Takoradi.

After dinner I returned to my bungalow, being careful to let Musa know that it was I who was coming and not a potential thief. I have a large living room, with a desk, a small dining table and two armchairs, a small bedroom, a shower room and an even smaller kitchen. Mensah tells me that when I wish to eat in the conference room, I should tell him and he will tell Mr Cade's cook, for it is he who prepared our meal this evening, but that the managers usually eat in their own bungalows during the week, since their hours of work vary, and in the conference room at weekends.

It has been a full day, and I have already learned a lot; tomorrow I will get to see the actual operation, and that is what I am really looking forward to.

24th July

The working day starts early here at the mine, and Mensah woke me with a cup of tea at half past six. Yeboah produced scrambled eggs and toast and marmalade at seven, and by half past I was in the conference room where Mr Cade met me and said that he was going to give me a conducted tour of the workings.

In the same building as the conference room there is a bedroom, a shower room and a study where Mr Cade stays when he visits the mine. There is also my office and a comfortable lounge, equipped with a full-size billiards table, where the latest newspapers and magazines from England can be read. On its shelves there are a number of books, some of which are about West Africa in general and the Gold Coast in particular, and I will certainly read some of those. A well-equipped kitchen completes the facilities available to the managers.

Around this building are the six bungalows occupied by the four managers, the mine superintendent and the chief of security, who I have yet to meet. There is another bungalow set a little further from the group which is used by visitors. All the buildings are in a clearing about two hundred yards across and are some distance from the mine workings.

The workings are spread over a large area, due to there having been a number of different companies and individuals on the site before Mr Cade bought them and formed the AGC. The previous prospectors did not have the resources to sink deep shafts and they worked pits, as I had done in Witwatersrand. Some of these are still producing a little gold, but the main activity is centred on two shafts which have been sunk since Mr Cade took over.

There were two substantial buildings and some impressive machinery in the centre of the area being worked. One building is where the chief engineer has an office in which he keeps plans of all the workings, a large well-equipped workshop and a storeroom housing the tools and spares necessary to keep the machinery up to scratch. The other building contains an office and the equipment where the chief chemist extracts the gold from of the crushed ore. The crusher is close by; it is fed ore from a moving belt, and when the resulting gravel is washed and the unwanted rock removed it is moved on another belt into this building.

Mr Cade took me into this building, which was guarded by one of the company's armed police, and Franz Werner showed me some of the latest gold that had been recovered. Mr Cade explained that at the end of each day the gold is taken to the strong room which was built into the bungalow of the chief of security, Sergeant Miller, and when a certain value was reached, usually once a month, it is sent by train to Takoradi to be put on the next sailing to England.

We then went to the heads of the two shafts that are currently being worked. These are not as well-equipped as those at Witwatersrand, and the lifts that carry the workers to and from the working level were fairly basic affairs, reflecting the lack of capital available to the original prospectors. The gold-bearing ore is brought to the surface by a winch in large iron buckets, and this device is driven by a steam engine.

Tomorrow I will descend one of the shafts and try to see whether it is being worked in a way that maximises the amount of gold recovered.

31st July

During the last week, I have familiarised myself with all the parts of the operation for which I am responsible, and have got to know the other managers; they are a good bunch, and I think that we can all work together to improve the profitability of the mine.

Mr Cade is leaving for England next week, and he has told me that he has every confidence that I will soon be able to see what changes are necessary to increase the amount of gold recovered. I have spent some time with the chief engineer, looking at his plans of the workings, and I am getting to understand the geology of the area beneath the surface. This may make it possible to predict where the vein with richest ore is to be found. But this is far from certain, and if a new shaft is sunk based on my judgement and no gold found, a lot of time, effort and money will have been wasted and my reputation will not be enhanced; I will take no chances, but equally I must show that I really am an asset to the company.

12th August

Mr Cade left for Takoradi and England this morning, so I now really have to show my colleagues that his faith in me is justified. I have been able to make a few minor changes to the way in which the two shafts are worked, but these have been more to improve the safety of the workers than to increase their output. Needless to say, Mr Williams resents anything that I do that he feels reflects badly on his responsibilities, and he would be delighted to see me make a mistake.

I have read several of the books in the managers' lounge about the Gold Coast, and I am particularly interested in the birds and animals in the country. There are evidently many elephants here and in the Ivory Coast, the country to the west of us, and also some pygmy hippopotami. There are any number of antelopes in the open grassland to the north, and some large rodents in the forest. There are several types of monkey, wild pigs, crocodiles and a variety of snakes, including pythons and very poisonous mambas and vipers. Large flocks of grey parrots inhabit the tallest trees, and some of them, when captured and kept as pets, very soon learn to mimic the voices of their hosts. The chief engineer has one in his office, and it repeats some of his choicest comments in a passable imitation of his Scottish accent.

30th August

I have discovered that George Thomas, the company doctor, or chief medical officer to give him his title, shares my interest in the local wildlife, and he has made several forays into the forest around the mine. He has very sensibly not ventured far from the workings by himself, and so has seen very little except the parrots, but he has asked me whether I would join him in a more ambitious expedition, for which we would need a native guide.

I said that I would be glad to go with him, and told him of my abortive efforts to climb to the top of Table Mountain, and how our guide there had saved the day when Rodney fell and damaged his leg. I said that I did not think that we should ask Williams who might be a suitable guide, for he was just as likely to arrange that we were lost in the forest. We agreed that we would both try to find someone who understands some English and knows the area.

20th September

Today I got a letter from Hermione, and I was delighted to learn that I am an uncle to Penelope. Hermione sounds so happy, and is especially glad that she has Mary to help her with the children. She says that Mama is not in the best of health, but that she loves the children dearly, and comes to see them almost every day.

I have now been here for almost two months, and I am really enjoying my work; I have not yet made any great improvement to the mine's output, but some of the small administrative changes that I have introduced, despite Williams' disapproval, are improving the efficiency of the workforce.

My cook, Yeboah, has recommended his cousin, Aggrey, as a suitable guide for the proposed expedition with George Thomas. Aggrey lives in a village about six miles from the mine, and has been a hunter all his life, providing food for his family and making a living by selling parrots and small animals as pets to Europeans. Yeboah assures me that Aggrey knows every path in the forest, and that he will be able to show us all the different animals and birds.

George has had no luck in finding a suitable guide, so we have asked Yeboah to get his cousin to come and meet us.

23rd September

Today we met Aggrey. When I got back to my bungalow after work he was in the kitchen with Yeboah, who proudly introduced him as the best guide and hunter in the region. I sent Mensah to get George, and together we tried to determine whether Aggrey was a suitable guide.

He is a small, wiry little fellow, obviously very strong and fit, and said in rather broken English that he would be proud to show us all the birds and animals in his forest, and that he could provide us with bush meat for a week if we wished. We said that we could only get away for two days at the most, and that anyhow we had not thought to spend a night in the forest. Aggrey said that in only one day he could not show us very many animals, and he then spoke with Yeboah in their language for two or three minutes.

Yeboah then told us that if we could spend one night out his cousin would provide two porters to carry our tents and sleeping bags, and that he, Yeboah, would accompany us and cook our meals. George said that small tents were indeed available in the company store, and that he could find groundsheets. It seemed to me that we would be sorely lacking in most creature comforts, but I was excited at the thought of what we might see.

We agreed a very reasonable sum for the services of Aggrey and the two porters and said that provided that the rains had finished we would set off in ten days' time. When Franz Werner and Cameron learned of our plan, they both said that we were ill-advised to penetrate deep into the forest, and that if we were not murdered by the porters, we would probably die of snake bites. I am somewhat concerned that Williams thought it an excellent plan, and I have to wonder whether he sees it as an opportunity to get rid of me.

He is not a pleasant fellow, and his morals leave much to be desired. A few days ago, I saw a young African girl, perhaps twenty years old, leaving his bungalow early in the morning; he told me later that she is a good friend of his, and he was sure that she would be a good friend of mine if I wanted. I told him in no uncertain terms that I did not want such friends, and that I did not think that his behaviour reflected well on the senior staff at the mine.

4th October

We returned yesterday from our expedition into the forest, and I know now why it is called a rain forest. We set off early on Saturday morning with Yeboah, Aggrey and the two porters. We were well-equipped to spend a night under the trees; George had found a two-man tent, groundsheets and sleeping bags, and Yeboah brought enough food for a couple of days. George had also brought a bottle of whisky; I did not ask where he had got it, as beer was the only alcohol allowed on the mine.

When we left the mine after a night of heavy rain, the weather was perfect; the sun shone and the temperature was in the high seventies, and although the humidity was high it was not unpleasant. I was surprised how soon Aggrey led us off the road onto a track into the forest. The tall trees shaded us from the sun, and as Aggrey and the porters hacked back the vegetation threatening to obscure the track the going was easy.

Very soon we saw many different birds, including the grey parrots, and George wrote a brief description of each species in his notebook. Aggrey pointed out where elephants had rubbed themselves against trees, and we saw their dung, but there was no sign of them. By noon we came to the edge of the forest and the land ahead was much more like the South African savannah. Here there were several different antelopes and a number of wild pigs. While we stopped for a rest and a light lunch provided by Yeboah, Aggrey and the porters went ahead to look for signs that the elephants were in our area. I did, for one brief moment, wonder whether we would ever see them again, and I rather doubted whether we would find our way back to the mine ourselves without them, but my doubts were dispelled when Aggrey returned with one of the porters. He said that the elephants were about an hour's journey ahead of us, where they were slaking their thirst on the banks of a small lake. Also, there were two pygmy hippopotami and several crocodiles. He had left the other porter there in case the elephants moved off before we got there.

Yeboah packed up his cooking equipment and we set off, Aggrey carrying the load of the absent porter. What had been an hour's journey for him turned out to be almost two for us, but when we reached the lake we were delighted to find that the elephants, seven of them led by an old female, were still there. They rolled in the mud on the edge of the lake; Aggrey said that this was because when it dried, the mud protected their skin from the sun.

While we watched them they moved off, back into the forest beyond the lake; we thought that we should move on, but Aggrey told us to wait, and sure enough the two pygmy hippopotami came out of the reeds only a stone's throw from us. I have seen normal hippos in the zoo at home, but these were much smaller, about twice the size of a good ram and much more heavily built. They were equally at home on the land or in the water, and we watched them for about an hour; before we left we saw a number of crocodiles on the edge of the lake.

By this time sunset was only an hour away; since we are close to the equator it sets at around six o'clock throughout the year. Aggrey said that we should find a good spot for our overnight camp, and he chose a place on the edge of the forest where we would be sheltered if it rained during the night. George and I managed to erect our tent and Yeboah lit a fire and started to prepare our evening meal. Aggrey and the porters made a shelter roofed with palm fronds and gathered enough wood to keep the fire going through the night; this would keep away some of the many mosquitos and other insects and hopefully deter any larger game or snakes from disturbing our sleep.

Yeboah served all of us with an excellent stew, consisting of guineafowl and a number of vegetables, some of which he had brought with him and some which he found near our camp. Fresh pineapple completed the meal, and after a mug of coffee laced with some of George's whisky we retired to our tent. I sincerely hoped that I would not have to leave the relative safety of the tent during the night. Sleep did not come quickly, but when it did it was a deep sleep and I was awoken at shortly after six the next morning by the sound of Yeboah starting to prepare breakfast; this consisted of scrambled egg, toast and marmalade, just as he often made for me back at the mine. A mug of strong coffee completed the meal, and by seven o'clock we were ready to move on.

Our path now took us through thick scrub, and Aggrey and the porters were kept busy clearing it with their machetes. They had told us that we might see leopards, although I thought that the noise of our progress would probably scare them away. About half an hour after we set off it started to rain; at first it was not heavy but within minutes it was torrential; the porters slung the groundsheet over a couple of branches and the six of us huddled there for about an hour until the rain eased off. We were all soaked to the skin, for the groundsheet had several times slipped off the supporting branches, but the sun had reappeared and it was not cold and Aggrey said that we should press on.

The chance of seeing any big game was now much reduced, since the animals had probably taken shelter in the thick forest, but the chance of being bitten by a poisonous snake was much increased. The rain had driven them from their usual hiding places and they were drying off in any patch of sunshine that they could find. Some of these were on or near the path, and Aggrey told us to watch out for them, and in the course of an hour or so we saw five or six snakes of at least three kinds, all of which looked extremely dangerous. Both of us were sensibly wearing high, leather boots but were still keen to avoid encounters with reptiles or any other forest dwellers.

Aggrey told us that we were now heading back in the rough direction of the mine, and since there was no chance of a hot meal, or even a mug of coffee, as there was no dry wood for Yeboah to make a fire, we only stopped for a short rest before we set off again. I have to admit that I was looking forward to a hot bath in the relative luxury of my bungalow.

It was then that the prospect of a hot bath was suddenly moved further into the future. As we came out of a patch of forest, our path led straight into a small, very fast-flowing river. Aggrey explained that what was usually a fordable stream had been fed by the recent rain further up country, and it was not possible for us to cross. There was nothing to do but follow the river downstream, although it was not flowing towards the mine.

I was concerned that we would run out of daylight, and that when we did not turn up at the mine a search party would be sent out to look for us. This would not do my reputation any good, so it was with great relief that we came upon a small village. It was on the opposite side of the river, but the villagers had strung a stout rope across, and since the water was only about three feet deep it was possible to cross. The water was very fast flowing, and without the rope we would have been swept away; as it was, we were soaked to the skin once more, but the porters managed to keep our kit dry and Yeboah balanced most of his load on his head.

Aggrey knew this village well; it was only five or six miles from his own, and he said that there was a good track to the mine, since several of the villagers worked there. One of the villagers told Aggrey that there was indeed at least one leopard in the area, and that it had taken several of their goats. The going was now much easier, although the rain had turned the murram surface of the track into a layer of slippery mud. Darkness fell before we reached the mine, happily also before our absence had been noticed. We paid off Aggrey and the porters, and George and I finished off his bottle of whisky. It had been a good expedition; we had seen elephants, crocodiles, pygmy hippos, wild pigs and any number of antelopes and birds, and George had sketches of many of them. We would very much have liked to see a leopard, and I hope that George and I may be able to make another expedition before too long.

We have learned at first-hand, that Africa is unpredictable, and that we were wise to hire Aggrey and the porters; without them we would probably not have seen so many animals and might never have found our way out of the forest. I will not be mentioning this in my next letter home, as Mama in particular would fear for my safety, and Papa would wonder if I was right to undertake such an expedition.

8th October

Today I wrote to Hermione, saying how glad I was to hear that she had a daughter, Penelope; I am so much looking forward to seeing my sister and her children, but I fear that it will be some time before I can return to Broadlands. I am pleased that Mary is being such a help with the children; she always was a cheerful soul and I am glad that having her child out of wedlock has not prevented her from having a happy life.

I told Hemione about my work and my colleagues here, and that I get on well with them; and I also said that I did not like Williams much. If I am to make a success of my position here it will be in spite of him and not with his help.

4th January 1903

We saw the New Year in with a senior staff party; the cooks produced a splendid meal, and the company rule regarding alcohol was relaxed for the occasion and this brought out some unexpected talents. Cameron — I still do not know his first name — has a fine singing voice, and did credit to a rendering of Auld Lang Syne. Franz Werner surprised us by proving to be a talented magician and performed a number of amazing tricks. George recited some of the Rime of the Ancient Mariner, by Samuel Taylor Coleridge; he would have recited the whole of that lengthy poem, but we all applauded enthusiastically after about ten verses and George got the message.

Sergeant Miller, our chief of security, is the person that I have seen least of. He is responsible for ensuring that the workers do not smuggle any gold out of the mine and that all the gold produced finds its way safely to Takoradi for onward transport to London. He usually keeps himself to himself but came out of his shell on this occasion and entertained us by recounting some of the more dramatic cases that he was involved with before he retired.

I was at a loss to know what I could contribute until I suddenly thought of *Last Man Standing*. I set out eighteen matches on the table, explained the rules of the game, and said that I would give a pound to anyone who could beat me. This opportunity was too good for Williams to resist, and he sat down opposite me. Needless to say, it was only a few minutes before he took the last match; he got up with ill-grace and tried to imply that I had cheated; since it was obvious to all that it was not possible to cheat he was told not to be a bad loser, and one-by-one, the others took me on and lost. Miller said that he thought that he remembered dealing with a case involving an allegation of obtaining money by false pretences made by a loser in this game in London, but he had never been let into the secret of the game.

The party ended at about three o'clock in the morning, and when I went to bed I was very glad to know that I did not have to get up in three hours' time; it is rare to have a holiday at the mine, but New Year's Day is one that we do have.

10th January 1903

The performance of the mine is assessed every six months, and today Franz gave us the result for the most recent period; this showed that the production of gold had risen steadily during the last six months of the past year. I would like to think that this was because of my arrival, but in fact it is mostly due to the many small workings all being brought under one management. I have had some success in suggesting which veins to follow up and which to ignore, but I need to do more than that if Mr Cade's confidence in me is to be justified. I have a feeling that there is a rich vein somewhere under our feet, and I need to find it.

15th February

George and I have decided that we must try to see the leopard that has been reported by several of the villages within a few miles of the mine. The rainy season has now passed, and we should be able to make good time on foot to the area where we would be most likely to see it. Mensah has told his friend Aggrey of our wish and he came to see us yesterday. He said that if we were willing to pay for a goat he was sure that we would be successful, and explained what we should do.

He would get the villagers closest to where the leopard was last seen to build a platform in a tree, with some cleared ground around it. A goat would be tethered to a stake in the cleared ground not far from the tree, and before nightfall we would settle ourselves on the platform. When it got dark, the goat would surely bleat, and this would attract the leopard; we would be equipped with torches and would get a fine close-up view of the creature before it vanished into the dark.

George thought this a fine plan and congratulated Aggrey; he enquired as to the cost of a goat, and asked how soon the platform could be built, as we did not want the leopard to move away from its present hunting ground. I had made no comment, and George asked if I was not in favour of the plan. I said that it was well thought out, but that I had one concern, and that was that leopards are well-known for their ability to climb trees, where they usually store their kills to prevent them from being eaten by hyenas, jackals, wild boar and vultures. I said that I felt that the leopard might prefer us to the goat, and that I was not confident that we could repel it if it climbed our tree, since we would be armed with nothing more lethal than our torches.

George admitted that he had not thought of that; Aggrey said that he felt sure that the two brave Englishmen would be more than a match for the leopard; I said that there was no way that I was going to offer myself as bait, and so we are no nearer seeing one than we had been. Perhaps there will be another chance, but for the moment we have no plan.

23rd February

I have lately spent a lot of time with Cameron, studying the many maps and charts which show the shafts and where all the pits were worked. Taken together it is possible to see in which rough direction productive veins run, but they give little indication of the depth at which they can be found. We have recently had delivered a large, steam-driven boring machine, ordered by Mr Cade in London, and this produces a circular shaft some six feet across, but it is a slow business, and much time is taken changing the cutters, which have to be resharpened frequently, especially when hard rock is encountered.

A small river runs through one side of the company's concession, and the recent flooding due to the heavy rain has brought a lot of new gravel to the surface, and now that the water level has fallen again about a quarter of our workers are now engaged in panning. This brings a real risk of small flakes of gold, and the occasional nugget, being stolen by the workers and hidden about their bodies when they finish work. Sergeant Miller and his policemen keep a sharp eye on the panners, but it is not possible to search every worker every day, and if it was done that would surely cause resentment.

The tunnels that radiate out from the shafts at various levels, some horizontal and some angled upwards or down, follow the ore-bearing veins until the amount of gold recovered is so little as not to be worth the time and effort. It is Franz's responsibility to say when work in a particular tunnel should be discontinued, and this is becoming ever more frequent. He has asked me more than once where I think that the next shaft should be sunk, but I am unwilling to make a recommendation until I am sure that I am right.

10th April

Today we had some very unpleasant news from London. When our last shipment of six boxes of gold was opened, one of them was found to contain not gold but a piece of iron. The difference in weight had not been noticed, neither had the seal on the box; instead of the company's seal, new wax had been impressed with a local coin of the same size, and since it was intact it had passed the cursory inspections by Sergeant Miller and the ship's purser. Needless to say, Mr Cade is far from happy, and has directed that the thief be identified and the gold recovered.

There are only two keys to the strongroom; they are different, and both must be used at the same time to open the door. I have one of them and the other is held by Williams. I have previously questioned why he has one, and not Sgt. Miller, and was told that it was thought unwise for him to have one since the strongroom is in his bungalow, and if he was overpowered by thieves they would have immediate access to one of the keys. I keep my key with me attached to the belt in which my diamonds are hidden, which I wear at all times.

11th April

As mine manager, I have assumed responsibility for the investigation, and naturally first asked Williams if his key had at any time been out of his possession. He swore that it had not and I had no proof otherwise. The only time that mine is not physically in my possession is when I am showering, and although I was loath to suspect Mensah or Yeboah, I was obliged to question them. Mensah said that on one occasion when I was in the shower,

Williams had asked him to let him have my key for a short time as he wanted to make sure that it had not been tampered with or copied. Williams had returned it within minutes, and Mensah had replaced it on my belt and not thought to mention it to me when I came out of the shower.

I went straight to get Sergeant Miller, and together we confronted Williams. He swore that he knew nothing of the theft, but a search of his room revealed a partially-used stick of red sealing wax, a crude but serviceable copy of my key, and a coin, on which Franz later detected traces of the sealing wax, all concealed in a pair of socks. Sergeant Miller took Williams straight to the mine's gaol, a fairly basic affair which usually only contains workers found trying to steal flakes of gold, and told him that he would remain there until the next visit by Mr Cade, when he would then be tried in accordance with local law, which might involve the death penalty.

Sergeant Miller is particularly embarrassed by this incident, for he accompanied the gold to Takoradi and handed it over to the ship's purser; he thought that Mensah was probably Williams' accomplice in the theft, but I felt certain that he was not, and when I returned to my bungalow, he told me that he realised how stupidly he had acted and said that he expected to be dismissed. I said that I was disappointed in him but that I did not think that he knew what Williams was up to and that he would keep his job but that he should learn by his mistake.

14th April

With Williams in gaol I have taken on his duties; they are mostly administrative, rostering the workers to the shafts, pits and panning, arranging the transport of gold and staff to and from Takoradi, and ensuring that the managers' servants are working satisfactorily. He also collects the mail for the London office and makes sure that it catches the next boat that called at Takoradi northbound.

I am glad to have this additional responsibility, as it gives me a greater understanding of the overall operation, but it will not stop me from my principal duty which is to find new veins and improve the profitability of the AGC.

20th April

All our efforts to find the missing gold have been unsuccessful until today, when Williams told Sergeant Miller that it was hidden beneath a floorboard in his bungalow. He is not finding the conditions in the gaol to his liking, and the fear of the death penalty has made him eager to cooperate.

I have written to Mr Cade, telling him that the gold has been recovered intact, and asking what he wanted done with Williams. It will be some time before I get a reply and this will enable Williams to reflect on his position. He has confirmed that he acted alone, and that Mensah did not know why he wanted my key.

15th May

A couple of days ago when I went out onto the verandah to have my breakfast I was surprised to find a small snake coiled up on one of the chairs. I had not seen one of this sort before and so consulted my book of West African snakes. This enabled me to identify it as a young Gaboon Viper, a very poisonous reptile. Although less than two feet long it was broad for its length, and a picture of an adult in my book showed it would grow to be five- or six- feet long. I pushed it off the chair with a stout stick, and as it glided across the lawn, I despatched it with several blows to the head. Felix had been watering the plants and was much impressed by my swift action; he said that it was a very bad snake, very dangerous, and that I was brave to kill it.

Yesterday when I returned from work I was strolling round the garden, looking to see whether the pawpaws were yet ripe, when Felix excitedly called me to come and showed me the mother or father of the snake that I had killed, coiled at the base of one of the lemon trees. This was very much larger, very much broader, and a different proposition altogether, and I thought that belabouring it with a mere stick would be unlikely to do it any serious harm and might irritate it, with serious consequences. Felix encouraged me to deal with it, but I told him that I had shown him how to kill bad snakes only yesterday, and that it was his job, not mine.

By this time, Mensah and Yeboah had come to see the fun, and the snake had made its way to the relative shelter of the flower beds. Felix went to get his machete, and with much excited shouting and trampling of the flowers the snake was driven into the open where its head was cut off. I gave Felix a small reward, and when he went off-duty he took the corpse with him.

This evening, when I told Franz of this while we enjoyed a beer, he told me that Felix had passed the snake to Charles' gardener, who had told

Charles that he had killed it in his garden, for which he was duly be rewarded. It was then passed to Cameron's gardener, where it earned a further small reward, and then via Williams' gardener to Franz's. Franz said that he had not questioned its provenance and had made a final donation. Whether or not the snake was eaten, it has made a useful addition to the wages of all four gardeners.

7th June

It is five years to the day since Ryneker sailed from Cape Town and out of my life. I often think of her, and I wonder if she ever thinks of me. If she had stayed in South Africa and we were married, she would have been a great help when I had the store, and later the hotel, but this place is no place for a woman, and there would be nothing with which to occupy her while I was at work. In fact I could not have taken on this job, and I doubt whether I would have found as good a position had I stayed in Jo'burg. I hope that she is happy and I am sure that by now she is married and has a family.

10th July

Today I got two letters from England. Mama is dead; she has for some time had difficulty breathing but has borne it bravely. I cannot imagine Broadlands without her, and I know that Papa and Hermione will miss her terribly. It is good that Quentin can be there for the funeral and to help Papa with some of the arrangements; I only wish that there was something that I could do. I will write to both of them tomorrow.

The other letter was from Mr Cade; he congratulated me on arresting Williams and recovering the gold. He says that I have justified his faith in me, and he has generously increased my salary, since I have taken on Williams' duties. There is, of course, very little here on which to spend it, and so most of my salary accumulates in my account with my bank in London, with just a few pounds each month paid locally for expenses such as hiring Aggrey and buying goats.

Mr Cade wants Williams to be sent back to England to be tried there. I went to see him and tell him of this and he was relieved that he would be getting out of the local gaol, where I have to say that the conditions are very unsanitary. I told him that because he had eventually co-operated in telling us where the gold was hidden, and because no attempt had been made to dispose of it, I would write a letter to be given to the judge when he was tried, suggesting some clemency in his sentence. In England he will escape the noose, but may endure some years of hard labour.

Mr Cade will be paying another visit to the mine at the end of December, so I hope that by then I will have done enough to justify his faith in me.

12th August

If I was at home, we would today be celebrating the first day of the grouse shooting season, the Glorious Twelfth; as it is I am abed, laid low with malaria. I have been taking the quinine tablets that Charles gives to all the managers, but this does not always prevent a mild case of the illness. I have no appetite, all my muscles ache and although I am sweating profusely yet I shiver. Charles says that I should feel better in a couple of days, so I will put down my pencil and try to get some rest.

16th August

I am feeling much better today and left my sickbed for my office. While I was unwell, I have had some ideas as to where we might find a new vein of gold-bearing ore, and I have got Cameron to make copies of his maps of several areas around where we are now mining. However, as soon as I started to look at them I suffered a blinding headache, so it seems that my recovery is not yet complete and I have returned to my bungalow.

20th August

I am once again fully fit and able to do a proper day's work. Nothing much has changed with the mining operation, but the paperwork has accumulated and it will be a day or two before I can clear my desk. I went to see Williams this afternoon; he is not in good shape and I wonder whether he will survive to stand trial later this year. I have asked Sgt. Miller to arrange for him to be able to take some exercise outside each day, provided that he is accompanied by one of his armed policemen.

3rd October

One of our shafts continues to produce well, but in the other, the gold is almost exhausted; some of the pits are producing satisfactorily but very little gold is being found by the panners and I have put them back to work in the better of the two shafts. There are now tunnels leading off the shaft in several directions and at different levels, but I am concerned that when these veins run dry there will be very little production.

4th November

What a day! I was checking that the shaft that we are no longer using was not flooding, for if it did it could make it dangerous to work the nearby pits. All was well and I made my way along one of the tunnels leading off the shaft. At the end, there had been a fall of rock from the roof of the tunnel and I was about to turn back when the light from my torch caused a glitter from the newly-exposed rock face.

I thought that this was probably what they call Fool's Gold, an iron ore that looks very similar to gold-bearing rock, but I broke off a piece and put it in my pocket to be shown to Franz. He was cautiously optimistic when he saw it, but said that he would have to test it to be certain that it was the real thing. He broke my bit of rock into small pieces and put some into a beaker of chemicals. After a short time, a broad grin transformed his usually expressionless face and he slapped me on the back. "It is gold, Frobisher," he said. "Now I must see what the yield will be." We agreed that we would say nothing to our colleagues about my find until he had completed his analysis and I left him to his work.

When he came into the lounge that evening, straight from his laboratory, he said that the gold content was about twenty-five percent higher than anything that we had previously found. Charles, Cameron and Sgt. Miller congratulated me and we celebrated with a few beers. I will go to bed a very happy man, but it remains to be seen whether this is the beginning of a new vein, the tail end of the one already worked, or merely an isolated gold-bearing area. I have a feeling that the former is the case and that my good fortune continues.

5th November

The news has already spread among our workers that a rich new vein has been found, and they all want to work on it. As yet we do not know how long or broad it may be, but from the rock brought to the surface today it looks as though we may be in luck. I have sent a report on the finding to Mr Cade and I am sure that he will be as pleased as we all are. He will be leaving London for Obuasi very soon, and may not get my letter before he leaves, and if so, it will be nice to be able to welcome him here with good news.

14th November

The new vein, which the workers now call 'Frobisher's Find', is producing well, and it is becoming possible to see in which direction it extends. If it continues in a relatively straight line I will have to decide where to sink a new shaft; if that hits the vein then we can access it from both ends and increase the production of gold.

25th November

I have decided where the new shaft should be and work started on it this morning. Hopefully, the boring machine will not break down, for it will take a lot longer to excavate the shaft by hand.

28th November

The boring machine has broken down, possibly terminally, and we have to complete the shaft by digging and blasting. Meanwhile, the work at the front of the tunnel from the original shaft is continuing at a good pace, and I estimate that it is about half-way to the new shaft's position. It remains to be seen whether my calculation for the position of the new shaft is correct; I very much hope that it is.

3rd December

Today, at the bottom of the new shaft, we found what must surely be the same vein that I found it a month ago. The ore looks very similar, and Franz has confirmed that the gold content is as high or higher than in the piece that I originally found; also it looks as though the vein is quite broad. We have to dig down a further five or six feet, so that the workers can work the vein as easily and efficiently as possible, but we should be able to start bringing out the ore in two or three days. Mr Cade is due to land at Takoradi on 20th December, so we should be able to give him a good Christmas present.

10th December

The new shaft is now in full production. I have devised a more efficient way of bringing the ore to the surface, and the vein is being worked towards the original shaft. I estimate that the two tunnels should meet in three or four days and it will then be a case of excavating them to the full width of the vein. At the same time we are excavating the vein in the opposite direction, and we hope that it will prove to be long and wide.

22nd December

Mr Cade arrived yesterday evening and I need hardly say how pleased he is with the progress at the mine since his last visit. He said that Ted Harris had told him that I had a nose for gold when he met him in Witwatersrand, and that I have certainly proved him right. He went on to say that he thought that I could be of even greater value to the AGC if I had a wider responsibility than just at Obuasi, and he offered me a position on the Board of Directors in the head office in London. My job would be to improve the profitability of their existing mines, and to suggest where new investments should be made.

I was very surprised by this, but I am also very pleased that my contribution to the profitability of this mine has been recognised, and I know that Papa will be very proud of me. It means that I will return to England sooner than I had expected, and that with the salary that goes with my new position I will be able to help Papa with restoring Broadlands.

My colleagues have all congratulated me on my promotion, and George said that without me he would never see a leopard. Cameron said that he hoped that I would find another rich vein or two before I left, and Franz said that he needed some new testing equipment and hoped that in my new position I could approve his request.

I have suggested to Mr Cade that Ted Harris be considered as my replacement here. His claims, my old claims, must be almost worked out by now, and he is certainly well-qualified; Mr Cade agrees and is going to write to him and offer him the position. If he accepts I will be so glad to have been able to repay him for the good word that he put to Mr Cade about me.

26th December

Our Christmas dinner yesterday was a very jolly affair. Mr Cade had very kindly brought a small present for each of us, and had bought a case of champagne from the store in Takoradi. This year we did have roast turkey, for many of them are to be found wild in the open country to the north of here.

Most of our African workers were gathered outside the headquarters building and were delighted when Mr Cade told them that as a result of the much-improved profitability of the mine they would all be getting an extra week's pay this month. The head labourer, who is a son of the chief in his own village, made a very grateful response to this good news in his halting English, and said that his men were proud to work for such a good boss and that he would see that they worked even harder in the year to come, at which they all cheered.

3rd January 1904

Today we had a most unusual visitor. Obuasi is in the Asante, or Ashanti region of the Gold Coast; the regional capital is the town of Kumasi, some thirty miles from Obuasi. The region has a long history of military prowess and is a kingdom within the Gold Coast. Its ruler is the Asantahene, who has complete power and controls all aspects of the region. This includes the mining concession at Obuasi, which pays an annual fee to the Asantahene. The Asantes have been successfully finding gold for many years, and the ruler sits on a golden stool when in council. All this and more I learned from one of the books in the lounge.

Since the country became a British protectorate, there has been tension between Accra, the capital of the country, and Kumasi, the seat of the Asantahene, who arguably wielded more power than the British Governor. Four years ago, the Asantahene was sent into exile by the British and at the present time, the Asantes are ruled by his deputy, the Mamponghene, who is more cooperative with his colonial masters, although still wielding absolute power in his kingdom.

Our visitor was no lesser person than the Mamponghene. He came in his traditional dress, carried on a sort of sedan chair, with a considerable retinue, to thank Mr Cade for bringing employment and prosperity to Obuasi. He presented him with a beautifully carved wooden elephant made from a very dark wood; it was about a foot high and had ivory tusks and a gold throne on its back. Although Mr Cade had been given no advance notice of the visit, he responded by giving his host a gold fob watch on a gold chain. This was very much appreciated by the Mamponghene, who was greatly entertained by the movement of the second hand. Mr Cade told us later that he had had nothing to give his visitor, and so rather than insult him, and suffer a great loss of face, he had given him his own watch, which he felt sure that the AGC would replace.

4th January

Mr Cade left yesterday; he is going back to South Africa to follow up what may be an opportunity for the AGC. He says that he will come back to Obuasi before returning to England, and he may be here again before I leave. It will be some time before Ted Harris arrives, if he accepts Mr Cade's offer, and there is still much work for me to do here. It may be that the new vein can be accessed by yet another shaft, but it is not easy to say exactly where this should be sunk, and it would be a costly mistake if it missed the vein. I shall give much thought to this, and will be spending a lot of time poring over Cameron's charts.

Williams has been sent back to England and will probably be tried in a few months' time. Sergeant Miller and I have both provided written statements about the theft, and if I am back home in time I expect that I will be required to give evidence in person. I had to feel sorry for the wretched man when he was put on the train to Takoradi in irons, escorted by one of the company police; he has lost a great deal of weight, his hair is unkempt and his skin is unnaturally yellow; at least he will be better cared for in an English gaol.

30th January

Charles and I were drinking a beer or two together this evening when he told me of a recent medical experience. In November, one of the workers had suffered a deep cut on one of his thighs when he was struck by a piece of falling rock. The wound became an ulcer, and Charles treated it appropriately for three weeks; but it resolutely refused to heal, and Charles was at a loss as to what to try. The man came to him and said that he had got permission to go to his home town and see the doctor there.

We have all heard tales of the powers of the Ju-Ju practised by witch doctors, but most of them are too fanciful to be believed. Charles had a professional distrust of anything but the medicine that he was taught, but could not prevent the man from leaving.

Ten days later, the man reported to Charles at his clinic and said that he was healed. Doubting this, Charles rolled up the man's shorts and examined his thigh. There was some discolouration of the skin, but not even a scar where the ulcer had been. Much surprised, and not a little impressed, he asked the man how his doctor had treated the ulcer. He replied that bones and the leaves of some plants had been boiled together, and then a piece of cloth soaked in the liquid had been bound round his thigh; this had been done for six days, after which the wound was healed. There was no doubt that it was indeed healed, and Charles could no longer disbelieve tales of the powers of African medicine; he tried to find out what plants had been used, but the man said that he did not know their names and they did not grow near the mine, and so Charles could not find out what was so effective. But he did say that he would never scoff at Ju-ju again, and that if he knew the recipe he could make his name and his fortune back in England.

23rd February

In the post brought up from Takoradi today, there was a letter addressed to Mr Cade with a South African stamp; on the back, the sender was shown as Ted Harris. I was sure that Mr Cade would wish me to open it, and I did so. I was delighted to read that Ted has accepted Mr Cade's offer, and hopes to be at Obuasi sometime in May. He has sent the same letter to Mr Cade in London. This means that I should be able to leave for home in June, and I will send a letter to Papa tomorrow with the good news.

Now that I know when I shall be leaving here, I must make sure that I can hand over the mine in the best possible state when Ted arrives. The tunnels from the new shaft are producing well and I think that we should perhaps excavate the shaft deeper to see whether there may be another vein beneath the one that we are working.

10th March

We heard yesterday that a leopard has been seen just two or three miles from the mine. The forest there is not as thick as that we encountered on our earlier expedition, and Charles said that we must try to see it. I would very much like to do so before I leave and I asked Mensah to summon Aggrey.

When he came this afternoon he said that he knew the area where the leopard had been seen and that he was certain that he could show it to us. I said that we would not sit on a platform in a tree, waiting for it to attack us, and he said that that would not be necessary. His plan is actually very simple, and reminds me of pheasant shoots at Broadlands. When the leopard's position on the day is known, he will get a line of villagers to drive it towards us.

This sounds much more sensible, and my only concern is that it may attack us when it is cornered between us and the beaters. The only firearms on the mine are the rifles of Sergeant Miller's police, and I am far from confident that I could bring down a charging leopard with one of them. We could not give Aggrey cause to think us afraid and so we said that it was a good idea and that he should set it up for Saturday, in three days' time.

We asked how we would have to reward the beaters and he said that the price of two goats would be good. We agreed this, without enquiring as to the going rate for goats, and Aggrey left us, once again assuring us that we would see the leopard. I feel that he is probably right, and hope that it is not too close an encounter. Charles seems to have fewer reservations than I about this plan and I hope that he is right.

13th March

We have seen the leopard; Aggrey's plan worked perfectly. Soon after sunrise we set off on foot to the edge of the thick forest, just over a mile from the edge of the mine workings. Franz had joined us, but Cameron pleaded that urgent work was necessary repairing some machinery. Aggrey positioned the three of us about fifty yards apart on the edge of the thick forest with fairly open ground, where the leopard was thought to be in front of us. The scrub bushes and tall grass would make it impossible to see the animal if it was not moving, but it would have to break cover when the beaters approached it.

There was no sign or sound of the beaters until Aggrey blew a loud note on a cow horn. They were about half a mile from us, and as they advanced through the bush, they shouted and beat on drums and tin cans; we could not see them, but it sounded as though the whole village had turned out. The noise got louder as they approached us, and I was tense with anticipation as I scanned the scrub in front of me. When the beaters were only about a hundred yards from us, I thought that the leopard must either not have been where Aggrey thought or it had got away round the edge of the drive.

And then, there it was. It had reached edge of the scrub, about thirty yards away, between me and Charles. It seemed undecided as to what to do next; the beaters were close behind, making a considerable noise, and it had clearly seen the three of us. It moved very quickly along the edge of the cover, towards Franz, who did not know that we had seen it and shouted to draw our attention to it. His shout scared it, and it retraced its steps until it was once more between me and Charles; then it leapt from the cover and dashed between us for the safety of the forest behind us.

We were all excited and delighted by the success of Aggrey's plan, and when the villagers emerged from the scrub we told him to thank them for their bravery. The price of goats turned out to be more than we had expected, but so had the morning's entertainment and we were very pleased to have seen the leopard at such close quarters. We gave Aggrey two pounds and congratulated him on the success of his plan, and he assured us that he could show us any animal that we wished to see. Charles has made several rough sketches of the leopard and has said that when he has completed them he will give one to me as a memento of the day.

5th April

It is now probably only a month until Ted Harris arrives to take over from me and I am trying to make certain that everything is in good shape. The tunnels off the new shaft are producing well and Franz is very happy with the amount of gold that each ton of ore produces.

I had a letter from Mr Cade yesterday, saying that he was looking forward to me taking my place on the board of the AGC and that the other directors were keen to meet me. It will be strange to be working in London after nine years in Africa; I suppose that I will have to find lodgings, perhaps a small apartment. I will be able to go down to Broadlands at the weekends, and I cannot wait to see Papa, Hermione and my nephew and niece.

6th May

Ted Harris arrived yesterday. I met him off the train and introduced him to the other managers over a meal in the conference room. He told me that when the claim that he bought from me was exhausted, he had bought a share in another, but that he had missed the satisfaction of being his own master and seeing the results of his own efforts. He has moved into the bungalow that Williams had, but will move into mine when I leave.

Today I took him round the mine and showed him the old and new shafts and the few pits that we are still working. He said that some of the shafts in South Africa had now been sunk to considerable depths, but that they required very expensive machinery, and while we could keep a high rate of extraction it need not be considered here.

He is very much looking forward to working here, and is grateful to me for having suggested him to Mr Cade; I said that if he had not recommended me to Mr Cade in the first place neither of us would be here and I would not have got a place on the AGC board. We drank to our past and future success in our new positions.

20th May

Ted has settled in well, and has already taken over most of my administrative duties. He gets on well with the other managers, and has spent much time with Cameron getting, as he calls it, a feeling for the land beneath his feet. I will be surprised if he does not repeat my success and find a new vein.

I am due to sail from Takoradi a month from today, on 20th June, and I will start packing up my few possessions next week. I came to Africa with very little, and will be leaving with not much more. I have some nice, wooden carvings which I have bought locally, a small nugget from my first pit at Witwatersrand, a silver paper knife that I found in the ashes of the Kimberley store and my two diamonds.

I am glad to say that I have achieved my goal of returning to England with a full purse, for although I have next to nothing in the bank here, my account with my London bank is not inconsiderable, and I will be able to help Papa with the cost of restoring Broadlands.

7th June

It is seven years since I said goodbye to Ryneker, and although I think of her much less often than I used to, this date never passes unnoticed by me. I might have been returning to England with a wife, and possibly one or two children, and I would have been proud to introduce them to my family. Papa could not have failed to like Ryneker, and Hermione would have loved to have a sister-in-law. We could have done so many things together, but I must not dwell on the past and the impossible future. I was never short of female company before I left for Africa, and I must admit that I am looking forward to renewing some old acquaintances and making new friends.

15th June

I leave for Takoradi on the train tomorrow, and this evening there was a farewell dinner for me in the conference room. Mr Cade's cook produced a splendid meal, and some champagne had somehow been smuggled in. As has become traditional on such occasions, when the meal was over, everyone had to contribute to the party by singing, reciting or otherwise entertaining their fellow diners, but before that started, Franz stepped forward and presented me with a gift on behalf of all the mine's employees.

It was a small, golden replica of the traditional, wooden stools that are common in the Asante region. It was fashioned, so he said, from gold found in Frobisher's Find, and I asked Sergeant Miller if I should not report all concerned for misappropriating the AGCs gold. He agreed that that would be the correct procedure but said that the gaol was not large enough to contain all those involved, and he was not certain how he should arrest himself. I thanked them all for the gift, and said how much I had enjoyed working with them, and that any success of mine, was a success of the whole team.

Franz, Cameron, Charles and Sergeant Miller all reprised their previous party acts, and I was keen to see what Ted would do. Imagine my surprise when he said that he would show us a game that he had learned from a chap in a bar in Cape Town before he sailed for Takoradi; he said that the game was called *Last Man Standing*, and that he would be glad to take on any of us. He could not understand why this was received with much laughter, but no one told him why. I said that I would be glad to try my luck and eighteen matches were laid out on the table. I knew that if he really knew the secret of the game, there was a good chance that I would lose, but halfway through the game Ted hesitated and made the wrong move; three moves later he lost.

He was surprised and asked for a return match, but I put him out of his misery and admitted that I knew the game, and I asked where he had learned it. He said that he had been having a drink in a bar near the port and had seen a chap playing the game, winning consistently and taking their money off all his adversaries. Ted had thought that the man's face was familiar, and when he remembered where he had seen it he waited until there were no more challengers and asked if he could have a game. When inevitably he lost, he asked the man if he would tell him the secret. His request was refused.

Ted then told him where he had seen him before, not in person, but on a number of 'wanted' notices in Jo'burg. The man was much concerned and pleaded with Ted not to turn him in. Ted said that he wanted to know why he was wanted and Sidney, for it was no other, told him that he had escaped from the Port Elizabeth gaol and had thought that by putting some distance between him and his erstwhile captors he could safely take up his financial practises in Witwatersrand, where there were plenty of rich prospectors and law and order was fairly basic. It had not been long however, before his fraudulent activity came to the attention of the local police, who learned of his arrest and escape from the Port Elizabeth gaol, and his picture appeared on posters all over the town, with a reward offered for information leading to his capture. He had then made his way to Cape Town, whence he hoped to get a passage to Australia.

Ted was sailing on the following day and saw this as an opportunity to do well out of doing good. He made Sidney tell him the secret of *Last Man Standing* and gave him fifteen minutes to make himself scarce before he alerted the police. After the briefest lesson, Sidney made off and Ted told one of the docks police that he thought that he had recognised a wanted man in the bar. Before very long the area was swarming with police, and as Ted made his way to his hotel he saw Sidney being dragged from another bar.

Because his lesson had been brief Ted had not correctly remembered all of the winning moves, and that is why he lost had to me. Everyone wanted to know the secret, but I said that if they all knew it there would be no opportunity for any interesting games. I told Ted that he was nearly there, and that I was sure that he would soon remember how to finish the game off, and I told the others that it was quite possible to learn by trial and error. When I retired to my bungalow the evening of my last day at Obuasi ended with the entertaining prospect of my colleagues making many attempts to avoid being the *Last Man Standing*.

When I returned to my bungalow, I found all four of my staff waiting for me. Mensah came forward and said that I had been a good master and they were sorry that I was leaving. I was then given a very beautiful little, ivory elephant, which they said was carved by a man in Yeboah's village from the tusk of a dead elephant that had been found in the forest not far away. I thanked them sincerely for the gift and the service that they had given to me, and said that I had arranged that they would all have an extra week's wages. They all shook my hand, and to my embarrassment Musa threw himself on the ground at my feet. I pulled him up and told him to make sure that no one disturbed my last night's sleep. I went to bed and before I drifted off to sleep, I wondered whether the dead elephant was perhaps one of those that we had seen; I hoped not.

16th June

Ted drove me to the station at Obuasi this morning and before the train left, we wished each other every success in our new positions. He is a very hard worker and I have no doubt that he will serve the AGC well.

The train left on time, which is by no means always the case, and I was in the Rest House at Takoradi in time to enjoy a gin and tonic at six o'clock. I have arranged to have a few days on the coast before leaving for England, and I am looking forward to being able to relax on the glorious, sandy beach, which stretches as far as the eye can see in both directions.

17th June

It is a very nice change to have nothing of any import to record. I walked along the beach for about two miles in an easterly direction and the only souls that I saw were a couple of fishermen, casting their nets from their wooden canoe about three hundred yards offshore. I waved at them, and they waved back; they shouted something, but I could not make out what they said; possibly an invitation to buy their fish.

The Rest House is well furnished and the food is excellent; I should have torn myself away from the mine and spent a few days here at some time during the past two years. I know that Cameron came here several times, but there always seemed to be something that kept me at Obuasi. Tomorrow a southbound ship is due to stop here and discharge some machinery for one of the upcountry logging companies. This will be something to watch and I will be interested to see how it is brought ashore by lighter.

18th June

The *SS Doune Castle* dropped anchor at eight o'clock this morning, and I was glad to see once again the ship that carried me to Cape Town more than eight years ago. It seemed that most of the inhabitants of Takoradi had gathered on the beach to watch. I mingled with them and moved towards where the ship's boat was going to run ashore, probably to pick up some fresh meat, fruit and vegetables, as it had on my voyage.

When the boat was beached a white man, obviously one of the passengers, stepped ashore carrying a leather valise. He was met by a smartly-dressed African and led away. I was wondering who he might be when I felt a tug on my shirt-tail, and when I turned around, I saw a partly-dressed girl with a large, white, enamel basin full of fruit balanced on her head. "Master," she said, "you give me white baby I give you pineapple." It was all that I could do not to burst out laughing; this was either the same lass who had propositioned my sailor friend all those years ago, or she was not the same and this may be an approach that has been tried by some of the local girls ever since white men first landed at their town, for a paler skin is evidently much respected. I declined her offer as kindly as I could and gave her a few coins for a pineapple and some pawpaws. Hermione will enjoy this story but I will not tell Papa.

When I returned to the Rest House I found the recent arrival from the ship sitting on the verandah perspiring heavily, enjoying a cold beer. He introduced himself as Trevor Roper and said that he was an engineer going to one of the logging companies to install the machinery that was offloaded from the ship. He said that he found the humidity very tiresome, and I did not have the heart to tell him that it was far, far worse in the forest upcountry.

The manager of the Rest House has been told by one of the crew who brought Mr Roper ashore, that the ship on which I am travelling is likely to be two or three days behind its schedule; he thought that this was because it had needed some repairs in Cape Town. I regret anything that delays my return home, but if I have to be delayed, this is as pleasant a place as any.

19th June

Trevor Roper left for Obuasi on the train this morning; he has not enjoyed his short stay here and I fear that he will enjoy even less the five or six weeks that he expects to stay at the logging camp; I hope for his sake that the machinery gets installed and up and running as soon as possible.

It was confirmed today that my ship will not be here until 22nd June, two days late; since there is nothing that I can do about it I will continue to enjoy this place. Today I walked for some distance along the beach in a westerly direction and was interested in the variety of items washed ashore by the tide. Some were obviously rubbish thrown overboard by ships and I thought this a pity, for the water was incredibly clear and it seemed that the rubbish desecrated it. There were bottles, none of them containing messages, wooden crates, coconuts and pieces of palm tree, a few dead fish, and what I took to be a dead porpoise. This had been dead for some time, and the smell had attracted crabs, gulls and rats. I gave it a wide berth and continued for another mile or so before retracing my steps.

21st June

The *SS Alnwick Castle* is confidently expected to arrive tomorrow; it is the same ship on which Mr Cade and I sailed from Cape Town almost two years ago; what a lot has happened since then. I shall be sorry to leave Africa, and this pleasant little town, but I am so much looking forward to getting home and seeing my family, and also to taking my place beside Mr Cade on the board of the AGC.

Chapter Eight
The Final Voyage

22nd June

The Alnwick Castle sailed from Takoradi at three in the afternoon, only four hours after her arrival there; two passengers disembarked and some provisions were taken on board. I have the cabin that Mr Cade had; it is probably the best of those for first class passengers and I suspect that Mr Cade specified it when he booked my passage. I have so much to thank him for, and I look forward to working with him in London. I have lost no time in entering for the daily run sweepstake, and I hope that my previous experience of the ship's speed may give me an advantage,

There are three other first class passengers, a middle-aged married couple and a man of about my age. The couple are nice enough and welcomed me on board; they have come from Perth in Australia and are returning to England for the first time in twenty-five years; they broke their journey in Cape Town, where they spent two weeks before joining the Alnwick Castle. The other fellow introduced himself as Nick Burton and said that he would show me around the ship, and that if I had any questions, he was the one to answer them. When I told him that I knew the ship well, he seemed to take offense and stumped off out of the lounge.

The couple, James and Sue Forster, said that he was rather difficult to get on with, and that they were glad that they would have me as company for the next ten days or so. The captain was the same as on my previous passage on the ship and he said that I was welcome to join him on the bridge at any time, but preferably to come alone rather than with Mr Burton. He told me that there had been a problem with the boiler before they reached Cape Town and that it had taken two days to repair it; they were now two days behind their schedule but would try to catch up some time before they docked in Portsmouth. I lost no time in increasing my estimate of the next day's run.

We sat down to dinner in the saloon at seven thirty, having taken cocktails in the lounge. Burton monopolised the conversation, and I can well understand why the Forsters welcomed my presence on board. As we finished our dinner Burton said that now that there were four of us we could play some bridge; I said that I did not play the game and the Forsters said the same, although I fancy that it may be that they did not wish to spend the rest of the evening with him.

Back in the lounge, Burton said that there were any number of games that two can play and started shuffling a pack of cards; I said that I had recently come across one called *Last Man Standing* and asked if he knew it. He said he did not; I said that I would be glad to teach him if he wished and he said that there was nothing else to do.

He handed the pack of cards to me, and he watched carefully while I shuffled them; I then laid out eighteen of them face down, on the table. "Ah, Pelmanism," he said. "I know that game; lay the rest of the cards down." I put the remaining cards to one side and said that in this game we only needed eighteen cards and that they were best left face down so as not to distract his attention.

I then explained the game to him and said that the object of the game was not to take the last card. He said that that seemed easy enough, and I let him start. I thought that he might not have been truthful when he said that he did not know the game but it was immediately clear that he did not in fact know it, and I spun out the first hand until I let him win. He said that it was an easy game, and I said that I usually won but that he must be a natural card player. He replied that he seldom lost at cards and he would like to show me by winning another hand.

I agreed and suggested that we play for a shilling; Burton said that was too little and we agreed on two shillings. When I won the hand, he said he knew where he had gone wrong and proposed double or quits. Four hands later, he owed me thirty-two shillings and I suggested that we call it a day. Burton agreed, he said that he could work out why I was winning and that we should play again tomorrow; I said that I would be happy to give him a chance to get his money back and he said that he wanted to continue where we left off, still playing double or quits. I said that risked me losing all my winnings on the first hand, but if that was what he wanted I would give him that chance. He asked the steward for a pencil and paper and retired to his cabin to work out how to win.

The Forsters had watched the evening's games without comment, but when Burton had left us, they said it was good to see him taken down a peg or two. He has told them that he is the managing director of a diamond-mining company, and he claims to be a friend of Cecil Rhodes, that his company has struck a very rich vein, and that he is going to England to raise the capital necessary to expand their operation. If he was in Kimberley at the same time as I was I never heard of him, and he does not strike me as the sort that Cecil Rhodes would mix with.

I must work out how to play this fish, for this is a good opportunity to increase my purse during the rest of the voyage.

23rd June

There was nothing of interest today as the ship ploughed her furrow in the ocean. Several of the crew remember me from my voyage, and I spent some time this morning chatting to them on the forward deck while they went about their work. The whole crew will go on four weeks' leave when they get to Southampton and another crew will take over the ship for its next voyage. One of them asked if I knew Mr Burton, and when I said that I did not, he said that he had heard a rumour while they were in Cape Town that he had sold his claim close to Kimberley for very much more than it was worth, having falsified the record of diamonds found by seeding the shaft. This deception involves 'finding' the same diamonds several times, and it is not the first time that it has been practised.

After dinner, Burton was quick to get out a pack of cards and said that he had worked out how to win; he repeated that we should pick up where we left off yesterday, and that the first hand would be double or quits for the thirty-two shillings that I had won. I agreed and he said that I should make the first move. After we had each made three moves I was in a winning position, but rather than administer the coup de grace I made a poor move and a few moments later he won. He said that he knew how he could always win, and waved the piece of paper on which he had made a number of calculations.

I congratulated him and asked if I could have the chance to get some of my erstwhile winnings back; he said that we could play all night as far as he was concerned, and that we should play the first hand for five shillings. I made a show of being reluctant to agree such high stakes but allowed him to convince me. His calculations proved to be as flawed as his account of the value of his claim at Kimberley, and it took less than an hour for him to lose sixteen pounds. He crumpled his piece of paper and said that he thought that he knew where he had gone wrong and that tomorrow he would show me. I told him that I did not want to beggar him, but he said that it was more likely to be me who was beggared and not to count my chickens.

I have enjoyed today, and the Forsters said how much they had enjoyed watching me beat Burton; we shall see how it goes tomorrow.

24th June

The repair to the boiler in Cape Town has proved to be very temporary, for it is once again playing up; we have had to reduce our speed quite considerably, and this has meant that my estimate of the day's run will be even more inaccurate than usual. More importantly, it also means that we will certainly be well behind schedule arriving at Southampton.

I resisted Burton's request that we played *Last Man Standing* after lunch but we sat down again after dinner. He said that if he did not win tonight he would not play again, but that he would be prepared to give me £10 if I told him how it was possible to win so often. I can imagine him trying to make a living by playing the game in public houses in England and I do not want to be responsible for the distress that this might well cause to some unwary souls, so I told him that the secret was not for sale.

The game followed its usual course and when I was ten pounds to the good I said that I thought that was enough and Burton reluctantly agreed. Having been in the same position myself when I first played with Sidney I know how frustrating it is not to be able to see how one's opponent always wins, knowing, as one does, that it must be possible to turn the tables.

27th June

Today, the captain told us that at our present speed it would be on 7th July or thereabouts that we arrived at Southampton, provided that the problem with the boiler got no worse. If it did, then we would put into Lisbon, where it should be possible to have the repairs carried out, but that would inevitably delay us for several more days. This was not good news, but since there is nothing that we can do about it we have to grin and bear it. Like me, the Forsters are keen to get off the ship as soon as possible, but Burton seems happy to enjoy the free food and drink on board for as long as it takes.

4th July

The highlight of the past week has been when I won the daily run sweepstake and pocketed fifteen shillings, otherwise there has been nothing of interest to record; the ship has kept going at its reduced speed and we have passed Lisbon; we expect to dock on 7th July. I have got to like the Forsters; they are well educated and have many interesting tales to tell about their time in Australia; we have agreed to keep in contact when we are back in England. Burton has kept very much to himself and does not join in our conversations; I suspect that he may be unsure whether news of his malpractice in Kimberley has travelled ahead of him and if so what sort of reception he may expect.

6th July

This will be my last diary entry. It is eight and a half years since the first one, and I am very conscious that I have been far from consistent. I had thought to write a few lines every day, but there have been many days, sometimes weeks, when I have written nothing, and there have been some days when I have put to paper in great detail a record of a particular event. Overall, I think that my diary gives a proper account of my time spent in several very different places under very different conditions.

I left Broadlands with the one thousand pounds that Papa had managed to find, and I said that I would return with a full purse. There were times when that seemed unlikely, for more than once I lost what I had managed to save; my time with Sidney was a lesson on who to choose as one's friends, and the destruction of my hotel and store left me with little more than I had when I landed in Cape Town. I did have, and still have, my two diamonds, and it will be interesting to see whether they have any value or whether I was naïve to buy them from a rather doubtful seller.

Despite the setbacks, I have been blessed with a great deal of good luck. I was lucky to meet Satish Modi and his family; I was lucky to get a job with the Ships' Chandlers; I was lucky to stake a claim that produced gold and above all I was lucky to meet Edwin Cade. My luck continued at Obuasi, and it has meant that I am returning to England with a good position in a respectable company.

My greatest luck, and my greatest loss, was meeting and losing Ryneker; it is no good thinking about what might have been, as I do on every anniversary of our parting, and I am learning to value our time together for the love that we shared, rather than regretting that it came to such an abrupt end. I truly wish her every happiness.

I am coming home with a full purse, and that was why I set sail for South Africa in January of 1896. I do not know exactly how much I have, for my salary is paid into my London bank, but it must be nearly twenty thousand pounds. More importantly, I can look forward to a steady income, which will enable me to help Papa with the upkeep of Broadlands.

I am not the Frobisher who landed in Cape Town. I have been the boss of a gang of labourers; I have been in love and in gaol; I have owned and lost a store and a hotel; I have made some good friends and met some less likeable characters; I have seen elephants and a leopard, and I have substantially improved the recovery of gold from a mine in the middle of nowhere. I have earned a place on the board of a major company.

When I put down this pen I will close this diary, raise a glass and drink a toast to my past and my future. Will I keep another diary? We shall see.

Frobisher's Other Diary

Contents

Further New Personae

Ashanti Goldfields Corporation — London

John Daw	Chairman of the Board
Stephen Carson	Deputy Chairman & Finance Director
Richard Beale	Director & Company Secretary
Alan Hughes	Director & Legal Adviser
Chris Roberts	Chief Accountant
Bill Franklin	Briefly a Director
Richard Waterman	Latterly a Director
Miss Press	John Daw's secretary
Sue Thompson	A comely secretary
Lisa Hill	Another secretary
Sally	Yet Another secretary

London & Paris

Reuben	A Jeweller
Victor Bisset	A French diplomat
De Velde	An art dealer
Flick Wilson	A Villain
Anton Dubois	Deputy Chairman of SARLEM
Betty	Ted Harris' fiancée

Obuasi & Bibiani

Ted Harris	Now General Manager
Alan Parsons	Bibiani Mine Manager
Edward Stokes	Obuasi Mine Manager
Louis Bucher	Bibiani Rest House Owner
Arnaud Leclerc	A French Prospector
Aggrey	A great Hunter

French Guinea & Senegal

Pierre Pichon (PP)	Lt. Governor of French Guinea
Georges Leroux	Siguiri Mine Manager
Henri Courmenier	A French Geologist
Jacques Bertrand	A French Civil Servant
Louise	His wife

Australia

Tom Heywood	Albany Mine Manager

At the Front

Capt. Fred Knight	Frobisher's senior officer
Lt. Dave Jenkins	A brother Mole

Chapter One
1904

10th July

It is now two days since I returned to Broadlands, and it seems as though there has not been a minute when I might put pen to paper. Indeed, I have to think whether I will continue to record events in my life. For certain they will be less dramatic here than some of my adventures in Africa, but they may perhaps be of interest to the next generation of Broads.

Papa met me at the station with a carriage when I travelled up from Southampton, and we went straight to Broadlands. Tony and Hermione, Arthur and Penelope, Mary and Rob, the house staff and many of the estate workers were outside the front door to welcome me home, and it was so good to see them and the old house again. I also got to meet Oscar, the dog who replaced Old Jock who had worked with our gamekeeper for many years. Oscar has taken to Papa and follows him everywhere.

Everyone was served with a drink, and it seemed that they all wanted to shake my hand and to hear about the black African savages that I had lived amongst. I told them that while I was away it was thoughts of Broadlands and its people that had buoyed up my spirits when I had disappointments, and that I looked forward to catching up with old friends and making new ones.

It was very good to see how well Mary fits into the family group, and it is hard to believe that she was once our kitchen maid. She was always a pretty thing, but now she has blossomed into a very good looking and self-assured young lady. Hermione's children obviously love her; she is good company for Hermione when Tony is away, and it is nice that her son Rob has playmates.

After half an hour or so we moved inside, and before long I was Arthur's best friend when I promised to tell him a story about Africa every night when he went to bed. Arthur is four and a half years old, and Penelope is two; they are lovely children and I am so happy for Hermione and Tony.

Quentin was not able to get away from his regiment for my arrival, but he will be here in a couple of days when Papa has invited some of our friends to dinner. It will be good to see him again, under very different circumstances from our last meeting.

12th July

Today I had terrible news. Edwin Cade had told me to contact his office when I had been back for a few days, and I did so this morning. His secretary answered the telephone and tearfully told me that Edwin had died of malaria in Obuasi. He had arrived there only a week after I left and had been taken ill almost immediately. He must have contracted the disease when he was there at Christmas. She told me that John Daw has taken over as chairman and would like me to call him when it was convenient. I have never met Mr Daw, but Edwin has spoken to me about him and has always said that he is a most knowledgeable and efficient director. I lost no time in calling him and I must say that he seemed very sincere in welcoming me to the board of the AGC and looking forward to meeting me. It was nice to hear that Edwin had spoken most highly of me, and he said that he felt certain that I would be a real asset to the company.

A memorial service for Edwin is to be held next week in his home village in Berkshire, and I said that I would very much like to be there. John, and he insists that as fellow directors we should use our given names, said that it would be a good opportunity for me to meet the other directors informally before the next board meeting, which is to take place at the end of this month.

The news of Edwin's death is not only very sad, but it means that I start my new job without his support, and without knowing just what responsibilities he had in mind for me. Will my fellow directors share Edwin's confidence in me, or will some of them resent the arrival on the board of someone who has not worked his way up the head office ladder?

13th July

Yesterday's luncheon party was such fun. Papa had intended to invite half the county, but Hermione persuaded him that a family gathering would be better at this time, and she was quite right. Tony's parents, Roger and Caroline Fellowes, made up the family group, and eight of us sat down to an excellent meal. Papa had brought several bottles of his best wines up from the cellar and Cook had done justice to the beef wellington and the sponge puddings.

It was after three o'clock when we left the table and retired to the sitting room for vintage port. Contrary to established custom, the ladies were asked not to absent themselves, and indeed showed that they appreciated a good port as much as their menfolk.

I was bombarded with questions about my time in Africa, and it was not long before I was asked about my diamonds and I was persuaded to get them. In their uncut condition they are not impressive, looking more like glass pebbles than sparkling gems. I was asked how valuable they were, especially the larger one, and I said that until I had the opinion of a dealer in London I really had no idea, but that I very much hoped that they were worth more than I gave for them, and Papa said that he was sure that I had got a good deal.

The three children joined us from the kitchen, where Cook had not only been keeping an eye on them but allowing them to finish off the treacle sponge, and I was struck by what a good-looking boy Rob is. There has been no mention of who his father was, and Mary has evidently never divulged his identity. It is so lucky for her that she has been taken on by Hermione, and that she has made the transition from kitchen maid to nanny so well. I reminded her that she had written to me before I left for Cape Town, wishing me well, and she blushed and smiled and said that it had been rather forward of her but that I had always been very kind to her and treated her more as an equal than a servant.

The party finished with Hermione playing some old favourites on the piano, and I went to bed thinking how lucky I am to have such a good, loving family.

18th July

Today was Edwin Cade's funeral. There was literally nobody there that I knew, but I met his wife and she introduced me to John Daw, who in turn introduced me to the other three directors of the AGC. After a very nice service there was a reception at Edwin's house and I had the opportunity to have a few words with my colleagues-to-be. They were very friendly, and without exception said that they had supported Edwin's proposal that I be brought back from Obuasi to take a place on the board, after having so much increased the profitability of the mine there. I am very lucky to have this opportunity, and I will do my best to justify Edwin's confidence in me and to make Papa proud.

25th July

I am really enjoying myself; as yet I have no onerous responsibilities and I am able to divide my time between Broadlands and Chestnut Cottage, which Tony and Hermione have made into a very comfortable home. It was originally built for the gamekeeper on the Fellowes' estate, but when that position lapsed it was very convenient for them to move in. It is within spitting distance of the senior Fellowes' house and only a short distance from Broadlands. I spend a few nights each week there, when I make good on my promise to tell Arthur stories about my life in Africa. He has already declared that he wants to go there as soon as he is nineteen, and is confident that he will find a lot of big diamonds.

I am concerned about Papa's health. He is still the life and soul of any party, and he still takes Oscar for a walk every day; that in itself is something of a trial for him, for Oscar is a young dog, and is more energetic than Old Jock, who was content to match Papa's speed, however slow that might be.

27th July

Two days ago, I went up to London in advance of tomorrow's board meeting and stayed at Papa's club. When I got off the train I went straight to a firm in Hatton Garden from which Papa bought Mama's engagement and wedding rings many years ago, and where Tony had taken Hermione to choose her engagement ring. It is a family firm and the proprietor has worked in the firm for more than fifty years, and although he was then an apprentice, and did not have cause to remember my father, he found the record of the sales in an old ledger.

He welcomed me and asked how he could be of service; was it another engagement ring he asked. I showed the diamonds to him and asked for his estimation of their value. He inspected each of them carefully through his loupe and asked whether they came from Kimberley. I asked how on earth he could tell that, and he said that diamonds were like people, outwardly not very different but as regards their characteristics quite different, depending upon where they were found.

I asked him how many carats each stone weighed, but he explained that it was only after they were cut that their weight was important; he did say, however, that he thought that the larger stone could be cut into quite an attractive shape. He said that he himself did not cut diamonds; that is evidently a very skilled operation, which can halve the value of a stone if not done properly.

He asked if he could keep them for a few days so that he could show them to a man whose only job in life was getting the best gem or gems out of every rough diamond with which he was entrusted. I said that that would be perfectly acceptable and that I would return within the week. I was offered no receipt for my stones, and felt that in view of the long association of the firm with our family it would probably be rude to ask for one.

6th August

John Daw has told me that the board meetings always begin at ten o'clock, so I made sure that I was at their quite imposing premises shortly after nine-thirty. The lady behind the reception desk knew who I was without asking, and welcomed me to the AGC; she said that she had worked for the firm for more than thirty years, and that if I needed to know anything that I could not ask another director she would be happy to help me. She is a motherly type, and said that I probably felt much as I had done on my first day at Eton; how she knew where I went to school I do not know, but she was quite right; I did feel distinctly apprehensive.

A smart, young lady came down in the lift; she said that her name was Sue and that she would take me to the board room on the fourth floor. It was a small lift, and if the circumstances had been different I might well have sought to capitalise on the restricted space; as it was I was careful to keep a respectable distance from her and to avoid looking at her figure. It is a long time since I was able, and indeed encouraged, to appreciate every one of Ryneker's attributes and I think that I must seriously consider making up for lost time.

Sue delivered me to the Board Room, and I was impressed by the quality of the furniture, the pictures on the wall and the other decorative items. John Daw and another director, who I remembered from our meeting at Edwin's funeral to be Stephen Carson, were already there, going through a pile of documents. John showed me which seat I should take and gave me a copy of the agenda for the meeting. The first item was to appoint me to the board of the AGC and to agree my responsibilities. Stephen said that he was sure that they would all like to hear something of my experiences in Witwatersrand and Obuasi and I made a few notes on the pad by my chair.

By five minutes to ten, the other two directors had joined us; Miss Press, who I was introduced to as John's secretary, and to whom I had spoken when she told me of Edwin's death, came in to take the notes. John called the meeting to order promptly at ten o'clock and asked for a minute's silence in which to remember Edwin, who he said had done so much to make the AGC the profitable concern that it is today.

He then said that the first item was the proposal that I should be appointed to the board of directors and asked for a show of hands by those in favour. I was relieved to see that all four hands were raised promptly, and they all shook my hand and said kind words of congratulation. I was then asked to tell them how I had become involved with gold mining and why I had been successful where others had not.

I said that at the age of twenty the possibility of making a fortune by a little hard work was very appealing, and that during a year and a half in Cape Town I had heard so many stories of gold making men rich, that I was determined to try my luck as soon as I could afford to stake a claim. And, I said, I had indeed been lucky, for with little or no knowledge of the practicalities of prospecting I had bought the title to a claim that not only produced river-bed gold but also rewarded the digging of shallow pits. During two years I developed the claim and was making good money and I thought to move to the diamond fields at Kimberley. Because of the success of the claim it was possible to sell it for a good price.

I told them how after the war against the Boers ended I had become the owner of a store, and then a small hotel in Kimberley, and that my initial success in that enterprise had gone up in smoke. I said that my good luck had, however, certainly returned when I met Edwin in Johannesburg, and continued when I found the big, new gold-bearing vein at Obuasi. I said that I very much hoped that my luck would continue in my new position, and that I looked forward to learning what my responsibilities will be.

John said that he always thought that people made their own luck, and that I was being too modest in crediting my various successes to good luck, but that he was sure that with or without luck I would make a valuable contribution to the future success of the company. He went on to say that my title would be Director of Development and Expansion and that I should seek to improve the productivity of existing mines and recommend where the company should either open new mines or seek to take over the operations of other companies. Both of these involve very high costs to the

AGC and may require me to travel quite extensively. I am flattered that I am considered competent to have such responsibility, and I very much hope that I prove worthy of it.

The other agenda items all referred to matters already in hand and I was given a pile of files which showed the background of each, which I could use to bring myself up to date. There was one file which dealt with possible acquisitions and another which gave details of all the known gold mines, and it is these that I will have to study and in some cases follow up, before I can make any recommendations.

When the meeting ended, John showed me to my office and said that I would need a secretary. The lady who had worked for Edwin for many years had decided to retire, but he thought that there were two in the typing pool who might be suitable, and he arranged for them to come and see me after lunch when I could make a choice. A light meal was served in the board room, after which I sat down in my office and began to go through the files that I had been given.

After half an hour or so there was a knock on my door and the first of the two possible secretaries came in. She was called Lisa Hill and looked to be in her middle thirties; she was well dressed and told me that she had worked for the company for almost ten years and that she had recently married her boss, the head of the accounts department. She said that it was only fair to let me know that they wanted to start a family before she got much older and that she realised that if she left to have a child when I was new to the job that might not be ideal. Her employment record that I had been given by the personnel manager confirmed all that she said and showed that she was not only a good secretary but also a very reliable employee.

I thanked her for letting me know and I told her that I would be making a decision before the end of the day. She said that whether or not she got the job she hoped that I would enjoy working for the AGC; I said that I hoped that her wish for a child would soon be realised.

I picked up the file for the second applicant and immediately saw that it was for one Sue Thompson. I wondered whether this might be the Sue who had brought me up in the lift, and was surprised that my heart suddenly seemed to beat more noticeably; but I told myself that Sue is by no means an uncommon name, and I was starting to read the file when there was a knock on the door and Sue entered.

It was indeed Sue of the lift journey, and I am somewhat ashamed to say that her arrival did give me something of a thrill. Of course she would get the job, but I had to have a plausible reason for preferring her to tell to John Daw. I blessed Lisa for giving me just that reason and proceeded to interview Sue. She is twenty-five years of age and has been with the company for four years. Her attendance record is excellent, and at her last annual review she expressed a wish to get out of the typing pool and do a more responsible and interesting job.

She said that she had heard of my successes in Africa and was sure that they would continue now that I was in head office; and that she would like to work for someone with such an important job. It seems that nothing discussed by the directors, in or out of the board room, remains a secret for very long. I went through the formalities of the interview and told her that she would hear before the end of the day.

She thanked me for seeing her and said that whether or not she got the job she hoped that I would enjoy my work. After she left my office I went to see John with the two files. He asked who I had chosen and I said that while Lisa was clearly the more experienced and qualified of the two I was concerned that she might be leaving us, either briefly or permanently, before very long, and that on that basis I thought that Sue was probably the wiser choice. He winked and said that he was sure that I was right, and that he would tell the personnel manager of my decision.

Before I left his office he said that he realised that I would have a lot to do in the next few days and not to worry if I had to be away from the office now and then. I said that I needed to call on my bank and that I had to find somewhere to live during the week, and that if I was to look like a director of a major company a visit to my tailor was probably also necessary. He said to ask him if I needed any help or advice settling in, and I said that I was sure that I would.

It has been a very good day; I have an interesting job and a responsible position in a well-respected company, and I can look forward to having Sue at my beck and call.

9th August

When I got to the office at nine o'clock this morning, Sue was already in the small room next to mine; one of the newest typewriting machines was on her desk, together with a notepad and pencil. I had seen from her file that she took short-hand, and I felt sure that I would have no reason to regret my choice. She said how pleased she was that I had chosen her, and that she was very much looking forward to working for me. She had laid out all my files and put a single rose in a small vase on my desk, and I thought that that was a nice touch.

John came in and asked if I had everything that I needed, and I told him that I did. He said that Williams' trial had been set for 20th August. and that since the court knew that I was now in the country I would have to attend as the major witness for the prosecution. I do not look forward to this, for the wretched man was certain to be found guilty, but since he had stolen from a company of which I am now a director it is clearly my duty to give evidence.

I left the office shortly after twelve, telling Sue that I would be back by two, and went straight to my bank; there the manager took me to his office and told a clerk to bring my file. While we waited for it he said how much the bank valued my custom and that I must have had an interesting time in Africa. When the details of my account were brought in, I was surprised to see that I had more than twenty-six thousand pounds to my name; this was good news, for it meant that I can certainly help Papa.

The manager said that with such a substantial balance I might wish to invest some of it, and that the bank would be glad to assist me in choosing a safe haven for my money. I told him that there were a number of expenses that I would incur in the next few weeks, but that when I had put all my affairs in order I would be glad to seek his advice.

From the bank I went straight to an agency that arranges for the purchase and letting of properties. There I told the manager that I wanted a small house or apartment in the area around Hyde Park Corner, and that I was open to renting at first and possibly buying later. He said that there were several properties on their books that he thought might be suitable, and that he could arrange for me to see them when it was convenient.

I told him that I could see two of them tomorrow between the hours of twelve and two and he said that he would make the necessary arrangements. I gave him my business address and returned to my office, where I spent the rest of the day reading the files that John had given to me.

10th August

Today I bought a house. It is actually a mews cottage close to the Brompton Road. It has a nice sitting room, a small kitchen and two bedrooms; I think that it will suit me very well while I am in London during the week, and I have no worries about leaving it empty during the weekends when I am down at Broadlands. It is partially furnished, but I need to buy a bed and some furniture for the sitting room; also I will bring a few pictures up from Broadlands.

It is empty at the moment, and I should be able to move in in a couple of weeks. I am sure that Hermione will want to come and see it, and probably stay for a night or two from time to time. Sue was very excited when I returned to the office with the good news and said that if I needed any help when choosing things like curtains she would be glad to assist me.

13th August

I came back to Broadlands for the weekend yesterday evening; Hermione had come for dinner, and she and Papa were very interested to hear about my week in London. I told them that I had been very warmly welcomed and what my responsibilities were. Papa said it sounded as though I would be making a lot of very important decisions, but I told him that I would make recommendations and it would be up to the board to consider them.

I also told them that I have a nice office and a nice secretary called Sue; Hermione said that she hoped she was not too nice as she had several of her unmarried friends lined up to meet me. I then told them about my little house, and Hermione straight away said that she must come and see it and that it would be lovely to be able to stay in London for a few days whenever she wanted. Everyone is agreed that I have made a good start to my new career.

16th August

Today, instead of taking lunch with my colleagues in the board room I went to see the jeweller who has my diamonds. I was welcomed effusively and taken straight through to the back office; there Reuben, as he has asked me to call him, said that his friend the cutter had reported positively on my stones, particularly the larger one. He was unable to tell me exactly what they were worth until they had been cut, but he was confident that they would fetch at least three thousand guineas and that he would be glad to buy them from me. I told him to tell his friend to go ahead with the cutting, and he said that if I returned in about three weeks' time he should be able to give me a firm figure. This is good news, for I have a very special purchase in mind when I have them sold.

17th August

At lunchtime today I paid a visit to a tailor in Jermyn Street that was recommended by Papa. Before I went to Africa I had no need of a tailor, for the clothes worn at Eton were all bought from an appointed supplier, and the dinner jacket that I occasionally wore in the holidays came off the peg at a local shop. I did wonder when I entered the premises whether I had come to the right place, for military uniforms and accoutrements were everywhere on display. I rather hesitantly asked the smartly dressed sales person whether they provided other than military clothing and he informed that there was nothing that they could not provide.

An hour or so later I left the shop having been measured from top to toe and side to side; I had selected material for two suits, two pairs of trousers, an evening suit for black tie events and a tweed jacket and plus fours. I was not sure that I needed the last items, but the proprietor, who had overseen the measuring, assured me that I would need them when shooting. Two pairs of shoes and half a dozen shirts completed my purchases, and when I enquired as to the cost of my new wardrobe I was told that it would be put on my account and that there was no need to pay now.

19th August

Today, Williams was tried and found guilty. I was asked to give evidence and told the court how the theft had been concealed until the box was opened in London and how the gold had eventually been recovered. I added that it may have been that Williams was resentful that he had not got the position of mine manager and wanted to get back at the company; I also said that until the theft he had carried out his duties satisfactorily. The judge sentenced him to eight years in prison, and said that without my statement he would have had a longer sentence. I saw him briefly before he was taken away; he said that he had been a fool and thanked me for speaking up for him. There was nothing that I could say to him.

12th September

I am well settled into my new life. At work, I have read all the files about our existing operations and possible acquisitions and I believe that I now know enough about the company to start making some positive suggestions. I have a good relationship with Sue, who is a good secretary and has introduced me to others in the company who can give me information not available in the files. I cannot pretend that I do not value her for other reasons, but I have been careful to keep our relationship strictly professional; I did take her round to show her the house one day at lunchtime but I have not taken her up on her offer to help me to furnish it.

I moved into it at the end of last month, and with Hermione's help it now looks like a real home; Papa has promised to visit when he is next in London, but I think that it will be best if he sleeps at his club.

My suits, shoes and other clothes were delivered to the office after I had a final fitting; and I have sold my diamonds. Reuben said that he would be glad to give me three thousand seven hundred guineas for them and I was happy to accept his offer.

I hope that I can now fulfil my last wish, which is to buy back our Gainsborough. Papa told me the name of the gallery that bought it and Sue has tracked down the man who bought it from them. I have spoken to him and told him of my interest and he has agreed to see me tomorrow. His name is Jan de Velde, and he makes no secret of the fact that he bought it at a low price with the intention of selling it on for a profit. Papa has never said how much he got for it, but to cover all the various costs of Hermione's wedding it must have been at least one thousand guineas for I expect that he needed a few guineas over after the wedding costs with which to take care of some of the most urgent repairs to Broadlands.

De Velde lives in Chelsea, in a large house off the King's Road. I was received by a manservant who took me to de Velde's study. As we passed through the hall, I saw that there were a number of large pictures gracing the walls; the Gainsborough was not among them, but they testified to de Velde's good taste.

He rose from the chair behind his impressive desk and shook my hand when I was shown into the room. He bade me sit down and told the servant to bring coffee and brandy. He asked, quite understandably, why I was keen to buy back the Gainsborough, and I told him that it was a portrait of one of my ancestors and that the proceeds of its sale had been needed for a special purpose at that time, but that that I was now in a position to return it to the family home.

He said that he had a number of people interested in the picture, but that he had some sympathy for my position and did not wish to enter into a bargaining round with me. He said that he would be satisfied with his profit if I paid fifteen hundred guineas, for which price he would have the painting taken to my office. I said that I would pay his price, but that I wished to see the painting to be sure that it was in no way damaged. He readily agreed and led me to a splendid sitting room where the Gainsborough hung in a commanding position. He said that it was one of his wife's favourite paintings and that he would be in trouble for selling it. The painting was undamaged and we shook hands on the deal. I cannot wait to take it back to Broadlands.

20th September

All the family were at Broadlands today, for I had said that I had a surprise for them. Quentin was able to get away from his regiment and Tony took the afternoon off from his solicitor's office. Hermione brought her children and Mary brought Rob, so eight of us enjoyed the sandwiches and cakes that Cook had made. After the meal, I said that I could reveal the surprise and brought in the large package that contained the Gainsborough. When I unpacked it and gave it to Papa he could not speak; he just gazed at it with tears in his eyes, and then hugged me for almost a minute.

Tony very soon took down the picture that had taken the Gainsborough's place, put another hook in the wall, and rehung the family portrait where it has been for so many years. When he could speak, Papa said that I could not have done anything that pleased him more, and that if it had been the only outcome of my time in Africa it would have been enough. I have got so much pleasure from being able to do this and seeing Papa's face light up when he saw the portrait.

15th December

As the end of the year approaches my thoughts go back to last Christmas at Obuasi; it was such a jolly affair. Since then so much has changed in my life; I have an interesting and responsible job, a little house of my own, and regular weekend visits to Broadlands and Chestnut Cottage. I so enjoy spending time with my nephew and niece and I have got to know Tony really well; he is such a good husband and father.

Their household would not be the same place without Mary and Rob, and the more I see of her the more I admire her; she was always good looking, but a kitchen maid's uniform does not do the wearer any favours. After she left service at Broadlands and before she came to be a nanny for

Hermione, she had spent some time taking lessons with a retired teacher, and he had not only greatly improved her grammar and diction but also developed her confidence and social graces. She can now hold her own in any gathering, and her cheerful demeanour makes her welcome anywhere. Most importantly, Hermione's children love her dearly and they get on well with Rob.

At the office I am working on two areas of possible interest to the AGC; one is in Cornwall and the other back in the Gold Coast; in the new year, I will be ready to put my proposals to the board and I hope that they will approve them.

26th December

Yesterday was the best Christmas that I have had for nine years, and very different from those in the intervening period. Quentin came down to Broadlands a few days earlier and we all gathered at Chestnut Cottage where Cook, helped by Mary, had prepared every ingredient of a traditional Christmas dinner. It was good to see them working together, for not so long ago Mary had been Cook's assistant, and now she was working in Mary's kitchen, but Cook clearly does not resent Mary's move upwards on the social scale, and Mary not only treats Cook as an equal, but does not hesitate to ask her advice.

Papa had wanted us to eat at Broadlands, but we persuaded him that Chestnut Cottage was better for the lunch and that we would all be at Broadlands for New Year's Eve.

Tony had decorated a Christmas tree, and there were any number of brightly wrapped presents around its base; Penelope was fascinated by the coloured lights. The children tore open their presents and squealed with delight when it so happened that they got just what they had put on their lists. Mary gave me a very smart silk tie, and I gave her one of the new leather handbags that are becoming fashionable

Papa, Quentin, Tony and Hermione had clubbed together and presented me with a pair of Holland and Hollands, to replace my Purdeys lost in the fire in Kimberley. They are lovely guns, and I look forward to trying them out when we have a small shoot on New Year's Day. Papa, Quentin and I returned to Broadlands after tea, and ended the day with a few glasses of port around a cheerful fire in the sitting room. Papa said how he misses Mama on these occasions, but that he does enjoy seeing the children regularly.

Chapter Two
1905

1st January

Today's shoot may not have been the affair that it used to be when Jackson was our gamekeeper, but enough of the estate workers turned out as beaters to provide the guns with some good sport. I was concerned that not having used a shotgun for so long, except when deterring the Boers, might have resulted in an embarrassing performance, but I am glad to say that I very soon was at ease with my new guns, and several pheasants paid the penalty of choosing to fly over me.

Papa is not too steady on his feet and likes to lean on his shooting stick, but his aim is as good as ever, and very few birds got past him. Tony, like me, was brought up to shoot from an early age, and has shot regularly on the Fellowes' estate. Quentin did not get too many birds; he was never much interested in sport shooting as a boy; but he won the small-bore cup at Wellington and several trophies when rifle shooting for his regiment. Hermione made up the number of guns to five and did well with her twenty bore. We were blessed with good weather and considering that we no longer have a gamekeeper or put any pheasants down the bag was a respectable twenty-seven pheasants, two woodcock and a pigeon; a good day's sport was had by all.

3rd January

Back at the office with the Christmas and New Year celebrations behind us, it is time for me to put a first proposal before the board. For many years, gold has been discovered in different parts of the British Isles, and some sizeable nuggets have been found, but the most consistently productive areas have been Cornwall and Wales, where mining for copper and tin has also produced gold. An area that has been worked for many hundreds of years is the South Crofty in Cornwall, where there are actually two mines; there has never been a massive production of gold, but it has consistently contributed to the profits of its owners.

There are also many other mines in the Gold Coast which are presently operated by indigenous prospectors; they do not have the capital to invest in the machinery necessary to extract gold on a large scale and there is little or no thought given as to which areas are likely to be most productive. Also, for the past fifty years or more there have been reports of rich veins of gold being found in Australia; I will research both of these possibilities further and report to the board.

15th January

At today's board meeting my proposal regarding South Crofty was approved in principle, and it was decided that Stephen Carson, the financial director, and I should make contact with the relevant persons in the company which owns it, express an interest, and find out whether they would be receptive to bids. This is my first real contribution in the six months that I have been here and I hope that it proves to be a positive one.

23rd January

Stephen and I have a meeting tomorrow with the chairman of the company operating the South Crofty mine. When Stephen contacted his opposite number on their board, he found that they had a cautious interest in talking to us, and from their published annual reports it seems that they are short of capital with which to develop the mine further. This may be an opportunity for the AGC to expand its portfolio.

25th January

Yesterday's meeting went well and there is certainly an opportunity to purchase at least a controlling interest in the company, but the finances are not attractive, and unless gold could be produced at twice the current rate there is no good reason for the AGC to invest. It was decided that I should visit the mines next week to see whether they could be made more productive.

31st January

Today, there was a most disturbing development in the office. I thought that Sue did not seem to be her usual cheerful self and when I asked her if there was anything the matter she said that she needed more money. I said that I thought that it was rather soon after the raise that she got when she became my secretary, and that anyhow, there were annual salary reviews and hers would not be due until August.

She then burst into tears and told me that she was pregnant and that if she did not get a raise she would tell everybody that I was the father. This horrified me. I said that no one would believe her, but she said that she would say that I had taken advantage of her when she went to see my house.

I went straight to Joh Daw and told him that her story was quite untrue, and asked what we should do. He said that he did not think that anyone would believe her but that she would have to leave. He called the personnel manager and told him to dismiss her with immediate effect, with a month's wages in lieu of notice.

I went back to my office and told Sue what had been decided; again she burst into tears, but this time said that she was sorry but the father had left her and she did not know what to do. I said that she should not have threatened me, but that she could tell people what she wanted. She said how much she enjoyed working for me and begged to be allowed to stay, but I told her that that was not possible and to go and see the personnel manager. I am sorry to lose her, for she was an excellent secretary. John said that he thought that Lisa Hill, the other candidate that I interviewed before choosing Sue, could fill the position until I got a permanent replacement and I said that I would be very happy with that.

1st February

Lisa moved into Sue's office today. She told me that everyone was surprised by Sue's attempt to blackmail me and that no one believed a word of what she said. I was very relieved to hear that. I said that I would not be looking to replace her until I had to, and that for my part I hoped that she would not start a family too soon. She smiled and said that we would have to see, but that she knew that she would enjoy working for me as she had never heard a bad word about me in the gossip in the staff canteen.

3rd February

I spent most of yesterday underground at the mines with their mine manager. He showed me all the latest tunnels being worked and it is evident that they have been producing copper and tin very efficiently. The proportion of gold, however, is very small, and I saw no reason to expect it to be possible to increase it. If the AGC wants to expand its interests beyond gold this may be a good opportunity, but gold alone can never support the operation of these mines and tomorrow I shall advise the board accordingly.

4th February

Today the board considered my report and decided against investing in South Crofty. There are two other areas where gold is being found that are interesting, French Guinea in West Africa, not far from the Gold Coast, and south-west Australia, and I will research these further. I am already planning a visit to Obuasi, for there are still a number of small operations not far from our mine where gold is being extracted in reasonable amounts, and I think that we might be able to increase their production without any great expense if we integrated some of them into our existing operation. I could combine this visit with one to the Guinea mines.

To travel to Australia to evaluate any prospects there would take a considerable time, and at this stage I would not wish to absent myself from England without there being a very strong possibility that such a voyage would be productive, and that cannot be guaranteed.

5th February

I have got into the habit of always going down to Chestnut Cottage for tea on Sundays. This gives me the opportunity to spend some time with Arthur and Penelope, and also Rob, who is now nine and a half years old, four years older than Arthur. They get on particularly well together, despite the difference in their ages, and both of them always ask me to tell them about Africa. When I said that I might be going there again for a short time, Arthur asked if he could go with me, but Rob said that it would be too dangerous for him, and that if anyone went with me it should be him.

While Mary was putting the children to bed Hermione said that she had something to tell me. I thought that perhaps she was expecting another child, but it turned out to be quite a different matter. It seems that Mary has always been attracted to me, even when she was the kitchen maid, and that since I returned from Africa her feelings have grown even stronger.

I had no idea of this, for she has always behaved with the utmost decorum, but we have enjoyed each other's company and I do look forward to seeing her every weekend at teatime on Sunday. Hermione asked whether I had any feelings for Mary, and I said that I did like her very much but had never thought that she might care for me in that way.

Hermione told me that Mary had invented the name Fisher as the father of her child and called the boy Rob since Rob and Fisher were an anagram of Frobisher. For some reason that affected me greatly, and I told Hermione that I thought that Mary was in many ways more attractive than some of the young ladies that she had contrived for me to meet. This conversation has left my mind in turmoil, and I need to think what my feelings really are.

15th March

I have been busy researching the mines in French Guinea. They are best described as artisan mines, not very different from the mines at Witwatersrand and Obuasi before deep shafts were sunk. Gold has been found there for many hundreds of years, and traditionally used in exchange for salt and other commodities, principally with the Ivory Coast, Liberia and the Gold Coast. The most productive area is around the town of Siguiri; this is situated on the Niger river and is more than five hundred miles from the capital, Conakry. I have no idea how I might get there but it would surely be interesting, and if combined with my visit to Obuasi might be achieved in a reasonable amount of time; I will see what the other directors think of the idea.

30th April

Tony and Hermione and their children, together with Mary and Rob, have moved into Broadlands from Chestnut Cottage. Papa said that it was ridiculous for just him and I to occupy the large house while the others were in much smaller accommodation. It is a good arrangement; Tony and Hermione have three bedrooms, one of which they can use as a private sitting room, and on the top floor Mary and Rob have three rooms to themselves; Cook has the other two. The old servants' sitting room beside the kitchen is now a playroom for the children, I have a room and the remaining bedroom is where Quentin sleeps when he comes to visit.

2nd May

Today, Mary and I went for a long walk around the Broadlands estate. It was a lovely, warm, sunny day and it seemed entirely natural that we should hold hands as we walked. I said that Hermione had told me about the anagram and that I was flattered that she had named Rob for that reason. I said how glad I had been when I learned that she was Hermione's nanny, and that when I got back to Broadlands how surprised I was to find her such an attractive and articulate young lady.

She said that in the letter that she had written to me just before I left for Africa she had wanted to say what she felt, but that as our kitchen maid that would not have been appropriate and I might have thought less of her.

Now that we are all living under the same roof at Broadlands, we will see much more of each other, and I hope that she will enjoy that, as I am sure that I will. It is a long time since I lost my last love and increasingly I feel the need for someone to replace Ryneker in my heart. I have a job which I really enjoy, and I would like to share that enjoyment with someone away from the office.

7th June

It is not yet possible for me to forget that this is the eighth anniversary of Ryneker's departure from Cape Town and from my life, but this year the sadness of that memory is to some extent lessened by my feelings for Mary. There will come a time, there surely must, when I do not remember this particular date with sadness, but rather enjoy it in the company of another. Whether that other will be Mary remains to be seen, but the possibility is by no means an unhappy one.

10th July

The board has decided that I should go to French Guinea and see whether, if the AGC was to buy out some of the small operators there, it could become a similar success to that at Obuasi. The centre of the gold mining is at Siguiri, which is close to the north-west border of the country with Mali, five hundred miles from Conakry. I know a little conversational French from my schooldays at Eton, but none of the technical words that I would need if I had to appraise a mining operation. I will find a tutor who can better prepare me for this journey, which I propose to undertake in August.

16th July

Another opportunity for a party. Quentin has been promoted to Major. This means that for the next two or three years he will be working in the War Office in London and will be able to come down to Broadlands at the weekend much more often. Papa once again emerged from the cellar with a couple of bottles of champagne and Cook provided us with a delicious dinner. We persuaded Quentin to tell us something of his time in South

Africa, and it seems that he was engaged in some fairly vigorous battles with the Boers. He evidently served well in action and was 'Mentioned in Despatches' after the relief of the siege of Kimberley. Papa said that he was carrying on in the tradition of great-uncle Arthur, and we all drank to his health more than once.

20th July

No small part of my preparations for my visit to French Guinea and the Gold Coast is how to travel when the ship deposits me at either Conakry or Takoradi. Siguiri is almost equidistant from Conakry and Obuasi, but to travel directly from Obuasi would involve passing through the northern part of the Ivory Coast, and it is most unlikely that there would be anything other than trails used by traders. I will go first to Obuasi and see whether such a route is possible, but am resigned to going via Conakry after visiting Obuasi, and I have booked my passage to Takoradi, departing from Southampton on 28th July.

I have sent a message to Ted Harris at Obuasi telling him of my forthcoming visit and the anticipated date of my arrival at Takoradi; it will be nice to see my erstwhile colleagues again and I expect that they will have made a number of changes since I left just over a year ago.

10th August

I arrived at Takoradi this afternoon after an uneventful journey on the *SS Braemar Castle* and spent the night in the rest house. I was the only person staying and I passed a pleasant evening in the company of the manager, who is the same as when I stayed on my way back to England. Tomorrow I take the train to Obuasi.

11th August

Ted met me at the station and took me straight to the guest bungalow in the Riley car which I had ordered shortly before I left and which was delivered six months ago; on the way he said that there was a rumour that the mine was going to be closed down, but I said that that was very far from the truth. Mensah was waiting for me on the verandah and said that he hoped that I was going to stay, but I had to disappoint him. After I had showered off the dust of the journey I went to the managers' lounge where they were all gathered awaiting me. I had brought with me from the ship a bottle of whisky, which made me doubly welcome, and over dinner, I told them the object of my visit. I will go and see the artisan mines in the bush some miles north of Obuasi, and if I think that they could profitably be brought under our management and developed, I will seek an audience with the Mamponghene in Kumasi and hopefully negotiate a further mining concession.

This would require a second mine superintendent, and the workers would be recruited from the present artisan prospectors, who would therefore not only not lose their present variable income but have secure jobs with monthly wages. The management of the mine would be done by the present team, who would divide their time between the two operations; the Obuasi mine is now running very smoothly under Ted, and should continue to do so under the new arrangement.

I did detect a slight concern as to whether two mines could efficiently be managed by a single team of managers, but when I said that the extra responsibilities would be recognised by an increase in their salaries, it was quickly agreed that there would be no problem.

Tomorrow I shall make a tour of the mine and make arrangements to visit the other goldfields on the following day. It is very nice to be back here, where my good luck led to the discovery of another rich vein, which in turn led to Edwin Cade moving me to the head office in London.

12th August

The Glorious Twelfth; Papa will be sad that he cannot travel to the northern grouse moors as he did for so many years, as a guest of several of his friends. It was to repay that hospitality that he worked so hard to reciprocate by laying on some good days at pheasants and partridges at Broadlands. But he will soon be out after those, joined by Tony, and that will give him great pleasure.

My tour of inspection of the mine today confirmed what I had expected; it is performing very well. Tony has recruited a replacement for Williams, a supervisor from one of the logging companies who had completed his contract and was going home. He has no mining experience, but the job is largely organisational and he has plenty of experience in charge of native workers.

The boring machine has been repaired and will be moved to the new mine if I get a concession. Cameron swears that it is a good machine, and has made one or two modifications to improve its performance and extend the period between breakdowns. Franz Werner says that he will have to decide whether to bring the rock to Obuasi for crushing and gold extraction or set up a second facility at the new mine. Either would involve some considerable expense, and it is one of the things that the board will require me to propose.

George was his usual cheerful self; he says that if we open a second mine he will have a small clinic there; a nurse in his present clinic has shown herself to be very responsible and he would put her in charge there on a daily basis and pay regular visits himself. He has made several more expeditions into the forest and has sketches of any number of birds, animals and reptiles, but he has not seen the leopard again.

14th August

On the day before yesterday Ted, Franz and I travelled to the goldfields in one of the mine's new Leyland steam-driven lorries; two were shipped to Takoradi three months ago and were put on the train to Obuasi. These vehicles are used to move men and machinery around the mine, and were chosen in preference to those powered by internal combustion engines as there is any amount of wood available here for use in their boilers but no petrol. The journey took just over an hour along a track cleared through the bush; today it was easily passable, but I doubt whether it would be in the rainy season.

The mining in that area is almost all done by individual Africans from the Gold Coast and several of the nearby countries, including the Ivory Coast, Mali and Guinea. There are a few Lebanese and a very small number of Europeans. Most of the mining is by panning and from shallow pits, but if what I was told is correct the area produces quite a considerable amount of gold every year, and has done for very many years in the past. I think that it would be necessary to sink a trial shaft before making a decision as to whether to integrate this operation with the mine at Obuasi; it is, of course, possible that the same vein as that at Obuasi runs under the area.

16th August

Yesterday the three of us were granted an audience with the Mamponghene in his palace in Kumasi. He welcomed us and led us to a room where many sorts of food were laid out on banana leaves on a large table; custom dictates that one does not mention the reason for the visit until one has enjoyed a meal. Pork and guineafowl, venison and *cutting-grass*, a rodent the size of a badger, and a variety of fruits and vegetables were washed down with beer or palm wine; the latter has a variable alcohol content, depending upon how long it has matured, and it is advisable to limit one's intake if important matters are to be discussed afterwards.

After the meal we were ushered into a well-furnished room and bidden to take our seats while one of the Mamponghene's entourage blew on a cow's horn. With the entertainment over we got down to the purpose of our visit. I said that the AGC might wish to take over the individual mining operations in the area north of Obuasi and replace them with a single operation similar to that at Obuasi, but that it would depend upon a trial shaft confirming the presence of gold in a sufficient amount. Employment would be offered to all of the present native workers, giving them an assured wage, and the AGC would of course pay for the concession a proportion of its income to the Ashanti treasury, as it did at Obuasi.

The Mamponghene said how much the AGC's Obuasi mine benefitted his people, and that he had great respect for its managers; he reminded us that we had all met when he visited the mine when Edwin Cade was last there, and he drew from a pocket in his robes the gold watch that Edwin gave to him on that occasion. I told him that Edwin had died quite soon afterwards and he asked that his condolences should be given to Edwin's wife. He then asked what proportion of the revenue we had in mind and I said that we proposed the same as from the present mine. He said that that would be satisfactory, and that he would do whatever was necessary to enable us to sink the exploratory shaft without any obstruction, and that if any of those presently prospecting there objected he would persuade them that it was in their best interests and that otherwise they would not be able to continue their prospecting. I wonder just how that persuasion would be applied.

Having reached agreement, we were treated to some sweet cakes and more palm wine, and I presented the Mamponghene with a Swiss cuckoo clock. I wound it up, set the hands at one minute to three, and placed it on the table at his side; as he reached to pick it up, the cuckoo duly appeared and burst into song three times. He was delighted, and asked for it to repeat its performance; I made it do so and then showed him how to wind it and set the correct time. He said that with the watch and the clock he would know the time whether he was in the palace or elsewhere.

The meeting ended with mutual expressions of respect, and we set off on the long journey back to Obuasi. I told Ted that he should get the exploratory shaft sunk as soon as possible and that he and Franz should then let me know in London whether the new mine was viable. There being no town in the area, we agreed to call it Obuasi Two and the original mine Obuasi One.

We got back to our bungalows in the early hours this morning, and after a few hours' sleep, I wrote a report for John Daw and made this entry in my diary. I hope that the shaft at Obuasi Two does prove the potential of the area, as it will be my first success after joining the board. I must now plan my visit to Siguiri, which will be overland from Conakry, as I have learned that it is not possible to travel directly from here. There should be a ship from Takoradi calling at Conakry in three days' time so I will complete my business here tomorrow.

17th August

This evening I joined the five managers in the lounge and brought John, Cameron and Sgt. Miller up to date with an account of our visits to the area of Obuasi Two and Kumasi. I said that if there proved to be enough gold at the new mine there would be much for all of them to do, not least or last to upgrade the track between the two mines so that it could be used by the lorries in the rainy season. I also said that Obuasi Two might guarantee their jobs when Obuasi One was exhausted.

After our evening meal, Franz said that he would very much like to have a game of *Last Man Standing* with me; he said that he had given much thought to it and believed that he could beat me. He laid out eighteen matches and we tossed for who should start; I won the toss and said that I would. After we had each made two moves, he was in a position where he could possibly win, but this was often the case and depended upon all his subsequent moves being the right ones. Confident that he would not realise the strength of his position, I played again and so did he; his move was the right one, and I found myself in a position where unless he made a mistake in his next two moves he was going to win. He made no mistakes and he won. I have never lost, except when doing so deliberately to raise a beginner's hopes, since Sidney taught me the winning moves, and I only lost this time because my early moves had been made without thinking to ensure that I had a winning position. I congratulated Franz on having worked out how to win. We had a return match with him making the first move and I won. In a number of subsequent games I won whether or not I had the first move and Franz said that he was surprised and disappointed.

He then told me that he had beaten all of his colleagues every time they played in the last six months and that none of them would now play with him. Cameron, who had studied our games intently and made notes on a piece of paper after every move, said that he thought that having watched how I played he could now beat Franz and laid out the matches again. He did not beat him in any of the three games that they played, and he said that his system needed refining but that he was near to finding the secret; Franz said that he doubted that.

18th August

Today I returned to Takoradi. As Ted drove me to the station at Obuasi he said that nothing had been said, but he sometimes felt that his colleagues thought that he did not have sufficient experience to be the mine manager; I said that they had probably thought the same about me when Edwin Cade brought me from South Africa, but that I had been lucky to find the new vein. I told him that if Obuasi Two was started it would be a good opportunity for him to show his managerial ability, for there would be a lot of decisions to take. He said that he looked forward to that and thanked me for my support.

I am back in the Guest House tonight, and I hope that in a couple of days' time I will be in Conakry.

19th August

The *SS Avondale Castle* duly anchored off Takoradi at midday, and by three o'clock we were on our way to Conakry. Three Frenchmen came aboard with me; they have been working in the Ivory Coast and like me are bound for Conakry. I thought that a game of *Last Man Standing* would be an opportunity to practise my French on them, for I do feel more confident since I took lessons before leaving London.

After dinner, I got their attention in the usual way, by laying out the eighteen matches, and before long one of them asked what I was doing. None of them would admit to speaking English, but I was well able to explain the rules and objective of the game in French, and he sat down opposite me. Inevitably he lost; his two colleagues told him that he had not played well, and one of them stepped forward to take his place. After he and then the third Frenchman had also lost they proceeded very noisily to criticise each other's play; I thought that I detected a feeling that they should not be beaten by a mere Englishman, but they spoke so rapidly and vehemently that I was not sure that I had translated correctly. After a short time, one of them was pushed forward by his friends and asked for another game. It took a long time to reach its end, because the two non-players continually told the player what and what not to do, frequently contradicting each other and emphasising their advice with much waving of their arms. When we finished playing, without a French win, one of them said my French was not good and he thought that they had only lost because I had not explained the game properly. They are not good sports.

It is only a short distance to Conakry, and we are expected to arrive there in two days' time. I am very much looking forward to my visit to Siguiri but not to the journey to there from Conakry; I have no idea as to how I will accomplish that but I am sure that it will be tiresome

21st August

We reached Conakry early this afternoon and I have a room in a very French hotel in the centre of the town. So far my attempts at their language have all been understood, and I have understood almost everything that has been said to me. French Guinea is one of a number of French overseas territories in West Africa; each is administered by a lieutenant governor who reports to a governor general in Dakar, the capital of Senegal. I have been told that the lieutenant governor's offices are in the hotel de ville and I will go to see him there tomorrow, for I think that I will need his assistance over arranging my trip to Siguiri.

22nd August

Today I met the lieutenant governor, Pierre Pichon, in his office in the hotel de ville. I had mistakenly assumed that he actually worked in an hotel, whereas I now know that that is what the French call their town halls.

I did not have a cuckoo clock to present to him, but I did have a letter to him from the commercial attaché in the French embassy in London. This letter introduced me as the bearer and said that the AGC, a major British mining company, was interested in investing in the Siguiri gold mine, and asked that all assistance should be given to me.

PP, as he told me to call him, is not much older than I and welcomed me to the country, or his country as he called it. He said that there was only one way of getting to Siguiri, apart from on the back of a camel, and that was in one of the lorries that regularly take supplies to the mine and return with gold. One of what he called 'the more comfortable lorries' is leaving early tomorrow morning, and he has given instructions that I should have a seat in it. It is more than five hundred miles to Siguiri and the journey takes two days, more if the lorry breaks down, which is apparently not uncommon. There is a rest house near the halfway point, and PP said that it is well run by a Frenchman and quite civilised, as he put it.

I was invited to his house for dinner and told him about the mine at Obuasi and how I had come to be a director of the AGC at such an early age. He joined the French diplomatic corps after leaving university and worked in their colonial office in Paris for eight years before being posted to Guinea last year. He said that the job was interesting, and that there were quite a number of Frenchmen in Conakry and at the mine, but that he missed female company. He expects to be here for five years and is concerned that he will be too old to find a wife when he leaves. I said that I had not yet found one and that he should not worry. All of our conversation was in French, and although I often had to ask him to repeat what he said, usually more slowly, I was pleased that we had not had to fall back on his English, which is no better than my French.

PP has given me a letter of introduction to the mine manager at Siguiri and he said that he hoped that my visit would confirm that it would be a good investment for the AGC, and that I should call on him when I got back to Conakry. He is a nice fellow and I hope that he finds a wife when he returns to France.

23rd August

I am at the rest house after an interesting journey from Conakry. The driver of the lorry was a Frenchman who smoked his evil-smelling cigarettes almost without a break. Another French passenger was an engineer returning to the mine after a week's leave in Conakry; he and I sat beside the driver on a very uncomfortable seat and it was a pleasure to get down every now and then for a call of nature. If this is what PP called one of the more comfortable lorries, I am glad that I am not travelling in one less comfortable.

The lorry was driven by a petrol engine, rather than by steam, for petrol can easily be brought by sea to Conakry. Behind the driver's cabin in a section of the lorry with a canvas cover, two Senegalese policemen armed with rifles sat on a wooden bench. It was explained to me that they would be guarding the gold on the return journey, and that they were used, rather than local police, as they were less likely to become involved in attempts to steal the gold. Behind them in the open part of the lorry there were a number of natives, some of whom were returning to work at the mine and some simply getting a free ride to their villages along the route. There were also some wooden crates containing spare parts for the machinery at the mine, and a number of large cans of petrol for the return journey.

The rest house is run by a Frenchman, and therefore the evening meal was better than I might have expected; the French seem able to produce good food under even the most basic conditions. He told me that the mine, or rather mining, had been worked at Siguiri for many hundreds of years, and that the gold produced had enabled the Mandingo empire to control a huge area of West Africa in the thirteenth and fourteenth centuries, and it was now a major contributor to the French treasury. Everything that I have found out about the mine leads me to believe that it would be a very profitable acquisition by the AGC and I look forward to seeing it for myself.

24th August

Our lorry staggered into Siguiri this evening and I have a room in one of the guest bungalows used by visitors to the mine. After what was a very tiring journey I was glad to be able to have a shower and change my clothes, and I now feel ready to tackle what I am sure will be another good French dinner. There are three two-room bungalows with beds, and another with a dining room, lounge and a small kitchen. Overall, it is very much like what there is at Obuasi.

The one other guest, Henri Courmenier, is a geologist from Marseille; he has been sent by the French government to assess for how long the mine can be expected to continue to produce gold at its present rate, which is not very different from the object of my visit. He has been here for two weeks and hopes to be able to complete his report and return to the relative civilisation of Marseille in the next few days. I am becoming increasingly confident to carry on conversations in French and I hope that I will be equally at ease when discussing technical terms tomorrow.

25th August

This has been a very interesting day. On arrival at the mine, which is less than a mile from the bungalow, I was taken to the wooden hut in which the mine manager, Georges Leroux, has his office and presented the letter of introduction that I was given by PP. I do not know what the letter said, but it did not seem to please its recipient and he asked me, in passable English, just why I was here. I told him the AGC were considering investing in the mine, with a view to increasing the amount of gold recovered and extending its useful life.

Georges said that the mine would still be producing gold long after we were both dead, but offered to show me around. It is very much bigger than I expected, and is in the form of a huge, open pit more than two hundred yards across. The sides have been progressively excavated at several levels, and the veins of gold-bearing rock are clearly visible. Large numbers of native workers are engaged in breaking up the ore and loading it onto lorries, which take it to the steam-driven crushing mill. The gold is then extracted in a large, corrugated iron shed. It is a much less complex operation than at Obuasi, where the ore is won from the rock at the end of narrow tunnels leading off a deep, vertical shaft.

At midday Georges took me to his bungalow, and over lunch told me a lot about the mine; he has been here for seven years and will be able to retire after another three. Because of the lack of facilities and the oppressive heat the position is well paid, and it is his ambition to buy a villa with a few acres of vines in Provence. He said that if the AGC could wait until he retired he would be grateful, and I said that if we did buy a share I was sure that we would want to keep him in his post, possibly for longer than three years if he wished.

This seemed to relieve him and during the afternoon he was much more forthcoming and showed me the various statistics from the past three years. The most interesting, of course, was the weight of gold extracted, and his records, which I have no reason to doubt, showed a slight increase year on year. I do not see any obvious ways of greatly increasing the amount of gold extracted, for it is an efficient operation which has refined the activities of the numberless native prospectors who have made a living here over the years. In this respect it is very much like the Obuasi operation, although on a larger scale, and it would certainly make a very useful addition to the

AGC's profits.

Georges said that I can return to Conakry on the day after tomorrow; it will be on the same lorry that I came in and will be leaving early in the morning with a week's gold production. The next lorry after that might not be for several days. There is little more that I can learn here so I have booked my seat. Over our evening meal my fellow guest, the geologist, said that he could not stand another week here and that he is also leaving on the same lorry as me.

26th August

I spent today making notes on the mining operation and the general area in which it takes place. There is no forest here and the land is generally bare of vegetation, with only scrub and grasses. The town of Siguiri is on the banks of the Niger river, which rises in the south of the country and rather surprisingly flows northeast, away from the sea, through the neighbouring country of Mali before turning southeast through Nigeria to the sea. Along the river banks there is quite dense vegetation but very few trees, as their wood is used either in constructing houses or for making charcoal. Further south, between here and Conakry, there is the same rain forest as in the Gold Coast.

28th August

I was up at six o'clock yesterday and we set off in the lorry before seven. Georges saw us off and, to my great surprise, handed Colt revolvers to Henri and me. He said that he was sure that we would have no need for them, but that as we were travelling with a consignment of gold it was as well to be prepared. He said that we should hand the guns in to the person who signs for the gold in Conakry. I had not thought that we might be attacked, but the presence of the armed Senegalese police was reassuring, and the driver showed me that he too had a Colt.

What was less assuring was the news that when gold was carried there was no overnight stop at the rest house, as this could encourage potential thieves; a second driver was on board, sitting with the police, and the two of them would drive for alternate four-hour shifts. The only stops would be to fill the fuel tank from the bidons on the back of the lorry. The gold was in a locked strongbox with the Senegalese, bolted to the wooden floor of the lorry.

It was estimated that the journey would take twenty to twenty-four hours, but by the time that night fell it felt as though we had been bumping along the track for at least that time, although we had only just passed the half-way rest house. During the night, our progress was much slower as the driver sought to avoid the worst holes in the track, and when dawn broke, we were still more than one hundred miles from Conakry.

The lorry came to a halt, and while the drivers refuelled it, Henri and I took advantage of the opportunity to 'see Africa', as the emptying of one's bladder is charmingly called by those who live there. With the refuelling complete we boarded the lorry for the last leg of the journey, but before the driver started the engine three black men carrying rifles emerged from the bush beside the road and shouted 'Descendez' and indicated that we should leave the lorry.

I was in two minds, whether to obey their instruction and die uselessly, shot down by the side of the lorry, or take them on with my revolver and probably die equally uselessly in the lorry. Happily, I was saved the necessity to make that decision, for the two Senegalese policemen, who had been sitting on their bench waiting for the lorry to move off, and whose presence under the canvas behind me was evidently unknown to the gunmen, opened up with their rifles. Whether or not they scored any hits I do not know, but our attackers vanished into the forest and our driver accelerated down the track. Henri was in a state of shock, from which he had only just recovered when we reached Conakry, and the driver, if I translated his French correctly, was of the opinion that our assailants were the illegitimate offspring of baboons and that this was the last time that he drove a gold truck.

We arrived back at Conakry just before eleven o'clock. Henri handed in his revolver and made straight for the nearest bar. I handed in mine and told the man, who seemed to be the one in overall charge of the mining operation, that the swift response of the Senegalese policemen had undoubtedly saved the day. I shook hands with each of them and I hope that they understood my thanks. I then joined Henri in the bar. The two drivers were already there, telling all and sundry how they had saved the gold and the lives of their passengers.

I will wait until tomorrow before calling on PP. Before I retire to bed this evening I will draft a report for the board on my visit to the Siguiri mine; in it I feel bound to mention the difficulty of moving the gold securely from the mine to Conakry.

29th August

This morning I went to see PP and told him of my visit to Siguiri. He had already heard about the attempted robbery and congratulated me on my safe escape. He said it was not the first time that the gold lorry had been targeted, and he feared that it was probably only a matter of time before the robbers succeeded.

I told him that I was much impressed with the way that the mine operated, and that I would be recommending to my board that the AGC took a substantial shareholding; he said that he welcomed that and thought that English participation might improve the overall efficiency of the operation, especially the security.

I asked how and when I might return to England and he said that it is rare for the Union Castle ships to call at Conakry. My best choice is evidently to take passage on one of the French ships that call on all their West African colonies, from Dakar in Senegal down to Cotonou in Dahomey. It is six days until the next such ship so I will have to be patient and see what there is of interest in Conakry.

3rd September

There is very little of interest to see in Conakry. There are shops and a few restaurants run by French men, and they also manage all the commercial enterprises. The local inhabitants seem very content to be administered by France, and their ability to earn a decent wage in such areas as the port or roadworks has clearly raised their standard of living. The nearby sea means that the climate is better than inland, for a good breeze comes off the sea on most days.

I shall not be sorry to leave tomorrow when I board a French ship bound for Le Havre. It will stop for twenty-four hours at Dakar, which I am told is a very agreeable place, more so than here. From Le Havre I should fairly soon be able to get a passage to Portsmouth or Southampton. By the time that I get home I will have been away for almost two months, and I must say that I am very much looking forward to seeing my family, and not least, Mary again.

4th September

I am on board the French ship Jacques IV. We left Conakry around midday and are due in Dakar tomorrow evening. This is a smaller ship than the Union Castle ships and is more designed for the carriage of cargo than for passengers. There is a more relaxed atmosphere than on the English ships, for it carries only a dozen passengers in a single class. But having said that, my cabin is well appointed and I cannot complain about the food and wine with which we were served at dinner. I think that all the cabins must be occupied, for twelve of us sat down to the meal.

My fellow passengers on this voyage are all French men with the exception of a married couple, also French, who are on their honeymoon. They evidently got married in Abidjan where he works, and will spend the ten days of leave for which he is due in Dakar. The others are a mixed bunch; two are water engineers who have been installing a piped water system in Cotonou, and three are from the Ivory Coast, where they have been establishing an area of cocoa plants, which apparently thrive there. The other four boarded with me at Conakry; I have no idea what they do, for their French is heavily accented and I only catch a word or two of what they say; and that is not very much, for they spend all their time together and do not even say much to their countrymen.

5th September

We tied up in the port of Dakar just before sunset and I was the only passenger to stay on board. The honeymoon couple bade me bon voyage and left for their hotel; the water engineers took with them their luggage, and presumably have work to do here, and the others went in search of bars, and quite possibly women. Dakar is effectively the capital of French West Africa, and the governor general resides here. According to a guidebook to the town in the ship's library, it is more developed towards European standards than the other French West African colonies and offers many opportunities in well-paid positions; I shall go ashore tomorrow morning and take a turn around the town.

6th September

Dakar is certainly more civilised than Conakry; some of the wide, well-paved streets are flanked with palm trees, and there are many bars and restaurants that from the outside appear to be smart and well-ordered. I lunched in one of them and was very pleasantly surprised not only by the quality of the food but also the cleanliness of the establishment and the demeanour of the waiters.

A little distance offshore is the island of Gorée; until some fifty years ago it was the base for the trade in slaves between West Africa and the West Indies and the southern states of America. I did not have time to visit it, but the remains of a fort are clearly visible from the mainland.

Before we sailed the honeymoon couple and the water engineers were replaced by another, very smartly dressed couple, and two businessmen. The couple introduced themselves and I learned that the husband is a civil servant who works in the office of the governor general, and that they are off on their once every two years leave. The businessmen, who are also very friendly, have been researching the possibility of opening a chain of stores in the French West African possessions. They complimented me on my French, and I must say that I am now much more confident in the language. The other four Frenchmen only just returned to the ship before we sailed, and I must say that I rather hoped that they would miss the boat.

7th September

I spent much of the morning talking with the French civil servant, Jacques Bertrand, and his wife Louise; he was interested to hear of the reason for my visit to Siguiri but said that he would be very surprised if the AGC was permitted to buy a share in the mine, as it was one of the most profitable operations in all of their West African colonies. I said that perhaps our investment could make it even more profitable.

After dinner I laid out matches on a table in the saloon and before long attracted the interest of the two businessmen. They both lost two games, and I was putting the matches away when one of the foursome came and sat down opposite to me and his three colleagues stood close behind him. Despite the language difficulty I managed to explain the game and he said that he understood and was sure that he would win; his colleagues nodded their confidence in his ability.

I felt sure that if I let him win the first game he would get up and tell all and sundry that it was not difficult to beat an Englishman at his own game, but if I won, which I would certainly do if he did not know the secret, his displeasure was certain, and he might make it awkward for me in some way. Having given thought to these unattractive alternatives, I decided that I could not allow the honour of my country to be besmirched and that I would risk the consequences of humbling him.

I won three games before he got up, grumbling in unintelligible French; one of his colleagues patted me on the back, but I was relieved when they all left for their cabins. I must choose my adversaries more carefully, for no one likes to be beaten without understanding why, and in the wrong company I might put myself at risk.

This is not a fast ship, and I understand that after calling in briefly at Nouakchott in Mauritania tomorrow it will probably be twelve days before we reach Le Havre. I am glad that Jacques and Louise are on board as otherwise I would have little opportunity for conversation.

18th September

The time on board has passed quite agreeably, but I am much looking forward to our arrival at Le Havre tomorrow. During the past days I have spent much time with Jacques and Louise; they wanted to take the opportunity to improve their English, so we have conversed almost exclusively in my language. He is an interesting fellow, aged about forty-five, who has been posted to several French overseas territories, including French Indo China and Canada. He has completed his tour of duty in Senegal, which he says he found very pleasant, and is now to return to the Ministry of Foreign Affairs in Paris with promotion to a higher grade. Louise especially welcomes this; she says that there was a very limited social circle in Dakar and that she looks forward to there being shops in which she can buy a new wardrobe.

I hope that I will be able to get a passage on a boat to England from Le Havre without delay; there is nothing useful that I can do there and I begrudge time wasted before I am back at Broadlands. It is more than seven weeks since I sailed from Southampton, and I have much enjoyed my new rôle. If the shaft at Obuasi Two proves to be productive, and if the board agrees my proposal regarding the Siguiri mine, then I feel that I will have justified Edwin Cole's confidence in me.

19th September

We docked at Le Havre this afternoon and I went straight to the shipping office to enquire about a passage to England. A boat from Falmouth is expected to arrive tomorrow and will probably depart on the following day. It is not a passenger ship, but it does have two cabins and the clerk in the shipping office suggested that I meet the ship and ask the captain if he will take me.

I have a room in a small but respectable hotel close to the port, and this evening I took a turn around the town. It will take me time to get used to the hustle and bustle of a European city but I am glad that my trip to Africa is behind me. I had an excellent meal in a small bistro that was well patronised by the locals, and I enjoyed a cognac or two with the manager of the hotel, who was interested in what he called my adventures. He was born here and has never left Le Havre, but he has an ambition to travel, as long as the destination is French-speaking.

20th September

I was down at the dock early and waited eagerly for the arrival of what I hoped would be my final ship. I did not have to wait for long; the Falmouth Lass eased her way to the dock before ten o'clock. Twenty minutes later the captain came ashore and I introduced myself and asked whether he would take me on the return voyage. He said that he was not expecting any passengers, but that for the sum of five pounds, which I suspect goes into his pocket rather than that of the ship's owners, he would be pleased to accommodate me. I would rather have landed closer to Broadlands, but am glad not to have to kick my heels here for longer.

The Falmouth Lass is due to depart at ten o'clock tomorrow and the captain wants me on board half an hour before that. I am so relieved that I will not have to hang around waiting for a ship, and I celebrated this evening by eating my dinner in the best restaurant that I could find. I have not previously eaten magret de canard, but it is a delicious dish, which I shall try to get Cook to make when I get home. A bottle of a fine wine complemented the duck and the cheese and I am ready for my bed.

21st September The Falmouth Lass is what I believe is called a coaster. We sailed on time and should be in Falmouth late tomorrow. I have a bunk in a cupboard, and for an evening meal I had a ham sandwich and a bowl of soup. The crew consists of the captain, an engineer and a first mate, who produced the meal and a succession of very strong, very sweet and very welcome cups of tea. There is no second mate. I have spent much of the time since we left Le Havre in the small wheelhouse with the captain. I think that he is glad to have someone to talk to, and I am glad to be able once again to hold a conversation in my mother tongue. The weather has not been good; it has rained for most of the time since we left and a strong wind has made the sea rough. Our course takes us parallel with the waves, and so the ship rolls every time that a crest lifts us up and drops us down on the other side; I am glad that I have not disgraced myself by falling prey to seasickness.

We have adjusted our speed so that we will dock in Falmouth in daylight, rather than in the night, and I will hasten ashore and seek the quickest way home.

23rd September

I got back to Broadlands late this evening, having travelled via Truro. Tony met me at the station and on the way to Broadlands, he brought me up to date with the latest news of the family. I had hoped for an early night, after a rather tiring journey but that was not to be. Papa was in good form, and had yet again taken advantage of the occasion to raid his cellar. Quentin is here; he was particularly interested in the attempt to rob the gold lorry and asked whether the attackers had French Army Lebel rifles; I said that when it was pointed at me I could only see a small round hole, and that made it difficult to identify the type. Mary was concerned that I had been in such danger, and Hermione said that the children will want to know all about my meeting with a black chieftain.

I am really looking forward to sleeping in my own bed tonight after having slept in a variety of beds during the past seven weeks; some have been reasonably comfortable, but none of them have wrapped me in comfort like mine here at Broadlands does.

24th September

Today I called John Daw and told him that I was back from my travels. He told me that the board was meeting in two days' time, and that they would be glad if I could be there and report on my findings in person. I will go up to London tomorrow and stay in my little house.

Papa is in good spirits and has been able to use the funds that I put at his disposal to make several necessary repairs to Broadlands. Now that Tony and Hermione are living there Papa does not have to do everything himself; Tony manages the estate and arranges for whatever needs to be done to the house or the farms.

I went for a long walk with Mary this afternoon; she said that she had missed me, and that after hearing of my adventures in French Guinea she hoped that I would not have to go there again. I said that if I did it would be because the AGC had invested in the mine, and that security would be one of the first things that we improved. I must say that absence really has made my heart grow fonder of her, and I think and hope that she still feels the same way about me.

26th September

Today's board meeting went well, I think. I gave to each director a copy of my reports on both Obuasi Two and Siguiri, and there was a discussion on each. We have not yet heard from Ted Harris about the trial shaft, but there was unanimous agreement that if it proves productive we should enter into an agreement with the Mamponghene along the lines discussed with him and employ all the native prospectors as workers. There is every prospect of this operation adding considerably to the AGC's profits, and I was congratulated for having suggested it.

We then discussed the Siguiri operation. This is a much less straightforward matter, for the company operating the mine is French, and despite the support that we have from the French commercial attaché here in London there is no saying how their board will react. It was decided that Stephen and I should go to their head office in Paris and offer to take a fifty-one percent share in the company. If that was not accepted we would drop the offer to thirty percent, but no lower.

After the meeting finished John took me into his office; he said that I had done well on my first major projects since joining the board, and that he hoped I would soon be bringing other proposals for their consideration. He said that Lisa Hill had been manning my office very ably while I was away, and that she is showing no signs of pregnancy yet; I told him that we get on well together and I will not look for a replacement until I have to.

I am pleased that my suggestions have received board approval, and I hope that our trip to Paris goes well, but I must then find other areas to exploit.

10th October

Today we heard from Ted Harris. The trial shaft on Obuasi Two has found gold-bearing ore at the same depth as the shaft on Frobisher's Find, and the gold content is the same; it seems possible that the same vein runs between them. If that is the case, it means that there could potentially be a huge expansion of our operation there, and I have told Ted to visit the Mamponghene and confirm our agreement regarding Obuasi Two, confirming his commission and the employment of his tribal workers. At the same time he should say that we may wish to carry out exploratory work on the land between Obuasi One and Two, and that we would propose the same arrangement if that was promising.

This is a very exciting development, and I have asked Ted to draw up a plan for a further trial shaft between the two mines; it should suggest where it would be sunk, when it could be done, and how much it would cost. I emphasised that this should not cause any reduction in the current work at the two mines and that additional labour would be needed. All the board members are very supportive of this expansion of our operation there and Stephen is already talking about increasing the dividends to be paid at the end of the year. This is rather premature, for even if our hopes are realised it will be at least six months before any gold can be produced, but Obuasi One has contributed significantly to our profits throughout the year, and Obuasi Two will soon be operational.

8th November

The French owners of the Siguiri mine, Société á Responsibilité Limitée d'Exploitation Minière (SARLEM) have at last agreed to see Stephen and me. It has taken some time to get a date agreed, but they have assured us that that was only because they were seeking confirmation that the AGC was a company with a good financial record and sufficient resources. We are going to Paris next week and it sounds as though they may be willing to do business with us.

10th November

Today is Arthur's sixth birthday and we celebrated it with a special tea party. Cook made a very fine cake, crowned with six candles, and there was a pile of presents for him to open. I gave him a very nicely illustrated book of all the animals in Africa; he is very interested in natural history and said that the book is just what he wanted. Papa gave him a gold sovereign, and said that if he still had it in a year's time, he would give him another; a clever way of encouraging him to save. After tea, we had the fireworks that should have been seen on 5th November.

13th November

A very interesting meeting today. We met with the SARLEM chairman and finance director, and Stephen and I at first got the impression that there was no real interest in sharing the profits of the mine, although our fifty-one percent investment could considerably improve those profits. The French were courteous throughout, but said that their government would never agree to an English company having a controlling interest in the mine. Stephen said that we understood that, and believed that if a figure of thirty-three percent could be agreed it would satisfy us.

The discussion continued over lunch in a very smart restaurant close to their offices; we had a private dining room for the four of us and no record was taken of what was said on either side. Their finance director said that despite their government's view, our investment would be very welcome, and that having seen the operation I would know that the production of gold could indeed be improved if more machinery replaced some of the manual work. I said that I wholeheartedly agreed and that that was why we had approached them in the first place,

The two Frenchmen asked if they could have a discussion in French and we agreed. They moved to the end of the long table but obviously did not believe that either of us could speak French, for they did not lower their voices. Although my grasp of their language is far from perfect, I had improved it while I was in French Guinea, and was able to understand most of what they said, without of course, giving any indication. It seems that they are short of capital, and that unless they can develop the mine, and move away from surface and near-surface mining, they believe that there is little chance of it having a long-term future.

I think that their chairman sees his well-paid position having a limited life and is keen to find a way to circumvent his government's position on the matter. They spoke for about ten minutes and then returned to their chairs and apologised for leaving us out of the discussion for so long. I had briefed Stephen on their position, but I had not been able to hear their final decision.

They came up with an example of what I think is a typically French way of getting what you want when you have been told that you cannot have it. They said that there were two areas in which our input would be very valuable. The first was modern machinery and the second was professional advice. Their first proposal, subject to the approval of their board, is that the AGC should provide, free of charge and amongst other things, boring and crushing machinery, the latest chemical means of extracting gold from its ore, conveyer belts to move the ore from the digs to the crushers and new lorries to transport the gold from the mine to Conakry and to move their personnel about the mine. Given the geographical size of their operation all this represents a very considerable capital outlay.

The other part of their proposal was no less interesting. They admitted that at this time, the mine is still really based on the methods of individual prospectors over several hundred years. No exploratory shafts have been sunk, and no work done to see whether there is a rich vein in the area which has given rise to the gold found on or near the surface. They feel that the mine manager, Georges Leroux, is doing what he is paid to do, but has neither the expertise nor the ambition to see whether the operation could be profitably expanded; I got the impression that they know about his plan to retire to a small vineyard in Provence as soon as possible.

They went on to say that what they needed as much as the machinery was the input of someone experienced in modern mining techniques and with a track record of success in developing existing mines. They said that the reason why this meeting had been so delayed, was because they had carried out research not only into the resources of the AGC but also into my background and more recent work. They said that they thought that I would be the ideal person to realise the true potential of the Siguiri operation.

You can imagine how this surprised Stephen and I. We asked if we might confer in private, knowing that they both very well understand English, and they suggested that we go to a café a few paces from the restaurant.

Stephen first asked me what I thought of their proposal. I said that I did not relish the thought of spending a few years at Siguiri but that we should first see how the financial part of the arrangement could work in our favour. SARLEM are very undercapitalised, and the cost of the equipment that they have asked us to provide is probably equivalent to the value of about twenty-five percent of their shares. If the mine prospered as we hoped that it would this amount could be repaid at the end of the first year, leaving them clear of debt; but if the AGC was to benefit on an ongoing basis, it would need that amount paid annually every year in the future. It would be up to SARLEM to find a way of doing that without breaking their government's regulations.

As regards my own involvement, I said that I would only consider working at Siguiri if I received a sizeable increase in my salary, the cost of which would be borne by SARLEM; since they would not know how much I was paid they could be billed for twice the actual amount, contributing to the AGC's profit from the arrangement. I said that I would not sign up for more than an initial two years, and that I needed to make some personal arrangements before finally committing to the posting. Stephen said that he quite understood, and that since SARLEM seemed keen to do a deal we had something of an advantage at the bargaining table.

We returned to the room in the restaurant and told the two SARLEM executives that we thought that a deal might be possible. We explained how the cost of the equipment would be repaid, and that we would need the same amount paid on an ongoing annual basis. When we asked whether this would be possible in the light of their government's regulations they said that it could probably be shown in their published accounts each year as consultancy fees or the cost of replacing old machinery, and that this was most unlikely ever to be queried.

As regards my salary, they realised that someone with my experience did not come cheaply, and that if the profit from the mine was increased as we all hoped there could be no questions asked. They accepted an initial two-year contract, but said that they hoped that it would be extended.

The meeting ended with assurances from them that they would put the proposal to their board, and that when it was approved the details could then be worked out and agreed by the two financial directors. We told them that our board's approval would also be needed and left them, not without suffering kisses on both cheeks. We returned to this hotel, where we went over the day's events and partook of a light dinner washed down with a glass or two of wine. If the SARLEM board approves the proposal the AGC will effectively have achieved a twenty-five percent investment at no cost once the machinery and other equipment is paid for. I have to hope that I will be able to make a real difference to the mine's profits, for it is on that expectation that the whole arrangement depends.

Stephen and I feel pleased that we have reached this agreement with SARLEM, and we will return to London tomorrow and seek our board's approval. I need to examine closely my personal life, and especially my feelings for Mary. I cannot imagine taking her to French Guinea, nor parting from her for two years, but a doubling of my salary is not to be dismissed lightly. Some very tricky decisions will have to be taken.

15th November

At today's board meeting Stephen went through our discussion with the SARLEM chairman and finance director. He said that there was no way in which the AGC would be permitted to buy even twenty-five percent of their shares, but that the agreement that had been reached had the same effect without costing a penny. He went on to say that the board should realise that I was not happy to have to go and work in French Guinea for two years, but that since the whole deal hinged on that the board should show its appreciation financially, as well as verbally; such a gesture would, once again, be at no cost to the AGC but could actually improve its profit.

Since I came to London I have had little contact with two of my fellow directors, Richard Beale, our company secretary, and Alan Hughes, our legal adviser, for they both have work outside the AGC and only appear at board meetings, and I watched them and John while Stephen made his report. I could not tell from their faces what they thought of the proposal, but John and Alan both made notes while Stephen spoke and Richard consulted a thick leather-bound book, the title of which I could not see.

When Stephen finished speaking, John said that he congratulated the two of us on finding a way into SARLEM, and he thanked me for being prepared to consider putting the company's wellbeing before my personal circumstances; he went on to say that he would like to hear from Richard and Alan and that there would then be a vote on whether to proceed along the lines proposed. Richard said that as there would be no actual investment in SARLEM, but rather an agreement entered into by the two boards of directors, the worst that could happen if SARLEM failed was that we would lose the cost of the machinery and equipment with which we were to supply them. On balance, he was in favour of the deal.

Alan took a very different view. He said that if we were dealing with an English company, subject to English law, it would be reasonable to proceed along the lines proposed, for we would have recourse through the courts if the other company failed to make good on its commitments. But in this case there would be no legal framework on which to hang the arrangement, and that if SARLEM defaulted on the deal we would not be able to recover a penny of our costs. Those costs might not be enough to damage the financial health of the AGC seriously, but its reputation would suffer considerably and it would certainly, in his opinion, make it very much more difficult to expand by entering into agreements with other companies, whether by take-over or partnership. It was on such activities that he saw the future of the AGC depending.

A silence followed Alan's contribution; Stephen and I looked at each other but said nothing. John thanked Richard and Alan for their input and said that it was time to vote. He personally felt that what Alan said made a lot of sense, and though it was tempting to take what amounted to a chance with SARLEM he had to exercise his duty on behalf of our shareholders. He said that the proposal now before the board was to take no further action with regard to the Siguiri mine, and he called for a show of hands by those in favour of that proposal.

This reversal of the normal procedure took me by surprise, but I was not surprised when Alan immediately raised his hand, and it was not long before Richard followed suit. Stephen and I made it plain that our hands would stay down and so the casting vote fell to John. He said that we had acted in good faith in our discussions with SARLEM but that he could not ignore Alan's advice, and he raised his hand; the proposal to withdraw was carried by three votes to two.

You can imagine how I felt. It was my recommendation in the first place after my visit to Siguiri to invest in the operation, and it was Ime, together with Stephen, who had achieved an agreement with SARLEM that we thought was in the best interests of the AGC. This has been my biggest responsibility since joining the board and it has come to nothing; I wonder whether I have a future here. My only consolation is that I shall not have to leave the country, and Mary, and spend two years in French Guinea; for that I am heartily thankful.

16th November

Yesterday I came back to my little house after the board meeting with very mixed emotions, and I have to admit that it took several glasses of a fine whisky to calm me down. After the meeting, John took me into his office and said that he realised how disappointed I must be; but he said that both at Siguiri and in Paris I could not have done more or better on the company's behalf, and it showed how right Edwin had been to put me on the board. He said that there would be many other opportunities for me to show my ability and that I should put the day's outcome behind me. I am going down to Broadlands tomorrow and will have to explain to Papa and the others what went wrong with my proposal; Mary, at least, will be glad that I am not off to Africa again.

Ed. In 1996, ninety-one years after the AGC Board voted against investing in SARLEM, AngloGold Ashanti, the result of an earlier merger between AngloGold and the AGC, bought an eighty-five percent stake in the Siguiri mine, with the other fifteen percent being owned by the country of Guinea (no longer French Guinea). Perhaps Frobisher was right.

17th November

As I expected, Papa is very surprised and angry that the AGC Board has decided against forming a partnership with SARLEM after all the hard work that I did. I said that while I thought that the proposed deal would have been to the benefit of both parties, I had to agree that our legal position would have been weak in the event that SARLEM defaulted. I also said that I would have had to go back to Siguiri for two years, and everyone agreed that they would not like to lose me.

Mary brought the children to see me and Rob, who will be ten in a few days' time, asked me what French people looked like. Arthur asked me to tell him again about the men who tried to steal the gold, and Penelope asked whether there were elephants and leopards in France. It took some time to answer all their questions satisfactorily, but it was so nice to relax with the family.

20th December

I have been going up to London for two or three days every week, staying overnight in my little mews house. Hermione has stayed there several times while I was away and it has benefitted from her feminine touch. She has brought up a few pictures, rugs and ornaments from Broadlands and the effect has been to make it much more like a home than a bachelor's retreat.

In the office I have been keeping abreast of reports of gold being found elsewhere in Africa. I believe that both Rhodesia and Tanganyika, a German colony, may prove to be of interest to the AGC, but it is too early to tell and it would be a very expensive exercise to set up an operation in either country.

Today I got another report from Ted Harris. Operations have just started at the new shaft at Obuasi Two, and the ore extracted has a good gold content; however, there are not enough workers to realise the mine's full potential. Ted has been to Kumasi and seen the Mamponghene and asked him to encourage more Ashanti men to work in the mine, for if the area between the two existing mines also contains gold we will want to increase our labour force considerably.

He was evidently received with all the usual courtesy, but the unspoken message was that he, the Mamponghene, was a chief and would only discuss serious matters with a chief from the AGC, as was done, he said, when I met with him in August. Ted said that he had no doubt that we would get what we wanted, for the commission that we would pay is very important to the Ashantis, but that a director of the AGC, preferably me, would have to go and parley with the Mamponghene.

This is not good news, for although Obuasi is very much preferable to Siguiri I have no wish to make another trip there just now. I took Ted's report to John and told him that I was not eager to go but that if he wanted me to go I would of course do so. He said that I had done my share of overseas trips, and that if the Mamponghene wanted a chief he could have one, and that he would go to Kumasi and try to reach an understanding. I am much relieved by this.

John has never been to the Gold Coast, and since Obuasi generates such a large proportion of our profits, he feels that he should see the place for himself, as well as negotiating with the Mamponghene. He has asked me to brief him thoroughly on the place and our people there. I said that they were all entirely dependable, but that with Obuasi Two in operation, and the possibility of another mine, Obuasi Three, between Obuasi One and Two, as we have never replaced Williams we need at least two mine superintendents, possibly three, and a doubling of our workforce. The latter could be supplied by the Mamponghene, but we would have to recruit the mine superintendents. Ted is presently working as mine manager and mine superintendent for both Obuasi One and Obuasi Two, and it is not reasonable to expect him to do all four jobs.

I also said to John that when I was at Obuasi I had heard that gold had for many years been found by artisan prospectors at Bibiani, which is about sixty miles north west of our mines, still in the Ashanti kingdom, and that if he had time it might be worth going there and seeing if there was an opportunity for the AGC.

22nd December

John is sailing for Takoradi on 3rd January, and in the New Year I will set about finding the men that we need down there. This will be my second Christmas at Broadlands with all the family and I am much looking forward to it. It is now eighteen months since I first returned from Africa and the time has passed very quickly. I have had some success, but I need to do more to justify my position on the board.

27th December

With Christmas behind us, and what a good time we had, it will soon be 1906 and a new year in which to show what I can contribute to the AGC. Recruiting two mine managers will be my first task, and then I will see where the AGC might profitably expand.

Chapter Three
1906

4th January

I returned to the office yesterday and set about seeking to recruit the men we need at Obuasi; I have placed advertisements in several newspapers, and also in the Monthly Miner, the technical journal published by the Confederation of British Mines. We need a deputy mine manager, who will report to Ted and have responsibility for both mines, and two mine superintendents. There are always men who have made their money in South Africa and elsewhere, come home and frittered their savings away, and are looking for further employment. Happily their skills at the mine are greater than their skills at managing their money, and I am sure that we will soon have a number of well-qualified applicants from whom to choose. Of course, not everyone wants to go to the Gold Coast, for in spite of its attractive name that country and the others in West Africa are known as the white man's grave. This is not wholly undeserved, for malaria, blackwater fever, dysentery, snake bites and other fatal encounters do take a toll on those seeking their fortunes there.

8th January

When I came to the office today Lisa handed me a letter which she said had just been delivered by hand; I imagined that it was from someone answering our advertisements, but when I opened it the first thing that I saw was the letterhead, proclaiming that it came from our old friend, the commercial attaché at the French Embassy. He presented his compliments, as always, and asked if it would be convenient for me to be his guest at luncheon today.

Since our board had decided not to become involved with the Siguiri mine my first reaction was to decline politely, but then I thought that a further meeting could do no harm, and it was sure to be a good lunch, and I sent word that I would be delighted to accept. When I got to the restaurant that he had suggested, he was sitting with another man at a table in an alcove at the back of the room. They both rose as I approached, and my host introduced his companion as Anton Dubois, the deputy chairman of SARLEM.

This was a complete surprise, and not a very welcome one, but I said that I was glad to meet him, that I had been impressed by their operation at Siguiri, and that I was sorry that my board had decided not to agree to the proposal that had been worked out in Paris. He said that he quite understood that there would have been risks entering into an agreement without a legal structure, but that was not why he had wanted to meet me.

He then said that his chairman had been much impressed when he met me in Paris, and that he had come to London to offer me a senior position with SARLEM. I would need to make occasional short visits to Siguiri but would be based in Paris, where the company would provide me with an apartment. My salary would be negotiable, and I would be given shares in the company and therefore receive annual dividends. My responsibilities would be much the same as with the AGC, but SARLEM wished to expand aggressively and I could expect to travel to East Africa, Australia and North America, and anywhere else where gold was found.

If I was surprised to see Anton Dubois when I entered the restaurant, it was nothing to my astonishment when I heard what he had to say. It took me a moment or two to gather my thoughts and think how to respond. The offer is, of course, very attractive, both from a personal and a financial point of view, and I am flattered that I should be thought worthy of the position. I thanked Anton sincerely and said that I needed time to make a decision; since my chairman is out of the country. Anton said that he quite understood but hoped that it would not be too long.

After the lunch I returned to the office and sat for some time trying to bring some order to the thoughts whirling around in my head. Would this be a good career move, to work for a foreign company? Would Mary want to come with me to Paris and be alone there while I travelled around the globe? Did I want to leave the rest of my family at Broadlands, with Papa not being in the best of health? It will be five or six weeks before John is back from Obuasi, and if I do decide to take up SARLEM's offer it would only be right and proper to tell him before I do. I wrote a letter to Anton summarising the position that I am in and assuring him that I would let him have my decision just as soon as my chairman returned.

Back here in my house I am thinking how I will break the news down at Broadlands at the weekend. Papa, Hermione and Mary will all react differently for different reasons, and I doubt whether that will help me in making my decision. We shall see.

11th January

The weekend passed very much as I thought it would. Papa was glad that I was thought suitable for such a job, but said that with Quentin in the army and me having been abroad for so many years, he had not had the pleasure of his sons' company that he would have wished, and that with Mama dead he felt very much alone, despite having Hermione and the children in the house. His health is not good, and I do not want his last years to be anything but happy.

Hermione said that it was a terrific opportunity for me and that she would often come and visit me in Paris. She also said that I ought to decide on my feelings for Mary, and to realise that if we were to get married it might be difficult for her to make the transition from nanny to the wife of a senior executive in a foreign country, with the social life that that would entail.

Mary, as always, put me and my life before any effect that it might have on her. She is a most kind and considerate person, and I am always so happy in her company; I get on well with Rob, and it would probably be good for him to have a second language if he and his mother came to Paris with me. I am increasingly leaning towards accepting the offer, but I need to weigh the pros and cons with great care, and Mary is one of the major considerations.

26th January

Three days ago, Alan and I started interviewing candidates for the three positions at Obuasi One and Obuasi Two. If we open Obuasi Three it can, at least initially, be managed by the staff at Obuasi Two. As I had expected, the candidates were a mixture of men who had worked in South Africa, both in the goldfields and the diamond mines, and some who had worked in different parts of Africa in a variety of jobs. There was also one man who has a shoe shop in London, and in his letter of application he said that he thought that a change of scenery would be nice.

By today, we had whittled the applicants down to five, two potential deputy mine managers and three superintendents. It would be very much preferable if Ted could choose the people to work with him, but that is obviously not possible and Alan and I feel sure that we could make the right choices.

31st January

We have chosen the men to go to Obuasi; two have to give a month's notice to their present employers and the third could leave tomorrow. The deputy mine manager has worked in South Africa, where he was in charge of three small open pit mines at Witwatersrand. I never met him when I was there, but I knew of the company owning those claims and it had a reputation as a well-run organisation. Since he returned he has been working for a company selling agricultural machinery, but says that he misses the excitement of every day expecting to find a really big nugget. We all shared that hope.

One of the two superintendents has worked for a timber logging company in the Gold Coast, and although he has no mining experience his past responsibility for a number of African workers should stand him in good stead. The other has worked with various responsibilities at a copper mine in Cornwall; he understands mining well and should have no difficulty in fitting into the Obuasi operation.

I was sorry not to interview the owner of the shoe shop; he has, however, promised to give me a good price if I go to him for a new pair of shoes.

I have booked passages for the three men to Takoradi, leaving on 2nd March, unfortunately, John will have left the mine by the time that they arrive there, but I have no doubt that he will approve our choices.

15th March

John returned yesterday and this morning we all met in the board room. He had much to tell us, and I had much to tell him.

He said that he had paid a successful visit to the Mamponghene in Kumasi, and that the AGC now had his full support for Obuasi Two and exploration for a possible third mine in the area between the two existing ones. We are assured of as many workers as are necessary, and the commission paid into the Ashanti treasury will be the same as now. John had presented him with a rather lovely pocket compass, set in a gold case; this rather useless gift had been received with much exclamation, and the Mamponghene had spent some time rotating the compass very quickly, hoping, predictably without any success, to confuse the needle and get it to point other than to the north. John was given a small model of the traditional Ashanti stool in solid gold, which he showed to us. It is a beautiful thing and John says that it will be displayed in the board room, but will be locked in the safe every night.

He went on to say that he thought that our mines were in good hands, and that he thought that Ted Harris particularly was a most competent fellow, doing more than one job very efficiently. I told him that we had selected a man who would lighten Ted's load, and also two mine superintendents, and that they should arrive in Takoradi any day now. John was glad to hear that and said that the increased efficiency of the mines would almost certainly offset the additional cost.

John then said that he had been able to pay a brief visit to Bibiani, which is in the western edge of the Ashanti kingdom, and he had been surprised by the amount of mining that is going on there. There are no deep shafts, but any number of shallow pits and horizontal tunnels driven into the sides of river banks and hills. Nearly all the people working there are Africans, from the Ivory Coast, Sierra Leone and French Guinea as well as local Gold Coast men. They have very little in the way of equipment, which would, in any case, be difficult to take there as the railway does not go there, and it is reached from Obuasi only by a track that winds its way through forest and scrub land for more than sixty miles. He thanked me for having suggested the visit, which he said had been very interesting, but in spite of the amount of gold being found he could not see how the AGC could operate profitably without heavy crushing machinery and other equipment.

It was then that I told him about the offer that I had received from SARLEM; he said nothing for some time and then said that it sounded as though it was a good offer, and that it confirmed the value of my experience and ability. He asked whether I was going to accept it, and said that if I did it would be a loss for the AGC but that he would not hold me to the three months' notice that my contract stipulates.

I said that I had given the matter considerable thought and that I decided not to join SARLEM, that I believed that I could continue to do good work for the AGC, and that my personal life would not benefit from a move to Paris. John and the other directors all stood up and shook my hand and said that they were glad that I was not going to leave. Miss Press went out and returned with a bottle of whisky and five glasses and we all drank a toast to the AGC's continued prosperity.

I will tell the family of my decision when I go down to Broadlands this weekend, and I am sure that no one there will regret it.

30th April

For the last five weeks I have suffered a recurrence of the malaria that I contracted at Obuasi. I am told that this is not uncommon, and that it may affect me for several years to come. I have felt very weak and have sweated a lot, and did not leave my room at Broadlands for three weeks. I now spend my time downstairs with the others, since the condition is not contagious, and I go out and sit in the sun whenever possible.

Mary has nursed me throughout, and has spent hours sitting at my bedside; she has shown a real interest in my work, and I have told her all about Obuasi One and Obuasi Two. I have had plenty of time to think about what John said about his visit to Bibiani, and I would like to come up with a feasible way of having a profitable operation there, in spite of the difficulties of its remote location.

10th May

I was back in the office today, and John and others congratulated me on my recovery. Lisa, who still is not pregnant, has kept me abreast of developments while I was away by sending important documents down to Broadlands for my consideration. Obuasi Two is now running at full capacity with the additional workers supplied by the Mamponghene, and exploratory work is going on between the two mines to see whether a third operation would be equally productive.

Ted has said that he is very pleased with the new men that we chose, and that he now has much more time to oversee the actual production of gold rather than attend to a multitude of administrative tasks. He has asked me, in a private letter, whether there is to be any involvement by the AGC at Bibiani; he accompanied John on his visit there and thinks that if all the individual native prospectors could be organised under a single management it could be a very profitable operation. But he agrees that to get heavy machinery there would be very difficult.

12th May

I have an idea as to how we might develop the artisan mining at Bibiani into a single profitable operation. The major difficulty would be to bring the very large, very heavy ore-crushing machine to the remote location. The boring machine is much more easily transportable, and so is the equipment for leaching the gold out of the crushed ore. Some fifty years ago an American designed, patented and put into production a device named after him, called a Berdan Pan. This is basically a large iron topless can, or pan, up to six feet in diameter and two or three feet high, which rotates, mounted on a canted spindle. In the pan there are two large, iron balls, and as the pan rotates these crush the ore that is loaded in it.

It is a very simple, cheap device, and has been much used in Australia and places in Asia with very satisfactory results, but although there is, or was, an English company with the rights to sell the Berdan Pans I can find no record of them being used here. To transport two or three pans to Bibiani, together with the steam-driven machines that rotate them, would be very much easier than to move a crushing machine similar to the one in use at Obuasi One. I have written an outline proposal along these lines and left it on John's desk; he will be in the office tomorrow and I wonder how he will react to it.

13th May

John has received my suggestion enthusiastically. He has asked me and Stephen to prepare a fully costed proposal to put before the board. Apart from the mining equipment there will be costs for transport, accommodation, management and the workforce; it will not be cheap, but it may be very profitable.

2nd June

I am engaged to Mary. I have wanted to ask her to marry me for a long time, but I was never sure of her feelings and was scared that she might not accept. As it is she asked me why I waited for so long, and said that she had begun to think that I was not the marrying kind. I am so happy; I have a job which I enjoy, a little house in London, and I will soon have a lovely wife; what more can I ask for?

I told Papa of my intentions last week and he said that I have made a good choice, that she has fitted so well into the family and is a very sensible girl; he said that he expects Quentin to be down next weekend, and Tony will of course be here, so we can have a family celebration. It is on occasions like this that he seems just like his old self. Hermione is delighted; she and Mary have been close and very good friends since she became their nanny, and both her children love Mary dearly. We will not get married until October or November, so there will be plenty of time to make all the arrangements.

Papa says that when we are married we should move into the gamekeeper's cottage so that we have a place of our own; it is only a stone's throw from Broadlands, and we will be able to go there to see Papa and Hermione's family whenever we want to. I know that Papa will want to invite a lot of his friends to the reception at Broadlands, and I will certainly invite my fellow directors. I am very busy in the office, working on the Bibiani project, and if we decide to go ahead with it I may well have to go there, and if so I would rather that it was before our wedding than after.

6th June

Stephen and I have completed our costing of the Bibiani project and it was discussed by the board today. It was agreed that it could only go ahead if we used Berdan Pans and I was able to report that these could be shipped from New York as soon as payment was made. John said that he had not spent enough time there to see where the mining camp might be situated, and that he supposed that we would have to have more lorries. All this has been taken into account in the costing of the project, and we must come to a further agreement with the Mamponghene to achieve the necessary number of workers over and above the existing individual prospectors, most of whom it was assumed would be happy to have the security of paid jobs rather than their present hand-to-mouth existence.

With two mines working at Obuasi there would be no spare equipment available to move to Bibiani, and we would need to duplicate much of it, and obtaining it will cost a sizeable sum. John said that the mine could make a great difference to the profits of the AGC if it proved to be successful, but that if it did not it could very well bring the company to its knees.

It was decided that I should go to Obuasi as soon as possible, and then go with Ted Harris to Kumasi to seek the Mamponghene's support before going to Bibiani to confirm that all our assumptions, from the suitability of the access track to the agreement of the prospectors, were valid. Most importantly, we should collect samples of the ore and have them analysed by Franz back at Obuasi.

I said that I would take a passage in the next ship calling at Takoradi, and that it was more convenient for me to go now rather than later, when I was getting married. This called for Miss Press to bring another bottle to the board room, where my colleagues drank to my health and that of my bride-to-be. This has worked out well, and I am looking forward to another visit to the scene of my earlier success; I hope that it can be repeated at Bibiani. Mary says that she will miss me while I am away, but that my return will be that much more enjoyable.

27th June

I leave for Takoradi tomorrow. I am looking forward to seeing Ted again and my other friends at Obuasi, and I have a long list of things to do at Bibiani. If all goes well there, and there are no problems with the Mamponghene or the present prospectors, I expect to be in the Gold Coast for no more than two or three weeks, and it will then depend upon there being a ship calling at Takoradi to get me home in good time to finalise the wedding arrangements. Mary says that she and Hermione are well able to do everything except have me measured for my wedding attire, but I have not told them that I took care of that when I was last in London.

28th June

Here I am, once again on board the *SS Alnwick Castle*; one might think that the Union Castle Line only has four or five ships, since I seem to travel on the same ones time after time, but in fact they have a large fleet and the reason that the Alnwick Castle calls at Takoradi more often than some of the other ships, is because its lesser draught allows it to anchor closer to the shore than the larger ones.

It will be nice to have nine or ten days in which to relax, and I will resist the temptation to demonstrate to my fellow passengers my skill at the *Last Man Standing*. I will spend my time going over my list of what I have to do at Bibiani and rehearse my approach to the prospectors there. I am sure that the time on board will pass pleasantly enough.

July 7th

I am back in the rest house at Takoradi. The train to Obuasi left before I disembarked, so it will not be until the day after tomorrow that I will leave here. The manager is the same as when I was last here; he asked whether my trip to Siguiri had proved successful and was interested to hear of our plans for Bibiani; he said that some of the few Europeans who prospect there stay at the rest house on their way home, and that from what they say, he believes that there is money to be made if the mining of the area is properly organised.

9th July

Ted met me at the station and took me straight to what is still called Edwin's bungalow; while I unpacked he brought me up to date with progress at Obuasi Two, which is exceeding our expectations. The Mamponghene will graciously receive us in three days' time, and before then we will go to the potential site of Obuasi Three, where the boring machine has just broken the surface.

At dinner, I met up with Franz, George, Cameron and Sergeant Miller. George told me all about his recent expeditions into the forest to see birds and animals and asked me to let him know what wildlife there is around Bibiani. Franz said that he looked forward to seeing what grade of ore is there, and Cameron, always pessimistic, said we would never get a crusher up that road. I told him about the Berdan Pans, but he said that he had never heard of them. Sergeant Miller said he had heard that it was a rather lawless area, being close to three other countries and a long way from any major town, and that a separate security unit with at least four trustworthy policemen would be necessary; I have included this cost in our proposal.

The three new men that we sent down four months ago seem to have settled in well and Ted said that they were all good workers, especially his deputy, Alan Parsons, who he thought might be suitable for the position of mine manager at Bibiani. This would mean recruiting another man to be his deputy here to oversee the operation of the two, possibly three, Obuasi mines.

The three servants that I had when I first came here from South Africa are still working here, and after dinner they were waiting outside to greet me as I made my way to my bungalow. I feel as though I have real friends here, of every class, and it is really nice to be back.

11th July

I have been to Obuasi Two, which is operating well and producing a very satisfactory amount of gold. I have also been to the site of Obuasi Three where I saw that the boring machine, which evidently still breaks down regularly despite Cameron's best efforts, is working about four feet below the surface. If my predictions are correct it should strike gold-bearing ore at a depth of about twelve to fifteen feet; I hope that it may reach that level before I return to London, it would be another feather in my cap.

12th July

Our meeting with the Mamponghene went well; he agreed that law and order is not always observed at Bibiani and said that he would instruct the local headman to provide us with workers, and tell his people that the AGC was a great benefit to all Ashantis and that any misbehaviour would not be looked on kindly. He said how glad he was that Obuasi Two was operating so well, and that he hoped that Obuasi Three would soon be doing so too.

14th July

We got to Bibiani this afternoon after an uncomfortable five hours' journey; the track, I cannot call it a road, was reasonable for the first ten miles from Obuasi, but then suddenly deteriorated, both the surface and in width; this is because a logging company is operating nearby, and they have improved the track to where their vehicles turn off it but not beyond. Improving the remainder of the track will be the first thing to do if we decide to operate here.

At the entrance to the town we were surprised and somewhat alarmed to find our way blocked by four warriors wearing their traditional dress and holding spears. Our driver enquired of them in their language why we could not pass, and he told us that the headman was waiting to greet us. It seems that the bush telegraph has got word from the Mamponghene that we are important people and are to be treated accordingly.

Sure enough, the headman appeared, dressed in colourful robes with monkey-skin cuffs and anklets; in perfect English he told us that we were welcome in his town and that if we needed anything we had only to ask him and it would be done. I said that we hoped that we would be able to bring great prosperity to his town and his people and that his help would be most valuable.

We then proceeded to the rest house, escorted by the four warriors, two running on each side of our car. I had been surprised when at Obuasi I was told that there was a rest house here; it is run by a Frenchman and caters for those European prospectors who are either recently arrived or about to depart with their hard-earned wealth. The facilities are fairly basic, but as always where there is a French influence around the kitchen one can expect the food to be very tasty.

And so it turned out to be; dinner was roast guineafowl, served in a delicious sauce, fresh vegetables and newly baked bread, all washed down with a good red wine from our host's personal store. His name is Louis Bucher; he told us that he came here as a prospector fifteen years ago; when I asked why he had chosen this back-of-beyond place, he confided that he had fled France, where he was wanted by the police for causing the death of a man who raped and killed his wife. He had rightly judged that the arm of the French law was not long enough to reach him here, and he had worked hard and accumulated enough money to finance the building of the rest house.

His partner, there is no one here to marry them, comes from the Ivory Coast and used to cross the nearby border several times a year and bring luxuries to sell to the prospectors. She still makes regular journeys, but most of what she brings is now for her and Louis, although she does still bring some things requested by the European prospectors.

Louis had heard that a foreign company was thinking of taking over the goldfield and had hoped that it was not a French one. He said that the only objections could come from the few European prospectors, but that since their permission to look for gold here came from Kumasi they would have to either work for the company or go home with what they had found. He thought that most of the African prospectors would be glad to get on the company's pay roll. Tomorrow we will go to where gold is being found and collect some ore samples for Franz.

15th July

This is another interesting place. To anyone with experience of gold mining it looks to be a very amateur operation, and indeed it is; several dozen men of several nationalities are scraping, digging, and in some cases tunnelling over an area of a square mile or so. There are no claims staked or registered, and such title as there is to any piece of ground expires when the prospector moves off it.

And yet gold is being found in remarkable quantities, considering the lack of a more professional means of extraction. Flakes and small nuggets are found in the dry river bed, and ore with a gold content is dug by hand out of tunnels driven into the river banks; this is crushed by heavy sledgehammers and the gold then extracted by mixing the rubble with mercury, which dissolves the gold; the amalgam is then heated to separate the two metals.

We spoke to a number of the native workers, in some cases through our driver as an interpreter, and asked whether they would be prepared to work for the AGC if we took over the mining here. Almost to a man they said that they would, if the pay was satisfactory, and that with the proper equipment much gold could be found. There were four Europeans on the site, two Germans, a Frenchman and an Italian; we told them that if analysis of the ore samples showed a sufficiently high gold content we would sink some trial shafts to locate the vein, and that if we found it we would offer them paid positions with the AGC.

The two Germans said that they had been here for long enough, too long said one of them, and that they were already planning to leave and go home. The Italian said that he would not wish to work for an English company, and that he would go to French Guinea, where he had heard that there was much gold. I told him that there was indeed, but that it was controlled by a French company; he said that was better than an English one.

The Frenchman, Arnaud Leclerc, said that if he was offered a position with the AGC that paid more than he was now making, he would be happy to work for us. I see him as a possible mine superintendent and told him that I was sure that we could come to an agreement

There is a level area of light scrub on which the buildings could be situated when it is cleared, and for most of the year a stream makes its way past that area to join the Niger river some miles to the north. There is evidence of a much larger river at some time in the past, and it is that which has brought gold to the surface. Two wells provide fresh water throughout the year. Overall I think that it is worth sinking two or three trial shafts; this could be done without incurring any great expense and might put the AGC on the path to a very profitable operation.

16th July

Today, Ted and I, together with Arnaud drove for some miles along the dry riverbed; there is no geological reason why the course of a river should follow the vein of a gold-bearing ore several or many feet beneath it, but when we stopped to examine the river bank, I found a small nugget at the base of it. That suggests that there is a vein of ore no deeper than the height of the bank, which varies between twelve and twenty feet. I asked Arnaud not to mention this back at the mine, and implied that his possible future employment depended on his silence. I think that he perfectly understood this.

17th July

Before leaving Bibiani we had a meeting with the headman. I said that we were encouraged by what we had found out, and that it was likely that before very long we would be back to sink some exploratory shafts; if the results were positive we would need all the workmen that he could produce, including carpenters to build the huts and machinery sheds. He said that in his town there were some of the best carpenters and hardest workers in Africa, and that we should have as many workmen as we needed. I told him that his cooperation was much appreciated and that we would be reporting favourably about our visit to the Mamponghene; this caused him considerable satisfaction.

I told Louis that if we returned, we would need all four of his rooms, probably permanently, and this obviously was good news for him; he said that if necessary he could build an extension to the rest house with two or more additional rooms.

18th July

On the way back to Obuasi we made a detour to visit the logging company that has improved the lower section of the track. The manager there is an Englishman and he is delighted that the AGC may operate in the area, as it will probably mean better communications with his head office in Liverpool. He said that if we paid for the fuel, he would get one of his machines with an angled blade to level the track all the way up to Bibiani; that should put Cameron's doubts to rest.

Back at the mine, I lost no time in giving our ore samples to Franz; he hopes to let me know tomorrow whether the gold content is sufficient to make worthwhile the risk of establishing a whole new mine at Bibiani. I am very conscious of what John said, that if we set up a new mine there and it does not perform as we projected the cost might be greater than the AGC can afford.

The next sailing from Takoradi to Southampton is not for another thirteen days, so I will be able to see how the work at Obuasi Three is progressing and discuss with Ted how we should structure the management of all four mines if we proceed with Bibiani. This delay to my return is a pity, as I miss Mary very much, but at least my visit to Bibiani was useful, and if all goes well here I will go down to Takoradi a few days before the ship is due and stroll along the lovely beach during the days and relax with my friend at the rest house in the evenings

20th July

Yesterday Franz gave us the good news that the ore that we brought back from Bibiani is very similar to that here and that the gold content is the same; that means that if it can be confirmed that there is a sufficiently strong vein it will be well worth while establishing a mine there. It all now depends on some trial shafts.

Today I spent at Obuasi Three; the boring machine continues to work and in the ten days since I was last here it is now boring very close to the depth at which I think it should strike the vein that I believe runs between Obuasi One and Obuasi Two. If it does, that will generate a significant boost to our profits. I will go back to Obuasi Three each day while I am here to see how it is progressing.

21st July

Today, I went with Charles on a short expedition into the local forest; we were accompanied by Aggrey, who evidently now always goes out with Charles; this is wise, because it is very easy to get lost. We had a good walk, and Charles saw two birds that he had not seen before. We were making our way back to the mine through the trees with Aggrey leading, when I noticed a patch of fresh blood to the side of the track. While we were examining it another drop fell into it and naturally we all looked up; about ten or twelve feet above our heads a newly killed antelope was caught in the fork of the tree, and beside the corpse, stretched along a branch, was a leopard.

This was clearly not the time to discuss whether it was the same animal that we had seen when I was mine manager at Obuasi One, and we looked to Aggrey for guidance. The leopard could easily drop on any one of us as we stood there, and could equally easily catch us if we turned and ran; I hoped that it had eaten enough of the antelope to satisfy its hunger, and that it did not consider us as a threat. Aggrey told us not to turn around and not to look the leopard in the eye; he said we should move slowly backwards along the track until we were out of sight of the tree and then, singing loudly, take another path towards the mine.

Charles was thrilled at seeing the leopard at such close quarters, and I have to agree that it was a splendid beast, but I would rather not be quite so close to it. Once we were safely in sight of the mine, Aggrey took full credit for taking us to see the animal, reminding us that he was a great hunter and knew every bird and animal in the forest; we added a few shillings to his usual payment and said that in future he must tell us in advance what it was that he was going to show to us.

24th July

The boring machine has reached the vein at Obuasi Three. It did so this afternoon, while I was standing watching its progress; Franz was with me and straight away collected some bits of the rock that it had brought up and hurried back to his laboratory at Obuasi One. I congratulated Cameron for keeping his machine going; it has become something like a much-loved pet of his, and he basks in any compliments that he receives on its behalf. He is usually a rather dour man, with little sense of humour, but as the machine delivered rock that was noticeably different from its earlier efforts he actually managed a brief smile of satisfaction.

I told Cameron that if the AGC Board decided to go to the next stage at Bibiani he would have to take his machine there to sink the exploratory shafts. He started to say that the track was not suitable, but I told him that it would be levelled and that Ted was going to send a gang of men to cut back the foliage on both sides. It would be up to him, I said, to deliver the company's next project, and that if the boring machine needed any new blades or other spares he should give me a list before I left.

27th July

My work here is done. Franz says that there is no appreciable difference between the ore brought up at Obuasi Three and that which we have been working for several years at the original mine, and that provided that there is enough of it there is no reason why it should not prove equally profitable. I am particularly pleased at this, for it was my suggestion that we see whether there was a connecting vein between Obuasi One and Two.

I will leave for Takoradi on tomorrow's train and enjoy a couple of days of well-earned rest while I write up my reports for the board on Bibiani and

Obuasi Three. I estimate that it will be at least two months before we can get the trial shafts sunk at Bibiani, and if we are to have the Berdan Pans ready to crush the ore brought up they will have to be ordered and paid for as soon as the board agrees to go ahead. That is one more financial risk that we will have to take, and it will not be the last.

1st August

I am on my way home on board the *SS Dunottar Castle*; this is one of the older, smaller ships in the Union Castle fleet and has been converted to carry timber, with only four passenger cabins. She arrived offshore Takoradi yesterday, and is now loaded with large trunks of the mahogany tree; this is much prized in Europe for making high-class, high cost furniture for high-cost, high-class homes. At Broadlands we have two small mahogany tables, acquired by grandfather Broad, and Mama was particularly proud of them.

There is only one other passenger, an English doctor who has been working for five years in a mission hospital in Cape Coast, the administrative capital of the Gold Coast; this will be his first home leave and he says that he has not yet decided whether to return for another five years. He was interested to hear that the AGC is expanding its exploration and asked whether there might be a position for a doctor. I told him that we already had one, but that if he kept in touch in England I would let him know if the situation changed.

11th August

We dock in Southampton early tomorrow morning, and I am so much looking forward to getting home and seeing Mary. It has been a pleasant voyage; the weather was good and the doctor was a good conversationalist and had many stories, some amusing and some gruesome, to tell of his work in Cape Coast. The captain, who spent more time talking with the two of us than on the bridge, was also an interesting fellow; he has been with the Union Castle Line all his working life, starting as a third officer, and is due to retire next year. His seniority entitles him to command one of their newest ships, but he says that he prefers the informality of the older, smaller ones.

12th August

I got back home this evening, and what a welcome I got from Hermione and Mary; Papa has gone to stay with some friends in County Durham for a few days grouse shooting, and I am surprised that he is well enough, for it can be fairly taxing walking through thick heather from drive to drive, but Hermione says that he thought that this would be his last time at the grouse, and that he will be back to see me at the weekend. I hope that he has a good time and bags a few brace.

Mary had much to tell me about the preparations for our wedding. A guest list has been drawn up, a marquee, table and chairs booked, and a menu decided upon; she says that Hermione has been a great help and that without her she would never have known what to do, since in her family weddings are very much simpler, and doubtless, cheaper affairs. The date chosen is Saturday, 11th October and Quentin has put in for leave then. I think that Mary is nervous that she will let me down in some way on the day, but I have assured her that I will be beside her throughout and that she has nothing to worry about.

15th August

Today there was a board meeting and I was able to report that Obuasi Three had come up to expectations, and that the Mamponghene would ensure that the necessary workers were available when production starts. There was general satisfaction that the third mine would soon be contributing to the company's profits.

I then took my colleagues through the report on my visit to Bibiani. I told them that Franz was very satisfied with the quality of the ore samples that I had given to him, and that the area was suitable for the establishment of the necessary buildings. I said that the local headman would cooperate and produce workers, and that while the mine was being set up there was good accommodation for the managers at the rest house. There was, I said, only one more thing necessary before we committed to the project and that was the outcome of two or three trial shafts.

If the board agreed I proposed that we should tell Ted to get that started, and that at our end we should order the spares for the boring machine, as it would be the first thing to test the site; luckily it is made in England so there should be no undue delay. A greater delay would be in getting the Berdan Pans to Bibiani, as they are made in America and the board must decide whether to risk ordering them ahead of the results of the trial shafts. If it waited on a successful result it would delay the start of mining by about two months; if the result was not successful we could use the pans at the other mines and the cost would not be wasted. It was decided to order the pans without delay.

John asked the other directors in turn for their views. Alan said that he saw no legal problems in what was proposed, and Richard said that his only concern was whether we could be said to have acted irresponsibly towards the shareholders if the venture failed. Stephen said that when Obuasi Three was in full production the cash generated would be more than enough to subsidise the Bibiani project without impacting adversely on the year's financial results.

John thanked me for what I had done on this visit and said that he saw no reason why we should not proceed, and that he believed to do so would be in the best interests of the shareholders; he asked Miss Press to type up the draft minutes as soon as possible and to give a copy to each director; we would then have two days to raise any problems before the minutes went into the company records and the necessary instructions were sent to Obuasi.

After the meeting he took me into his office and said that the other directors were very impressed with what I had achieved, and that he hoped that my absence from the country had not delayed my wedding. I told him that it was not until October and that he would be getting an invitation in due course.

18th August

No objections have been raised to the draft minutes of the board meeting, and so I am sending the necessary instructions to Ted and have ordered the Berdan Pans and the spares for the boring machine; with luck it should be possible to start sinking the trial shafts in about two months' time. I had hoped that to save time the pans could be shipped straight from New York to Monrovia, the capital of Liberia, America's only presence in Africa, and thence to Bibiani, but I have found that it would not be possible to move them overland from there and they will have to be shipped via London and Takoradi.

There are many arrangements to be made, not least the staff changes that I agreed with Ted. Subject to the board's agreement Ted will be appointed general manager of all the AGC's mines in the Gold Coast; Alan Parsons, now his deputy, will become mine manager at Bibiani, with Arnaud Leclerc as his mine superintendent and we will recruit someone to be the mine manager responsible under Ted for the three mines at Obuasi.

23rd August

I am now spending five days each week at the office and it is very convenient to have my little house to stay in. Mary has said that she would like to stay there with me one week, and as we are engaged I do not think that any eyebrows will be raised; it would be nice to have her to myself for a time and I am sure that she will add a few more feminine touches to the place.

We have three applicants for the position of mine manager at Obuasi One, and we will interview them next week; I always have one of the other directors with me when we interview, for they all have much more experience of choosing staff than I do. The owner of the shoe shop has applied again, and this time I will see him, if only to enjoy his company for a short time for I feel sure that he must be a lovely man.

28th August

Today we interviewed the applicants for the position of mine manager at Obuasi One. I was right about the shoe shop owner; he is a most engaging fellow and said that he thought that managing a mine could not be more difficult that persuading people that a particular shoe was more their style and then getting them to pay for it. He had a shop in Cape Town for a few years and still gets his leather from South Africa. He knows shoes, he knows Africa, but sadly he knows nothing at all about mining and I can find no good reason to employ him.

The man that we chose, Edward Stokes, returned to this country from Australia a year ago; he worked as mine superintendent for two different companies and, interestingly, has used the Berdan Pans, which he says are very efficient for most types of ore. He is available immediately, and I will get him on his way to Obuasi as soon as possible.

8th September

Mary came up to London with me today and immediately set about cleaning my house; I do not remember getting it dirty and had no idea that it needed cleaning, but before I went to the office she asked for some money so that she could go and buy soap, scrubbing brushes, dusters, polish and any number of other things. This will give her something to do while I am out, but I do worry about how I will be required to change the habits of a lifetime when we are married.

When I got back from work the lights were on, the fire lit and there was a bottle and a glass beside my chair, the table was laid and a hot dinner was in the oven; there was also a distinct smell of disinfectant and polish.

After dinner Mary came and sat beside me on the little sofa and said that she had something important to tell me; I asked if it was something that had happened today and she said not, it had happened a long time ago. She said that she had never told anyone who Rob's father was, but that if we were to be married it was important that I should know, and that I might not want to marry her. I said that there was nothing that could cause that but that I did not want there to be any secrets between us.

She was very tense and clearly anxious, and when she told me I could entirely understand why Rob's father is Papa. She said that it had happened one afternoon in February of 1896 and that it was as much her fault as his. Papa had drunk rather more port than usual after his lunch and had gone to get another bottle; on his rather unsteady way to the cellar he met Mary, gave the cellar key to her and asked her to bring a bottle to the sitting room. Mama was out with Hermione and before she knew it, Papa was fumbling with her dress. She said that he did not force himself on her, and that she did not resist because she felt more flattered than afraid.

There was never any further intimacy between them, and when she had to leave Broadlands Papa opened a savings account in her name and paid an amount into it every month. He also paid for a retired schoolteacher to give her lessons to improve her vocabulary and general deportment. There never was a Mr Fisher. When she became Hermione's nanny Papa often went down to Chestnut Cottage to see Hermione and the children and always showed great interest in Rob's progress, without giving Hermione any reason to wonder why.

When she finished this account Mary looked up at me with tears in her eyes and begged me to understand and forgive her. There was such confusion in my brain that it was a minute or two before I could trust myself to speak; when I did I said that there was nothing to forgive, and that she should know that I had had a very intimate relationship with a girl in Cape Town and that I could easily have put her in the same condition. I told her that I loved only her, and that I always would.

She threw herself into my arms and thanked me a thousand times for my love and understanding. She has told no one of this, not even Hermione, and I see no reason why anyone else should ever know. Mary said that she would go to bed and that tonight she would sleep in the second bedroom, but, with a twinkle in her eye, that she would not make a habit of it.

I sat down with a glass of whisky and played over the evening's drama in my mind. I cannot think less of Papa, and I applaud his support of her after she left Broadlands. I am trying to work out the relationships that Rob and any child of ours would have. Rob is clearly my half-brother and will also be my stepson when we are married. Our children will be Papa's grandchildren, but would also have been his step-children if he and Mary had been married, and he would have been my brother-in-law. Mary will be Papa's daughter-in-law. Heaven knows how I fit into the picture; I am off to bed, it may be clearer tomorrow.

9th September

It took me a long time to get to sleep last night; I kept turning over in my mind all the various relationships, but I never for one moment thought that I would not marry Mary. I came down to breakfast this morning to the smell of bacon and eggs frying on the stove, and toast, butter and marmalade was already on the table. I kissed Mary and told her that as far as I was concerned nothing had changed and that we should continue to make the arrangements for the wedding next month. She gave me a cup of coffee and said how worried she had been, and how happy she was that I still wanted to marry her. I left for the office with a feeling that there was nothing that could stop our marriage.

12th September

The working week has passed very pleasantly; all the necessary arrangements have been made for the trial shafts at Bibiani, the equipment, including the Berdan Pans, has been ordered and should be in place by the end of November, and the staff changes are finalised. Ted is very proud to have been appointed general manager, but says that it will not stop him from taking a personal interest in what happens at every mine.

Back at my house every evening I have had a taste of what married life will have to offer. Mary is an excellent cook, having learned the trade in the kitchen at Broadlands; she is tidy to a fault, and often I cannot find something that I have put down in a particular place because Mary has tidied it away; I will have to break her of that habit. But just having her in the house with me has been a delight and the next month cannot go quickly enough.

23rd September

I did not go up to London yesterday, and it will be some days before I do; I have a severe recurrence of the malaria symptoms, and the doctor says that it was probably brought on by my recent visit to the Gold Coast; or I may have been stung again by a mosquito while there. Whatever the case, it cannot be certain that I will be well enough to get married in three weeks' time. Papa, Hermione and Mary all came to my bedroom and discussed what was best to be done. Mary was tearful and said that everything was spoiled, but Papa said that she should cheer up and not cry over milk that was yet to be spilled.

Hermione said that although the invitations had gone out, it would not be difficult to send out another lot, and Papa said that he had no doubt that the firms supplying the marquee and the food would accept a change of date. The general feeling was that a postponement of a month was wise, and Saturday, 15th November was decided upon. I will be unable to do much to help with the change, but they have told me not to worry and to concentrate on getting better.

10th October

I am out of bed, and taking gentle exercise, but I would not have been well enough to get married next week; as it is, I am catching up with work papers that Lisa has sent to me, and I am glad to see that all is going well in the Gold Coast mines. No less importantly, to me at least, are the arrangements for our honeymoon; luckily I had not finalised these before I fell ill and so there were no cancellations to be made. I have persuaded Mary that we should go to Paris for a week; she was rather doubtful at first, but I had much enjoyed my brief visit there when we met the SARLEM people and I am sure that Mary would enjoy seeing the city. I have asked Lisa to make the necessary travel arrangements and to book us in a first-class hotel; since I started working in London I have not had many major expenses, apart from buying and furnishing my house, and my balance at the bank can well afford a little luxury on what may be a once in a lifetime trip.

22nd October

I went back to the office today. Mary wanted to come with me, but I said that she should stay at Broadlands and help with the final arrangements for our delayed wedding. The Berdan Pans arrived from America while I was ill and they, together with the spares for Cameron's boring machine, are now on their way to Takoradi. The new mine manager for the Obuasi mines has already arrived there, and preparations for a temporary camp at Bibiani are well-advanced. Everything seems to have progressed well during my absence, and if there are no untoward developments work on the trial shafts should start before the end of November.

14th November

Tomorrow I marry Mary. Almost all of our forty invited guests have been able to accept the change of date; the marquee is erected on the front lawn; it and the church are filled with flowers, and the weather looks to be set fair. Quentin is my best man and Papa will give Mary away; this seems rather ironic under the circumstances, but she has no male relatives and says that she finds it rather appropriate. Hermione is Mary's maid of honour, and the three children are her attendants. I have not seen Mary's wedding dress, but Hermione says that it is beautiful and was made by Betsy's sister.

Mary has, in fact, very few relatives, and only a sister who is in service in Kent and an aunt, who evidently does not really approve of Mary lifting herself out of her class, will represent her family, but Cook and Betsy are invited guests and Hermione has said that she will take the four of them under her wing and has seated them next to guests who will not cause them any embarrassment. The other Broadlands staff and the estate workers will all be in the church and will enjoy some refreshment afterwards in a tent beside the marquee.

23rd November

The honeymoon is over and we are back at Broadlands. Paris turned out to be an excellent choice and Mary was so excited to see the sights. We had marvellous meals, strolled along the banks of the Seine, visited museums and one night went to a nightclub in Montmartre. Mary said that she thought it very naughty but was quite prepared to imitate some of the acts when we returned to our hotel. She was very impressed by my attempts to speak French, and I was glad that my trip to Siguiri had improved it sufficiently to get by with some of the Parisians, who resolutely refused to admit to any knowledge of our language.

It seems ages since our wedding, but I remember as if it was yesterday how lovely Mary looked in her wedding dress, and how smart Papa and

Quentin were in morning dress and regimentals respectively. My speech was well received, the food and drink could not be bettered, and the sun shone throughout the day. Much of the success of the occasion was down to the hard work put in by Hermione, and my tribute to her in my speech was warmly applauded by our guests. She has been such a comfort to me and no one could hope for a better sister. Papa was in really good form, although I fear that occasions like this do tire him greatly. Tony Fellowes congratulated me on winning such a lovely bride but regretted losing such a good nanny. I shall remember every detail of the day for a very long time.

26th November

Back to work today, and I was glad to find that all is going well at Obuasi. Obuasi Three started to produce gold and Franz is evidently pleased with the weight per ton of ore, which is the yardstick by which mines are judged. The Berdan Pans and the boring machine and its necessary spares have arrived at Bibiani, in spite of Cameron's gloomy predictions, but we got news only yesterday that starting the trial shafts has been delayed.

The two German prospectors, who said that they were ready to leave, now say that they should be compensated for going and refuse to leave the site where they have been digging. Ted has been to see them and pointed out that we have offered to employ them for more than they were earning by themselves, but they say that they should be paid what they would have earned during the next two years; even if we agreed to that in principle, who knows how much that would have been? Every day of an operation such as theirs yields a different result, sometimes gold and usually nothing. Their site is not only where we want to position our machinery, but also close to one of the freshwater wells and we cannot risk that being contaminated if they start to play dirty tricks. Ted has asked what he should do. I went and saw John and Alan and told them of the problem. Alan said that since they had no legal claim to their site, and we had the permission of the Mamponhene, they had no leg to stand on. John said that as they had declined our offer of employment we should not be drawn into a discussion about the value of two years' work, and that to compensate them could result in some of the other workers taking the same stance.

I said that I thought that we should ask the Mamponhene to let the Germans know that permission for them to work there was withdrawn, and get a few of his warriors from Bibiani to escort them over the border into the Ivory Coast, and to make it clear that they should not return. I am sure that the Mamponghene will be only too happy to make it possible for us to start boring, and we know that there are the necessary warriors available in Bibiani.

This was agreed; it will keep the AGC at arm's length from the actual expulsion and send the right message to the other workers. I have told Ted of our decision and asked him to do the necessary in Kumasi; the delay to the start of boring is a nuisance, but better to solve the problem now than have potential trouble-makers on the site.

26th December

What a splendid Christmas we all had at Broadlands. Papa was in great form, and delighted the children with his imitations of a bear and various other animals. Mary and I had brought presents for everyone from France, and we were given a number of things for our house in London, it will now look like a proper family home. Rob very much likes staying there; he calls the second bedroom his room and has started to decorate it accordingly. He enjoys seeing the sights of London with his mother, but is equally happy to stay at Broadlands, where Hermione treats him as one of her own while Mary and I are in London.

I hope that the new year will bring continued success for the AGC, and especially that the problem with the Germans at Bibiani can be resolved quickly; I look forward to hearing from Ted with news of his meeting with the Mamponghene.

Chapter Four
1907

10th January

Today, we got news that the Germans have left Bibiani. The headman provided four warriors in full battle order, equipped with spears; they went to the Germans' hut at six in the morning and invited them to pack up their belongings and be ready to leave in an hour's time. They then went with them to the border and handed them over to the Ivorian police, who had been tipped off in advance of their arrival by a French friend of Louis Bucher who lives in the Ivory Coast near to the border. The Germans were surprised to find that they were expected.

The Ivorian Police greeted the Germans and asked to see their documents. They had nothing to show that they were allowed to enter the Ivory Coast, and certainly not to prospect for gold; since they had brought with them the gold that they had found during the past few months and such prospecting equipment as they could carry it seemed that they had hoped to continue their mining. They were arrested and Louis was told that they were to be taken down to Abidjan and put on the next ship out of the country. A satisfactory ending to what might have been an ongoing problem. Arnaud is now our mine superintendent at Bibiani and he and Alan will be glad to see the backs of the Germans. Boring of the trial shafts can now begin, and we will soon see whether the mine will be a profitable one.

16th February

Today we heard from Ted; the first gold-bearing ore has been brought to the surface at the Bibiani mine and put into the Berdan Pans to be crushed. To Cameron's surprise and Ted's delight the machine worked very efficiently and produced pieces of exactly the size that Franz prefers. A second trial shaft will now be sunk, and if that taps the same vein as the first the boring machine will be used to cut shafts wide enough to enable workers to excavate the side tunnels from which the ore will be cut.

10th March

Quentin is engaged. He and his fiancée, Pamela, came down to

Broadlands for lunch today and he introduced her to all of us. Her brother works with Quentin in the War Office and they met at some military celebration. She seems to be very nice, and Papa is certainly very taken with her and thinks that he knows one of her uncles; Hermione said after they had left that she thinks that she is exactly the right girl for Quentin, pretty and homely, as she put it. They have not yet set a wedding date but think that it will probably be towards the end of the summer.

25th March

The second trial shaft has come good, and Bibiani will soon be earning its keep. Ted says that Alan Parsons and Arnaud Leclerc work well together, and he will only have to visit Bibiani about once a month unless there is a major problem there.

14th May

I see that it is nearly two months since I wrote in this diary; that is because all is going well at our mines. We heard yesterday that Bibiani is yielding its riches, and all three operations at Obuasi are in full production. The Berdan Pans are proving to be most effective, and even Cameron admits that they are just as good as, if not better than, the very heavy and cumbersome crusher that we have at Obuasi; I think that we may buy some more pans and phase out the crusher.

My responsibilities are for development and expansion, and I think that so far I have been able to fulfil them; the original Obuasi operation has been expanded considerably by the addition of Obuasi Two and Three, and we have developed the Bibiani mine. All are locally managed very efficiently and there is no requirement for me to be involved on a day-to-day basis, even if that was possible, although I will be told of any problems that require head office attention.

While there are no such problems I have lately been giving thought as to where the AGC might expand further. There are any number of mining operations in Canada, some large and some small, and it may be that one or more would be a profitable addition to the AGC's portfolio of mines. It would take time to research even a few of them in person, but it might be time well spent.

Also, much closer to our existing operations, Ted says that there are reports of gold being found at Iduapriem in the Gold Coast. This place is near Tarkwa in the southwest of the country and is not very far from Takoradi. It would not be difficult to add an operation there to our existing operations in the country, and I have asked Ted to go there as soon as he can and let me have a full report.

21st May

Mary is pregnant; I am about to be a father! Not immediately, but probably in November. Papa is thrilled that he will have another grandchild, and Hermione is so pleased for Mary. Rob says that it would be nice to have a kid sister. My house in London is not really big enough for four people, and I think that Mary and the children will spend most of their time in our cottage on the Broadlands estate. There will be so many things to do to prepare for the baby; I am sure that it will be a boy, but Mary says that she thinks that Rob is right and it will be a girl. I do not really mind; I will love him or her so much.

3rd June

When I got to the office this morning, Lisa told me that Victor Bisset, our friend in the French Embassy, would like to call on me at midday if it was convenient; I asked what this was about, but she said that she had no idea. I told her to let him know that I would be glad to see him, and wondered what on earth he wanted. Promptly at twelve o'clock, Victor arrived and told me some surprising and rather disquieting news that he had received from the French consul in Abidjan.

When the two Germans that we had had evicted from Obuasi reached Abidjan, the capital of the Ivory Coast, one of them had gone to the German consul and told him that he thought that a man wanted by the police in France was working at Obuasi, and had given him Louis Bucher's name. The German consul was evidently not much interested in the story, but had found it his duty to pass it on to the office of the French Consul.

He had asked one of his staff to see if Louis's name was on the list of wanted persons circulated by the French general intelligence directorate once a year to all domestic police forces and overseas missions. Louis's name was not on the list, and there the matter would have ended were it not for the persistence of the German, who was enraged when the consul told him that the French police were not looking for Louis Bucher.

It seems that one evening in Bibiani, after having drunk several beers with the Germans, Louis had let slip the reason why he had left France many years before, but had not said that he had changed his name. The German persuaded the consul to pass the matter to the office of the English police commissioner in Cape Coast, since he was responsible for law and order in the Gold Coast, together with a copy of the list provided by the general intelligence directorate. The commissioner, who was not much interested in the German request, and had no wish to undertake the arduous journey to Bibiani himself, sent one of his native policemen, a sergeant, to go first to Obuasi and thence with Ted Harris to Bibiani to investigate the allegation.

At Bibiani, in the presence of Ted and Alan Parsons, the sergeant interviewed Louis; he produced a number of photographs of men wanted in France, together with their names, but since it was more than fifteen years since the photographs were taken and his name did not appear on the list Louis had no difficulty in convincing him he was not one of the wanted men. Ted arranged with the headman for the sergeant not to want for food and drink that evening, and on the next morning he left for Cape Coast to report to the commissioner that there was no wanted man at Obuasi. By this time the Germans had left Abidjan and were not in a position to cause any more trouble.

When I reported to Victor that the enquiry had come to nothing, despite it having been passed by the German consul to the French lieutenant governor to the English police commissioner in Cape Coast he smiled and said that he had been kept up to date with developments, or rather the lack of them, by the French lieutenant governor in Abidjan, and that he was glad that the investigation had come to nothing. When I asked why he smiled, he said that he had been in Paris at the time of the crime and that it had become something of a cause célèbre, with much public sympathy for the man accused and convicted of a crime of passion. How he had escaped from police custody was never established, but it had seemed likely that a door or two in the prison had carelessly been left unlocked.

Like Victor, I am glad that we will not be losing Louis, whatever he may or may not have done; he runs the Bibiani Guest House well, and we will be making much use of it before very long.

7th June

Today is the tenth anniversary of my parting from Ryneker, but I no longer have an empty feeling in my heart when I remember her. I loved her, and she loved me, but I now have another love, one that I hope will last for the rest of my days.

Mary and I went out for dinner at a restaurant not far from my house, and looking at her across the table I thought how lucky I am to have her as my wife.

15th July

This evening there was a full house at Broadlands; Quentin was there for the weekend, and Tony and Hermione and their children, and Papa had invited Mary, Rob and I to dinner. After dinner he beckoned Quentin, Hermione, Rob and me to his side, put his arms around us, and said how proud he was to have four such fine children.

This announcement clearly came as a huge surprise to Quentin and Hermione, who at first looked puzzled and then, as they understood the meaning of what he said, looked delighted. Tony, who is Papa's solicitor, obviously knew about Rob's parentage before today, but had never broken the professional confidence by which he learned it.

It certainly was news to Hermione, and I do not think that Mary had told Rob who his father was, but he dearly loves the man that he now thinks of as his grandfather, and I do not think that the change of rôles will affect him. Quentin is not one to worry over such matters, and was the first to shake Papa's hand, followed by Hermione, who kissed him and said how happy she was to have a little brother.

Mary joined Rob and me at Papa's side and Mary kissed him and said that she was glad that everybody now knew the truth. I shook his hand and said that Rob could not have had a better father, but that I was glad to take over that role. What might have been a very awkward situation had passed very happily for all concerned, and I am glad that it is now out in the open.

Papa said that he was tired, kissed us all and went to bed, leaving us to digest the change in our new relationships. Tony told Mary that if she wanted to change Rob's name to Broad it was a simple matter that he would be happy to help her with. Mary hugged Hermione and said how grateful she was for being taken on as a nanny, which had led to her becoming part of the family before tonight's announcement. I think that everybody was glad to be part of such a happy family; Mary, Rob and I certainly were as we went back to our cottage.

16th July

Papa died in his sleep last night. The doctor says that there was no specific reason but that he had simply come to the end of the road. This has obviously overshadowed last night's news, and there will be much to do arranging the funeral. Tony told us this morning the main provisions in Papa's will; as the oldest son, the Broadlands estate and house pass to Quentin, together with one quarter of his residuary estate, after a number of small bequests to long-serving household staff and others. Hermione, Rob and I each get a quarter, and Mary and I get the freehold of the cottage in which we have lived since our marriage. Mama's jewellery is to be divided between Hermione and Mary.

Quentin still has much of his military career ahead of him, and has neither the will nor the experience necessary to manage the estate, although he wishes that he and Pamela, and any children that they have, are able to stay at Broadlands for weekends and holidays as he does now, and to live there when he retires. The house is quite big enough to accommodate two families, his and Hermione's, and he asked Tony to draw up whatever documentation is necessary to legalise the arrangement.

He also said that he would be very happy if Tony managed the estate, and that he could either be paid to do so, with the revenue from it going to Quentin, or be paid nothing but have the revenue for himself. Tony said that it was a very kind offer and asked for a few days to discuss it with Hermione and decide which option to choose.

Papa in his wisdom has ensured a very equitable division of his personal estate, although the sums that we will each receive are very much less than they would have been if grandfather Broad had been a better judge of horseflesh; each of the three families benefit, and since no one wants to leave Broadlands, the estate remains effectively undivided. I will continue to contribute to the upkeep of the house, and I think that Hermione will also do so; that is only fair, as otherwise Quentin, usually away from Broadlands, would have to foot all the bills himself.

24th July

Today Papa's funeral took place in the village church and he was buried next to Mama, as he had requested. I was very gratified by the large number of his friends who came to the church and afterwards to the reception at Broadlands; he was well-liked and respected in the county and I doubt whether he had an enemy in the world. Broadlands seems very empty without him, and for five days after he died Oscar lay outside his bedroom door and could not be coaxed into leaving; however, he has now switched his allegiance to Mary, much to the delight of her children; he came with her to the funeral and sat quietly by her side in the church and while Papa was buried. I am glad that he is not going to pine any longer, and I hope that he has many more happy days at Broadlands where there are rabbits galore for him to chase.

1st August

I was back in the office today for the first time since Papa's death; it seemed strange to leave Broadlands without saying goodbye to him, but the estate is in good hands, for Tony has agreed to manage it as an employee of Quentin, so Tony will have a salary and the revenue from the farms will go towards the upkeep of the house and estate.

We have heard from Ted about his visit to Iduapriem; it is a very different operation from Obuasi and Bibiani as it is an open cast mine, a large pit from which flakes of gold and occasional nuggets are dug out of its sides. This is alluvial gold, and it is likely that there is a vein of ore close by. It is owned by the local chieftain, who charges prospectors a fee to be able to work there. The total amount of gold produced by the many prospectors is not great, but in Ted's view it could be significantly increased if the mining was run and organised by a single operator.

He met the chieftain, who seemed agreeable to dealing with a major English company rather than a number of individuals, and he produced an estimate of the costs and revenue. The profit would not be great, but it would be another string to the AGC's bow in the Gold Coast and would deter competitors from getting a foothold in the country. I will raise the matter at the next board meeting.

18th August

There was a board meeting today, and it was agreed that Ted should come to an agreement with the chief, and that we would make preliminary arrangements so that we could start mining when one of the four mines that we are currently operating became unprofitable. We would make an annual gift to the chieftain and then have what amounts to first refusal to take over the existing mining operation. I will advise Ted of the board's decision.

The usual review of the productivity of our mines took place, and it was noted that all were contributing satisfactorily; the Bibiani mine was proving particularly profitable, and it was agreed that letters of appreciation should be sent to the mine manager and mine superintendent, with a copy to Ted.

When John asked whether there was any other business to discuss, Stephen Carson shocked us all by saying that he wished to leave the AGC as soon as it was possible. In response to John's enquiry as to why he wished to go Stephen said that he had been offered the position of chairman in one of the Canadian mining companies that we had evaluated and considered as a possible acquisition. He had accepted the offer and was expected to start as soon as he could. He asked that the contractual requirement for three months' notice by directors be waived. John said that he would be a loss to the AGC, but that he did not wish to stand in Stephen's way, and that provided that our chief accountant could hold the fort until a replacement finance director was found he would release Stephen at the end of the week, and that he wished him every success in his new position.

The meeting broke up with all of us congratulating Stephen and saying how sorry we were that he was leaving. I am particularly sorry, for I have got to know and like him well during our negotiations with SARLEM and when discussing the costs of opening our new mines. He is a very able man, and I am sure that he will do well in Canada; if we do decide to take an interest in a mine in that country our paths may well cross again. John told me confidentially that he is surprised that Stephen has got such an important job, and that he hopes that is not out of his depth; he is an excellent financial man but has no practical mining experience.

21st August

Yesterday, there was a party in the office to say goodbye to Stephen. The directors and senior staff all attended, and John gave him a silver salver with the names of the four Gold Coast mines inscribed on it. Stephen said that he would write to us when he had settled in, and that if the AGC did decide to operate in Canada he would be glad to do what he could to help, as long as it was not in competition. The party ended with all of us singing 'For he's a jolly good fellow'.

24th August

Not a good day; it seems that Stephen is not such a jolly good fellow after all. John was out of the office this morning and so it was to me that Chris Roberts, our chief accountant, came with the bad news. Since Stephen left Chris has been bringing himself up to date with some of the accounts that Stephen usually managed personally. When checking the reserve account he could find no trace of a very considerable sum of money. The account is kept well-funded so as to be available for any unexpected contingency, such as a flooded mine, or to be able to take swift action if a desirable acquisition becomes available at short notice.

Chris had searched all the other accounts to no avail, and had then contacted our bank to see whether the money had perhaps been invested in something without his knowledge. The bank manager said that the money had been transferred to an account in Canada ten days previously on Stephen's instructions, and that he had assumed that the AGC was going ahead with an investment in one of the mining companies that we had investigated. Chris was fearful that he would be thought to have stolen the money, but I told him not to worry and that he should find out the details from the Canadian bank.

When John came in after lunch I was breaking the bad news to him when Chris came in and said that our bank manager had given him details of the transfer; it was to a new personal account in the name of John Smith in a bank in Toronto. Our bank had acted in good faith, for Stephen was an authorised single signatory for all our accounts.

John immediately contacted the police and in no time a detective chief inspector from the fraud squad was with us. John explained the position and asked him to alert the Canadian police to apprehend anyone trying to withdraw funds from the account. It is not possible for Stephen to be in Canada yet, and John asked that every effort be made to find him. The DCI left promising immediate action and said that all ports will be advised to detain him if he tries to leave the country, and that he will keep us up to date with developments.

25th August

Just when we thought that nothing worse could happen, we got news that it had. The Canadian bank told our bank that on the day after the funds were transferred, before we were aware of the theft and before the Canadian police were alerted, a man came to the bank, correctly identified himself as John Smith with the agreed password, and withdrew all except one hundred

Canadian dollars from the account in cash. Both banks have acted perfectly correctly, and there is therefore no chance of recovering any of the money from them; if we are not to sustain a considerable loss, Stephen has to be found and persuaded to return the money.

When we told the DCI of this development he said that he would examine all the passenger lists for ships due to sail to Canada and the United States in the coming weeks, and also double the surveillance of passengers leaving for those destinations.

28th August

Stephen has been apprehended; he was caught yesterday when trying to board a ship leaving Southampton for Perth in Australia with a young lady, and has been transferred to a prison in London pending further investigations. We are of course delighted that he has been caught, but cannot understand why he was hoping to go to Australia when the money is presumably still in Canada. John was required to go and confirm his identity, but was not permitted to speak to him; the DCI said that he would be interviewed today and that he would let us know if Stephen was prepared to assist with the recovery of the money.

29th August

The DCI told us today the result of the first interrogation of Stephen. He did not deny the theft, but said that he had thought it the only way out of a situation that he was in. He had taken a mistress a couple of years ago and had managed to keep it from his wife until two months previously. Although he promised to end the affair, she was so enraged that she threatened him with a visit from a local villain, after which there would be no point in him having a mistress. She also said that she would divorce him, and that unless he was able to give her very much more money than he had, then the local villain would go to the next stage.

The DCI said that there was indeed a man in the area where Stephen lived, one Flick Wilson, who had a reputation for vigorous enforcement, but who had never been convicted, and that he did not doubt that the threats could have been carried out.

Stephen's first intention had been to get the money from the AGC account and pay off his wife, but when he had it he resented the idea of his wife getting it, although he was quite happy to be divorced. If he kept the money he could expect a visit from the villain, so he decided to move the money out of the country and move himself and his mistress to Australia, from where he would access the money and live happily ever after. He chose to move the money to Canada because he has a cousin there who was willing to help him.

With his dream shattered, Stephen was now willing to go down any route that would save him from his wife's threats, and said that he would recover the money from his cousin if he could expect leniency when sentenced. The DCI saw this as an opportunity to put the villain behind bars, by pointing out to Stephen's wife that it seemed that she was guilty of incitement to violence or murder, and if she did not give evidence against him she would risk a custodial sentence. It was not clear how she knew the villain, although it seemed possible that Stephen was not the only one who had strayed from the marital path.

Since it was the AGC who would be bringing charges against Stephen, it was possible to reduce them from theft to misappropriation of funds, which carried a lesser sentence, provided that the money was recovered from Stephen's cousin, and John was agreeable to that. The DCI was also prepared to go along that route and it is now up to Stephen to arrange with his cousin to return the money to our bank.

2nd September

Back in the office after the weekend we were all eager to find out what progress had been made in recovering the money. The DCI told us that Stephen had been able to contact his cousin who was prepared to return ninety percent of the money if he was not prosecuted, but that he had already spent almost all of the ten percent that had been agreed with Stephen for facilitating the movement of the money on a new house, a boat, a car and some jewellery for his wife. John said that ninety percent was a lot better than nothing.

I went to see Stephen in prison this afternoon and I was shocked by his appearance; he has lost a lot of weight and is very apprehensive about the outcome of his trial. He has agreed to plead guilty, and is doing everything that he can to assist the police in their investigation of his wife and the villain. His mistress has also visited him and told him that if she could not go to Australia with him she wished him well and would find someone else to take her. Poor chap; the only thing that gives him any satisfaction is the thought of his wife going to prison, and he looks forward to testifying against her.

John says that we should now draw a line under the whole wretched business and get back to mining for gold. It will be several weeks until the trials are held, more if the villain is also put on trial. Stephen's wife has identified him, and he is now in prison awaiting formal charging. The police hope to be able to pin various outstanding cases of grievous bodily harm, assault and even murder on him.

It has been a stressful time in the office, and it has been a joy to go back home at the weekend and be a part of a loving family. Rob thinks that it is pretty special to have two fathers, one of them also being his grandfather, and is not at all embarrassed by the situation. Mary expects our baby in about ten weeks' time and is having a perfectly normal pregnancy; having already had one baby she says that she is not scared as she was on the first occasion and that she so looks forward to having another baby to care for.

12th September

We heard from our bank today that they had received a considerable sum in Canadian dollars and that in accordance with John's instructions it has been credited to our reserve account. Chris reckons that Stephen's cousin and the charges levied by both banks account for about eight percent of the original amount, and John is relieved that it is not more.

We also heard from the police that Stephen's trial will start on 19th September, and that it is expected that his wife and Flick Wilson will be tried a week or two later. The DCI has dug a number of unsolved cases out of the files and hopes to be able to pin several of them on the villain. The two of them deny knowing each other, but a witness will testify that he has on several occasions, and specifically when Stephen was in Paris with me, seen the villain, who is well-known in the neighbourhood, entering Stephen's house in the evening and leaving early on the following morning.

At the last board meeting we discussed the need to replace Stephen with a new finance director and to appoint a new deputy chairman. John proposed that Alan Hughes should fill the latter position, saying that his legal knowledge would be particularly valuable in that post; Richard Beale and I both endorsed the proposal. As regards the finance director, we were all agreed that Chris had performed very well during the difficult time after the detection of the theft, and it was agreed that he should be given the director's job for a trial period of three months; if he continued to impress, he would be confirmed in the post.

When 'Any other Business' was to be discussed, I floated the idea that Ted should be made a director of the AGC, remaining in situ in Obuasi. Since joining the company and his arrival in the Gold Coast he has been responsible for implementing the board's decisions to open Obuasi Two and Three and Bibiani; he has also suggested that we should consider operating at Iduapriem. He seems to be well-received by the Mamponghene and the local chieftain in the southwest of the country, and now has the complete respect of all the managers under him. As a director he would be able to make more local decisions without referring to the board, and would inspire even greater respect from the native chiefs.

John endorsed what I said about Ted's achievements and said that it was certainly something to be considered; he directed that it be an agenda item at the next board meeting.

19th September

Stephen's trial started and finished today; he pleaded guilty to misappropriation of the company's funds and was sentenced to two years in prison. John said on his behalf that he had been an excellent member of the AGC Board for a number of years, and that he was sure that it was only the unfortunate situation in his private life that had driven him to crime. The DCI said that his cooperation had led to the arrest of an individual that the police had linked with a number of serious crimes, and that it was the behaviour of his wife that had been the major reason for his fall from grace. The judge said that without these statements in his favour he would have gone to prison for five years. Stephen left the courtroom looking a lot less worried than when he first stood in the dock; I will try to visit him in prison before long.

3rd October

The trial of Stephen's wife and her low-life lover began today; they are jointly charged with conspiring to commit murder and both have pleaded 'not guilty'. It will last for some days and when it is over he will face several other charges and the police are hopeful that he will be put away for a number of years. I will not attend every day of the trial, but I hope to be there when the verdicts and sentences are announced. Fortunately there have been no problems at the mines while we have been distracted by events rather closer to home.

While my time in London has been much occupied with the effects of Stephen's crime, the weekends at home have been much occupied with preparations for the baby. His or her arrival is now confidently forecast for 15th November, or a day or two either side of that date. The nursery is equipped with a cot and various items designed to encourage the child to sleep peacefully night after night, although I do not think that anyone has any faith in their effectiveness.

Hermione has been an enormous help to Mary, for although Mary had Rob it was in rather different circumstances, without the loving support that now surrounds her. She is in very good health, and the regular checks on the baby's progress have all indicated that a very healthy child is on its way. All three children are very excited, and all have produced lists of names, male and female, from which they want us to choose one; Mary and I have several favourites of our own but will wait until we have a baby on which to bestow one.

11th October

At midday we were told that the jury were expected to return their verdict when the court resumed after the break for lunch, and John and I hurried to the court. In an effort to get a lesser sentence, Stephen's wife had said in her defence that she had only wished her husband to get a bad fright, and that she would testify that it was her lover's idea to kill or maim him. The prosecution clearly did not entirely believe her, but the charge against her had been reduced to one of enticement to commit grievous bodily harm and she was found guilty of that. She was sentenced to three years in prison.

The charge against Flick Wilson had not been reduced; he was found guilty of conspiring to commit murder and was sentenced to twelve years in prison with hard labour. I went to visit Stephen with the result of the trial and he was pleased to know that he would be free before his wife. He wanted to know whether divorce proceedings could be started while he was in prison and I said that I would find out and let him know.

14th October

Quentin and Pamela were married yesterday in our local church and the reception afterwards was held at Broadlands, the third such occasion in recent years. It was a very fine affair. Quentin was in his dress uniform, as was his best man, a brother officer, and there was a good turnout of both county and military friends. Hermione was Pamela's maid of honour, and her children were once again the bride's attendants. Pamela looked very lovely and I am sure that she is just the girl for Quentin; she comes from a military family, so is no stranger to the periodic moving from one post to another that all army families have to suffer.

16th October

At today's board meeting John said that the reputation of the AGC had been tarnished by recent events and that several shareholders had withdrawn their investments. There was no doubt, he said, that our mines were operating very profitably and that it would be possible to pay substantial dividends at the end of our financial year, but it would be very timely if we could announce some new activity to catch the eye of potential new investors and the mining fraternity.

I said that perhaps this was the time to take over the Iduapriem mine, and announce to the press that the AGC now had five mines in the Gold Coast. Alan said that some might say that all our eggs were in a single basket, and that it might be wise to look for an opportunity in another country. The matter was discussed at some length and it was eventually agreed that when I returned to work from leave after the birth of our baby I should spend some time evaluating possible acquisitions and report to the board in three months' time. This suits me well, for by that time I should have a month of fatherhood behind me and will probably be glad to retreat to the calm of the office.

10th November

Yesterday, Mary thought that the birth was imminent, but it was a false alarm and we all resumed waiting; I am the only one who has no experience of the event and consequently am much more prone to worry over things which are evidently quite normal. I am often told to have a drink and sit down out of the way.

12th November

I am a father, and Mary and our daughter are doing well; we have called her Sarah. I took Mary to the hospital yesterday afternoon and waited there until she produced Sarah at half past six this morning. She is such a beautiful baby, and I am sure that she already knows that I am her father. Mary says that it was an easier birth than when she had Rob and she is eager to get back to our cottage, but she has been told to wait until tomorrow. Hermione came to see her niece and brought gifts from the children, so Sarah's cot is now festooned with cuddly toys awaiting her arrival.

I came back to the cottage this evening, to make sure that everything is ready for their arrival tomorrow and to catch up on my sleep. It is such a shame that Papa did not live to see this day; he was so looking forward to welcoming another child into the family.

13th November

Mary and Sarah came home this morning and my whole family is now around me. Mary says that Sarah slept well last night, but we cannot hope that that will continue. When Mary brought her children to meet their new cousin, Rob was very proudly showing her off. I now have a month here at home and I am so happy.

20th November

It is a week since Mary and Sarah came home and I am rapidly learning the routine; only Mary can provide the nourishment at this stage, but I gladly do what I can to assist with the other tasks. We are lucky that so far Sarah is a happy baby and does not seek attention more than once a night.

28th November

Sarah is putting on weight and seems to respond to our attention; she is the best baby ever!

10th December

In a couple of days I have to go back to work; it will be strange not to have my daily routine entirely matched to Sarah's requirements and not to be able to help Mary, but Hermione will come to our cottage every day and they both say that I should take a break from the duties of fatherhood. There will be much for me to do in the office, but alone in my house in the evenings I will wish that I was here at home with my family.

13th December

All the staff congratulated me on becoming a father when I got to the office and Lisa had put a vase of pink flowers on my desk. I continue to live in fear that she will announce that she is pregnant, for she is an able secretary and manages my office well in my absence. John was not there, but had left a note welcoming me back and saying that there were some decisions to take at tomorrow's board meeting. On the agenda there is an item 'Appointment of a Director', and I assumed that this is a result of my suggestion that Ted should join the board; or perhaps to confirm Chris as finance director; we shall see.

I looked at the last monthly report on the productivity of the mines; Obuasi One is producing less gold than it did, and at some stage we will have to decide whether it is worthwhile sinking another shaft; it may be that we have exhausted that vein. Obuasi Two and Three continue to produce well, and Bibiani is still exceeding our expectations. There have been no problems with the workmen there; they seem to be well pleased that they have steady employment rather than having to depend on their own efforts to win gold from the ground.

14th December

The board meeting produced only one surprise, and that was the agenda item regarding the appointment of a director. John said that since Stephen left he felt that the board should be strengthened, as he put it, and that he had in mind a man that he had met who had mining experience in both South Africa and Australia, one Bill Franklin. He was very willing to travel to evaluate opportunities but he wanted to be based in England. John said that he had invited Bill to join us for lunch when the meeting was over and that afterwards he would be interested to hear what we thought of him.

My first thought was that it seemed that this Bill's responsibilities might well conflict with mine for development and expansion, and I said as much to John. He agreed and said that I had very effectively addressed those responsibilities in developing our Gold Coast mines but that any further expansion would have to be further afield, and that it could involve long periods out of the country. He thought that this might not be an attractive proposition for me now that I had a young child.

I said that he was quite right, but asked what would my responsibilities be if not for D and E? He said he had given thought to this and that the AGC and I would both be best served if my title changed to director of mining. Our mines in the Gold Coast are our only mines at the moment, but the position would clearly bear responsibility for mines in any other country where we might operate in the future.

With that settled I felt unable to raise the question of Ted's position at this meeting; not only could it mean three new directors being appointed, Chris, Bill and Ted, but it might seem superfluous to have a director resident in Africa and another in London with much the same responsibilities. I do have a debt of gratitude to Ted for my first introduction to Edwin Cade, but I think that I have probably settled that by getting him promoted to the position of general manager.

The last item on the agenda was to consider whether Chris's appointment as finance director should be confirmed, and this was unanimously approved. I am glad for him; he is a nice fellow and very conscientious, and he has done well to mitigate the effect of Stephen's crime.

When the meeting finished John asked Miss Press to bring Bill Franklin into the board room. He is a good-looking man of about forty-five and his tanned complexion bears evidence of years spent under the tropical sun. John introduced him to all of us and over lunch Bill gave us an account of his mining career. Like me, he started out as a prospector in Witwatersrand and was lucky to have a claim that produced some sizeable nuggets. After a few years there, with money in the bank, he moved to Australia, where gold was being found in a number of places in that vast country. There he had more good luck, and after five years was able to buy a share in a new mine in Western Australia. That too prospered and he returned to England last year as a rich man.

He said that gold was in his veins, and although he had sufficient funds to live comfortably without working he could not imagine having nothing that needed to be done each day. John asked whether he would be prepared to travel overseas to look at possible acquisitions and he said that he enjoyed travelling, and since he had no family it was not a problem to be away from England from time to time, but he had spent enough time in Australia and it took so long to get there and back that he would rather not have to go there.

When the lunch was over, John thanked Bill for coming and said that he would talk with his fellow directors and be in touch very shortly. After Bill left John asked us for our impressions of him. I said that his early career had been very much like mine, and that if anyone had a nose for gold it was probably him. Richard said that it would be useful to have a director who was prepared to travel to evaluate possible acquisitions, and Alan said that he thought his experience could be very useful to the AGC.

John thanked us for our contributions and said that now that he knew Bill better he was sure that it would be in the AGC's interests to add him to the board and that he proposed his appointment with the title director of business development, with responsibility for identifying new areas where the AGC might operate. We were all in favour of this and John undertook to contact Bill and discuss terms of employment. This is very satisfactory from my point of view, as I was not looking forward to having to leave my family for long periods while I travelled the world seeking more gold. I know that Mary will be delighted.

17th December

John has been in touch with Bill Franklin, who has agreed to join the AGC with effect from 2nd January. He and I must work closely together, for it will be up to me to consider his proposals and put them before the board. I will tell him that I believe that I think that there may be an opportunity in Tanganyika, near a town called Bindura, and that we are aware of many mines in Canada.

21st December

The office has closed for the Christmas break and I have been much engaged in erecting and decorating a Christmas tree in the sitting room at Broadlands, where the two families will celebrate Christmas together. Rob and Hermione's children are making coloured paper chains, and parcels wrapped in brightly coloured paper are accumulating under the tree. Rob wants a dog for Christmas; Arthur wants a gun and Penelope wants a kitten; I have left it to Hermione and Mary to decide which of these wishes, if any, can reasonably be granted.

There was a Christmas party at the office yesterday, and John told everyone that it has been a good year for the AGC; the Bibiani mine has done particularly well in the eight months since production started. I noticed that Lisa was not drinking anything and when I offered her a glass of wine, she said better not as there was a chance that she was pregnant; she asked me not to tell anyone else yet. I am of course, happy for her, but I will miss her cheery efficiency and will have to fish in the typing pool for a replacement.

26th December

What a lovely day it was yesterday. Mary and I together with Rob and Sarah went up to Broadlands after breakfast and put our presents under the tree with the others; Tony, dressed up as Santa Claus, then handed them all out. Although there were no pets unwrapped, the children were delighted with everything that they did get. Christmas lunch with all the trimmings was washed down with more than one bottle of wine, and the plum pudding was brought in on fire by Cook. It was sad that Papa was not there with us; he did so love every excuse to have a party and Christmas at Broadlands had always been one of the highlights of the year when I was a boy.

We stayed at the big house until it was nearly dark and then I lead my family back to our home, where Mary and I sat down with a nice cup of tea and a slice of a very fine Christmas cake. Sarah, bless her, had slept through most of the festivities; she is a very contented baby and Mary says that she is much less trouble than Rob was.

Chapter Five
1908

1st January

Tony and Hermione brought their children down to our cottage last night to see the New Year in. There is no shoot today, so we were able to raise a glass or two to toast 1908. The past year has had its ups and downs; Papa's death cast a dark shadow on all of us for a time, but that was lifted by the arrival of Sarah. In the office I believe that I have earned my keep, and I look forward to making a mark in my new position.

10th January

Bill has been in the office for a week and has taken over Stephen's office and his secretary. I have shown him all the work that we did when we considered expanding into Canada. He has a lot of personal experience in Australia, and in South Africa, although he says that it is probably too late to make a worthwhile investment there. Brazil is another place where gold is being mined profitably and it may be worth a visit.

Lisa is quietly confident that she is pregnant, but says that she would like to work for at least another four more months; I am glad, as this gives me time to find a suitable replacement. I am making detailed records of each of our mines, when production started, when new shafts were sunk, annual production of gold, the managers and the number of employees, the machinery in use and the other assets. This should have been done long ago, for while we have multiple operations in a fairly small area it makes it possible to see where we can move men and machines from one location to another when necessary.

3rd March

I seem to have very little time for my diary these days, although I should be able to discipline myself and write a few lines every evening that I am alone in my London house. At weekends I catch up with my family and Hermione's and I am thrilled by Sarah's progress; she is nearly four months old now and is a proper little person; she usually only wakes us once during the night and soon goes back to sleep when she has been fed. Hermione says that she wishes that her children had been so thoughtful.

Bill has gone to Cape Town and from there will go to Tanganyika; on his way back he hopes to stop over in the Gold Coast so that he can see for himself where the AGC's profits come from.

21st March

Sarah is four months old and is a very lively baby; I think that she is eager to be able to crawl, walk and run and she finds her present limited capabilities very frustrating. It is a real joy for me to greet her when I get home on Friday evenings and I like to think that she recognises me as her father. Mary says that is rubbish and that I will have to wait for quite a bit longer before she greets me as Dada.

Today Lisa told me that she wants to leave at the end of April; I asked her if she thought that any of the typists would be a good secretary for me and she said that Sally would probably suit me very well. She is evidently in her late thirties, married with two children and not likely to have any more. She has worked for the AGC for about five years. I said that if she is interested I would like to see her and Lisa will arrange that for tomorrow.

22nd March

Lisa duly brought Sally to meet me and I think that she will be a good replacement; she is a very competent shorthand typist, has a good sense of humour and is keen to have a more interesting job than her present one in the typing pool. We agreed that she would work alongside Lisa for a week before Lisa leaves, so as to get to know the ropes, and most importantly how and when I like my morning cup of tea. I think that we will get on well together.

Bill should have arrived in Cape Town by now, and may have gone up to Witwatersrand to see how the mines there are doing on his way to Tanganyika. Before he left I asked him whether with his experience of the country he thought that there might be an opportunity for the AGC in Australia; he said that it is a huge country and much of it is not only undeveloped, it has yet to be explored by white men. Some of the natives are quite friendly and are happy to work for the prospectors and farmers while others are quite prepared to cut your head off; it is as well to find out which sort you are dealing with.

There is a lot of gold there but much of it is in inaccessible areas, and where it is possible to get to it, there are already individual prospectors or large companies with officially registered claims. It would not be easy to manage an operation so far from its head office in England, and if it did not come up to expectations it would be a costly failure.

10th April

Mary and Hermione had planned a surprise party for the children today, and some local children of similar age were invited. There were games on the lawn at Broadlands and tables were set out with sandwiches, cakes and lemonade. The weather was perfect, and I so enjoyed sitting in my chair in the sun with a cup of tea watching the young enjoy themselves. Rob is very good with younger children, whether relations or others, and is quite prepared to lose a game that he could easily win. Sarah is still desperately anxious to crawl, but still has to settle for shuffling along on her backside.

20th April

Both Lisa and Sally were in the office before I got there, and Lisa was sorting out the various papers on my desk and telling Sally where they should go; some are projects on which I am currently working and some, such as the Canadian and Iduapriem exercises, can be stored for future reference if necessary. Lisa leaves at the end of the week, and I must ask Sally what would be a suitable leaving present.

24th April

Lisa left today; I took her out for lunch and gave her a bottle of perfume that Sally told me that Lisa used; she has worked very well for me and I wish her well with raising a family; I know how rewarding it is. The staff had collected a nice sum for a leaving present and at the end of the day in the board room, she was presented with a variety of toys and garments for the baby. John said how well she had worked for the AGC, and that if she wanted to come back at some time in the future there would be a job for her. She is a very popular lady.

26th April

This weekend we are taking the children to the zoo; they are very excited about this and have asked me whether I saw all the animals in the zoo when I was in Africa. I told them that I was sure that there will be lots of animals that I have never seen before, and that I am just as excited as they are.

Before then I have to complete a report for the board which shows the relative efficiency of our four mines in the Gold Coast. The weight of gold produced from one ton of ore is the standard benchmark, but it is also important to know the cost of that production, taking into account all the overheads such as staff costs, machinery depreciation, local 'commissions', etc. I have gone into great detail, and I think that it will not only be useful now but also will help us to evaluate the profitability of any other operations that we consider. At this time, it looks as though Bibiani is the best performer.

Chapter Six
1912

1st October

Yes, 1912; this the first entry in my diary for more than three years. Why? It seems that when Sally replaced Lisa and they sorted out the papers on my desk my diary was mistakenly put into storage with a lot of other documents; and there it stayed until yesterday when I asked to see Ted's report on the Iduapriem mine. To Sally's great embarrassment, and to my delight, my diary was in that folder. I do not normally take it to the office, and I cannot remember why I did so then, but whatever the reason I never thought to see if it was in the storage room, where most things gather dust undisturbed over the years.

For some time I hoped that it would turn up so I did not start another diary, but I recorded events of interest, both at the office and at home, on sheets of paper which now take up a considerable part of one drawer of a filing cabinet in the office and much of a drawer in my bureau at home. I will try to edit them and put the sheets together in chronological order, but in the meantime I will bring this diary up to date with a summary of my home life and record the major events of the past four years at the AGC.

At home Mary is the same lovely lady that I married seven years ago. Rob is now studying land management at the Royal Agricultural College at Cirencester and Sarah is almost five years old, a very different little girl from the one that I took to the zoo. Over the years, we have made some improvements to our cottage, mostly involving plumbing and electricity, and is now a really lovely family home.

Quentin's regiment has moved to Wiltshire, where there are several large training areas, so we have seen less of him and Pamela lately; they do not yet have any children.

Hermione is a wonderful mother, and her children are a credit to her. Arthur has just started his first term at Charterhouse and Penelope, who is now aged eleven, will go to a boarding school in a couple of years. Tony is doing a great job managing the Broadlands estate; it is now on a sound financial footing and there is no longer any need to worry about whether it can be kept intact. The tenant farmers are all very supportive of Tony's plans, and he gets further support from Rob, who comes home for the holidays from Cirencester with all the latest modern ideas about farming.

All is well on the home front.

In the office I have been kept busy. When Bill returned from his trip to Tanganyika he said that there was a real opportunity to invest in the mine at Bindura; he did not recommend buying it, but said that it was undercapitalised and not well-managed and could be much more profitable if a more professional structure was put in place. This was discussed by the board and meetings were held with the mine's English owners, and it was agreed that the AGC would buy fifty-one percent of the shares and put in a new mine manager for a minimum of two years.

Bill was happy to go there, and by the time that he returned eighteen months ago the productivity of the Bindura mine had improved considerably and the management of it was much more efficient. He has not yet been to Obuasi, buthopes to go there before too long. John is very happy that he was able to recruit Bill, who is already more than paying his way in the AGC. Three months ago he left for Canada, where he is visiting a number of the mines there; I get regular reports from him but so far there are no obvious opportunities.

Our first mine in the Gold Coast, Obuasi One, continues to become less profitable; the weight of gold per ton of ore has decreased and Franz says that it will soon cost more to mine and extract it than it is worth. Obuasi Two and Three are both performing well, and could do better still if some of the workmen are switched from their ailing parent mine. Bibiani is now our most profitable mine ever and it has made a real difference to the area; the number of workmen has increased steadily and Louis has extended his rest house.

At the last board meeting, I raised the matter of the Iduapriem mine; I have studied Ted's earlier report, which was brought up from the storeroom, happily with this diary, and I think that it may be the time to become involved there. When Bill returns from Canada I think that he should go to the Gold Coast and meet Ted; he has not yet seen our operations at Obuasi and Bibiani, and he can form an updated opinion on the Iduapriem mine. We continue to pay an annual sum to the local chieftain to protect our right to operate there if we wish and it may be time to exercise that right;

especially as he is probably also being paid by other companies or individuals for the same exclusive right.

I think that what I have written here summarises the events during the time when this diary was gathering dust in the storeroom, and I will continue to record in it, as previously, anything of interest at home or at work.

20th October

It was agreed at today's board meeting that Bill should go to the Gold Coast after a reasonable time back in England. He is due back from Canada at the end of this month, so I would expect him to go early next year. I would very much like to see for myself the mine at Bindura, but to go there and back with only a few days at the mine would take at least ten weeks, more if I had to wait at Cape Town for the return voyage, and I cannot justify that time out of the office or away from my family. From what Bill has said it is a very different operation from that at Obuasi, but our investment is proving to have been a good one.

5th November

Bill will not be coming back, or going to the Gold Coast; he has been arrested by the Canadian police on a number of charges relating to his time in Australia. It was quite by chance that at one of the mines that he visited near Quebec he was recognised by a man who had worked at the Australian mine in which Bill had a half share. In Australia he was known as Frank Williams, his real name, and he changed it to Bill Franklin when he booked a passage to England to avoid being exposed, having defrauded his Australian partner over a number of years.

He was wanted by the Australian police under his real name, and they had not realised that he had left the country under an alias; it was unlucky for him that one of his Australian superintendents, who had left the company a year or so after the theft was discovered, had moved to the same Canadian mine that Bill, as he was now known, had visited on behalf of the AGC. Bill Franklin denied having been Frank Williams, or having ever been to Australia, but his erstwhile employee was not deceived and reported the matter to the police.

Bill, or Frank, is now in prison in Quebec, and will be returned to Australia as soon as may be. Canada has had an extradition treaty with a number of countries since 1877, and where there is no treaty then rendition, involuntary return, to some countries has been practised. Cooperation between British colonies is the rule rather than the exception, and in one way or another Bill can be certain that he will soon be facing a long prison sentence in Australia.

When we heard this unwelcome news from our friend in the fraud squad, John immediately asked Chris to check all our accounts; Bill, as we still think of him, had no access to any of them, but now that we know about his past criminal activity it is as well to be sure. Chris reported that there was no irregularity. Bill's work at Bindura has in fact benefitted the AGC considerably, unless of course he has misappropriated either funds or gold there. I have instructed our chief accountant there to carry out a very detailed examination of our local bank accounts and to compare very carefully the records of gold produced with the records of gold shipped to England.

John has taken this very personally; he introduced Bill to us and recommended his appointment as a director; he feels that his lack of judgement has damaged the reputation of the AGC and at an extraordinary board meeting he offered to resign. All four of us absolutely rejected the idea; since Edwin Cade died he has led the AGC through a period of profitable expansion and he cannot be blamed for being deceived by Bill any more than we can. It is not as though the AGC has suffered any financial loss; our red faces are the only outcome and we will soon put this behind us. Meanwhile we have received one application to replace him as a director from an acknowledged criminal, lately out of prison, who said that he felt that his experience suited him well for a senior position in a company with a record like ours. I did not put the man forward for interview, but I had to smile at his cheek.

At the meeting it was proposed that as a temporary measure only I should take over Bill's responsibility for business development; this I do not welcome, for it should involve the foreign travel that I have tried to avoid since I got married, but in these troubled times I must put the company before my personal convenience. Before his arrest, Bill had reported that there were no realistic opportunities in Canada for the AGC, and in the short term at least there is nothing in our sights overseas.

Chapter Seven
1913

3rd January

The Christmas holiday passed very happily and it was nice to be able to put the recent problems at the office behind me and simply enjoy being with my family. This year the Christmas tree and the ceremony of opening the presents was at our home, and Mary had made a great effort decorating the tree; the pile of wrapped presents under it was as big as ever and the turkey and plum pudding were delicious. On Boxing Day Tony and I took our guns out and our wives and children did their best to drive a few pheasants over us; the children enjoyed shouting and beating their sticks against the trees, and between us we got six brace of nice birds; Tony will give a brace to each of the tenant farmers.

The markets are unsettled at the moment and the price of gold has risen as a result; John has said that we must take advantage of the situation and do whatever we can to increase production. I reminded him that at the last board meeting, I had suggested the Bill should go and see the mine at Obuapriem, and that Ted had already said that it could be worked profitably. This would result in a much greater increase in our total production than would result from small increases at Obuasi and Bibiani.

John supported the idea and told me to make it an agenda item for the next board meeting; in the meantime I have to see what management and machinery we could put in place at short notice.

23rd January

At today's board meeting, it was unanimously agreed that we should exercise our right of first refusal at Obuapriem, and that we should get the mine operating as soon as possible. It has always been agreed with the local chief that we will employ all the indigenous prospectors and will need a great many more, and because his 'commission' is a percentage of the output he will ensure that we do not lack for workers.

The management of the mine poses a problem. It is too far from Obuasi for it to be managed from there, and it would not be wise to put a newcomer to the AGC in charge of this fledgling operation. It is clearly my responsibility to get the mine up and running as soon as possible, and much as I dislike the idea I think that I will have to go there for at least six months; by the end of that period I hope that one of the mine superintendents at Obuasi or Bibiani will be considered ready for promotion and can be moved to Obuariem as mine manager.

Meanwhile, we will need to recruit two more mine superintendents, one for Obuapriem and the other to fill the vacancy at Obuasi or Bibiani. We will also need more Berdan Pans and the machinery to drive them, at least two lorries, material to construct housing and sheds, and any number of other things. A list of these requirements was drawn up by Ted when he visited the mine some years ago and I will now place the necessary orders.

I will leave in about a month's time and I will ask Ted to be ready to join me at the mine while we get it up and running. He knows the chief and the area, and there will be more to do than one man could achieve on his own; between us we should be able to manage the preparation of the site and when the operation starts we can act as mine manager and superintendent until those posts are filled.

I do not look forward to telling Mary of this when I see her at the weekend; I know that she will say that it is in the best interests of the AGC and that of course I must go, but she will not be happy. She is so supportive of me, and will always put my career before her life. At least she has the children to occupy her time and Hermione and her children will be frequent visitors.

1st March

I am once again on my way to Takoradi and due to arrive there in ten days' time. By the time that I get there, much of the material and most importantly the Berdan Pans, should have got there before me, and it should be possible to start getting the buildings up and the machinery in place. I am looking forward to working with Ted, we have so much in common. When the mine is operating I am sure that the board will agree to him becoming a director, and I hope that in due course he will join us in London.

It was hard to say goodbye to Mary and the children; Rob wanted to come with me and Sarah said it was only all right if I brought a parrot back with me; ever since her first visit to the zoo she has been obsessed with parrots and now she wants one that she can teach to speak. African Greys are well known for that ability, and I have seen several that have demonstrated it. Mary was brave in front of the children, but I know how much she will miss me and how much I will miss her.

Hermione told me that she will see Mary every day and that I should not worry.

11th March

We anchored offshore Takoradi at midday and I am now in the rest house with Ted. He met me at the wharf where passengers disembark from the ship's boat; it is good to see him again, he has been so supportive of me in my role in London and has done an outstanding job in this country. We were very pleased to see that a lot of the crates of cargo offloaded from my ship were marked 'AGC Takoradi'. Ted says that there are already quite a number at the mine, so we should be able to make a start without delay.

We passed the evening over a few beers; we reminisced about Witwatersrand and Cape Town, and I brought him up to date with events at head office; he did not know the details of the sins of either Carson or Franklin and when I told him the full sorry stories he said that we should take more care when choosing directors; I said he did not know how true that was, but I gave no hint of my plans for him.

12th March

Today we first called on the local chief. He greeted Ted like a long-lost brother and said how honoured he was that he had brought a big chief from London to his humble village. I gave him a Swiss Army knife, and he gave me a very nice ebony carving of a man's head. He was fascinated by the knife, and spent some time pulling out and replacing the various tools. I said that his reputation as a wise man, able to see the future benefits of working with the English, was much talked of in London, and that the benefits to his people would be considerable. I also reminded him tactfully, without actually saying so, that his commission would be directly related to the mine's productivity, and that that would depend upon the number, quality and honesty of the workers.

I said that if there were any thefts of gold we would assume that they had been taken to be given to him, their chief, and that we would naturally reduce his commission accordingly; he said that his men were known to be the most honest and hard-working in the Gold Coast, if not the world, and that we need not fear on that score, but that if any man did steal gold he would be punished according to local tradition. I thought it best not to enquire further into that.

18th April

We are making good progress; two residential bungalows are taking shape and a big shed to house the extraction process, a workshop and a vehicle maintenance pit are nearly complete. The Berdan Pans arrived before I did and next week we plan to set them up and connect them to the steam engine that powers their rotation and tilting. Ted reckons that we should be ready to start production in three weeks' time; I think that that is a bit optimistic, but he knows the country and its workers better than I. In fact, even now, the mine is producing small amounts of gold, for while there is nothing else for the workers to do until the machinery is all working we have encouraged them to continue their individual efforts; the difference being that we get to keep the gold and they get paid to find it.

14th May

The mine is not yet operating, and Ted's forecast has indeed proved to be optimistic. The buildings are completed and the Berdan Pans are in place, but the steam engine stubbornly refuses to work. I have sent word to Obuasi asking Cameron to come down on the next train to Takoradi, where we will meet him, and work his mechanical magic on the engine.

18th May

The steam engine surrendered to Cameron, and is now up and running. We fed the first load of ore into the Berdan Pans yesterday and Franz, who came down from Obuasi with Cameron, was very pleased with the result. He has left the mine superintendent at Obuasi in charge of the extraction plant there and will stay at Obuapriem until that operation is running smoothly. Ted has returned to Obuasi, but I will stay here and keep an eye on the operation for a month or so.

29th June

With the new mine now running well I am taking the opportunity to visit Obuasi and Bibiani. The next ship calling at Takoradi for England is not for another three weeks, and I would like to see how the new men that we selected in London are performing on the job.

1st July

Back here at Obuasi One, it is almost as though I have never been away; it is ten years since I first arrived here with Edwin Cade, and I was here four years ago when we investigated the possibilities at Bibiani. George greeted me enthusiastically and said that he would show me his latest drawings of the local wildlife; I said that I looked forward to that, but that he need not organise another expedition into the forest with Aggrey while I was there. Sgt. Miller said that the policemen that he had recruited at Bibiani seemed to be honest, but that he was keeping an eye on them and paying occasional unannounced visits to check that they were performing their duties properly; my original house staff, Mensah, Yeboah and Musa, all came and welcomed me.

8th July

I have visited all three mines and found nothing out of order. Obuasi One is indeed proving less productive; one reason being that the length of the tunnels leasing from the main shaft is now such, that recovering the ore mined at the head of the tunnel takes much longer than it did. The quality of the ore is also lower than it was, and we will have to decide whether it is worth sinking another shaft in the area, with the hope of striking a richer part of the vein, or whether we should close it.

Obuasi Two and Three are producing very well, and the breadth of the vein at Obuasi Three particularly makes it much easier to move the ore from the tunnel head to the shaft.

11th July

I could not leave Obuasi without making a journey to Kumasi, where the Mamponghene received me with all the usual ritual. I said that his men were working well for us at all four mines, and that we were particularly pleased with Bibiani, which I would be visiting next week. He said that he heard that we were now mining at Obuapriem, where a minor chief of an insignificant tribe was helping us, and he hoped that we would not be disappointed. I said that we could not complain, but told him that it would be difficult to have as good a relationship as we had with him. We could not avoid drinking several cups of palm wine before we left, and I must admit that I recall very little of the return journey to Obuasi.

12th July

The journey to Bibiani on the now well-levelled road was not only quicker but also less uncomfortable than previously. Ted and I called first on the headman and told him that we were pleased with the work that his men were doing. We then went to the rest house where Louis welcomed us with a refreshing drink; he is very grateful that his real identity was not exposed when he was questioned by the policeman from Cape Coast; he has built two additional guest rooms and Alan Parsons, the mine manager, and Arnaud Boucher, erstwhile prospector and now mine superintendent, are using them for a very reasonable cost.

We then went to the mine, where a single shaft is serving three tunnels; this produces as much ore as the Berdan Pans can handle, and we must think as to whether production could be increased with another set of pans. Arnaud explained that while the shaft and tunnels were the main source of gold he still had a number of workers on the dry river bed and its banks, both of which continued to make a useful contribution.

The boring machine, once the bane of Cameron's life, is now in the capable hands of one of the local villagers. He has spent several years repairing assorted types of machinery and so far, has persuaded it not to break down. Edward firmly believes that the local 'witch doctor' has cast a spell on it, and while it continues to work, I am happy to go along with the idea.

Ted and I, and Alan and Arnaud, dined with Louis and his lady; Alan has some good ideas for increasing production and Arnaud is very supportive; having worked for several years as a prospector among the local African prospectors, he knows many of them well and is evidently well-liked, and he has no trouble getting them to do his bidding. Alan is wise enough to encourage this situation and the result is a happy, well-managed mine.

14th July

We resisted Arnaud's invitation to stay another day at the mine and celebrate his national day with him and returned to Obuasi yesterday. With my business completed, I allowed Charles to take me for a short trip into the forest where he showed me several birds that I had not seen before. We were accompanied by the worthy Aggrey, who promised not to bring us again into close contact with the leopard.

Back at the mine, I asked him if he could get an African Grey parrot for me in the next two days, and he assured me that not only could he get a parrot but, if I wished, he could get a pygmy hippopotamus or a crocodile. I did not see either of those fitting well into the Broadlands estate, and I told him that this time a parrot would suffice. He told me, unsurprisingly, that he knew where to get one of the best parrots in the country, that it had been in captivity for some time and already spoke fluently.

16th July

Today, Aggrey delivered a parrot. It is a good-looking bird and came in a cage made of wooden strips woven together to form a base and then bent upwards to form the bars that retained the bird. It seemed to me that if it wished it could very quickly destroy the cage with its powerful beak and gain its freedom, but Aggrey assured me, again unsurprisingly, that it was used to the cage and had no wish to escape. We shall see. It cost the princely sum of five shillings. It does indeed seem to have a small vocabulary, but since it is in the local language I have no idea what it says; I asked Aggrey to translate, but he said that it was not something that I would want to hear.

This evening I dined with all the expatriate staff and congratulated them on how well they had got the new mines into production. I said that it had been a difficult time recently at head office, but that we had been confident that the mines, the really important parts of the AGC, were well-managed and did not need our immediate attention while the more pressing local problems were addressed. Ted said how pleased they all were that I was now in charge of all mining, and that they hoped that I would soon identify new possibilities.

17th July

Back at the Takoradi rest house I am told that the *SS Braemar Castle* is now not due until 21st July. This gives me enough time to pay another brief visit to Obuapriem before I leave the country, and I will be interested to see how the work there has settled down. I am accompanied by the parrot, and I am hoping to teach it to say 'Hello Penelope' before we get back to England, but that may be a wish too far.

21st July

The parrot and I are established in our cabin; I have brought with me a supply of palm nuts, which I am assured are its favourite food, but it will have to get used to something less exotic back at Broadlands. There are only four other first class passengers, and I do not think that any of them are likely to want to play *Last Man Standing* with me; I shall pass the time writing up my reports and teaching the parrot.

31st July

We dock at Southampton tomorrow morning and I shall be glad to be on my way back to Broadlands. The parrot now says 'Hullo', not 'Hello', but 'Penelope' is still beyond it; I am sure that it will have every opportunity to learn that when it is in its new home. As I foresaw, it has discovered that it can force apart the wooden slats that act as bars on its cage, and on one occasion when I returned to my cabin it was perched on the edge of my bunk and greeted me with a perfect 'Hullo'. I was so delighted that I gave it a couple of palm nuts before returning it to its cage. When I do not want it to be active I put a cloth over its cage and it thinks that night has fallen and seems to go to sleep. When I remove the cloth it shows off its limited vocabulary, and if it does that when I present it to my niece, we will all be delighted.

1st August

Tony met me at the station and I am now back at Broadlands. The parrot performed perfectly when I gave it to Penelope, and she has not ceased trying to increase its vocabulary; tomorrow we must see if we can get a rather more secure cage.

It was lovely to see Mary again, and Hermione and all the children, and a reunion like that almost makes it worth being away from home; Mary says the same, but that I should not make that an excuse to make frequent overseas trips.

2nd August

Back in the office I was able to report that Obuapriem is now fully operational and that our four other mines in that country, with one exception, have increased their production by almost five percent. The exception is Obuasi One, and we will soon have to decide whether to sink another exploratory shaft or close it down.

20th December

Christmas is almost upon us once again, and I see that it is more than five months since my last diary entry. My excuse is that nothing of great importance or interest has happened, either in the office or at home. The parrot, for which I feel a certain sympathy, has responded to Penelope's constant encouragement and can now manage 'Hullo Peppy'. Tony says in private that it is a stupid bugger, and I have to hope that it does not learn that phrase and come out with it at an embarrassing moment. Sarah is only six years old, and if she has to learn words like that it should be when she is older, and not from a parrot.

At a board meeting this week Alan Hughes said that he would wish to stand down as an executive director from the board of the AGC at the end of next year. He is a partner in a firm of solicitors and feels that he should give them more of his time. John said that he was a valuable member of the board and would he reconsider his decision. Alan said that he thought not, but that he would be glad to be a consultant to the AGC on legal matters if they wished. John said that that would be much appreciated, and better than losing him completely.

Quentin is down for the weekend; he is now second in command of his regiment and says that the government is taking steps to make the army, and indeed the navy, better prepared should the unrest in the Balkans boil over into war. He does not look forward to being involved in another war but says that if you join the army you cannot complain if they ask you to fight. He survived the Boer war, but a war in Europe is likely to be fought against a more professional enemy, and it is well that we are taking the possibility seriously.

Rob is back from Cirencester for the Christmas holiday, and spends much time with Tony, learning the practical side of land management. Tony says that he is a bright lad, with some good ideas of his own, and that in time he will be able to manage the Broadlands estate as well as anyone else.

Arthur and Penelope, now fourteen and eleven years old respectively, are doing well at their schools and are the envy of Sarah, who when not tormenting the long-suffering parrot asks why she cannot go to a big school where they do not come home every day. That day will come all too soon. Meanwhile I delight in her presence at home and wish that she would never grow any older.

Mary and Hermione are the backbones of our two families and are dearly loved and much appreciated by all of us; they work so well together, remember to buy presents and cards for everyone's birthday, organise parties at home and trips to zoos and the pictures, and generally ensure that the children enjoy almost every moment of their lives. They are strict when necessary, always kind and fair, and will listen until the cows come home to stories about a sick lamb or a bird with a broken wing; the children are so lucky to be so loved.

31st December

Christmas is behind us and the new year beckons; I wonder what it will bring.

Chapter Eight
1914

10th January

John said today that we must prepare for a very different year; it is not a time to seek to expand the AGC's portfolio of mines but rather to ensure that they are operating at maximum efficiency. The price of gold continues to rise, and so do our profits, but international tension has seen the value of many companies much reduced. My responsibility is to see that our mines do not want for any equipment and that the workforce is at the optimum level. I am lucky to be able to rely on Ted to let me know if he needs anything.

10th June

While the past months have been uneventful at home and in the office they have been anything but calm on the international front. Alliances have been made between European countries, and even countries as far distant as Japan, and there is a tension which can surely only explode into war one day soon. John has said that if England becomes involved in a war, it will be up to each individual to do as his conscience bids; but war is expensive, and the AGC must contribute as much as possible to the war effort by maximising gold production.

28th June

The Austrian Archduke and his wife have been assassinated; that may be the spark which ignites the tinderbox in Europe.

28th July

Here we go; war declared between Austro-Hungary and Serbia.

3rd August

Germany has declared war on France and invaded Luxembourg and Belgium

4th August

It had to happen; England has declared war on Germany.

John called the directors into the board room and said that we must see how this affects our mining operations. In West Africa the Germans have a colony in Togo; this is a small country immediately to the east of the Gold Coast. Our goldfields must be very tempting to the Germans but it must be doubtful whether they have the means to attack the Gold Coast, and the mines are all a long way from the border between the two countries.

The situation in East Africa is very different. Tanganyika is a German colony, and there is no way that the mine at Bindura could be defended should the Germans move to take it over; they would probably wish the mine to keep on producing gold and simply steal it before it could be shipped to England. I fear for our staff and workers there and hope that they come to no harm, and it is frustrating to have no news from there.

It is being widely said that the war will be over by Christmas, and at the moment there is no compulsory enlistment into the army; there has been a surge in the number of volunteers and the government seems confident of a swift victory. The AGC does not employ many people at its head office, and so the impact of the war on our day-to-day work will be little, if any.

18th September

It seems less likely that the war will be over by Christmas. The Germans made large territorial gains before we brought them to a halt, and it will take time, and probably the loss of many lives, before the situation can be reversed. There are posters everywhere now saying that 'Your Country Needs You', and this has boosted the number of recruits; but I wonder how long it will be before enlistment becomes compulsory rather than voluntary.

20th December

With no good news from the front, and no news at all from Bindura, Christmas this year will not be the jolly occasion that it has been. The children, of course, are not aware of how serious the situation is, and we will try to make it a happy time for them. Rob is talking about enlisting, but I have said that he should finish his degree studies first and see if there is still a war when he completes the course in a couple of years' time.

Arthur says that he hopes that the war is still being fought when he is eighteen, so that he can go and fight, and has asked for a gun for Christmas so that he can learn to be a good shot and kill lots of Germans. Penelope wants another parrot so that they can have babies, but quite apart from the impossibility of finding another bird in England we have no idea as to whether ours is male or female. Tony has taught it to say 'Bloody Kaiser', but it has not progressed beyond 'Hullo Peppy'.

Sarah, who was eight last week, wants a pony; this is probably the most realistic of the children's wishes, and Tony has said that he will see whether there is one for sale around here; all the horses are being taken to France, some for the cavalry and some to pull the guns and supply wagons.

Mary, bless her, just asks that I do not volunteer to go and fight. I do not like the idea, but I have talked about it with Tony and we think that there may come a time, all too soon, when we cannot ignore the call to arms.

28th December

It was not possible to celebrate Christmas as we used to, but we made it as enjoyable as we could for the children. There was no pony under the Christmas tree for Sarah, but Tony has promised to keep his eyes open. The parrot now says 'Bloody Kaiser' almost non-stop, and has to have its cage covered to shut it up. There will be no shoot on New Year's Day.

Chapter Nine
1915

10th January

In the office the talk was more of the war than of our mines. There is still no news from Bindura, but the Gold Coast mines are producing well. John called me into his office and we had a long talk about enlistment. He is not liable to be called up, on account of his age, but it seems likely that men of my age will soon be conscripted. I would rather enlist voluntarily, and I told John that I was seriously thinking of it. I said that if I did, I would suggest that Ted was made a director and stayed at Obuasi, effectively doing the same job as I now do in London.

John thought that was a very practical solution, and said that he understood my wish to get involved in the war, and that my job would of course be there for me when I returned. Richard Beale is a few years older than I, and will probably not be called up unless the war goes on for a long time, and Alan Hughes is in much the same position, so the AGC will not be without experienced men to take it through the war.

14th January

Tony and I had a long talk this afternoon and decided that we should enlist on Monday. He said that he thought the tenant farmers are more than capable of keeping the estate going, and that Rob knew enough to be able to contribute when he was down from Cirencester. I told him that I had discussed it with John Daw and that he accepted that I should go.

After dinner at Broadlands we told Hermione and Mary of our decision. It was no surprise to either of them, for we have talked about it for some time, but they are both very upset now that we are really going. We tried to convince them that it would be only a short time now before the war was won, but I think that they know, as we do, that victory will not come quickly or easily.

We agreed how we will tell the children tomorrow and went to our beds with much on our minds.

15th January

Tony and I went to the recruiting centre and officially enlisted. We were weighed, measured and examined by a doctor, who jocularly pronounced both of us fit to die on the field of battle. Because of our backgrounds we were selected as officer material, and were told to expect a summons to the training depot at Aldershot, probably within two weeks. We determined to make that time as happily memorable as possible for our families.

1st February

We go to Aldershot tomorrow and are advised that the training will take six weeks; during that time we will be assessed as to which part of the army we are best suited for. I shall take this diary with me; although I think that I may have little time to make entries, but I will carry a little notebook and record events of interest.

Our last dinner together was not a festive one; everyone tried to be jolly, but it was not possible to ignore the fact that one or both of us might not be returning to Broadlands. The children are least affected by our decision; Arthur, of course, wants to go with his father, Penelope hopes Tony can bring back another parrot, and Sarah says that there may be more ponies in France than here.

4th February

It is Sunday, and my first opportunity to record my life as a soldier. We have been given kit and told how to clean it to a ridiculous standard; we have been marched up and down the barrack square; we have been bullied by physical training sergeants and taken on long runs in freezing weather, dressed only in vests and shorts, and we have spent some time on the rifle range. We have also, I am glad to say, sat in cold classrooms and been taught something about warfare, but I am not yet confident that I am ready to fight the Huns.

18th February

The last two weeks have passed so rapidly that I find it hard to pick out individual events, but our instruction has been much more focussed on what is expected of a junior officer. Leadership is the first requirement; the men must be sure that you know what is what and that you care for their wellbeing. We are told that communications are often far from perfect on the front line, and that an officer must be prepared to act on his own initiative in the absence of specific orders.

In the countryside close to the barracks, there is a trench system similar to the one we can expect in France, and we have practised moving around in it in dense smoke at night. We have also practiced going 'over the top', which is when all the men in the trench go forward to attack the enemy. The quicker you are up and running the less likely you are to be shot.

25th February

Tomorrow we are interviewed by an officer who will decide which branch of the army we will be posted to, when we are commissioned in two weeks' time. Tony and I have agreed that we will both ask to join Quentin's regiment; it is an infantry regiment and has already seen action.

26th February

Tony will be joining Quentin and I will be joining the 257th Tunnelling Company in the Corps of Royal Engineers. These decisions were made because Tony proved to be an excellent shot with a rifle, as well as with his twelve bore shotgun, and because I know about mines. I am not yet sure why that is relevant but I will no doubt soon find out.

We have been told that we are excused duties tomorrow so that we can get our officers' uniforms; it will be nice to get away from the barracks for a few hours.

27th February

Mary met me at our Mews house at lunchtime; it was lovely to see her again, and I wondered when, if ever, we would be just the two of us together again. In the morning, I went to the tailor who had fitted me out when I first got back from Africa, and who already had my measurements. This time I said that I needed the uniform for the unit that I was to join and was told that it would be ready to collect on Friday.

I then went to the shop of the shoemaker who had applied for the position of mine superintendent. He was delighted to see me and provided me with two pairs of shoes, a pair of leather boots and a pair of gaiters, all, luckily, at very reasonable prices, since my uniform and accoutrements were not cheap.

9th March

This was our last week of training, and it has been the most interesting. We have been talked through several actual recent engagements and shown how the outcome of each was decided. I had a morning with an engineer officer and he told me all about mining in warfare. It consists of digging tunnels, one hundred yards or more in length, which end under an enemy emplacement that is causing problems and possibly preventing us advancing. It may be a machinegun post or a command bunker. The end of the tunnel is then packed with high explosives, which are detonated when the attack is made.

This is obviously important work, but it must be not only very dangerous but extremely unpleasant. The tunnels are as narrow as possible, prone to flooding and collapse, and without any fresh air; there is also the possibility that the enemy will detect the tunnel beneath them and ensure that it and all in it are destroyed. It will be quite different from Witwatersrand or Obuasi.

12th March

I am now Second Lieutenant Frobisher Broad, and I have the uniform to prove it. I collected it from the tailor yesterday, and Mary and I spent a last night together in London before we both returned home today; she is resigned to my going, and puts a very brave face on it, especially in front of the children. I have been told that I can expect a Movement Order and a rail pass to Dover in the next few days. Tony has already got his, and he leaves in two days' time. In a way, I am looking forward to joining my unit in France; I know that it will be dangerous and that I may not return, but there is a certain satisfaction in knowing that you are doing your duty for your country, along with very many others from all walks of life.

I shall not take this diary to France with me but I will keep a record of important events in a small notebook and enter them in the diary when I return.

15th March

This is the last entry in my diary for I do not know how long. I leave for France via Dover tomorrow. I am as ready as I can be, and my greatest fear is that I may be found wanting when the lives of others depend upon me. My training has been very short, and I hope that it is not too obvious to the men that I will be in charge of; so much may depend upon our respect for each other.

I have told the children that I hope to be back for Christmas, but that until then they must be a great help to their mother. Rob is away at Cirencester for much of the time, but is looking forward to keeping an eye on the estate when he is here. Sarah said that she will help her mother every day if I will bring back a pony for her at Christmas; we really will have to get one for her before long.

Mary will look after this diary while I am away; she says that reading about things that I did in Africa will make me seem nearer to her when I am in France. She is such a lovely person; I am so lucky to have her, and I pray that I will return and be able to love her for the rest of my life.

18th March

I have joined my unit in France; we are about five miles behind the front line and the men are enjoying a brief rest in this little village. In their last operation they lost two of their comrades and their officer when a tunnel collapsed before it was completed. He was evidently well liked, so I have much to live up to. They all have been miners; some were tin miners in Cornwall, and two come from the South Crofty mines that I visited in 1905; most of the others are coal miners from mines in England and Wales.

My senior officer, Fred Knight, is a regular army captain; he joined the army a few years ago when he returned from mining in Australia; he seems to be a pleasant fellow and welcomed me to the Moles, as 257th Tunnelling Company is known. There is one other second lieutenant, Dave Jenkins, a Welsh miner by trade, a sergeant, two corporals and about fifteen men. A corporal and seven men are my squad. We have been told to expect another task soon, so I must get to know my men and let them get to know me before we start tunnelling.

I have sent a letter to Mary, telling her that my address is Army Post Office No.11, and asking her to give me any news that she gets of Quentin or Tony, and to let them know that I am so far safe and well.

21st March

Last night we were moved up to just behind the front line and Captain Knight briefed me on our task. On a slight rise, about one hundred and twenty yards from our trenches, a well-protected German machinegun post is able to prevent any advance by our troops without a very heavy loss of life. Our task is to set a mine beneath it and blow it up. Dave is going to help me plan the operation, as he has already done several, and my corporal will also be involved.

22nd March

We have started tunnelling. It is a miserable business; we start from our trenches, which are a muddy mess, and have to get down gradually to about ten feet so as to avoid detection by the Germans. We also have to avoid breaking out into one of the many shell holes between the lines, but that is more a matter of good luck than good planning. When we are under our target we tunnel upwards before placing the explosives.

Only one man at a time can be at the face of the tunnel; he pushes the spoil behind him to another man, who loads it onto a sledge which is pulled back to the start of the tunnel by a third man. If there are no problems, the tunnel grows by about a yard every hour, when the man at the front is changed. Two shifts are working twenty-four hours a day, and it will take five or six days before we are under the German position.

I have told my men that I will take a turn at the front of the tunnel when the shift changes; this enables me to see whether it is running in a true line and whether any section needs to be shored up. Luckily, the ground is firm and fairly free of large stones, but the man at the face works in cramped, airless conditions, made worse by the water that inevitably collects on the tunnel floor. I hope that our efforts are not in vain.

29th March

If my calculations have been correct we should now be under the German position at the optimum depth and the next task is to enlarge the face to make room for the explosives; these are pulled up on the sledge that was used to take the spoil back. Handling the slabs of TNT is a nerve-wracking business; in theory, they are stable until a detonator is used, but we still take care not to drop them.

The mine will be detonated to coincide with an attack from our trenches tomorrow morning, and I have been briefed as to when to wind the handle on the electrical generator; I only hope that we have got the mine in the right place. All my men have been moved back from the front line for a well-deserved rest, but they will be very much hoping for a good result when the mine blows.

30th March

It worked! Thank heaven, it worked! I wound the handle and the German post seemed to rise in one piece from the ground in a ball of flame and smoke before breaking up and falling back to earth. Our infantry climbed out of the trenches and charged forward, and within ten minutes, a large section of the German line was in our hands; now it has to be held against the inevitable counter attack.

Fred and Dave congratulated me on a fine first operation and I passed that on to my troop. I cannot hope that all our operations will go so smoothly, but I am lucky to be working with such good men and I hope that between us we can make a real contribution.

16th April

I got a letter from Mary today; all is well at home and Hermione has heard from both Tony and Quentin. Their regiment has been in action a lot, but they are all right. They cannot say in which part of the line they are, for our letters are censored so that nothing of strategic importance is given away if the post falls into German hands. Our unit is moved from place to place, depending upon where there is a target for us, so it is quite possible that I will meet up with them one day.

3rd June

Quentin has been wounded and is in a hospital in England. I got a letter from Hermione telling me this, but saying that she has been to see him and that I should not worry. He evidently took a bullet in one lung while standing on the top of the trench and encouraging the men forward. As second in command he did not need to be so exposed, but he was never one to avoid danger if it did some good. I hope that he recovers quickly but is not considered fit enough to come back to France.

10th September

I have been out here for six months, the hardest six months of my life. We are not tasked to dig a tunnel every day, or even every week, but when we do it is always a very stressful time, and I am so fortunate to have such good men under me; we have almost become a family, and when we are waiting for our next operation we talk about what we did before the war.

My men are intrigued that I spent so long in Africa mining gold, and some want to know whether there will be jobs doing that after the war.

I get letters from Mary or Hermione every so often, usually two or three at a time, and I so like hearing how the children are. I do not know when I will get back home, but seeing them again will be one of the best things. Quentin is recovering from his wound, but will not be fit enough for active service and is likely to be posted back to the War Office. I have told Mary to tell him that he and Pamela can live in my mews house; it would be good to keep it warm.

10th December

We have been busy lately, and have had one or two really good results. Our colonel, who I have never met, came to visit our unit while we were resting after our last operation and said what a difference we were making. The men were pleased that they were thought important enough to have their hands shaken by a senior officer and our morale certainly got a boost. We are not winning this war as quickly as we were told that we would, but it is nice to have our efforts appreciated.

30th December

Christmas for us was a quiet time; we were not required to dig a tunnel and spent the time in a village behind the lines where the men were able to get a bottle of beer or of wine and relax for a few days, some of them in the company of French girls. We three officers were billeted in the house of a well-to-do French family, who looked after us as well as was possible, given that they were almost in a war zone. Our men had billets with other families, and on Christmas day we all pooled our rations and ate our lunch in the village hall with many of the villagers. They all brought a bottle or two of wine and some brought fresh bread, cheese and meat and vegetables that we had not seen for a long time.

There was a piano in the hall, and one of my men turned out to be an accomplished pianist, and we sang many songs to his accompaniment. The French also sang their songs, and it was a very happy and relaxing time.

Chapter Ten
1916

16th January

Life is back to normal, and we are about to dig another tunnel. We have been lucky so far, with no flooding or roof falls, and I pray that our good luck may continue. The other section under Dave Jenkins have not been so lucky; the Germans detected their tunnel and blew the roof in, killing two of the men and wounding Dave. The other men in his unit have been transferred to mine until Dave is replaced by another officer.

8th March

I got a letter from Hermione today with the worst possible news; Tony has been killed. He was leading his men in an attack on a German bunker when he was shot by a sniper and died instantly. His body was recovered after the attack, which was successful, and has been buried in a cemetery behind our lines. Poor Hermione! How do you tell the children that their father will not be coming home?

Quentin's regiment is not having good luck, but then I do not suppose that any regiment is; this war is proving very hard to win.

7th July

After two very busy months, which I am glad to say were very successful, all the men in the company are to have ten days' leave in England. I can hardly believe that I shall soon see Mary and the children and Hermione and hers. I will take this notebook with me and leave it at home and at some stage will add the entries to my diary.

20th July

I never thought that I would be so glad to be back at Broadlands; not least is the pleasure of having dry clothes and sleeping in a comfortable bed without the sound of guns. But it is not the same without Tony; Hermione is bearing up, and her children get some relief from knowing that their father died being very brave, for which he got a Mention in Despatches.

Mary was so happy to see me, and admitted that she had half-hoped that I might be slightly wounded and sent back to a hospital in England like Quentin. Sarah asked if I had brought a pony for her, and I promised that she shall have a pony after the war.

Quentin has been back at the War Office for several months, and if he cannot get down to Broadlands I will go and see him and Pamela in my London house. He must be so sorry that Tony was killed, having served with him in the same regiment; and apart from anything else he will have to find another manager for the Broadlands estate when the war is over. Rob is in his third year at Cirencester and we all think that he could probably fill that position very ably if he wanted to.

27th July

My leave is going all too quickly; I have to report in Dover in two days' time. Mary and I have spent a day and a night in London, staying with Quentin and Pamela in our mews house; it was good to see him but he is not very well and I am surprised that he is back at work in the War Office. One lung is virtually useless, and he gets very out of breath with only the least exercise. I hope that he gets better.

29th July

This is my first entry in another little notebook. I have said my goodbyes and am on a train on my way to Dover, where I will stay overnight in the transit camp. The last ten days have been so good and I cannot help wishing that I could have stayed at home; but there is still work to be done, and strangely I look forward to seeing my men again; we have become a very tightly-knit little unit, and I think that they feel that I will keep them safe, although that is not really possible.

31st July

I have rejoined my unit and we are awaiting orders for our next task. I am proud to say that all my men returned from leave; that is not always the case for some take the opportunity to desert.

Chapter Eleven
1918

13th December

With the war over I am back at Broadlands, having been demobilised, 'demobbed' as they call it. I was so lucky to get through it all unscathed, unlike Quentin and poor Tony, the more so, as I might so easily have been killed only a few days before the end of hostilities. Dave Jenkins and I shared a small, damp dugout just behind the line of trenches, and I left him there shaving when I went to see my men. I was a few yards down the trench when a German shell landed smack on our dugout.

I was knocked over by the blast, but the zig-zag form of the trench system is designed to prevent the blast and shrapnel killing all nearby and I was unhurt. Our dugout was completely destroyed and Dave was killed outright; so unlucky after surviving so many mine tunnels and within sight of the end of the war. Happily, the little notebook in which I have recorded life at the front is always in my pocket.

20th December

How different this Christmas will be from the last four. I have all my family around me, but it is only two and a half years since Tony was killed and although Hermione puts on a very brave face in front of the children I know how deeply she misses him.

Quentin and Pamela will be down here for a week spanning Christmas and New Year, and I hope that he is better than when I last saw him. He has asked Rob, who came down from Cirencester with his degree this year, to manage the estate until he can find another manager, but he tells me that if Rob makes a go of it he can have the job permanently. I know that the tenant farmers all like and respect Rob, so they will do all that they can to ensure that the estate is profitable, for their sakes and his.

There are still so many shortages in the shops that our two cooks cannot give us quite the Christmas dinner of earlier years, but having our own farms means that we do not go short of fowls, pork, eggs, butter or cream.

The orchard has provided enough apples to last for months, and the vegetable garden produces potatoes, celery, broccoli, carrots and onions aplenty; we shall not starve.

27th December

Christmas was such a lovely time for all, and I am glad that Hermione was able to enjoy it; when the children are having such fun it is hard to be sad. The star of the show was Sarah's pony. Rob had been told by one of our farmers where he could find one, and it was kept in one of our stables for a couple of days without Sarah suspecting anything. Hermione gave her the saddle and Rob gave her a pair of riding breeches. Quentin gave her a very nice whip and Penelope gave her a hard riding hat, so as soon as I took her round to the stable, accompanied by all the family, she was able to do a quick change and mount up. It is a very docile pony and she managed to stay in the saddle, even when it trotted for a bit. She now wants to sleep in the stable by its side.

Chapter Twelve
1919

1st January

Quentin and Pamela, Hermione and Mary, Rob and I today made the traditional calls on our tenant farmers. At each house we were given an apple and a piece of cheese, to ensure a good harvest, and we provided a glass of whisky. This ritual used to be delayed until the second day of the month when there was a New Year's Day shoot, but it is evidently more likely to work its magic if held on the first day of the year.

Quentin and Pamela are going back to London tomorrow and I will go with them, for I am going to the office for the first time in nearly four years. I will sleep in the second bedroom in my house and it will be nice to be able to talk over some of our wartime experiences with Quentin. I do not know exactly how he was wounded, and he has told me that he saw several of the explosions caused by our mines but never knew just how the Moles did their work or whether my men had dug them.

Saying goodbye to all at Broadlands this time will not be as emotional as when my leave was up, for I will be back at the weekend, but it is always hard to leave Mary.

2nd January

It was strange to be back in the AGC offices; everyone shook my hand or clapped me on the back and said how pleased they were to see me. Sally had put a big vase of flowers on my desk and over my office door there was a sign saying 'Welcome Back', it is as though I have a second family here.

John took me into his office and said that he would bring me up to date with how the AGC had fared over the last four years; he looks older, but has lost none of his enthusiasm for the job that he has now done for the fifteen years since Edwin died. He told me that Richard Beale, who has been deputy chairman and company secretary since Stephen Carson's trial and imprisonment, is not at all well and has not been to the office for five months. Chris Roberts, now the finance director, has taken on the role of company secretary, and since Alan Hughes is no longer a director but a consultant John, Chris and Ted Harris, who is still in Obuasi, have been the only people running the company.

John said that we needed to recruit another director, and since the AGC was performing well it should not be difficult to attract someone suitable. Meanwhile he wants me to become the deputy chairman. This was a very pleasant surprise, and I said that it was an honour and that I would do my best to justify his faith in me. I will still be responsible for all mining operations, with Ted providing on-the-spot management in the Gold Coast.

I was then briefed on the situation at each of our mines and I was glad to hear that all are doing well, with the exception of Obuasi One which was closed down last year. The German military presence in Tanganyika was defeated by our East African troops, and there was no fighting over the Bindura mine, which continues to improve its production. I now have to look for new opportunities in the post-war world.

2nd March

In future I will only record in this diary events of significance. My work in the office is mostly much the same from month to month, and at home my life is a continual delight, which makes up for my having missed four years of the children's development.

Rob is running the estate very competently, and I think that Quentin will confirm him as the permanent manager very soon. Arthur is now nineteen and will soon complete his first year at Oxford, studying law. Penelope is apprenticed to the local vet, and has her sights on eventually having her own practice; the parrot has not increased its vocabulary. Sarah has moved up from her pony to a young horse and wants to compete in show jumping events in a few years' time.

Mary gets lovelier as she gets older. She has become involved in various local clubs and committees and is much liked and respected in the village and further afield. She is adored by me and all the children.

Hermione has got over losing Tony, although I do not think that she will ever forget how happy they were together, and is able to enjoy life once again. She and Mary are such good friends, and she always been a very special sister to me.

And Quentin; he has not recovered completely from his wound and I do not think that he ever will. He says that his job at the War Office is boring, and I would not be surprised if he retired from the army, and he and Pamela came to live at Broadlands as he has always intended.

7th June

We have a new director on the board of the AGC; he is Richard Waterman and he comes to us from Lloyds Bank, where he has been responsible for diversifying into other activities. He will research the financial strength of any operations in which the AGC shows an interest and suggest related activities in which it might become involved. He seems a nice chap and I look forward to working with him.

10th August

Hermione has a beau, Chuck. He is an American colonel, the military attaché at their embassy in London, and they met by chance in Harrods store. She was looking at some china, as was he, and he asked her whether she could recommend something as a suitable present for the ambassador's wife, who was having a fiftieth birthday party. The purchase made they retired to the tea room where they found that they had much in common, despite their very different backgrounds. Romance blossomed over a period when she met him in London several times, and today he came down to Broadlands for the weekend.

I find him pleasant and very interesting; well-suited to Hermione. I hope that something comes of this, although he is likely to be posted back to America next year. His wife died before the war and he has no children. He comes from Twin Falls, Idaho, where his family has a potato farm; his somewhat unusual ambition, when he retires from the army, is to avoid growing potatoes and have a house in the country not far from Boise, the state capital, where he can breed pedigree dogs. Oscar seems to approve of this, for he has taken to Chuck and seldom leaves his side when Chuck is at Broadlands.

14th September

Today in the office was an unusual one. Sally told me that there was a man in reception who wanted to see me, but would not say why. Normally I would have him sent away, but for some reason I told her to have him brought up. He was well-dressed, middle aged and had a confident air about him; he introduced himself as Tom Heywood and said that he had a proposition that he thought might interest the AGC. I asked Sally to bring some tea, and said that I would like to hear what he had to say.

Tom was a miner in Western Australia for almost twenty years, always working as an employee of a mining company rather than as an individual prospector, lately near to Albany. He has no scientific background, but he does have years of practical experience, and he, like me, has a nose for gold. When he suggested to his boss that the company should look for gold in a particular area a short distance from their mine he was told to do his job and not try to do anyone else's.

His father died in England and he resigned shortly afterwards; he then spent some time studying the geological records of the area before returning to England, where he intended to find a job. He found a good one, selling mining machinery and equipment, but could not rid himself of the idea that he knew a place where there was gold waiting to be found. I said that we had considered operating in Australia but had decided not to, but that his experience might be valuable to us elsewhere if he was interested.

He said that he was not looking for a job with the AGC, but that he had a proposition that might interest us. He said that he would go back to Australia, stake a claim on the area that he had in mind, and have one or more trial shafts drilled. He was confident enough to pay for all this himself out of his savings, and if he found gold in sufficient quantities he would transfer ownership of his claim to the AGC, who would operate a mine there, and he would want thirty percent of the profits.

Despite the problems involved in running an operation so far from the head office this seemed to me to be an arrangement where we could not possibly lose. Tom would pay for his passage, the cost of the claim and hiring the men and machinery to make the trial shafts. If gold could be mined profitably there were one or two small mining companies in the area that could probably be bought by the AGC to do the actual mining.

I left Tom in my office and went to see John; he said that he had never been involved in any such arrangement, but that he agreed that there was no risk to the AGC and that he would support such a proposal and called an Extraordinary Board Meeting. Richard is still not well enough to come to the office, but John holds his proxy vote and I have a permanent proxy vote on Ted's behalf. Chris said that he found it hard to believe that there would be no cost for us, but that if it really was the case he could see no objection and I brought in Tom who repeated what he had told me. It did not take long for Tom to convince the others, and the proposal was agreed unanimously.

Over lunch in the board room, it was agreed that Tom would sail to

Australia as soon as possible and keep us advised as to his progress. I will do further research on the companies mining in that part of western Australia, to see which might be receptive to a takeover bid. John asked Tom whether if the project was successful he would be prepared to manage the operation for a year or two, and he said that he would.

It has been a unique day in my experience, and if Tom is proved right, and there is gold to be mined profitably at that place, it will turn out to have been an important day for the AGC.

10th December

Richard Beale died yesterday. He served the AGC well, and his input in the board room will be missed; there will be a good turnout at his funeral.

20th December

Hermione is engaged to Chuck. I am so glad for her, although I fear that we will lose her to America. Arthur and Penelope both like him, but it remains to be seen whether they will stay here or leave this country with their mother. Chuck will be staying at Broadlands for the Christmas holiday, and we will all get to know him better.

Chapter Thirteen
1920

17th July

Hermione and Chuck were married yesterday in London. It was a nice ceremony with only a few guests, some of our county friends and some of Chuck's friends in the Embassy, including the ambassador and his wife. The reception was held at the Savoy hotel and the happy couple left for their honeymoon in Italy.

1st August

We have a long report from Tom in Australia. Two trial shafts at his claim have proved very positive and he has received a lot of enquiries from companies and individuals wanting to buy it from him. One such was from his erstwhile employers to whom he replied that they had their chance when he worked for them. He has suggested two small companies operating in the area who might be suitable ones for the AGC to take over. One of them is also on my list of possible acquisitions and has English owners, so I will make contact with their head office and see if they are interested. Tom has meanwhile stopped all activity on the claim awaiting our decision.

20th August

At a board meeting it was decided to proceed with takeover negotiations with our preferred target.

31st August

Takeover terms have been agreed and Tom advised accordingly.

2nd October

Chuck has been told that he will be posted to Texas in February. I am glad that we will have Hermione and him at Broadlands for Christmas.

28th December

It was a really good Christmas; Chuck has fitted into both families very well and I am sure that he will be a good husband to Hermione. Arthur is going to stay in England and continue to study law. We will keep an eye on him and he will come to Broadlands whenever he wants to. Penelope thinks that if she can qualify as a vet in America her first customers will be Chuck's dogs, and she will be going with her mother.

10th February 1921

Chuck, Hermione and Penelope sailed from Southampton to New York yesterday. We all saw them off at the quayside and waved until the ship was out of sight. Arthur took the parting from his family well and is now the not-so-proud owner of Penelope's parrot.

20th March

We heard from Tom today that what is now the AGC mine in the district of Albany, Western Australia, is up and running. The quality of the ore is very good, and it seems that Tom was quite right in thinking that the area would be productive. At the board meeting when this was discussed John said that most people would not have taken the time to see Tom in the first place, let alone paraded him in front of the board, but that my instinct, even at a distance of almost nine thousand miles, had once again proved to be right.

31st March

I got a letter from Hermione; they are now at Fort Worth in Texas where Chuck, now promoted to full colonel, commands a regiment of engineers. She says that life is very different there, but that she and Penelope are enjoying it. She sends her love to everyone here, especially to Arthur.

1st April

John called me into his office this morning and told me that he is going to retire at the end of the year, and that he wants me to take over as chairman of the AGC with effect from 1st January 1922. You can imagine my surprise. I said that it was a great honour but was there not one of the other directors better qualified for the position. John said that apart from Ted Harris I was the only director with practical experience of mining, and that I had also shown good commercial and management qualities since becoming deputy chairman. He said that he had spoken with the other directors and that they were all very supportive of the proposal.

4th April

At Broadlands for the weekend, we all celebrated my forthcoming promotion; Mary said that she had been happy when she was Cook's assistant, but that she would be happier still as the chairman's wife.

28th December

There was a leaving party for John today, and on behalf of everyone in the AGC I presented him with a solid gold signet ring, engraved with the AGC crest on the face. The gold came from the Bibiani mine. He said how much he had enjoyed his time with the company and the personal friendships that he had formed; he praised the technical skill of those who worked at the mines and the support that they had from their colleagues at head office.

He ended by saying that I had worked my way up from being a prospector, and that several of my decisions when in a managerial role had considerably increased the profitability of the AGC. He closed by saying that he wished everyone in the company every success and happiness. I led the staff in singing 'For he's a jolly good fellow', and this time there was no doubt about it.

2nd January 1922

With another happy Christmas behind me, and another busy year ahead, when I got to the office this morning the sign on my door proclaimed my new title, and many of the staff came and congratulated me. I have not moved into John's office; mine is quite big enough and I do not want to seem to be throwing my weight about.

It is almost exactly twenty-six years since I arrived in Cape Town and I can hardly believe that in those twenty-six years, I have gone from being a dock worker and a grubby but enthusiastic prospector to being the chairman of a well-respected international company.

I have a loving wife, a fine son in Rob and a beautiful daughter, and I have been able to contribute to the upkeep of Broadlands, which was one of the reasons why I went to Africa in the first place. If only Papa had lived to see this day; he would have been so proud of me.

Chapter Fourteen
1922

4th July

I have now been the chairman for six months, and it has been a period when I have been introduced to a variety of matters, some of them, such as the Chamber of Commerce, not related solely to mining. I have been invited to join a club, some of whose members are senior executives in other mining companies, some of whom I have met since I moved to London. I will certainly join, as it will enable me to keep abreast what other mining companies are up to, and what acquisitions might be possible.

John is a member of a gentlemen's club in London, and he has suggested that I might like to become a member; he is on the committee that runs the club and would be glad to sponsor me. It has sporting facilities, including tennis and squash courts, as well as the obligatory billiards tables. I know very few people in London, and this would be an opportunity to make new friends. Also it would be somewhere to go of an evening when I am up in London alone. Chris advises me that the membership fee, which is not inconsiderable, can be reclaimed from the company as a legitimate expense, and I have thanked John and said that I would like to take up his offer.

Following the death of Richard Beale and the departure of Alan Hughes the AGC Board now consists of only three directors in London, Chris, Richard and myself. The only other director is Ted Harris, who is still based in Obuasi. Richard Waterrman has turned out to be a useful addition to the board, although his recent employment has been in banking he has a degree in chemistry and was formerly involved in research into the extraction of elements from their ores. Anything that would reduce the cost of extracting gold would make a big difference to our balance sheet and could mean that a previously unprofitable mine could indeed turn a profit. I want him to meet Franz and discuss how we might make some changes to our procedures, and he should see our operations in the Gold Coast for himself.

18th July

Today I got a letter from Hermione, with very sad news; Chuck died three weeks ago as a result of a car accident. He was on his way home after celebrating a win in a football match by his alma mater, the University of Texas, in Austin. It is a distance of nearly two hundred miles, and it may be that he fell asleep at the wheel. She is so unlucky; she is in her mid-forties and has lost two husbands. She says that she has not yet decided whether to stay in America or return to England; she has made a number of friends in Fort Worth, and Chuck's pension would enable her to live there comfortably, but she very much misses seeing Arthur. She proposes to come over and make a decision while she is with her family and friends here. I so much look forward to seeing her again, and I hope that she decides to stay.

Arthur has a job as a solicitor and he will be thrilled to see his mother again; it is almost eighteen months since she left England and I know that although he has a good job as a solicitor which keeps him busy, he still misses her a lot. Hermione does not say whether or not Penelope will be coming with her. Her parrot has not taken on board that the war is over and still says 'Bloody Kaiser' loudly and often. It will be interesting to see whether it manages a 'Hullo Preppy' if she does come. Mary, of course, very much wants her good friend to stay in England at Broadlands.

I have written to Hermione saying how sorry we all were to hear of Chuck's death, but how happy we will be to see her again when she comes to England. I have asked her to let us know as soon as she has firm travel plans, and whether Penelope will be coming with her.

3rd August

Today I got a very interesting letter from Tom in Albany; the chairman of the locally-owned company that he used to work for, whose claim is adjacent to ours, has approached him and asked whether the AGC would consider selling the mine. This is a remarkable development; we have only been producing gold for a little over a year, and that is from land that they refused to consider when Tom suggested it when he worked for them, but its profitability is common knowledge.

Tom is naturally much amused by this turn of events and says that he does not know whether the AGC would be interested in selling the mine; but it is producing gold at a very satisfactory rate, which is why it has attracted a potential buyer.

I called Chris into my office and showed him Tom's letter. When he had read it, he sat back and said nothing for some time and I could see that his accountant's mind was balancing the pros and cons of the proposal. What he suggested was very much the same as what had crossed my mind, and together we put together a deal that we thought would benefit all the parties concerned,

The claim had cost us nothing, for Tom had charged us nothing when he signed it over to us; we had bought a lot of additional machinery, including Berdan Pans, and spent a lot of money on the buildings and other necessary infrastructure. Chris had all these costs listed, as well as the costs of the labour force and the management.

We could not expect the new owners to pay Tom thirty percent of their profits, and we would have to come to another agreement with him. If he wishes, we could include in the deal a proviso that he can continue to be the mine manager for an agreed period at an agreed salary. We would come to a separate agreement with him to compensate him to some extent for his loss of his thirty percent of the profits. Since he has put this sale forward I do not believe that he still expects to keep his original income, but he may be pleased to have a lesser day-to-day responsibility for the profitability of the mine.

The deal that we will propose is that we will sell the claim for an agreed sum, less than its true value but sufficient to more than cover the costs that we have incurred getting the mine operating, and we will be paid twenty-five percent of each year's profits for twenty years. If the mine continues to perform as it is at present this will be a worthwhile investment for its buyers and will considerably improve the AGC's profits. The only risk as far as the AGC is concerned would be if the mine failed in the next twenty years, but since it is likely that we would have recovered very much more than our initial costs long before then there would be no loss on our balance sheet.

I asked Richard Waterman to join us and Chris and I talked him through the proposal that we would ask Tom to convey to his former employers. Richard said that he could see no way in which we could incur a loss, and it was agreed that I would instruct Tom to respond to the potential purchasers. We would also let him know how we proposed to compensate him. I hold Ted Harris' proxy vote when a matter needs an immediate decision so we were able to hold an extraordinary board meeting and formally agree to proceed as proposed.

10th August

Today we heard from Hermione; she sails in ten days' time and will be with us before the end of the month. Penelope, who is training to be a vet, will come with her, but plans to return to Fort Worth and complete her training. We are all so pleased that they are coming, and we will try to make them so welcome that they will not leave us again.

18th September

Today we heard from Tom that our proposal to sell the Albany mine has been accepted, and the necessary formalities at that end should be completed by the end of the month. Tom is prepared to stay on as mine manager on a renewable two-year contract and says that he is happy with the arrangement that we proposed regarding his personal remuneration. Chris is seeing to the transfer of the funds agreed as the purchase price, and we should not have any further involvement until we receive our share of the year's profits.

This sees the end of the AGC's brief involvement in Australia, which came about as a result of Tom's visit to our offices just three years ago. The outcome is very financially satisfactorily, and with Tom hands-on at the mine we can be certain of a good return for a number of years. When Tom does return to this country I will seriously consider offering him a seat on the board.

1st October

Hermione and Penelope arrived at Southampton yesterday morning and we were all there at the quayside when their ship docked; it is getting on for two years since they left from the very same berth, but a healthy tan is the only noticeable change in their appearance. Arthur was the first to throw his arms about them, closely followed by Mary, Sarah, Rob and me; we drove to Broadlands in two cars, Hermione in one and Penelope in the other, and by the time that we got home we had all heard much about their lives in America.

The parrot was the first thing that Penelope wanted to see, and we all held our breath as she removed the cover from its cage; for the past few days we had been rehearsing it in 'Ullo Preppy', but our efforts proved to have been in vain when it nodded its head and greeted her with an emphatic

'Bloody Kaiser'.

A short time after we got home, Quentin and Pamela arrived from London; Mary had asked Cook and Betsy to come in and prepare and serve our dinner, and Quentin was more than happy to produce from the cellar several bottles of what he insists on calling 'his' wines, on the rather tenuous basis that they are in the house that Papa left to him. How Papa would have loved to have been here.

There was so much to talk about events on both sides of the Atlantic that it was very late before we called it a day. Hermione has rallied well since Chuck's death and seems to be able to enjoy our love and company in her old home. She will tell us more about his death and what she plans to do, when she is ready. Until then we will all do everything that we can to make her put the past behind her and enjoy the present.

1st November

Hermione has decided that she will make her home in England; she will return to Fort Worth briefly in a couple of weeks' time, settle her affairs, and hope to be back in England for Christmas. We are all so pleased. Penelope, who is now twenty, will go back to America with her mother and stay there until she completes her training at the end of next summer. She will then see whether there is a suitable job for her in the area that she knows around Fort Worth and Dallas, and if there is not she will come back to England with a degree and find a job with a veterinary business.

8th December

I have been elected as a member of John's club; he accompanied me yesterday on my first visit. It is a very smart place, just off Piccadilly, and apart from the written rules applicable to members there is a great deal of protocol as to dress, guests, bar bills, etc. I had a game of billiards with a member to whom John introduced me and afterwards we had an excellent, very reasonably priced dinner; I am very glad to be a member. I am glad to say that there is no initiation ceremony, as there was when I joined the club in Cape Town.

28th December

Hermione and Penelope arrived on 23rd December and Christmas at Broadlands was something like it used to be; of course the children are all grown up now, but not too old to enjoy some of the games that we used to play in the evenings before bed time. After New Year, Penelope is going to see whether there might be a job for her with the local veterinary practice when she has finished her training, for I think that she is thinking that family life at or near Broadlands might be preferable to making her way alone in Fort Worth or Dallas. I do hope that she stays here.

Chapter Fifteen
1923

3rd January

We saw the New Year in with all the usual jollity, and on New Year's Day we had a small shoot. It is a long time since we put down any pheasants or partridges, but the birds seem to appreciate the calm of our estate and find it a safe haven to which to move from the land of some of our neighbours, who still take their shooting very seriously. Quentin, Rob, Hermione and I made up a small line of guns, and Mary organised the others to drive plenty of birds over us. I do like my Holland and Hollands, and between us we bagged a very respectable twelve brace. It was a lovely day, very reminiscent of the days when Papa organised the shooting.

10th January

Back in the office today I found a letter from Ted waiting on my desk. It is an unbelievable eighteen years since he joined me in Obuasi, and in all that time he has never been back to England. He is entitled to four weeks' paid leave every other year, and although the AGC pays the cost of the fares, he has always preferred to take some time off in Cape Coast, the administrative capital of the colony, or Abidjan, which is very French and rather more civilised and relaxing, although he says that he can never relax completely when he is away from his beloved mines.

It seems that on his last few visits to Cape Coast he has met and got to like the daughter of one of the British colonial officials, and they have decided to get married. They want the ceremony to take place in England, and Ted has asked whether he can spend a month here in April. He says that he would be quite happy to leave Franz in charge of the mines.

I have replied, congratulating him and saying that of course he can, and I think that this would be a good opportunity to give Richard some first-hand mining experience, and I asked him whether he would like to spend a few weeks at Obuasi while Ted was on leave. Subject to the shipping schedules he should arrive there about a week before Ted leaves, so that he can get a general briefing, but he need not stay there until Ted returns as

Franz will be there.

I put this to Richard and he responded enthusiastically, so I have replied to Ted telling him of the plan and to let us know the date on which he will leave Takoradi.

Cameron, in fact, is the only other one of our expatriate staff in the Gold Coast who has never taken any home leave, and Franz and George have taken much less than their entitlement and have accumulated quite large sums of pay in lieu. Cameron says that if he went home he would have to stay with one relation after another, and that he would spend his time counting down the days until he could get on the ship and return to Obuasi. He is a strange chap and a good engineer, and his pay in lieu of leave credit is very considerable.

2nd April

Ted and Betty, his fiancée, arrived in Southampton two days ago and came into the office this morning. Of course he knows no one here in London and I introduced him to the senior staff. Betty is a very pretty girl, and I can only think that it was a lack of suitable males in Cape Coast that has kept her unmarried. They will be married in two weeks' time in Haywards Heath in Sussex, where her grandparents live. Her parents have already returned to England on leave, and Chris and I and our wives are invited to the wedding.

After a light lunch in the board room, Ted asked if he could have a word with me. We left Betty telling Chris all about life in Cape Coast, what little life there was for a young woman, and took our coffee to my office. I thought that I knew what he would say, and I was not wrong. He said that Obuasi was even less of a place for a wife than Cape Coast, and that reluctantly he would be giving me six months' notice that he was resigning, to give me time to find a replacement. Betty would stay in this country with her grandparents until he came back to England.

I told him that I had anticipated his news but that there was no question of his resigning; we needed his experience on the board, and I would like him to have my old title, director of mining. He was so pleased to hear this that he jumped up, spilling the rest of his coffee, and shook my hand vigorously for some time. He said that with his savings he thought that they could buy a small house just outside London, and that he would be so glad to continue to work for the AGC.

I told him to give some thought as to how we should rearrange the management structure at the mines, and asked if he could come in one day before the wedding to discuss it, if he was in London. He said that he had some ideas and that he would be in touch very soon. He and Betty then left on a sight-seeing trip of London; he a very happy man now that he has a secure future with the AGC.

17th April

The wedding was a very happy event; a number of relations of the bride and groom were there and also one or two who had worked in Cape Coast and were now back in England. Mary said that it brought back memories of our wedding. Before the happy couple left for their honeymoon in a rented cottage in Cornwall Ted said that he would be back in the office when his leave expired in ten days' time. I told him that a few days either way was no problem; he is, after all, a director of the company and there is no timeclock on his comings and goings.

Richard arrived in Obuasi a week before Ted left, so he had plenty of time to be briefed on our operations there. Before he left London, he said that he would try to get to Bibiani and Iduapriem if he had the time, and I hope that he manages to do so. In my discussion with Ted about the necessary management restructuring when he left Obuasi he said that he thought that it would be sensible to have a general manager, since rank was important when dealing with Africans, and that Alan Parsons, mine manager at Obuasi, was the right man for the job. He thought that Arnaud Leclerc, presently mine superintendent there could move up to mine manager; he worked there for several years before the AGC took over the mining and is well-respected by both the headman and the workers. Since the closure of Obuasi One Bibiani has been the most productive of our mines in the Gold Coast, and it makes sense for Alan to remain there; the mine managers at Obuasi Two and Three have shown themselves to be very capable, and under the watchful eye of Franz, can be relied upon to maintain a good rate of production.

17th May

Hermione returned to America at the end of January, and I had a letter from her today saying that she expects to be back here finally, early in June. I know that she wants to get involved in local affairs and she is not one to sit around doing nothing. Penelope has enrolled in a course that will enable her to sit the exam in this country for her degree in a year's time, and whenever possible, she is working with a local vet to get practical experience. It seems that the whole family will be living at Broadlands again before very long, and it is only sad that Tony Fellowes is not alive and with us.

20th July

Richard is back from the Gold Coast. He visited all our mines and the local dignitaries at each and also made a courtesy call on the Mamponghene in Kumasi. He was very impressed with the competence of the expatriate managers and superintendents, and with the excellent relations that they have with the workforce. He says that although he knows next to nothing about mining he does know when a business is on a sound financial footing, and that contented and competent staff are just as necessary as a healthy balance sheet.

1st October

Quentin has retired from the army. Because of his wound he will get a good pension and he and Pamela will move into Broadlands before the end of the year. For the time being they are continuing to live in my house in London while the accommodation at Broadlands is rearranged.

Quentin and Pamela will move into Papa's suite; Hermione and Penelope, and Arthur when he is at home, will occupy the rooms that Mary and I have had and we will move back into the gamekeeper's cottage with Sarah, who will be going to university next year to study drama. Rob, who has been managing the estate fulltime since he came down with his degree, has converted the old groom's quarters by the stables into a very cosy little habitation. He says he prefers to live closer to his work, but we suspect that it is the ability to spend some private time with female company that is the chief attraction.

20th December

Another Christmas is almost upon us, and this year there really will be the whole Broad family around the dinner table and the Christmas tree. Rob and Arthur, who see very little of each other these days in the normal course of events have become great friends, and spend a lot of time in Rob's lair. Similarly Sarah and Penelope seem to have much in common, and their conversation centres on boys and fashion. We three Broad children and Mary and Pamela have plenty of stories to share, Quentin about the war, Hermione about America, Mary about her life here as Cook's assistant and me about my time in Africa. This is such a happy time; I wonder how we have deserved it.

Chapter Sixteen
1924

10th January

Today, I paid a visit to my doctor in Harley Street; I did not feel at my best over Christmas, although I managed to conceal it from the others, and I wanted to know whether there is a serious problem or just something that will pass. I have a permanent slight pain in my stomach and very little appetite; sometimes the pain is acute.

After a thorough examination the doctor, who is a good friend of the family and has been a guest at Broadlands on several occasions, said that he would like me to spend twenty-four hours in a London hospital where a number of tests could be carried out. I said that there would be no problem if the stay was during the week, and after he consulted a colleague who is a specialist in diseases of the stomach it was arranged that I should go to St. Bartholomew's Hospital on Tuesday of next week.

I am, naturally, concerned that it is thought necessary for me to undergo further tests, but I am keen to get this behind me as soon as possible. I shall tell Mary, who noticed that I was not on top form at Christmas, and ask her to spend next week with me in my mews house.

16th January

The worst day of my life. I think that I said that when Ryneker sailed away from me in Cape Town, but this truly is the worst. I spent yesterday in the hospital, where I must say everything is done to make the patients feel as much at ease as is possible. The consultant who saw me, and who arranged for a series of tests, was very pleasant and instilled great confidence.

Before I was discharged this morning, I met with him in his room in the hospital. He explained that he could not be certain at this time, but that he very much feared that I may have a progressive cancer. He gave me a list of foods which would be most easily digested, prescribed some medication for the pain, and has made another appointment for me in a month's time.

Naturally I asked him for his prognosis; he said that if he was right the cancer was not operable and could not be cured, but there was a chance that it could be contained and prevented from spreading. I asked how long I could expect to live if it continued to spread and he said six to nine months.

Mary was waiting for me when I got back to our house and must have seen from my face that my news would not be good. She is such a loving, caring person that all her thoughts were for me, and not for her and anyone else. I said that the consultant had said that he could not be certain, and that we should be as optimistic as possible. I will take the medicine, which I believe is morphine, and eat the various foods that he suggested. We will not say anything to the family until after my next visit to the hospital, when there may be good news.

19th January

I have decided to say nothing to my fellow directors until after my next hospital visit, but I will start to prepare for my departure from the AGC, for even if I live for some time I cannot carry out the duties of chairman while in constant pain.

Richard is best suited to succeed me as chairman, and I know that Chris and Ted will be happy to work with him in that rôle; there should probably be a fourth director, but it will be up to the three of them to choose one.

Sally caught me wincing after a particularly sharp stab of pain; I said that it was indigestion, but I will probably have to tell her, in the strictest confidence, before very long. In the meantime, I must try to carry on as naturally as possible. Happily there are no major projects or potential acquisitions at the moment.

14th February

I was back in the hospital yesterday for a further examination and more tests and there is no good news. I told the consultant that I was having to take more of the morphine to counter the pain, and he said that he could tell that the cancer was spreading; he said that it was probably closer to six months than nine that I could expect to live.

Back here at my little mews house I told Mary the bad news and for the first time she broke down, threw her arms round me and sobbed uncontrollably. I said that we must both be as brave as we could for the sake of the children, and that we must tell all at Broadlands when we return tomorrow. We sat together on the sofa, with arms around each other, saying nothing for a long time before we went to bed.

15th February

This afternoon I told the family the bad news. Naturally they were all stunned and mostly in tears. I said that I wanted to enjoy what I could in the next months, and that they could help me in that by being as normal as possible and not showing concern for my condition. For my part, I will try to do as much as I can to conceal the pain that I am increasingly suffering and to be as outwardly cheerful as possible.

27th February

At today's board meeting I told my fellow directors of my situation. Their concern was genuine and I felt both sad and guilty that I would be leaving them before very long. I said that the AGC was a strong company and that I knew that it would continue to expand under their guidance. I told them that I was proud to have been chosen to lead the company, albeit for an all too short time, and that I felt that Richard should succeed me. Chris said that he strongly agreed and that if Ted felt the same it should be put in the minutes there and then, and so it was. Richard said that with my record I was a hard act to follow but that he was honoured to have their support and would do his best to ensure that the AGC continued to be thought of as one of the leading mining companies.

Sally was tearful when I told her, and said that she had so enjoyed working for me; she asked if she would have to go back to the typing pool and I said that I was sure that Richard would want her to work for him.

I will go back to the office once more to say goodbye to all my friends there, but I do not want to work there again knowing that my time there is really over. What I do need to do is to have a word with Chris about the widow's pension that Mary will get.

I have a substantial balance with the bank, and my shares in the AGC can be transferred to her after my death; she will also be the owner of my little London house, so she will be comfortably off. Rob is making a good job of managing the Broadlands estate and Sarah is doing well at drama school.

Hermione has Tony's Army pension and Chuck's widow's pension and her share of Papa's estate, and can continue to live at Broadlands. Arthur is studying law and Penelope will soon be a qualified vet; there is every likelihood that both will soon have good jobs.

I wish that I had seen more of Quentin since I returned from Africa, but he and Pamela are now enjoying a well-earned life of leisure in the family home.

The Broadlands house and estate are, for now at least, in good shape and there is no foreseeable reason why they should not continue in that state for several generations to come.

This will be the last entry in my diary. I have said my goodbyes at the office, where I was touched by the genuine compassion and regret that so many expressed. I had told Richard that there should be no presentation or speeches; I would say personal goodbyes to all that I knew well.

Chris gave me a printed summary of the pension entitlement that Mary will have, together with a statement of the shares that will be transferred to her. I thanked him for the good work that he did when Stephen Carson ran off with the money and for his subsequent work as a director and company secretary.

I had an emotional ten or fifteen minutes with Ted. He said that if it was not for me he would still be trying to scratch a living out of the ground at Witwatersrand. I said that he would surely have risen above that, and that his service to the AGC in the Gold Coast had more than justified my confidence in him. He said that he had received messages from the staff at all our mines expressing their sadness at the news of my illness. I wished him a long, happy life with Betty and much success

I have known Richard for only a short time, but he has proved to be more than a competent member of the board. He makes friends easily and is enthusiastic about any project, large or small. He knows more about mining than he will admit, and I am sure that it will not be long before he suggests that the AGC diversifies and seeks to make its profits from something other than gold.

My last surprise, just as I was about to leave the building, was when Sally brought Lisa to say goodbye to me; the two of them are good friends and have kept in touch since Sally replaced Lisa as my secretary. The two of them were in tears, but I told them that apart from consigning my earlier diary to the archives for four years they had made my life so much easier and that I owed them a great deal. When I left the building, all the staff lined up just inside the front door and I shook hands with each of them as my time with the AGC came to an end.

This evening I am alone in my house. Mary wanted to spend my last short visit to London with me, but I told her that it was a trip that I wanted to make on my own. Back at Broadlands, for as long as may be, I will spend my last days remembering the happy times that I have spent in so many places and with such a loving family. I believe that I have lived as Papa would have wished and I will not disappoint him in my death.

Printed in Great Britain
by Amazon